SIX SISTERS
DOUBLE BLIND Book 6

DAN ALATORRE

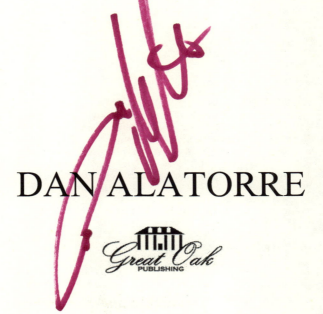

SIX SISTERS *DOUBLE BLIND Book 6*
© 2023 Dan Alatorre. © This eBook is licensed for your personal use only. This eBook may not be re-sold or given away to other people. Thank you for respecting the hard work of this author. © No part of this book may be reproduced, stored in a retrieval system or transmitted by any means without the written permission of the author. Copyright © 2023 Dan Alatorre. All rights reserved. This is a work of fiction. Names, characters, places, and incidents either are the product of the author's imagination or are used fictitiously, and any resemblance to actual persons, living or dead, businesses, companies, events or locales, is entirely coincidental.

OTHER THRILLERS BY DAN ALATORRE

NOVELS

<u>**Double Blind Murder Mystery Series**</u>
Double Blind, *a murder mystery*
Primary Target, *Double Blind book 2*
Third Degree, *Double Blind book 3*
Fourth Estate, *Double Blind book 4*
Five Sparrows, *Double Blind book 5*
Six Sisters, *Double Blind book 6*
Seventh Avenue, *Double Blind book 7 COMING SOON*

<u>*Jett Thacker Mysteries*</u>
Tiffany Lynn Is Missing, *a psychological thriller*
Killer In The Dark, *Jett Thacker book 2*

<u>**The Gamma Sequence Medical Thriller Series**</u>
The Gamma Sequence, *a medical thriller*
Rogue Elements, *The Gamma Sequence, book 2*
Terminal Sequence, *The Gamma Sequence, book 3*
The Keepers, *The Gamma Sequence, book 4*
Dark Hour, *The Gamma Sequence, book 5*

A Place Of Shadows, *a paranormal mystery*
The Navigators, *a time travel thriller*

CONTENTS

Acknowledgements

SIX SISTERS

A Note From The Author
About The Author
Other Books By Dan Alatorre

ACKNOWLEDGMENTS

I would be remiss if I didn't occasionally make reference to the many people who helped me in my writing journey. I was encouraged at a young age by many people - my mom and dad, my brothers and sisters, classmates, co-workers... When I took writing more seriously, I met many people in critique groups and through social media who guided my storytelling abilities. Some are still friends who have become bestselling authors, while others are merely fond memories now, but as I write, they are always over my shoulder, whispering in my ear the things they helped me learn so long ago.

Certain information on weaponry, explosive devices, and methods of physical attack are intentionally vague or exaggerated in this book so if some kid picks up your Kindle, they won't learn enough to do the things described in the story.

Such inaccuracies may be irritating to a trained eye, but I hope you can appreciate my rationale.

CHAPTER 1

"AND NOW, LADIES AND GENTLEMEN..." The handsome young magician strutted across the darkened stage, the spotlight following his every move. He tugged at the lapels of his tuxedo. "The finale of... the tragedy of the six sisters!"

The 10 A.M. Saturday show had a sold-out crowd—a good sign for the start of the magic act's two-week stay in Tampa—and the magician had informed his assistants that he planned to milk as much drama from these hour-long performances as he could.

He turned and waved his hand at the six cages that, a moment ago, had descended from the ceiling and been draped in blue velvet curtains. Colorful laser lights beamed out from behind them, a thick white fog from an offstage smoke machine covering the stage floor.

Racing to his left, the showman flung his hand at the first cage, a fireball flying from his fingertips and landing at the base of the velvet-cloaked enclosure. A puff of smoke went up from the bottom of the first cage, and its velvet curtain snapped upwards, revealing it to be empty.

The crowd gasped as the voluptuous female assistant who had been locked inside just an instant prior, had now vanished.

Cage by cage, master magician Sinclair O'Lair launched fireballs at the remaining enclosures, and each time a puff of smoke drifted upward to show the cage also was now empty.

Five of the magician's scantily-clad teammates had been locked inside the first five cages, along with a female volunteer from the audience to occupy cage six.

Now, all of the assistants had vanished—as had the beautiful volunteer.

The crowd gasped, and slowly broke into applause, but O'Lair didn't slow down.

"Not yet! Not yet!" He raced to the last cage. "Because legend says the youngest sister, who was most pure of heart, sacrificed herself to save her sisters. Behold!"

Once again, the blue velvet curtains plummeted down over all of the steel enclosures. The cage bottoms erupted in smoke a second time, and their velvet curtains immediately soared back up toward the ceiling of the massive expo hall.

The clouds of white vapors curled upward, dissipating as they climbed, and revealing that all of the magician's beautiful assistants had returned to the cages. And each was now dressed in a brightly-colored ballroom gown.

Only the sixth cage remained empty.

The crowd broke into thunderous applause.

"And of course, there were six sisters..." O'Lair smiled at the audience. "So, join me in welcoming back the fair young maiden in the story—our volunteer—who has saved the day. Give her a big round of applause!"

He pointed to the rear of the expo hall.

The spotlights swung to the back of the huge room, stopping on the doors behind the seated audience.

There was no one there.

The applause continued as Sinclair O'Lair glanced around. "Well, she's supposed to be right there. Maybe she got lost."

The crowd chuckled. O'Lair lifted a hand and extended one finger, looking upward and swinging his arm in a circle. "Let's have our terrific spotlight operators help our beautiful volunteer find her way to the stage."

The bright lights drifted over the crowd. The magician's five assistants descended from their cages, stiff smiles glued onto their faces, looking back and forth at one another as their dainty ballroom gowns swirled and swayed.

One of the blonde assistants rushed to the sixth cage, leaned through the steel frame door, and peered inside. "Oh!"

She recoiled, turning her face away from the enclosure.

Sinclair O'Lair ran to her side. He put his hand on her shoulder and peeked past the bars of the cage.

Blood lined the floor of the mock enclosure.

The magician gasped, his jaw dropping.

The secret trap door lay open, revealing the escape ladder that descended from the cage and into the hollow recesses of the stage floor, where a yellow guide rope would lead the volunteer to a hidden exit. From there, a waiting stagehand would escort her around to the entrance of the hall and slip her inside while the smoke bombs kept the audience's eyes up on the stage, setting up the big reveal and the show's grand finale.

But everything in and around cage six was covered in blood.

A huge pool of crimson stretched out from the base of the ladder, inching its way to an ancient, rusty drain in the middle of the concrete floor. Two long streaks went from the thick pool and toward the exit door, their markings getting lighter as they neared the exit, like a paint brush running out of paint. In the middle of the red pool rested the magician's dagger, covered in blood.

But the beautiful volunteer from the audience was nowhere to be found.

Master magician Sinclair O'Lair's face turned white. He dropped to his knees, jamming a fist into his gaping mouth. "Wh—what happened?" Sweat glistened on the handsome young man's brow; saliva trickled from the corner of his lips.

Whimpering, he stretched a trembling hand out to the edges of the trap door and the base of the cage, sliding a fingertip along the edges before holding it up to his face.

The bright spotlight illuminated the showman in stark white light, his chest heaving.

The magician's washed-out complexion told the crowd that this wasn't part of the act. The audience members gasped, loud rumblings going up among them. People hurried toward the exits.

"What happened?" His voice wavering, the handsome young magician stood up, staggering from the cage. Blood covered the palms of his hands and the knees of his tuxedo pants. "I don't... What happened?"

His eyes widened, his gaze going to his shapely blonde assistant as she stood by the bloody cage.

"What happened?" he cried, holding his blood-covered hands out at his sides as the crowd's rumblings turned to screams. "Somebody tell me what just happened!"

CHAPTER 2

As Officer Mark Harriman rushed toward the Florida State fairgrounds expo hall, Mrs. Diaz from Guest Relations trotted alongside him and gave the rundown on the crime scene.

Magic act.

Random female volunteer is missing.

Blood everywhere.

"What a way to start the morning," he mumbled. Harriman scribbled on his notepad and stuffed it back into his uniform shirt pocket, sweat beading on his brow. He turned to his partner. "Rope off the expo hall with crime scene tape and get the names and IDs of everyone in the act. We're gonna want to talk to all of them."

Officer Jim Rondo nodded. "Will do, Mark."

"I'll radio in for some more units so we can start interviewing everyone who was in the crowd.

Maybe we'll get lucky and somebody recorded the whole thing on their phone." Harriman stopped, glancing at his partner. "And Jim—there'll be stagehands. People who work behind the scenes. Get them, too. The detectives are definitely gonna wanna talk to them."

As Rondo disappeared into the sea of people enjoying the events at the fairgrounds on a warm sunny day, Harriman turned his attention back to the woman from Guest Relations.

"Okay, Mrs. Diaz. Where did you say I could find the person who runs the magic act?" He glanced at the large sign near the door of the expo hall, with its ten-foot-high rendering of a handsome young man in a tuxedo pulling a rabbit out of a top hat. Harriman took in the sign's colorful lettering, announcing the amazing magical feats of Sinclair O'Lair, magician extraordinaire, and pointed to the enormous illustration. "That guy."

The woman gestured to a distant part of the parking lot, acres of grass filled with vehicles from all over. "Traveling acts usually have a trailer, so we have them park way out in lot K or L. But the magician and his people are here for the whole run of our midsummer event—two and a half weeks of boat shows and RV shows, remodeling shows, concerts... They have a lot of equipment trucks, so we let some of them park behind the expo hall during their stay. Right now, they're all still backstage, waiting for you. That's what the 911 operator told us to do."

"Good. That's perfect." Harriman wiped another round of sweat from his forehead. "Lead on, ma'am."

In the air-conditioned coolness of the expo hall's back rooms, the woman from Guest Relations introduced Officer Harriman to the participants in Sinclair O'Lair's traveling magic act—five buxom women in costumes that were barely rated PG: short shorts, tight corsets, fishnet stockings, and an abundance of stage makeup—and half a dozen men dressed in black from head to foot.

But not the handsome young man in the tuxedo who appeared on the big sign outside.

Harriman frowned. "Where's your boss, Sinclair O'Lair?"

Several of the assistants opened their mouths, but Mrs. Diaz beat them to the explanation. "Mr. O'Lair has had a bit of a… situation."

A snicker went up from the magic staff. The African-American assistant shook her head. "Meltdown is more like it."

"He's Jello," the redhead said, snorting.

Harriman turned to his guide.

"Mr. O'Lair is in the office." Mrs. Diaz turned to a nearby door, putting a finger to her mouth. "He… may need a moment."

A slender blonde assistant with well-toned legs and a bustier that barely kept her contained, chuckled. "She means he's in there crying like a baby."

Harriman cocked his head. "Crying?"

"Uh, sobbing, actually." The Guest Relations lady shrugged. "Apparently, he's the sensitive type." She moved toward the office. "He's in here."

Turning the knob, Mrs. Diaz pushed open the door. Inside, the handsome young man in the tuxedo lay curled up on the floor next to a pile of crumpled tissues, quivering as tears streamed down his cheeks.

He lifted his head and glanced at Harriman, bursting into sobs. "I don't understand it." O'Lair grabbed another Kleenex from the box on the floor next to him. "The blood! There was so much blood!" He shook his head and then blew his nose, his red, swollen eyes coming up to meet Harriman's again. "I just—I don't know what happened!"

Sighing, the officer stepped out of the room and pulled out his notepad. "Okay, we'll start with someone else. *Anybody* else." He glanced at the assistants and stagehands. "We've got an apparent murder. Who wants to tell me what happened out there?"

The slender blonde with the well-toned legs pulled a chair from a nearby table, plopping down and crossing her ankles on the edge of a wooden cargo box. "Officer, we've had a rough morning." Her voice carried a southern accent laced with harshness. She slid her hand along the hem of her low-cut bustier and pulled a crumpled pack of cigarettes from between her substantial breasts. One shake of the pack produced the tip of a disposable lighter, which she snagged. A second shake of the pack launched a cigarette halfway out. She slipped the tobacco stick between her shiny red lips and flicked the lighter, holding the flame under the tip of the cigarette until it glowed.

The representative from Guest Relations wagged a finger. "Oh, I'm sorry, Ms. Scarlet. This is a no smoking facility."

"Yeah?" Scarlet turned and blew a stream of smoke toward Mrs. Diaz, scowling. "The roof rafters in the main hall are still fogged over from the eighteen different types of pyrotechnics we set off during our performance, and y'all think one cigarette is gonna make a difference?"

Mrs. Diaz cleared her throat and adjusted her collar. "Well, I suppose under the circumstances…"

"Thank you, sugar." Scarlet's gaze moved to Harriman. "Maybe I can help move things along, Officer…"

"Harriman," Mark said, making another note on his pad.

Nodding, the buxom blonde looked him up and down. "Well, Officer Harriman, the volunteer was selected at random, the same way we do every night. None of us had anything to do with the death of Mrs. Gabriella Romain."

Harriman's head snapped upright. "What name was that? Who did you say?"

"Gabriella Romain," Scarlet said. "The volunteer. A fancy-schmancy Tampa socialite whose sad and untimely death is about to screw this magic show out of two hundred and fifty matinee ticket sales at ten dollars apiece."

Harriman took a deep breath and let it out slowly, his eyes wandering to the exit door. "If your random volunteer really *was* Gabriella Romain, she's a lot more than just a dead socialite." He extended his hand and massaged his neck. "I, uh… I need to ask all of you to keep quiet about the identity of the victim for now."

"Why, Officer?" Mrs. Diaz furrowed her brow. "What's going on?"

"Trust me," Harriman said. "We need to keep that name under wraps."

CHAPTER 3

Detective Sergio Martin paced back and forth over the crumbling asphalt alleyway, checking the time on the gold Rolex Daytona watch strapped to his wrist. Frowning, he looked up and down the cluttered lane.

Where is he?

Rusty blue dumpsters lined the old brick walls of the warehouse exteriors, smoldering in the heat and filling the stagnant air of the alley with the stench of whatever the business owners had discarded. Nearby Tampa Bay offered a healthy reek of low tide to the port's warehouse district.

Heart racing, Sergio wiped the gathering sweat from his temples and the beard stubble lining his jaw. His toned, athletic frame had yet to completely cool down from the workout he'd logged earlier at the gym, and the heat of early summer wasn't helping.

But a fair amount of his perspiration was caused by the anticipation of the meeting he was about to attend with the drug dealers inside the warehouse.

He grabbed the bottom of his sports coat, flapping it back and forth to send air over his t-shirt and jeans, but his bullet proof vest prevented his actions from being effective.

He clenched his jaw and checked the watch again.

Come on, Lavonte!

Up the street, a dingy van with the words Southeast Seafood Distributors on its side, complete with a jumping dolphin logo, sat empty near a large, brick building bearing the same name. Fast food wrappers littered the dashboard of the dirty vehicle. A few feet away, a rusting metal sign at the corner said "Processing Plant." Above that, an ancient Coca-Cola billboard displayed the faded remains of a bikini-clad, olive-toned woman, and a large broken clock whose corroded arms had come to a stop at five minutes after three.

Wiping his damp palms on his jeans, the detective resumed pacing.

Lavonte would be late to his own—

The noise of a large engine reached his ears, its rumbling growing louder and louder. At the end of the alley, a shiny red pickup truck with supersized tires appeared, its chrome exhaust pipes sparkling in the sunlight and its sound system thumping out some indiscernible hip-hop tune.

The raucous sound shut off with the engine, and a muscular African-American man with a bald head and a thick beard jumped out of the driver's side of the vehicle. Smiling at Sergio from behind Pit Viper sunglasses and half a dozen gold chains, Lavonte Jackson held out his arms to the detective as he approached. "Greetings, my brother. How we doin' on this fine, sunny morning in May?"

Sergio let Big Brass wrap him in a bear hug, putting his arms around his friend in return—albeit with much less enthusiasm.

The massive man kept his thick arms around the detective. "I ain't feeling the love, brother."

"You're late." Sergio pried himself out of Lavonte's grip. "I've been out here sweating my butt off for the last fifteen minutes. It's too hot for this jacket."

"Complain, complain." Big Brass smiled, peering at the roof line of the building he'd parked in front of. "Out of all the people I could've gotten to play the role of my bodyguard, I chose my man Sergio. You should feel honored."

"You mean I was the only one dumb enough to say yes."

Big Brass shrugged. "Same difference. And you needed that jacket to look like a drug dealer's bodyguard." Chuckling, he clapped the detective on the shoulder. "Or your version of it."

Sergio fanned the bottom of his sports coat again. "It's almost noon. We should have scheduled this meeting for earlier in the morning."

"Drug lords don't do early mornings."

"Well, we're late either way." Sergio took a step toward the front door of the aging warehouse. "Let's get in there."

"Hold up, hold up." Lavonte shook his head. "Not here. Back door."

"What?" Sergio turned around. "Yesterday, you said we needed to go in at the front entrance of the fish plant."

"Change of plans. I got a text from Carmello an hour ago saying to go in through the back door."

The two men peered down the alley to the rear of the building.

"I don't like it." The detective frowned, running a hand over his chin stubble. "There's less visibility, and fewer escape routes if something goes down."

Big Brass lowered his voice. "Your boys scoped the place out, right?"

"They did," Sergio whispered. "SWAT's been here since six this morning, watching the place from every adjacent rooftop and all the nooks and crannies of the surrounding buildings." He nodded at the dirty seafood van up the street. "The cheeseburger wrappers all over the dashboard of that delivery van are my signal that we're good to go. The Coca-Cola clock says it's five minutes after three, meaning five people have gone inside. But the van's headlights haven't turned on once since I've been here, indicating that your old friend Carmello hasn't shown a hair on his drug dealing head yet. So even though you and I are technically late, I guess we're cool. Once we're in, if Carmello even pulls up in his little Mercedes Roadster, SWAT will arrest him for conspiracy. If he's carrying a gun, that violates his parole."

"Okay, then." Lavonte gazed at the rear corner of the old fish processing plant. "Let's walk."

They headed down the alley, Big Brass glancing wildly at everything, out of the corner of his eyes. Every smelly dumpster, every broken window.

Sergio cracked a thin smile. "You're pretty jumpy for a drug dealer."

"There's an old saying. Hope for the best but plan for the worst." The bald black man tugged at his collar. "Me getting killed would be the worst."

"No, no, no. That's the completely wrong mindset." Sergio hooked a thumb at his sports coat-covered chest. "*Me* getting killed would be the worst." He quickened his pace. "Now, step it up, big fella. Your buddies are expecting us."

Big Brass maintained the same slow pace. "My guy, when you're going into a meeting with a bunch of anxious drug dealers, I find it best not to run on in."

Sergio slowed down.

"And I'm not a drug dealer," Lavonte said.

The detective scanned the alleyway. "You sold illegal drugs in the Greater Tampa Bay area for more than ten years."

"I like to think of myself as an entrepreneur who was meeting the needs of an underserved market."

"It was underserved because your product was illegal."

Big Brass shrugged. "That's not my fault."

They stopped at a set of rusty steel doors.

Taking a deep breath, Sergio glanced at Lavonte. "Which one of us is supposed to go in first?"

"You go." The big man glanced over both shoulders. "I'm not in a big rush to do this. Might be a suicide mission."

"Gee, thanks for inviting me, then." Sergio stared at the door.

Here goes nothing.

Holding his breath, he put a hand on the metal handle and pulled the heavy old door open an inch. When gunshots didn't ring out, he opened it further and stepped inside.

The rear of the dim warehouse was quiet. Sergio stepped into a small room of metal shelves spanning from floor to ceiling, filled with cardboard boxes and big plastic bottles. Bits of dirt and other debris littered the wet concrete floor.

He inched forward, followed by Lavonte. Heart racing, the detective used one hand to push aside a stray spider web and kept the other hand nestled against the butt of his Sig Sauer service weapon.

A tiny shadow darted away on his right side, just out of the light of the doorway. Sergio peered into the blackness just fast enough to spot a greasy, fat rat scurrying behind a cardboard box on a shelf.

The detective looked at Lavonte. "Nice place you got here." He stepped to one side, holding his hand toward what appeared to be the entry into the main warehouse—two double doors with small, dirty windows.

Big Brass held his hands in front of himself, massaging his fingers as he stood in place and stared at the doors.

"It's not a suicide mission." Sergio swallowed hard. "Probably."

The big man continued rubbing his hands, his feet firmly in place and not budging.

"Look." Sergio moved closer to his friend. "Carmello extended a hand to his top producers, his main rivals, and you—right? And you said the word on the street is, he's looking to expand his drug network statewide. He wants to buy into their lines and expand them, and buy your vitamin delivery routes—which used to be your drug distribution routes—to help that expansion." The detective looked at the dirty windows on the double doors, then turned back to Big Brass. "So he's not likely to whack *you*, a necessary piece of a deal that should net him some big time money."

"Right. Right." Lavonte shifted his weight from one foot to the other. "Even so, have your SWAT boys ready with their fingers on the triggers, just in case. Your police-issue nine millimeter pea shooter isn't going to keep us safe, Mr. Pseudo Bodyguard."

Clenching his jaw, Sergio patted the back of his jacket, where his gun was tucked into his belt. "It'll do enough for this job." He looked at the doors to the main warehouse one last time. "Showtime, amigo. I'll go in first, then you follow."

"Why do I not have a gun?" Big Brass hissed.

"Because the nice people at the Tampa Police Department don't trust you." The detective put a hand on the door and leaned toward the dirty glass. "Here we go. Get ready to meet five of your favorite armed drug dealers."

Exhaling a long, slow breath, Big Brass moved behind his friend and crept toward the door.

CHAPTER 4

The pungent smell of fish was even stronger inside the main warehouse. Sergio winced, his heart pounding as he glanced around the large, silent room.

Water covered the warehouse floor. It looked as if the entire place had been hosed off after the last shift, leaving puddles here and there on the wet concrete. A large tank, the size of a swimming pool, stood at one end of the warehouse; several smaller plastic bins lined the side wall, with a long conveyor belt stretching out in front of them. Rectangular stainless-steel tanks stood at the other end of the line.

But no people were visible.

Heart pumping, Sergio pulled out his service weapon and gripped it tightly, holding his breath as he tiptoed toward the center of the room.

Where is everyone?

The warehouse appeared to be completely empty. The only sound was a hose or faucet somewhere, dripping water onto the wet, concrete floor.

Putting his hands on his hips, the detective glared at Big Brass, whispering. "Did you get the wrong day?"

"No," Lavonte hissed. "It's the right day. As much as I didn't wanna see five drug dealers this morning, it might be worse that they aren't here."

"Well, according to the surveillance guys, they came in." Sergio scanned the walls of the odorous warehouse, scrunching up his nose and keeping his voice low. "Maybe the smell in this place knocked them all out."

Big Brass maintained his position by the double doors, clinging to a steel shelf. "What did you expect? It's a fish processing plant, brother." He nodded toward the swimming pool-sized vat on the far side of the room. "That cistern over there holds the fresh catches in seawater until they're chopped up and processed on the line. The good stuff goes into the steel tanks until it's shipped out, and the scraps and guts go in the bins—or on the floor. Couple times a week, it all gets automatically flushed down the drain into the bay."

Sergio checked behind the empty scrap bins, pointing his gun to wherever he looked. "That sounds eco-friendly."

"More than you'd think. I understand a lot of sharks come into the bay for that crap, like clockwork. It's like shark Thanksgiving out there on cleanout days. Carmello only uses this place because ain't nobody gonna come snooping around. The smell keeps people away."

"It'd keep me away." The detective nodded, approaching the stainless-steel containers. "Your vast knowledge of the fish mongering business is impressive, but what happened to the five—"

The body of a man lay inside the first metal bin. A gunshot wound was visible in his chest and another one in his forehead.

The corpse rested on two other bodies, their torsos and bloody faces clearly visible. Each had been executed in the same manner as the first. The next stainless-steel bin held the remaining members of the planned meeting.

The massive hole in the first victim's skull told Sergio that the victim was already deceased, but the detective put two fingers to the man's throat to check for a pulse anyway. There was none.

Sighing, he lowered his gun and stared at the five dead drug dealers. It had been a setup, the worst of all possible outcomes.

Sergio shouted across the warehouse to his friend. "Lavonte, you can come out now. I think the meeting has been canceled."

Big Brass crept over to Sergio and peeked over his friend's shoulder. "Damn."

"Yeah." The detective pointed at the bodies using his gun. "Do you recognize any of these guys?"

"They're not Carmello's people," Big Brass said. "The guy on top is a boss from up state, in the panhandle." He looked at the other dead men in the bins. "I recognize one from a Miami deal we did back in the day—a big player. The rest, I don't know." He turned to Sergio. "Looks like somebody took out a lot of potential rivals."

"They sure didn't kill each other. Not like this." He eyed his friend. "Would Carmello do this?"

Big Brass nodded, sweat forming on his upper lip. "The man's been known to go crazy sometimes." Swallowing hard, he pulled at his shirt collar. "But if Carmello did this, where'd he go? You said SWAT's been watching this place all morning."

Clutching his service gun, Sergio turned around and leaned against the edge of the stainless-steel bin as he visually searched the warehouse for a means of escape.

How could Carmello get in and out of here if SWAT was watching the entire exterior of the building?

If he spent the night here, okay—he got in before SWAT arrived this morning. But he's either still here, which would be the stupidest move ever after killing five people, or he got out.

How?

Somewhere in the silent processing plant, another drop of water fell to the soaked concrete floor. Its faint, solitary sound echoed off the warehouse walls.

Sergio scanned the glimmering floor, his attention going to the round cover of a storm drain in the middle of the room.

The detective bolted upright. "I think that's where he went."

Big Brass turned as Sergio raced toward the storm drain. "You're not going in there."

"Yes, I am." Sergio grabbed the edges of the heavy steel lid and heaved it upwards.

Two muzzle flashes burst outward from the large drain, the gun held by the hand of an African-American man wearing a tan suitcoat.

Reeling backwards, Sergio gasped as he dropped the storm drain cover and landed face-first on the warehouse floor. Big Brass ducked as the bullets zipped past his head and ricocheted off the steel roof rafters. As the steel drain cover hit the concrete with a loud *clang* and fell on its side, Big Brass sprinted back to the double doors.

The heavy cover spun in a circle, wobbling back and forth like a giant coin, its metallic whirring growing louder and louder until the lid finally came to a stop.

Lifting his head from the concrete floor, Sergio narrowed his eyes as he hauled his gun out. "Well, we definitely know where Carmello went now."

Lavonte's eyes went wide. "You're not going in there!"

"No choice." Sergio got to his feet, gripping his weapon with both hands. "SWAT didn't see him come in, so they sure won't be able to apprehend him wherever this storm drain lets out—and I'm not losing a killer."

The detective shoved his gun into the opening and fired twice, the loud blasts reverberating through the fish warehouse.

Cringing, Big Brass covered his ears. "Was that necessary?"

Sergio nodded. "Now he's headed back to however he got in. If we don't follow him, he'll get away." He knelt down and leaned back as he stared at the hole.

"By we, you mean *you*," Big Brass said.

"Yep." Gritting his teeth, Sergio crept toward the drain opening, peering over the edge into the darkness.

"Okay," Big Brass said. "It's your funeral."

"Let's hope not." The detective clutched his weapon as he glanced over at his friend. "SWAT heard those gunshots just now. They'll be coming in. Get outside first and let them know it was me."

"Yeah…" Big Brass frowned, looking toward the exit. "Send the black man outside to deal with a bunch of hyped-up cops after shots were fired in a dark warehouse. What could possibly go wrong?"

"Tell them I said to swarm the building." Sergio popped the magazine out of his gun, verifying the number of remaining rounds, then rammed it back into place. "And tell Max to look up the city's easements for these storm drains so they can meet me wherever this one comes out."

Big Brass grimaced.

"Relax, would you?" Sergio said. "They know who you are. But… you know—raise your hands, just in case." He stepped to the edge of the storm drain.

"Lordy." Big Brass shook his head. "You're gonna get yourself killed one of these days—and me, right along with you."

"Maybe," the detective said. "But not today. Now, go."

SIX SISTERS

Gripping his gun, Sergio crossed his arms over his chest and dropped himself into the hole.

CHAPTER 5

Sergio's feet hit the bottom of the concrete storm drain with a jarring thump and a small splash. An inch or so of water trickled past his shoes in the oval pipeline, and a light breeze carried air past his face.

Clutching his service weapon to his chest, the detective looked back and forth in the near-darkness. Reflected light came from a distant turn in the long, narrow tunnel.

Sunlight. That's the way out.

A glance at the water moving by his feet confirmed his conclusion.

Carmello could have parked an escape car farther up the storm drain, though.

Which way did he go?

Sergio held his breath, straining to hear any noises from the fleeing murderer.

A series of small splashes echoed up to him from downstream.

Footsteps. He's on the move.

Bolting forward, the detective rushed through the storm drain as he extended his weapon. "Tampa police department! Stop running and give yourself up!"

Other openings went by over his head, concrete circles sealed with heavy steel drain covers. The bend in the tunnel bounced in his sights as he ran. "Police! Stop running!"

The arm in the tan suitcoat swung around the corner ahead, brandishing the large handgun again.

Two more gun blasts lit up the darkness.

Sergio threw himself forward, crashing to the floor of the tunnel as he covered his head with both hands. A connecting spillway was visible to his right. Scrambling across the wet concrete, he rolled into the spillway just as another volley of shots exploded into the concrete drainway.

At his feet, a collection of dark brown shadows scattered. Cringing, he reeled back and kicked outward, scattering the shadows. High-pitched squeals came from whatever his shoes collided with.

Sergio flinched.

Rats.

Terrific.

The vermin dispersed, racing out of the spillway and across the main storm drain. Two more shots fired from his attacker, lighting the tunnel as they ricocheted off the tunnel walls by the rats.

Collecting himself, the detective counted how many shots the killer had fired.

Two now, and two before, when I first jumped in. Then three, plus at least ten in the warehouse—two for each body.

So, seventeen?

He's empty, or close to it.

Holding his breath, Sergio leaned out of the spillway.

Another gunshot flashed in the drain, whizzing past his head.

The detective recoiled, gasping.

Okay, not empty. He's using a twenty-round magazine. Got it.

Gritting his teeth, Sergio pointed his service weapon into the storm drain and rolled out of the spillway, firing off three rounds at his attacker.

Footsteps from up ahead again rapidly hit the water of the drain, quickly fading.

Huffing, Sergio pushed himself to his feet and hurled himself toward the fleeing gunman.

"Once again," he panted, "the guy who hates running finds himself doing cross-country."

At the corner, he thrust himself over onto the far wall and fired off another shot. His bullet bounced off the concrete and drifted into the light at the end of the tunnel.

Squinting, Sergio spotted a rickety steel ladder and a pair of legs in tan suit pants, wiggling upward through a vertical access shaft. The rusty ladder shook and banged against the concrete wall.

The detective frowned.

Another opening in the storm drain. Carmello's about to get away.

Breathing hard, Sergio pointed his weapon toward the escape hole and inched forward. The drafty air in the tunnel shifted, from a slight inward breeze to a push outward and toward the water of the bay, lifting his hair and dropping it over his forehead.

Carmello will have a car close by, and maybe a driver waiting.

If it's his Mercedes, I'll never catch him on foot—and SWAT won't know where we are yet.

I have to stop him before he gets to his car.

Gritting his teeth, Sergio raced toward the rusty ladder.

He might be just sitting up there, too, with a gun pointed right at this hole, waiting for me to stick my head out so he can shoot me.

So…

Does he want me dead more than he wants to get away?

As the wind in the tunnel increased, Sergio stopped just before the overhead exit access. Gasping and sweating, he gripped his gun and poked his head into the storm drain opening, withdrawing it again as fast as he could.

Nothing.

Clear blue skies.

It's a parking lot. And I bet his Mercedes is there, waiting to drive him away.

Not on my watch.

He grabbed the side of the rickety ladder with his left hand and kept his gun pointed upward at the opening, placing a foot on the bottom rung.

As he climbed, the gentle wind in the tunnel turned into a rush, and a roar came from behind him. The ladder vibrated in his hands.

He turned to see a massive wall of water bouncing back and forth against the curved walls of the storm drain.

His jaw dropped as the water rushed toward him.

What the heck is that!

Sergio sprinted upward as the rusty ladder bounced against the concrete wall. The tsunami of tunnel water crashed into him like an NFL linebacker, knocking his feet off the rusty steel step and dragging him down. He hung on, holding his breath and gripping the flimsy ladder with his fingertips as his legs were pulled by the ferocious current. Pieces of debris slammed into his head and shoulders, hammering his hands and slapping his face.

As his lungs strained for air, black dots gathered in the corners of his eyes.

The rushing water ebbed a bit, slowing enough to allow him to force his head above the waves and gasp for air.

The hand in the tan suitcoat was there, a .45 caliber gun pointed at Sergio's face.

He ducked, squeezing his eyes shut and hunching his shoulders.

The muffled sound of the gunshot was loud enough to be heard over the rushing water. The bullet slammed into Sergio's back like a baseball bat. His Kevlar vest prevented the bullet from penetrating, but the force of the massive impact knocked the air out of him.

Sergio's waterlogged clothing and the extra weight of the sports coat and bullet proof vest dragged him under the water.

Shoving his feet downward as hard as he could, the detective managed to pop his head a few inches out of the churning water and grab another quick breath. This time, the tan-sleeved hand and the .45 were nowhere in sight.

As Sergio pulled himself forward, another watery roar filled the air. He threw his arms around the rickety steel ladder as the next surge of water came crashing down the pipeline toward him and smashed into his face.

It yanked his right hand from the ladder, stripping away his service gun and carrying the weapon away. Clinging by one hand, Sergio's shoulder strained as if it would pop out of the socket. He squeezed his eyes shut, holding onto what little breath he had left, his lungs burning as the churning water pulled and slapped at him. The rusty steel of the ladder cut into his fingers as he strained to hold on.

His grip slipped a fraction, his pinky finger coming free of the rail, then his index finger.

Hang on or you'll be swept away through the pipe.

He clung to the ladder, his fingers on fire with pain.

A moment later, the monstrous waves subsided and the churning surface lowered.

Gasping, Sergio forced himself to stand in the chest-deep current, slouching into the storm drain wall as he flung the water from his eyes.

The business end of the .45 swung into the hole again.

Sergio grabbed the barrel and twisted it away as the muzzle flashed. His hand stung with the burn of the blast.

Letting go of the ladder, he took a quick breath and slapped both of his hands onto the killer's gun, plunging himself under the water and lifting his feet so the weight would force the gun from his opponent's hand or drag the drug dealer into the hole with him.

Underwater, Sergio kicked and flailed against the current, holding tight to the .45—and working to keep the business end pointed toward anything but him.

The weapon dragged him upward.

Sergio slammed into the concrete walls of the storm drain, pain surging through his fists. He lost his grip on the wet steel of the gun barrel, and the .45 jerked upward, away from him.

Panting, Sergio resurfaced. Streaks of blood ran from his knuckles.

The exit hole above him was nothing but clear blue sky again.

He grabbed the rusty rails and hauled himself up the rickety steel ladder, pausing just below the top to peek out.

A man in a tan suit lay on his back next to the opening, gasping for air. A black Mercedes waited no more than twenty feet away in an empty parking lot.

"Police!" Sergio shouted desperately. "Don't move, Carmello!"

Groaning, the drug dealer bolted upright and raised his weapon, firing once. Sergio ducked under the rim of the storm drain, then leaped upward and out of the hole, grabbing the gun and throwing himself on top of the killer. He slammed the killer's hand into the asphalt again and again until the gun came loose and skittered away.

Carmello shoved the exhausted detective away and rolled over, getting to his feet and staggering toward the Mercedes.

"Stop, now!" Sergio stretched out his hand and grabbed the .45, squeezing the trigger. Two shots blasted into the front of the criminal's vehicle and a third shot punctured the front tire.

A burst of steam rose from the hood as the Mercedes sagged on its flattened wheel.

Carmello turned around, his hands in the air, as he slumped backward onto his car. "Okay." He gasped. "I give up."

Sergio cocked his head, keeping his eyes on the drug dealer. "Keep your hands up and turn around, Carmello."

The drug dealer nodded, barely upright, his breath coming in short gasps. He lifted a dripping hand and pointed at Sergio. "You... you was with Big Brass." He shook his head. "That double crossing mother—"

"Enough!" Sergio gripped the gun with both hands and leveled it at Carmello's torso. Water dripped from his chin. "Turn around and put your hands on your head!"

The drug dealer sagged against the car, wheezing, his arms at his sides. "I shoulda killed Lavonte when he left the business." He put a hand on the side of the car. "Figures that bald-ass traitor would pull something like this. Bein' friendly with the police done turned him."

"Last warning." Sergio took a step toward the suspect. "Turn around, hands on your head."

"Or maybe you got bought off, cop." Carmello's eyes narrowed. "Does this double cross go beyond that vitamin hustler Lavonte?"

Frowning, the detective crept forward. "I said, put your hands on your head."

"That's it, isn't it?" Carmello smiled. "You're just working for a different snake in the grass. Well, son, lemme explain things. You have had your last good night's sleep. Somebody's reach done exceeded their grasp, and I'm gonna figure out who."

Less than five feet away, Sergio kept the .45 aimed at the killer. He shook his head, exhaling. "Last warning, then I start putting holes in that nice suit of yours. I'm too tired for this crap."

"Uh huh." Camello's smile widened as he raised his eyebrows. "Me, too."

The drug dealer wheeled around and heaved open the Mercedes door, snatching a gun from the passenger seat. Sergio threw himself forward, slamming himself into Carmello and crushing the drug dealer's body against the car. He grabbed the killer's new gun with one hand and held onto the .45 with the other.

Carmello wrapped his free hand around the detective and pushed himself forward, knocking

Sergio off his feet and taking them both down onto the asphalt. The detective landed on his back, Carmello crashing down face-first on top of him. The impact knocked the wind out of Sergio.

As the detective grappled to keep both weapons pointed away from him, Carmello's eyes went wide. The drug dealer pushed down on Sergio and raised himself upwards, howling as he hurled his forehead straight down toward Sergio's skull.

The detective turned his face away. Carmello's head smashed into the asphalt.

The drug dealer sagged on top of Sergio, moaning as the fight went out of him. Sergio pushed him off and got to his feet, grabbing his attacker by the collar and kicking the second gun out of Carmello's hand.

Sweat dripping off his nose, Sergio shoved his suspect against the Mercedes and pressed his forearm across Carmello's chest, raising the .45 caliber weapon. "Any more stunts like that and this will end very badly for you." He clenched his teeth, his pulse throbbing. "Are you finished?"

Carmello panted heavily, his foul breath reaching Sergio's cheek. Blood trickled down the side of his face.

Sergio shoved him again. "Are you finished?"

"I'm done." The drug dealer mumbled, his hands dangling at his sides. "It's over." He lifted his head just enough to look Sergio in the eye. "Call me an ambulance."

"Okay." Sergio wheezed. "You're an ambulance. Now, turn around and put your hands on your head."

Lights and sirens illuminated the brick walls of the warehouses around the parking lot. A SWAT van came around the corner, followed by two police cruisers and several TV vans. Overhead, a Tampa PD helicopter swung into view, hovering over the old brick warehouses.

Sergio managed to keep his grip on his suspect until the reinforcements took over. They locked handcuffs around Carmello's wrists and dragged him toward the SWAT van.

"Carmello!" Sergio shouted. "Try not to die before they can request medical attention. We need information from you."

The drug dealer turned his head around over the protests of the SWAT officers holding him. "I got nothing to say, pig. I didn't do anything wrong."

"I think… the guys in the warehouse…" Sergio took a breath to slow his pulse. "They would disagree—if they weren't dead." He glared at Carmello. "Once we ID them, we'll know what your whole takeover plan was. I bet they have a lot of employees who might want to settle the score for taking out their bosses and putting them out of work. Police custody might be the only safe place for you."

Carmello scowled, blood dripping from his forehead as he staggered to the back of the SWAT van.

Exhaling, Sergio leaned back against the Mercedes and closed his eyes. "Oh, man. I could use a nap."

"Sergio." One of the SWAT officers approached the soggy detective, carrying a towel and a bottle of water. "Let's get you cleaned up." He draped the towel over Sergio's shoulders.

"Thanks." After a few deep breaths, Sergio held out his scratched-up hands. They were bruised and swelling, but clenching them and unclenching them a few times indicated that no bones had been broken. He took the water from the SWAT officer. "I guess I'm gonna live."

"For a little while." The officer chuckled. "Carly's waiting in the recon van—and she's really steamed. When Big Brass came out and said you jumped into the storm drain, I thought she was gonna have a heart attack. That was a real cowboy move, my guy."

Sergio peered at the recon van, nodding. "And now I have to hear all about how I broke freaking protocol or something." He took a swig of water and looked back at the officer. "Well, getting the bad guys is what's important, right? And we did that."

Sergio walked toward the SWAT van, dabbing his face with the towel. As he approached, he pulled his phone from his pocket. Water dripped from it in a stream.

Terrific.

The van's back doors opened and Sergio's partner appeared, red-faced and stern.

"Carly." Sergio smiled. "How nice to see you."

Scowling, Detective Sanderson moved to one side as Sergio climbed into the van, then she slammed the door shut behind him.

CHAPTER 6

SERGIO FLINCHED. "You seem upset, Carly."

"You are so irresponsible!" His partner glared at him, her face growing redder. "If anything went off plan, you were supposed to take cover and wait for backup. You *knew* that. And instead, you… you…"

"Chased the bad guy down and arrested him."

"You broke protocol. Again." Carly lowered her voice. "And stupidly risked your life—again—by blindly jumping into a storm drain. Anything could have happened in there! Carmello might have had ten of his thugs waiting in there for you, and—"

Sergio waved a hand. "Oh, there was no way."

"You didn't know that!"

"And what did you know?" He faced his partner. "I was up all night planning this, same as you. The reconnaissance team didn't even see

Carmello go into the warehouse. Then, he somehow managed to kill five guys right under the noses of a hundred cops who were watching the building with you. And he'd have put a few holes in me and Lavonte if he were a better shot." Wiping his face with the towel, Sergio turned away. "I'm sorry if I broke protocol, but with backup like that, I'll take my chances going down the storm drain."

Carly sighed, lowering her head. "Okay, you're right. It was a mistake in the surveillance, not seeing how Carmello could have gotten inside." She peered up at him. "But that's not an excuse for breaking protocol."

Sergio shrugged. "I saw it a little differently when the bullets were zinging past my head."

"We have the rules for a reason." Carly held her hands out. "You can't keep doing stuff like this or people will get hurt. Pulling a stunt like that…" She shook her head. "If I were your boss, I'd recommend a suspension."

"Hmm." Sergio took a swig of water. "Good thing you're not my boss, then."

Detective Sanderson huffed. "Your behavior was completely irresponsible, and—"

"Come on, Carly." Sergio looked at her, his voice softening. "We got the bad guys. It's a win, and it was a team effort. It's all good."

His partner put a hand to her head. "When are you going to listen to me and stop taking such excessive risks?"

"It wasn't excessive." Sergio sat down on one of the bench seats in the back of the van, dabbing his neck with the towel. "I knew you wouldn't let anything happen to me."

Leaning against an equipment shelf, Carly dropped her hands into her lap. "You don't get it. I worry that—"

There was a knock on the back of the vehicle. As the van's rear doors opened, the SWAT officer's face appeared. "Detective Sanderson? Ms. Fox from Public Relations is asking if she can borrow Sergio for a quick interview before the news crews head out."

Carly's eyes stayed on Sergio. "He'll be there in a sec."

"Ma'am, she says it has to be now if the reporters are going to make a teaser for their noon broadcasts and get a full segment edited in time for the five o'clock news."

"Okay." Carly looked away and waved a hand. "Go."

"Thanks." Sergio scrambled out of the recon vehicle. "You can finish yelling at me later."

"I'm not interested in yelling at you," Carly said. "I'm interested in you staying alive."

"Really?" Turning around, he grinned at her. "Well, I'm encouraged."

Outside the van, the Tampa PD's designated Public Relations expert, Avarie Fox, stood a few feet away, her short golden locks shimmering in the bright midday sunlight.

Sergio took a position next to the slender and beautiful PR expert, walking quickly away from the recon van. "Thank you for rescuing me," he whispered.

"It's the least I could do." Avarie smiled. "After all, you saved my life once."

Sergio nodded. "And I am gonna keep trading on that for as long as you'll let me."

* * * * *

Inside the van, Carly picked up a clipboard and stared at it, then tossed it back onto the equipment shelf and peered out the window. Outside, Sergio walked next to Avarie, smiling at her, their shoulders almost touching as they made their way toward the reporters.

A twinge went through Carly's insides.

She returned to the equipment shelf and picked the clipboard up again, heat rising in her cheeks.

She studied the page, but nothing on it registered.

Huffing, Carly threw the clipboard back onto the shelf and put her hands to her head, pushing her hair back and lowering herself onto the bench seat.

* * * * *

"So…" Avarie clasped her hands at the waist of her blue suit skirt, slowing her walk towards the reporters. "They'll ask a few questions about the operation. Keep your answers short and factual."

"Got it." Sergio beamed. "Actually, I was wondering if you were free later. I have to meet my mom and sister this evening, but what about after that?"

"After?" The petite PR rep furrowed her brow. "I don't know…"

"What about lunch, then? I know you have to do this press conference, and I've gotta do a debriefing with Deshawn, and—"

"Sergio!" Across the parking lot, the SWAT Commander waved a hand and lifted up a hand-held radio. "Chief Clemmons wants to talk to you."

Sergio waved back, then turned to Avarie. "And apparently the chief needs me for something."

"The chief?" She raised her eyebrows. "Maybe you're getting a commendation."

He walked backwards, in the general direction of the SWAT Commander, keeping his eyes on the blonde PR rep. "A commendation? You think so?"

"Nabbing Carmello is a pretty big deal," Avarie said.

"Yeah." Sergio glanced over his shoulder at the commander, then back at her. "Well, so what about having a late lunch with me, then?"

"Maybe I could squeeze you in." Avarie smiled. "What time?"

"Two?" He continued walking backwards—but slower—as he held his hands out. "But I have to leave by five to meet my mom and sister, and there'll be a ton of traffic, so we'll only have three hours to eat."

The PR rep folded her arms across her dark blue suitcoat. "Tell you what. Give me the key to your condo and I'll have lunch waiting for you when you get there."

Sergio stopped, his mouth hanging open. "Really?" He dug his key ring from his pocket.

"Sure." Avarie strolled up to him and held her hand out. "The Italian place on the corner delivers, right?"

CHAPTER 7

Avarie walked toward the waiting reporters, smoothing nonexistent wrinkles from the fine fabric of her skirt. The thrill of the drug bust had gripped her insides for the better part of two hours, waiting in silence with the others in the unmarked police van as the SWAT members moved into place around the fish processing plant. Now, it was time to help shape the message that the news reports would deliver to their audiences.

She approached the press conference like a major league baseball player taking batting practice, with certainty and confidence, prepared to answer any and all questions the local media might bring up. The success of another important Tampa PD operation would allow Avarie to present the police department in the best light—as was her goal for the day, and her job overall.

A recent serial killer running loose in Tampa, coupled with several unrelated prominent murders, had caused the local citizenry to become uneasy with their police force. As TPD's top brass corrected things internally, Avarie had been contracted as a public relations expert to remind the people of Tampa just how good their police officers actually were.

The petite professional, with her winning smile and big blue eyes, was quite a change from the semi-unpolished spokespeople the department had used in the past. Her well-tailored blue suit showed off her slender, attractive figure while offering a stark contrast to the grittiness of the port's warehouse district surrounding her.

The twenty-seven-year-old blonde made a few statements to the reporters about the morning's operation, then fielded their questions amidst the flashing lights of almost a dozen SWAT vehicles and Tampa police squad cars.

A quick glance at her phone as she wrapped up indicated that the entire press conference had taken less than ten minutes—a good sign. The three journalists didn't ask difficult questions; they seemed genuinely thrilled to have been invited to watch the takedown from a distance with her, and they were putty in Avarie's hands after that.

She had extolled the heroics of the men and women in blue to the reporters—and she had highlighted Detective Sergio Martin, the main actor in the morning's efforts.

Looking over her shoulder at the squad cars, she pointed out Sergio to the news people as the handsome detective spoke on a hand-held radio.

SIX SISTERS

Cop after cop came up and high fived him or patted him on the back.

"So? Any other questions?" Avarie turned back to the news crews, clasping her hands in front of herself. The reporter from Channel Eight appeared satisfied, as did the one from Channel Thirteen. They moved away and rendezvoused with their respective videographers, talking about the best angles to do their story coverage from, and lighting options.

The third reporter, independent news journalist Kerri Milner, slid her computer satchel off her arm and opened it, removing a small tripod and a half-eaten apple pastry. The skinny, twentysomething brunette was the only member of the media to record Avarie's press conference with a smart phone.

Kerri squatted, taking a bite of her leftover breakfast as she arranged the legs of her tripod. She pushed a strand of her short, brown locks over her ear. "You know, Ms. Fox, making Detective Martin out to be a star might not be your smartest career move."

"It's not a career move." Avarie bristled. "He *is* a star. He's got the most high-profile arrests in the department, and his conviction rate is one of the best in the state. Only his partner, Detective Sanderson's, is better. And Sergio goes where some other cops won't. I've seen it. So have you."

"Oh, I know. I get it." Kerri stood up, squinting in the bright light. "He takes risks. It's a flex. But—"

"It's not just that he takes risks." Avarie looked over to where Sergio stood, his shirt now off as he dried off his muscled torso with a towel from the EMTs. "He… he does the math. Sergio assesses a situation and makes a decision, following through without hesitation. How many other cops would have jumped into a dark storm drain to chase after a suspected murderer, not knowing how many other killers might have been down there? Or gone into a trailer knowing a hostile murderer was inside with a gun?" Her gaze returned to the reporter. "Sergio—Detective Martin—does that. He's one of those rare people who's willing to put his life on the line, again and again, to keep the rest of us safe."

A smile tugged at the corners of the young reporter's mouth. "Hey, if you're crushing on the guy, that's cool. Just low key the fangirling. You don't want to appear biased."

Putting her hands on her hips, Avarie narrowed her eyes. "Are we off the record?"

"Yeah." Kerri nodded. "Sure."

"We've been out a few times." Avarie sighed. "Work-related stuff, until the other night. I asked him out on a date. Dinner. That was it."

"Now you sound disappointed." Kerri glanced toward Sergio. "I thought he had a reputation."

"He… he's bouncing back from a relationship that ended recently." Avarie shrugged. "I'm trying to respect that. The fact that I'm interested in him romantically doesn't affect the way I represent his work or do my job."

Kerri nodded. "Well, I don't think the other reporters picked up on anything." She took another bite of her pastry. "Not to throw shade, but the airhead from Channel Thirteen wouldn't know it if she walked in on you and Sergio *in flagrante delecto*, and that Karen from Channel Eight is so focused on herself, she'd be hard pressed to notice anyone else." She smiled at Avarie and stuffed the rest of her pastry into the mouth. "Is he a good kisser? I bet he is. He's got those Latin lips."

Avarie withheld any other reaction than a smile. "So, how's the independent news business?"

"LOL. Too far? You know, I don't roll that way, but I'd give the boy a try." Kerri chuckled, brushing the crumbs off her hands. "FlashFire News is bussin—but it's a lot more grinding than I thought it'd be. But if I keep publishing the truth when the others won't, it'll hit it big. Meanwhile, I make ends meet by doing freelance stuff like commercials. I pulled a short stint recently with a TV production crew that's trying to make livestream shows to sell to networks, but it didn't pay much."

"I can sympathize with getting a startup business off the ground." Avarie nodded. "But I've seen some of your news stories. You're smart. You'll make it—*no cap*."

"Thanks. And I really appreciate you inviting me here today, for reals." Kerri looked around the parking lot, with its crumbling asphalt and sagging, trash-laden fencing. Broken windows were everywhere on the ancient brick warehouses that surrounded the crime scene. "There was a good chance this flex would've fizzled out into nothing—a burn, right in front of the local TV cameras." Kerri's eyes returned to the PR rep. "I guess you're a risk taker, too. Watch out for Sergio, though. Word is, the guy's a player, and I don't wanna see you get played."

The young reporter placed her phone into a clamp on top of the tripod and stepped in front of it, moving backward and forward until her face and shoulders filled most of the small screen, while still keeping the warehouses and squad cars in the shot.

As Avarie walked toward the unmarked SWAT van that had brought her, Sergio climbed into a police cruiser and departed.

She reflected on the young reporter's unanswered question.

"Is he a good kisser?"

It had been a nervous date, at first—Avarie had been nervous to ask Sergio out. But before the appetizers had even arrived, they'd settled in.

Good food, good beer, good talk. Laughter and another round of drinks, followed by more talk and more laughter. None of it seemed forced or awkward. There was a flow, an easiness, to the night. A harmony. She had bridged the difficult gap between working together and asking the handsome detective out, and it had worked. Avarie was able to enjoy herself, enjoy Sergio's company, and relax.

Mostly.

Because even though the entire evening went well, it was still *she* that had asked *him* out—and as the night drew to a close, the inevitable question of "what now" loomed in the air.

In the parking lot of the restaurant, he suggested they go back to his place…

Her heart jumped a little.

...to drop off his car, and let him drive her home in hers. He'd catch an Uber from her motel.

She accepted at first, slightly flustered by the misdirection she allowed herself to have, then declined because it would be an unnecessary waste of time and money. She only had two beers over three hours; she could drive herself home.

Then, upon hearing what she'd said—and wondering if she had just turned down a night of something more—she hesitated but couldn't think of a way to backtrack. Her brain was a jumble of conflicting thoughts and self-doubt.

She made it worse when, as she pulled her car into the parking lot of his condo, she parked in the visitor spot, turned the engine off, got out, and walked with him toward the elevator.

As they strolled side by side, she fumbled with her key fob. He'd already said no—or, more precisely, she turned him down if he had been offering to add to the evening.

Just be happy with a nice first date, Avarie. Take the W.

Sergio stopped next to the elevator and pushed the call button, turning to her. "Well, thanks for asking me to dinner." He smiled. "I had a great time."

Clearing her throat, she tried to think of something to say in return—anything—that wasn't just a reply of "me, too."

Nothing entered her thoughts.

"Roscoe!"

Sergio glanced to his left. A massive brown dog smashed into him and took him to the ground.

Tail wagging full speed, the big furry canine stood with his front paws on Sergio's chest, licking him furiously.

"Holy cow!" An African-American man rushed forward, limping on a boot cast. "No, Roscoe!"

Sergio scrunched up his face, laughing. "Roscoe! Chill, buddy."

With some effort, the owner clipped a leash onto the dog's collar and pulled him off. Sergio sat up.

"I'm sorry, Sergio." The man panted. "He got away from me, and I can't move too well with this foot." He pointed at his cast, then glanced over his shoulder, gesturing to a small boy and girl as they raced down the sidewalk toward him. "You know how Roscoe gets when these two hooligans come over."

The young children plowed into the detective without slowing down. "Sergio! Sergio!"

The momentum carried the detective over onto his back again. He patted their heads, his feet sticking up in the air. "Hi, kids."

"Will you take us to the pool?" the boy asked. "We packed our bathing suits."

Sergio gently lifted the children off him and plopped each one on the grass. "I think it's kinda late for swimming, isn't it?"

"You two get up now." The man frowned, straining to keep the rowdy dog from rejoining the melee. "Can't you see Mr. Sergio's trying to talk with this young woman? We don't wanna be rude."

As the children went to their father's side, Sergio sat up, grinning. "Avarie, this is Jason and Janine. You already met Roscoe. And the owner of all three is Mr. Givens here."

The man nodded, holding onto the leash. "Nice to meet you ma'am. Sorry to interrupt your evening."

Roscoe pulled his owner forward and began to lick Sergio again.

"Let's see if the pool's open!" Jason raced away down the sidewalk, his sister on his heels. Roscoe broke free of his owner's grip and bolted after them.

"What!" Mr. Givens put his hands on his knees, gasping. "Roscoe! Get back here!"

At the end of the sidewalk, the children turned left. Roscoe ran straight ahead, barking wildly at something in the hedges.

Mr. Givens turned to Sergio. "Can I bother you to help me corral him, Sergio? He's faster than me but he always listens to you."

"Yeah, sure." Sergio got to his feet and clapped the dirt from his hands. "You go get your kids. I'll get Roscoe." He turned to Avarie, pointing toward the hedges. "So, I kinda need to—you know—help get the dog before he chases a raccoon into the street or something."

"Oh. Okay. Yeah." Avarie hooked a thumb over her shoulder, shrugging as she took a step toward her car. "It's getting late anyway, like you said."

I know when Karma has spoken.

"Okay." He grinned at her. "I guess I'll see you tomorrow, then."

"Yeah. See you tomorrow." Nodding, she turned away.

Sergio trotted off into the darkness.

"Come on, you maniacs." Mr. Givens limped along the sidewalk, the leash swinging from his fist. "Too much sugar. That's what I get for taking you to McDonald's when your mom drops you off."

Avarie drove herself home, barely noticing the city as it passed by her car windows in the darkness, replaying the almost-moment in her head.

What happened?

One second, we're about to have a romantic moment—I think. The next second... the night is over? "See you tomorrow?"

Really, Avarie?

She envisioned Sergio leaning in, his warm hands framing her face, his lips coming close to hers...

"Ms. Fox?"

A uniformed officer tapped Avarie on the shoulder. "The van is ready to head back to the station, ma'am—if you're ready to go."

"What? Yes. Absolutely." She glanced at the officer in the fish warehouse parking lot, a tinge of heat rising to her cheeks as her thoughts careened back to the present. "I'll, uh..." Avarie cleared her throat. "I'll be right there."

CHAPTER 8

IN THE SWAT VAN, Carly stopped typing her after-action report and pressed her phone to her ear, a knot gripping her insides.

"Carly?" the nurse said. "Are you still there?"

She wasn't. Not anymore.

The detective's gaze drifted over the drab gray interior of the van, unfocused.

I should have known when the doctor tried to call me directly.

Carly swallowed hard.

After Doctor Mendez's nurse said the word "cancer," Carly didn't hear anything else.

She couldn't even breathe.

Cancer.

Death.

She exhaled a long, slow breath. Outside, in the sunshine of a beautiful May afternoon, the uniformed officers roped off the crime scene and the coroner tagged the bodies.

Inside the van, the detective sat alone.

I'm going to die. Not in decades, like everyone thinks, but in months, or maybe weeks.

Darkness swept over Carly like she'd fallen down a well. The light grew smaller and smaller as blackness encompassed everything, her thoughts focused on the word that echoed in her head.

Cancer.

She forced herself to refocus on the nurse's call.

"I'm sorry, ma'am. I didn't get any of that. Could you repeat it please?"

"Of course, Carly. That's actually fairly common in these situations." The nurse cleared her throat. "What would you like me to repeat?"

"All of it." She took a deep breath and held it. "Everything."

And this time, could you say something else? Could you tell me I heard you wrong?

"Okay," Mendez said. "The lab results from the biopsy confirm you have ovarian cancer. Now, this type of tumor is very treatable, and we caught it early, but Doctor Mendez wants to run more tests so we can determine if it has spread and metastasized, so we'd like you to come in for that. What would be your availability for a full consultation and layout of an ongoing treatment program?"

Carly shook her head. "That's not... I need to know—I need to know if I'm going to die. Like, how... how bad is this? Am I going to die in a month, or..."

"I understand." The nurse's voice was reassuring and stable. "And the answer is, we can't say for certain. Doctor Mendez says we caught it early, so statistically a patient in your situation would have upwards of a ninety-five percent chance of making a full recovery if we start treatment right away. But if you look on the internet, you'll see a lot of horror stories—so don't do that. Those are often advanced cases where the mortality rate is very high, but many times a patient diagnosed with an advanced case is also an elderly woman, and the ability to respond to treatment is diminished. That's not the case here. You're young and healthy."

Carly snorted. "And full of cancer."

"We find it's best to keep a positive outlook," the nurse said. "There's an excellent chance you'll live a long, happy life. I think that's the thing to focus on. That and a rigorous treatment plan."

Sighing, Carly nodded. "So… how soon do we need to start? Like, should I make plans to leave work and come in right now?"

"No, no, no."

Carly breathed a sigh of relief.

"First thing tomorrow morning would be fine. Doctor Mendez knows you have a very busy schedule at the police department, so she asked Roberta to squeeze you in. We can see you at seven A.M."

"Tomorrow?" Carly said. "That's Sunday."

"Yes, ma'am. Oncology doesn't do bankers hours."

The detective's jaw dropped. "Oh, wow."

Tomorrow morning? Sunday morning? It's that serious?

First thing?

"Oh, boy." The detective nodded. "Okay. Whew. I'm... Wow."

"I know news like this can be a shock," the nurse said. "But don't let it be. As I said, we need to do further tests. The sooner we start that, the sooner we can lay out your treatment plan, and the better your results will be."

"Thank you." Carly put her hand to her forehead. "I'm just about to head to the office, and I have an appointment this afternoon, so I'll look at my schedule for tomorrow and see if I can rearrange something, to..." Huffing, she shook her head. "What am I saying? This is obviously more important. Yes, I'll be there first thing in the morning."

"And of course..." The sound of typing came over the line. "...there's the other complication in your particular situation. Have you given any thought to what we discussed?"

The detective exhaled.

The other complication. As if ovarian cancer wasn't enough.

Yes, I know about the other complication.

And no, I don't know what I'm going to do about that.

CHAPTER 9

Sergio hopped out of the squad car as it pulled up in front of the Tampa Police Department headquarters. He raced up the steps and sprinted through the lobby, smiling as he made his way to the men's locker room for a quick shower before meeting with Chief Clemmons.

A commendation from the chief? That would be awesome.

If you collect enough of them, do they turn into a raise?

Turning the corner to access the locker rooms, Sergio nearly crashed into Mark Harriman.

"Sergio!" The younger officer stepped backwards, patting Sergio's arms. "Good to see you."

"Same, bro." Sergio wiped the sweat from his forehead, his gaze going to the locker room door. He looked back at Harriman, trying to be fast but not rude. "The bosses keeping you busy?"

"Yep. Got a missing persons case at the fairgrounds that I have to get back to. Looks like a pretty important case, too."

Sergio nodded, stepping past his friend. "View every case as important. A detective's gold shield is made out of sweat and headaches, you know? Keep after it."

"Will do. You take—" Harriman scrunched his face up. "Oof. What is that smell?" Leaning forward, he sniffed Sergio. "It's you. What happened, did you have canned tuna for breakfast and spill it all over yourself?"

"I had an accident at a fish processing plant." Sergio moved toward the locker room door. "I'm trying to get a quick shower. I have a meeting with the chief."

He resisted the urge to boast about a possible commendation for nailing Carmello.

"Shower. Good idea," Harriman said. "The chief's not going to want that odor in his office." The younger officer fanned his nose and turned toward the lobby.

"Tell me about it." As Sergio put his hand on the locker room door, he stopped and turned back to his friend.

He's smaller than me, but we're roughly the same size...

"Hey, Mark," Sergio said. "You, uh… wouldn't happen to have a spare set of street clothes in your locker, would you?"

* * * * *

"Detective?" Chief Clemmons' secretary hung up her phone and nodded at Sergio from behind a paper-strewn desk. "The chief will see you now."

Sergio got up from the waiting room sofa and pushed open one of the two large wooden doors that kept Chief Cass Clemmons' office separate from the rest of the busy police department. Inside, the chief sat at his large desk, his eyes on a file folder in front of him. On the chief's right was a State of Florida flag, hanging from a flag stand, and next to that stood Sunny LaPierre, State Attorney for the Thirteenth Judicial Circuit, whose jurisdiction encompassed all of Hillsborough County, including the city of Tampa.

The stocky blonde lawyer folded her arms across her chest and scowled at Sergio as he entered the large office.

Clemmons didn't look up from the folder. "Please have a seat, Detective."

"Thank you, Chief." Sergio slipped into a chair at the front of the massive wooden desk. "I got here as fast as I could. Things were pretty hectic out at the port."

"Hah!" LaPierre frowned. "I'll bet."

Sergio swallowed hard and shifted in his chair.

"This is the case file for the fish processing plant operation." The chief closed the report and sat back, resting his hands across his belly. "Including your after-action report—your *very brief* after-action report." He looked at Sergio. "Quite a morning, Detective."

Sergio smiled. "Well, thank you, Chief. Just—you know—doing my job."

"Oh, really?" Lapierre sneered, stepping out from behind the chief's desk. "I'm glad you're so proud of your work, Detective Martin, because I came over here to tell you in person that we're releasing your suspect and dropping all the charges."

"What!" Sergio's jaw dropped.

"Carmello will be out on the street again within the hour," the State Attorney said, "and we don't want you making any errant statements to the press. Consider yourself lucky he didn't file assault charges against you."

"How—" Sergio shook his head. "He killed five people. How does he get his charges dropped? We have the murder weapon! I took it from him myself!"

Sunny LaPierre waved her hand. "Carmello's lawyer is claiming his client found the murder weapon in the parking lot right before you came out of the storm drain."

"Did he just happen to get covered in gunshot residue in the parking lot, too?"

"He's claiming he was shooting aluminum at the shooting range before he happened to run into you."

"He was in the storm drain!" Sergio gripped the sides of the chair. "The only shooting range that maniac has been on is the one he created in that fish warehouse!"

LaPierre picked up the file from the chief's desk, brandishing it at the detective. "Technically, you didn't identify him in the storm drain. Your statement says you identified him face-to-face when you came *out* of the storm drain. His comment is, he was heading to that meeting in the warehouse when you confronted him—at which time he had no choice but to take out his gun for self-protection, because you were not dressed as a police officer, and you did not identify yourself as such. And you lost your service weapon!"

"Not on purpose," Sergio said.

"What if a child found it?" LaPierre threw her arms in the air. "Your service firearm is out there—and it's loaded, right? What if some kid comes along and starts playing around with it and accidentally shoots himself?"

Sergio gritted his teeth. "Well, first he'd have to go swimming in the bay where that storm drain comes out, and hold his breath to a depth of about forty feet. And there are sharks, so…"

"Okay, smart guy." She leaned on the arm of the chair next to him, looming over him. "What if some drug dealer finds it instead, and uses it in the commission of a robbery-homicide? How about that? At a time when we finally have the department's image on the upswing, one of our detective's guns is used to hold up a liquor store and kill the owner." She walked away, shaking her head. "That would be perfect for the press to hammer us with in a slow news cycle, wouldn't it? Meanwhile, Carmello says after he was apprehended and compliant, you assaulted him and shot up his personal vehicle. He says there's over twenty thousand dollars' worth of damage to his Mercedes."

Sergio huffed, looking at the chief. "Oh, this is crazy!"

"This is the law!" LaPierre leaned toward Sergio, her face growing red. "The irresponsible way you dealt with Carmello has created enough reasonable doubt to allow a jury to find him innocent, so he's going to be released." She slapped the folder down onto the chief's desk.

Sergio put his hands to his head, looking at Chief Clemmons. "Sir, I can't believe you're gonna let that happen."

The chief shrugged, pursing his lips. "I have to let it happen. That's the law. A little less… *flamboyancy* might be in order next time, Sergio."

LaPierre sneered, folding her arms again. "Your stunts don't make my job any easier, you know."

"Well, we're all here to make sure Sunny LaPierre's job is easy." Sergio shook his head. "I have work to do. There are a bunch of dead drug dealers in a fish warehouse that need to be investigated. But let's all be sure to play nice so Counselor LaPierre can keep her Wednesday morning golf dates with the local judges at private country clubs like Avila."

"Hey!" The attorney wheeled around. "My schedule is just as busy as yours, Detective. My department puts in—"

"Okay, okay." The chief raised his hand. "That's enough. Sunny, let me speak with my detective for a minute." He stood, walking to the door and opening it. "Thank you for coming by, counselor. We'll talk more later."

"Of course, Cass." LaPierre stepped out of the office. "Enjoy the rest of your day."

The chief eased the large door shut and strolled back to his desk, picking up the folder and opening it again. "You know, she has a point." He rested his rear against the edge of the desk and looked at Sergio. "Even the judges that like us can get a bit picky when they feel we're bending the rules into a figure eight. So watch yourself. Chasing a suspect down a storm drain and having a fistfight might make for a good news story, but it can create a big legal mess that could cost the city millions—again." He set down the file. "Or did you forget about driving your partner's car into the bay after nearly running down a group of school children on a field trip?"

Sergio sighed. The high-speed chase had been an embarrassment, obscuring the fact that he got a dangerous murderer off the street.

"I'll assign another detective to the fish warehouse murders. Gianelli, or Haskins, maybe. You—"

The detective cringed. "Gianelli? Sir, that's my crime scene. I was there."

"It's not your scene. It's the scene of whoever I assign it to, and I'm assigning it to somebody else. I need your talents elsewhere."

Nodding, the detective chewed his lip. "What's more important than a multiple homicide case?"

"Drug dealers kill each other in the street all the time. I'd like you to look into something more… sensitive. You should be building bridges with people like LaPierre. She's an ally. She can help you. Think about your long-term future with the department, not just what looks exciting today, but a dozen or so years down the road."

Sergio sighed. "To be honest, Chief, for the last year or so, I've been trying to hang onto my job with both hands." He looked up at the gray-haired police chief. "Lieutenant Davis seemed to be working overtime to get me fired until he ended up running the parking meter department."

"We understood that was mostly a personality conflict between you and former Lieutenant Davis." Clemmons nodded, putting his hands on the edge of the desk. "Sergeant Schmertz has nothing but good things to say about you since you started reporting to her."

Sergio leaned back in his chair. "Well, Sergeant Schmertz is a smart lady."

The chief smiled. "I'm pretty smart myself." He stood, walking back around behind the big desk. "I have a knack for recognizing talent. You're an up-and-comer, Sergio. You always have been. And you could go high up in the department. You set a great example for the people around you—when you're not breaking the rules and earning reprimands."

"Sir..." Sergio grimaced. "In a police department, everything above the rank of Detective starts getting political. I'm no good at that stuff. My job is out in the field."

"So was mine, fifteen years ago." The chief sat pulled his chair forward and down. "But there comes a point where you wake up in the morning and your knees don't feel so good, and all that pizza and beer are turning into a spare tire around your midsection that won't go away with a workout. Fast forward a couple of years, you're married, and your perspective starts to change a little bit. You're thinking about spending quality time with your wife, and coaching your kid's baseball team—and *not* running through the streets of Tampa getting shot at." He wagged a finger at his detective. "The future comes, Sergio. Whether you're ready or not. Think about that, so one day when you decide that moving up in the department is something you want to do, you haven't screwed things up for yourself so badly that you can't actually do it."

"Chief, I just..." Sergio squirmed on the seat. "It's not me. Now, Carly—there's your future Chief of Police. But not me."

"Oh, I'm very aware of Detective Sanderson's qualities," Clemmons said. "I'm just trying to emphasize that it's not a bad thing to have your eyes open to future possibilities." He leaned forward, folding his hands on the desk and looking at Sergio. "And to maybe have a game plan."

"Yes, sir." Sergio nodded. "And thank you, too. I... I appreciate you telling me all this."

The chief pointed to a wall of framed pictures. More than a few were of him as a young, uniformed officer, and then as a detective. Other prints showed him being sworn in as Chief of Police, and standing with various political figures at events. "When I was your age, I wasn't looking down the road, either. I was making headlines, like you are." He looked at Sergio. "But I managed to not make the mistakes you're making. Marriage. And a family. It... civilizes a man, Detective."

Sergio's tone was contrite. "Yes, sir."

The clock on the wall ticked a steady rhythm in the large, quiet office. Chief Clemmons got up from his desk and peered out the window, the Tampa city skyline filling the panoramic glass. "Now, we'll make this morning's mess a non-issue." He peered at Sergio over his shoulder. "Believe it or not, Sunny came over to tell you in person as a favor to me. She won't make a big deal of Carmello's release, and we'll squash any news reports about this morning. That'll keep your name in the good graces of the public, too."

"I'm not asking for that," Sergio said.

"Son, don't you know when somebody's doing you a favor?" The chief faced his detective. "If Carmello wins a lawsuit against the city, that's a career killer for you. You'd be lucky to land in the motor pool with Davis."

Sergio winced. "Yes, sir. I see what you mean."

"Now, I'm willing to make all this go away..." Clemmons stepped back to the window, clasping his hands behind his back. "...but I have a favor to ask in return. We assigned you and Carly to work the Carmello case because of your close relationship with Lavonte Jackson, and also because Carmello has been a murder suspect in the past—"

"He still is."

The chief turned and glared at Sergio.

"Sorry." Sergio slunk down in his chair. "Go on."

"Since Carmello has been a murder suspect before," the chief said, "it wasn't a big stretch to loan you out to Narcotics. Now, I'm going to assign you to Missing Persons."

Sergio cringed like he'd been punched in the gut. "You're pulling me off the homicide division?"

"No, it's temporary. You're on loan."

"To Missing Persons?" Sergio groaned. "Why don't you just admit my career is getting flushed down the toilet?"

"Because it isn't." The chief turned back to him. "I, uh… said this was a favor, and there may be a homicide aspect to it—although I certainly hope not."

Taking a deep breath, Sergio nodded, his insides hollow.

Accept your fate with dignity. If it's a done deal, it's a done deal.

Looking up at his chief, the detective worked hard to exude interest and not the overwhelming disappointment he felt about his new, low-level assignment. "Who's gone missing—and is presumed murdered?"

"Her name is Gabriella Romain." Cass Clemmons' voice was low, his face grim. "And she's my niece."

DAN ALATORRE

CHAPTER 10

THE CHIEF ADJUSTED THE computer monitor on his desk. "A friend over at the Miami-Dade Metro Police sent this over." He typed on his keyboard and slid the mouse to a file on the screen labeled Personal. "There was a food service technician that witnessed a scuffle in a café. He was cleaning the soda lines, down behind the counter. The diners couldn't see him, but he noticed two men and a woman at a nearby booth, and he happened to overhear their conversation. Later, he saw the lady's face on the news, so he alerted the Metro cops. They retrieved this video footage from security cameras at the café."

As he clicked the file, the chief sat back and pushed the computer monitor in Sergio's direction.

On the screen, a young man and a young woman sat in a booth inside a nearly-empty café.

From the body language, it appeared that they were having a disagreement, but were keeping their voices down.

The man's face was visible—mouse brown hair, bad complexion, a ratty mustache—but the woman's back was to the camera. All that showed of her was slender shoulders in a tank top and long, auburn hair.

The young man waved his arms and scowled, shooting a hand across the table and catching the woman in the face. The impact sent her head back, her red hair flying.

She lowered her head, her hand going to her cheek. She grabbed a napkin from the table and put it to her face. It came away streaked with mascara.

Her companion wagged his finger in her face.

From a nearby table, a dark-haired man in a suit stood up. He'd been dining alone, but now went over to the booth, sliding into the seat across from the woman and boxing the younger man in. The stranger was good-looking—attractive enough to be a model, physically fit —and wore an expensive-looking suit that complimented his athletic build.

"I'm going to ask each of you some questions." The stranger had a slight Spanish accent, the kind certain people adopt when they aren't actually Latin but live in the Miami area among a lot of Spanish-speaking people for a while, and want to blend in. "Don't speak until I tell you to. For now, just nod."

The younger man scowled. "How's about you get back up and go mind your own business? This is between me and my girlfriend."

The dark-haired stranger grabbed the young man by the neck with one hand and bashed his head into the table, face-first. When the boyfriend lifted his face again, blood streamed from his nose.

"I try to speak clearly, but I will repeat myself this one time." The stranger took the mascara-stained napkin and handed it to the boy. "I'm going to ask some questions, but you *don't* speak, *cabrón*. You just nod, or your face gets introduced to the top of the table again. Now, nod if you understand."

The redhead girl and her companion nodded.

The dark-haired stranger was calm, not raising his voice. "Okay." He looked at the girl. "It seems like Mr. Every Mother's Nightmare is giving you a hard time, miss. That ends now. Do you live with this moron?"

She nodded.

"Mm-hmm." The stranger said. "Not anymore. You're moving out today."

The boyfriend sat upright. "Hey!"

The stranger's hand darted out again, finding the young man's neck and slamming his head into the table once more, and keeping it there. Groaning, the young man put his hands to his face, blood oozing out from under his fingers.

"He's not very quick on the uptake, is he?" the stranger said. He looked at the cabrón, keeping the young man's face pressed to the table. "This is not up for debate." Leaning his other elbow on the tabletop, the stranger peered at the redhead and reached into his suitcoat pocket, taking out a business card. "Here is the address of a hotel downtown. Nonni, who has been your server at this establishment today, is in the back office calling you an Uber. You are going to leave here and go straight to the place where you have been staying with this clown, and you are going to pack all your stuff—and anything else you want from there—and you are going to go to the hotel on the card."

He tightened the grip on the boyfriend's neck, sending a whimper up from the table's Formica surface.

"When you get to the hotel," the stranger said, "ask for Andre. Tell him you are a friend of Teodoro, and that you need a room, some writing stationery, and a pen. He will set you up, don't worry. You're going to spend the next couple of hours enjoying a luxury suite. Maybe take a hot bath, enjoy a refreshing adult beverage from room service... and then you write down what you need to start a new life. List the items needed and how much they're going to cost. New car, airplane ticket, whatever it is."

The stranger eyed her, his demeanor relaxed and soothing. "When I visit the hotel this evening, have the list ready. I'm going to hand you however much money you wrote on that list. Then, you're going to start a new life." He glared at her boyfriend. "And you're going to start it without this *idiota*."

Gripping the young man's neck, Teodoro held his hand out. "You. Brainless. Give me your driver's license."

The young man wiped his bloody hands on his shirttails and dug into his pocket, producing a wallet. His head pinned to the table, he took out the license and handed it to Teodoro.

Holding the laminated document at arm's length, Teodoro shook his head. "Pittsburgh. I should have known. I never met anyone I liked from Pittsburgh." Throwing the license back to the man, Teodoro looked at the redhead again. "So let me guess. He talked nice to you, promised you nice things, and then a few months in, he's acting like he can't stand the sight of you and you can't do anything right."

She nodded.

"I know the type. Here's a lesson, girl. If it looks too good to be true, it is. Especially when all those sweet lovey-dovey words are pouring out of the mouth of a moron like this one."

Teodoro turned his attention back to the young man.

"Okay, cabrón. Here's your deal. I think you should move back up north, because if I hear anything about you contacting this girl, or looking for her, or even uttering her name in a bad dream, you are going to disappear off the face of the Earth—*comprende*?"

The man nodded.

"They'll be lucky to find scraps of you in Biscayne Bay after the sharks take a dump, because I will cut you into little pieces and feed you slowly to those maneaters while you scream for help from the deck of my boat. I will peel the skin off your face and bait crab traps with it while you watch."

Clenching his teeth, he lowered his mouth to the young man's ear.

"If I ever hear anything about you again, three hours later you will have disappeared.

Understand? Have you ever heard of Carlos Pesamantos? Do you know who that is?"

The man nodded.

"Well," Teodoro said, "I'm part of his world—and you crossed into it today. And once you walk in, there's no walking out. So now you have to make a decision. Do you want to live to become an old man, doing whatever it is you do—but doing it somewhere else, where you and I will never, *ever*, run into each other again? Because Florida will not work out for you."

The man lifted his head an inch off the table, looking at Teodoro.

"You may speak."

"I... I'd like to live to become an old man." The cabrón swallowed hard. "Somewhere else. Not in Florida."

"Wise choice." Teodoro let go of the younger man's neck, but maintained eye contact. "Here's what happens next. You are going to stay here in this café until it closes tonight. You're not going to get up and go to the bathroom, you're not going to make a phone call." He hooked a thumb at the counter. "I know the people that work here, and if they say you moved an inch from this booth before closing time, what's going to happen? Speak."

The man's voice was a whisper. "I... become shark bait."

"Ah. That's right." Teodoro smiled. He looked at the girl. "What's your name?"

She pointed to herself. "Me? I'm Sasha."

"A beautiful name for a beautiful young lady. Ms. Sasha, my name is Teodoro. Now, I am of Italian descent, but some people, when they hear my name, they think it's a Spanish nickname—Tio D'Oro. Uncle of gold. And that's what I am for you right now. I am your uncle of gold. I am your passport out of Hell, bestowing a once in a lifetime favor upon you. Don't screw it up."

"I won't," she said. "Thank you."

"Okay." Teodoro smiled. "Your gratitude is appreciated."

The server approached the table and nodded to Teodoro.

He peered toward the big windows at the front of the café. "Your car is out front, Sasha. Get going, and make sure you make a comprehensive list when you get to the hotel. Everything in the world that you need for a new life needs to be on it."

"Thank you, Teodoro." She got up, smiling at him as she grabbed her purse and headed for the door. The server walked outside with her, guiding Sasha to a light blue, four door sedan.

A moment later, the car pulled away from the curb. When it was out of sight, the server re-entered the café. "She's safe now, Teo."

"Good. Thank you, Nonni." Teodoro turned his attention back to his hostage. "Get comfortable, hot shot. You're going to be here for a while."

Teodoro stood up and walked out of the café slowly, without looking back.

* * * * *

"That's... pretty intense, sir." Sergio folded his arms across his chest and stroked his beard stubble.

The chief clicked the next file on the computer screen. "And this video was obtained from a security camera in the hallway of the Essex House hotel in Miami."

The recording showed Teodoro in the hallway, knocking on the door to a suite. Two large men stood next to him, one on each side.

The door opened, revealing the young woman from the diner, dressed in nice jeans and a blouse, with her hair wrapped up in a towel. A white robe lay crumpled up on the bed behind her; on the far side of the big suite, an open bottle of champagne rested in an ice bucket on the desk, next to a glass that was three-quarters empty.

"Sasha." Teodoro stepped into the luxurious hotel room, wearing a dark suit. His two accomplices stayed in the hallway, one of them holding the door open with a massive hand. "Good to see you've made use of the amenities," Teodoro said. "Andre hooked you up?"

The young lady smiled. "Yes."

"Good. Where's the list?"

She walked to the desk and picked up a sheet of stationery, handing it to her guest.

"A hundred and forty thousand dollars." Teodoro nodded. "That sounds like a good start. And no more Mr. Idiot from Pittsburgh, right?"

Sasha giggled. "Right."

"Good girl." He held a hand out to his men. "Filipe, I need one hundred and forty thousand dollars, please."

One of the massive thugs handed Teodoro a few stacks of cash. The Uncle of Gold held them up in front of his face and fanned through them.

"This is one hundred and forty thousand dollars, Sasha." He held the money out to her.

As she reached for it, the two men raced forward, grabbing her. One forced his hand over her mouth as the other pulled out a roll of duct tape.

She kicked and flailed as they gagged her.

"You're as stupid as Mr. Pittsburgh," Teodoro said. "I told you, if it looks too good to be true, it is."

Sasha heaved against her assailants, emitting only muffled cries through the tape over her mouth. The next strips of tape bound her arms, then her legs.

Teodoro stuffed the bundles of cash into his suitcoat pockets, walking to the desk and pouring himself a glass of champagne. "But as promised, today begins the first day of your new life."

* * * * *

The video went dark. Chief Clemmons clicked the mouse, taking the images from the screen.

Sergio leaned against the chief's office wall, exhaling a long, slow breath.

"Two weeks later," Clemmons said, "during the execution of a drug raid at the port of Miami, the Metro cops inadvertently stumbled onto a shipping container slated for Venezuela. It was stuffed with twenty-eight women, all of them dead. Sasha was one of them." He shook his head. "No ventilation, no food, no water… The Miami-Dade Coroner said they died from heat exhaustion, probably after about seven days. The port workers had been complaining about the smell."

"Do we know it was the same woman?" Sergio asked.

The chief nodded. "The Metro police ID'd the body in the shipping container as Sasha Manitoba. That's the same name on the driver's license she used to check into the hotel. They grabbed a screen shot from the security camera at the café when she got up to leave. It's a positive match. They also showed the waitress and the soda repair guy her picture and they both said it was the same woman. It's her, across the board. Doubtful anyone else would know to use the name Sasha at the hotel anyway."

He faced Sergio, his face ashen.

"And that's the guy my niece got mixed up with—Teodoro Romain. I told you his reputation—his brother is a big drug dealer in Miami, and apparently they've branched into human trafficking. There's all kinds of wild stories about this Teodoro guy, but so far the Miami PD haven't been able to pin anything on him. He came to Tampa a few months ago, and Gabriella... managed to get on his radar screen."

The Chief lowered his head and put a hand to his mouth.

His niece's antics around town were somewhat known, but not openly discussed. Gabriella had a reputation, too—a part-time model, part-time cruise ship entertainer, and full-time party girl. She'd been picked up a few times for marijuana possession and once for solicitation at the Tampa Yacht Club, to the everlasting embarrassment of her uncle.

Nobody on the force blamed Chief Clemmons for the actions of his niece. She was an adult and she seemed to enjoy being the black sheep of the family.

"Her, uh..." The chief cleared his throat. "Her social media accounts say she met Teodoro at a club, and that they've been together ever since. Last week, they flew to Vegas and got married." The elder lawman's shoulders sagged. "Now, she's missing, Sergio. I'm worried what might have happened to her."

Chief Clemmons shook his head. "I tell myself... that Teodoro wouldn't... wouldn't have stayed with Gabriella all this time if he was going to just get rid of her the way he got rid of that girl from the café, but... It's my sister's kid. I can't afford to guess wrong."

Sergio moved away from the wall, a pit in his stomach, his thoughts reeling.

If this crazy Teodoro guy gets tired of Gabriella, or even if he's just had a bad day, she could end up in a shipping container or a crab trap.

I guess I'm being assigned to Missing Persons to make sure that doesn't happen.

He turned to the chief. "Where was Gabriella last seen?"

"At the fairgrounds, this morning," Clemmons said. "Mark Harriman came to see me just before you arrived. He said a woman claiming to be Gabriella Romain went missing a few hours ago during a stage performance—a magic act, with a volunteer from the audience. When they lifted the curtain, she was gone and everything was covered in blood." He sighed, looking away. "They're… interviewing witnesses right now, and I dispatched a squad car to the residence, but nobody answered the door. I'd like to think my best investigators would help me out on this, so I'm asking you to head up the case. I'm asking Detective Sanderson, too—to oversee things. She'll catch up with you later today. She has some meetings here first."

The highest-ranking member of the Tampa Police Department gazed at Sergio from behind the large desk, in the massive office, with the executive view of the city behind him and all the buttons of power at his fingertips.

But all Sergio saw was a man who needed help.

He tried hard not to also see the man who could send him to the motor pool for the rest of his career if he was unsuccessful.

"Okay." Clenching his jaw, Sergio headed for the door. "Tell Harriman I'll be there within the hour."

CHAPTER 11

Her thoughts reeling, Carly sat quiet and still in the passenger seat of the SWAT van as the driver pulled out of the fish warehouse parking lot.

The crime scene she was leaving was an untidy one. Several dead bodies had yet to be identified, and the actual purpose of the meeting they were supposed to attend was still a mystery.

Obviously, the murders were part of a bigger plan, but what? A new drug kingpin taking over? An attempt by Carmello to expand his drug business while streamlining the number of people taking a cut of the profits?

But although those facts kept working their way into her thoughts, they were pushed right back out again by the ones the nurse at Doctor Mendez's office had delivered.

Cancer.

It was a relentless thought.

What do I tell Kyle? What do I tell our boys?

The cross-country hiking trip her husband and sons had undertaken would last most of the summer, starting with the four weeks they were currently enjoying in the mountain ranges around Utah's Park City, and ending with a second, four-week trek along the Mississippi river that ended in New Orleans. In between, the hikers got a week off at a Holiday Inn in St. Louis.

Carly pursed her lips.

What do I know that I would tell them, anyway?

Carly and Kyle were currently separated. She wasn't sure if it was a good idea to get into the details of her illness with him at the moment. On one hand, he had been her loyal husband for over a dozen years, and discussing something like this with him would have been automatic. On the other hand, he would very likely be her ex-husband soon, and her divorce lawyer might feel there were good reasons not to share the information with him.

The boys.

What does someone with cancer tell their children? How does that news affect them?

They'll be scared. They're such brave little men, but a child losing his mother—a child of any age—it has to be devastating.

She imagined bad grades during the school year, as they watched their mother lose all her hair from chemotherapy, or days of stress on their young faces when she was too ill to get out of bed.

It'll be hard on them. They're already worried about the unpredictable waves of nausea that keep coming over me for no reason.

Well, we know the reason now.

Don't tell them. Not about the cancer. Not until you have to.

Don't ruin their summer with news like this. Wait for the results of the second set of tests, and until after the treatment schedule is planned out.

She nodded, staying silent as the big van rolled onward toward the station.

Protect your children from the thing that will scare them—the thing that they'll see is scaring their mother.

Then, tell them the truth.

She gritted her teeth and balled up her fists.

You will tell your brave sons the truth, Carly, and then you'll answer their questions—every question they can think to ask.

And then you'll fight this thing with all your might so you can stay with your boys and watch them grow into men and husbands and fathers and grandfathers.

You fight, Carly.

You fight this thing, and you beat it.

* * * * *

Sergio grumbled as he climbed into his car and headed out of the TPD parking lot, cursing and pounding the steering wheel.

"A Missing Persons assignment." He shook his head. "That's just great."

He pulled into the street, frowning as he gripped the steering wheel.

I know it's the chief's niece, but come on. There are fifty guys who could do this case just as well as me. Maybe better.

Sergio shook his head. "Oh, and I can just hear Carly, too. 'Be a team player, Sergio. Help him out. It never hurts to do a favor for the higher-ups.' Sheesh. He assigned her to oversee things? To oversee me, that's what *that* means. I have a babysitter."

Grumbling, he slouched behind the wheel.

The fairgrounds was twenty minutes away without traffic, but a quick wardrobe change was in order first. Borrowing Harriman's blue jeans and golf shirt—as poorly fitting on Sergio as they were—had been a welcome relief from his fish-soaked ensemble. But once he started working the case at the fairgrounds, there was no telling how long he might be stuck in the smaller officer's uncomfortable attire; maybe all night. Switching into his own clothes wouldn't just be an improvement in comfort, it would eliminate an unnecessary distraction and allow him to do a more thorough job.

A few minutes later, Sergio drove his sedan into the lot at his condo, still steaming about the assignment.

"Five minutes before the chief says his niece is missing, he's telling me I need to get married," he muttered, exiting the vehicle and slamming the door shut. "What's that all about? Softening me up with some crap about family and marriage and long-term perspective so I'll take the case? Like I have a choice. He's the Chief of Police. If I don't help him out, then what? The motor pool?"

He opted for the staircase near his parking spot instead of going to the elevator; it was at the other end of the building and he was too wound up to wait for it anyway.

He bounded up the steps, taking them two at a time.

"Married. How does that change anything?" Sergio approached the door to his unit, pulling Harriman's Polo shirt over his head.

And how is that any business of his? I'm a cop. A detective, and a good one, married or not.

So if I get married, I'll be chief one day? And if I stay single, I'll be working missing persons cases for the rest of my career?

He threw open the door to his unit and stepped inside.

Married. Who needs to get married to have a career? I already have a career!

Marriage.

Avarie appeared from the kitchen, dressed in blue jeans and scrolling through her phone with one hand, while carrying a delivery box from Antonio's Pizza in the other. "Hey there!" She smiled at Sergio. "Hungry?"

He stormed into the living room.

Sheesh. Who wants to get married?

"Hello?" Avarie said. "Detective Martin, there's a strange woman in your condo with a pepperoni pizza."

"What?" He turned around to her, balling Harriman's shirt into a knot. "Oh, hi. Hey—would you want to get married?"

She recoiled, her jaw dropping. "Wow. If that's a proposal, it's gotta be the least romantic one I ever heard of."

"What?" Sergio's brow furrowed. "Proposal? I—"

"I mean…" She moved between the living room sofa and the love seat, setting the pizza on his coffee table. "I'm flattered, of course. But for some reason I imagined the man—fully dressed, probably—" she glanced at his bare, muscular torso "—but not necessarily. And he'd get down on one knee, with a big bouquet of flowers and a little velvet box." She looked at the pizza carton. "I envision this happening in a nice restaurant. But maybe that's just a silly schoolgirl's fantasy."

"Okay." Sergio put his hands up. "Hold it."

She twirled around, swinging her hands out at her sides. "Some fortunate women are out in a little rowboat when a man asks for their hand, on a quiet, scenic little lake. Others get asked at the office, with all their co-workers around, and it's a complete surprise."

"Avarie—"

"Although I have to say…" She moved behind the loveseat, putting her hands on the back of the chair "…this was definitely a surprise."

"Okay, stop." Sergio took a deep breath. "I wasn't asking if you would want to get married."

"No?" She turned away, peering at him over her shoulder. "I'm pretty sure those were your exact words."

"Well, I mean, yeah… but…" He ran his hand over his beard stubble. "It was more like, would you *want* to get married?"

"Oh. A subtle distinction?" Avarie scrunched her face up, looking toward the ceiling as she put a finger to her lip. "No, you said the same thing both times. But I'm afraid my answer must be no."

Sergio nodded. "Because what I'm trying to ask is…" He looked across the living room at her. "Wait, what? You said no?"

"Of course," Avarie said. "How long have we known each other? A few months? We went on one date. That's hardly—"

"What difference does it make how long we've known each other?" Sergio huffed. "My mom and dad were only going out two weeks when he knew he wanted to marry her."

"Did he *propose* after two weeks?"

"He waited until they had been dating for a year. What's your point?"

Avarie opened the pizza box and took out a slice. "I don't think it's incumbent upon *me* to have a point. I believe you asked me if I wanted to get married." She took a bite of her pizza.

"Uh, yeah," Sergio said. "But I didn't mean do you wanna get *married*. I meant… like, do you *want* to get married? Like, I'm not asking you to marry me, I'm saying would you ever want to get married one day?"

"Oh." Avarie nodded, swallowing her mouthful of pizza. "Nope. I'm still not seeing what the difference is."

"Whatever. But if I *were* proposing, you'd say no?"

"I would. I did." She took another bite of pizza. "And you're making it pretty clear you're not proposing. I'm feeling a bit hurt and used right now. You'd have gotten the pizza without the ruse."

Sighing, Sergio sunk into the chair, putting his head in his hands.

Avarie chuckled, lowering herself onto the armrest and stroking his arm. "Are you having a bad day? Did your meeting with Chief Clemmons not go well?" She lifted the slice back to her lips. "Should we talk about this later, like adults? Or possibly drunken adults?"

Sergio nodded. "Yeah, maybe."

"Good, because I need to eat and run." Avarie stood up, going to the kitchen. She grabbed her keys and her purse. "Clemmons just texted me and asked me to run cover for a missing persons case at the fairgrounds."

Sergio looked up. "Me, too. That's where I'm headed. I came home to change, then I'm supposed to meet Mark Harriman at the expo hall." He looked at Avarie, his brow furrowing. "When did you change clothes?"

"On the way here." Avarie bit another chunk off of her pizza slice. "Gotta run now, though. The chief wants a low profile on this thing, and he thinks the media might try to blow it out of proportion. I'm supposed to get out there and make sure they don't." Holding her slice of pizza in her teeth, she slipped her purse strap over her arm. "I'm not sure why a missing persons case warrants that kind of caution, though."

"Because the missing person is his niece." Sergio got up and pulled the dangling slice of pizza from Avarie's lips, jamming it into his mouth as he headed to his bedroom closet for a change of clothes. "And because she might be dead."

CHAPTER 12

Detective Sanderson took a breath and squared her shoulders. Chief Clemmons' receptionist was nowhere in sight, and Lieutenant Marshall's text said to meet him at Clemmons' office right away.

She looked at her phone and re-read the new message, confirming its contents. It had come in just as the SWAT van pulled into the Tampa PD parking garage, but offered no context as to why Deshawn wanted to meet her.

And why here, of all places?

Carly stared at the big double doors of the chief's office. A gap of about an inch was visible between the two wooden barriers.

Am I supposed to just go on in?

Reaching out her hand, Carly extended a finger and tapped on one of the doors. "Chief Clemmons? Did you want to see me?"

She pushed the door open another inch, revealing the short, squatty figure of Sergeant Mona Schmertz and the athletic frame of Lieutenant Deshawn Marshall. The pair stood at the far side of the room, the conversation between the heavyset new sergeant and the tall African-American lieutenant barely more than a murmur.

Carly swallowed hard.

This doesn't look good.

"Ah, Detective Sanderson." The chief stood up from behind his desk, smiling and extending his hand. "Come in—and don't look so glum."

She entered the big office.

He's smiling, but I have no idea why.

It can't be from this morning's fouled-up drug bust.

"Here, have a seat." The chief gestured toward the chairs in front of his desk.

As Carly sat down, Sergeant Schmertz and Lieutenant Marshall strolled over.

"I have good news." Clemmons beamed. "The politicians are done with their fiscal wrangling, and the new budget has been approved."

"That's, uh, wonderful, sir." Carly nodded, folding her hands in her lap.

What's that got to do with me?

"Well," he said, "it's wonderful news for our newest sergeant, and after all the chaos that's been going on around here over the past few months, I thought you might like to be here when I announced the news."

Behind her, Schmertz chuckled.

Carly shifted on her seat.

Ugh.

It's not bad enough I lose out on a promotion to Sergeant Schmertz, now I have to congratulate her publicly for beating me out for the job?

But it's been weeks since Schmertz took the job. Why would they make a special announcement now?

A twinge went through Carly's insides.

Oh, please don't tell me she's getting promoted again. She's barely tolerable as it is.

But either way, congratulations are obviously in order, so be gracious and acknowledge her.

Turning, Carly held her hand out to the rotund Ms. Schmertz, trying to sound sincere. "Congratulations, Sergeant."

Clemmons laughed. "No, no, no, Carly. The announcement is about *you*."

The detective peered over her shoulder at the chief, her mouth hanging open and her cheeks growing warm.

I must have missed an email or something.

This cancer business has already gotten me completely distracted. That's going to be a problem.

But right now, I'm in a meeting with the Chief of Police for some reason.

She looked at Chief Clemmons, shrugging. "I don't understand."

* * * * *

From the passenger side of Sergio's car, Avarie scrolled through her phone as the detective weaved in and out of traffic.

"Now, I get it." Avarie lowered the device and looked up at Sergio. "Chief Clemmons wants to keep this situation with his niece from embarrassing the department. You know the media. 'If the Chief of Police can't protect his own family members, how can he protect the rest of us?' He's right." She sighed, peering out the window. "In a slow news cycle, reporters can really run wild with a story like that. And it's gotta be bugging the chief personally." Avarie lifted her phone and swiped her finger across the screen, sending page after page of websites past. "Think the guy knew he was marrying the niece of the chief of police?"

"I don't know." Sergio frowned, gripping the wheel. "But it's skating over the thin ice if you're a criminal."

"Or putting it in the chief's face," Avarie said. "A move like that kinda says how powerful this guy is. That he's not afraid."

Sergio nodded. "So, who is Teodoro Romain trying to impress?"

She glanced at her phone again. "According to the news sites, he recently bought a big house on Bayshore Boulevard and a historic landmark theater in Ybor City. I'd say he's trying to impress everyone."

"It's unusual for a criminal to draw so much attention." Sergio pursed his lips. "There's something else to it." The detective glanced at his companion. "Can I borrow your phone? Mine kinda got waterlogged in that storm drain. I need to request a new one—and a replacement service weapon."

"Sure." Avarie handed Sergio her phone. "Want me to drive while you do that?"

"No, I got it." He tapped the screen, glancing up to correct the direction of his vehicle as it veered over the center line.

"Are you sure?" Avarie pressed herself into the passenger seat. "Last time you drove while distracted, we almost ate the tail of a dump truck."

Sergio put the phone to his ear. "If you're worried, tighten your seat belt."

"Yep." She nodded, her hands going to her fastened seat belt straps and pulling them more snugly across her hips. "I was just thinking that."

* * * * *

"Me?" Carly's jaw hung open.

They're finally promoting me to Sergeant?

She had worked as Acting Sergeant under former Lieutenant Davis, logging extra hours for weeks and performing the duties of the position, ostensibly as a kind of audition for the job. In the end, St. Petersburg Police Detective Mona Schmertz had been brought in to become TPD's newest sergeant, and Carly's efforts appeared to have been a scheme by Davis as a way to make his department look more cost effective than it really was.

Losing out on the promotion after all that—especially to Schmertz, an outsider—was a blow. Clemmons had told her it was a very close vote, but that didn't do much to temper her disappointment.

Carly cleared her throat. "I'm sorry, sir. You just... caught me a little off guard, that's all." She managed a smile.

Lieutenant Marshall and Sergeant Schmertz stepped forward and congratulated her.

As Carly shook hands with her co-workers, Chief Clemmons leaned back in his chair, a wide grin stretching across his face. "After we promoted Mona, I mentioned to you that as soon as the budget mess was cleared up, we'd be looking for you to fill the other vacant sergeant position. You were the selection committee's next choice after Mona, and we're within ninety days of the interviews, so HR said we're good to go." He folded his hands across his belly. "That is—assuming you're still interested in the job."

A twinge went through Carly's insides.

How will a new, more demanding work schedule affect my treatment schedule?

Lieutenant Marshall clapped Carly on the back, laughing. "Of course she's still interested. Right?"

Carly put a hand over her abdomen.

Deshawn's smile faded. "Right, Carly?"

It was a big promotion, and one she had worked hard for. It would mean a better financial situation for her and her two young sons, as well as the possibility of a more regular schedule.

It meant security, and the recognition of all the hard work she had done, not just as Acting Sergeant but also in her role as a Tampa Police Detective.

Carly massaged her fingers, shifting on her seat.

I'd be a fool to turn down the promotion after all that, but…

A wave of nausea washed over her. Pain gripped her lower abdomen.

Deshawn's face fell. He loomed over his friend. "Carly?"

The detective looked up at him, then to Clemmons, as she tried not to wince. "Chief, may I speak with you privately, please?"

* * * * *

"That's right." Sergio held Avarie's phone to his head, speaking with the equipment clerk as he exited the interstate. "Sergeant Schmertz and Chief Clemmons know all about the lost weapon and phone, so they'll sign off on the replacements."

"Okay, Detective," the clerk said. "I'll rush this through for you. I heard it was a real wild scene out there this morning. Try to have a better afternoon."

"I will." He nodded. "Oh, and Claire—could you have the new equipment brought out to me at the state fairgrounds expo hall? I'm being attached to Mark Harriman's case from this morning. Sorry, I don't have the incident number yet."

"Mark Harriman? Sure, one second." The sound of fingers typing on a keyboard came over the line. "That's a missing person's case, Sergio."

The detective frowned. "I am well aware."

"What happened?" The clerk chuckled. "Did you get in trouble again?"

"Thank you for all your help, Claire."

"Okay, Detective. Stay safe."

He ended the call and handed the phone back to Avarie. The PR rep was halfway through her second slice of pizza.

Sergio snatched the slice from her and stuffed the end of it into his mouth.

"Hey!" Avarie smacked him on the arm. "You can have your own piece, you know. The box is right there on the back seat. You just have to ask."

"Sorry." Sergio smiled, his voice barely intelligible through his full mouth. "This one looked good."

Huffing, Avarie leaned over the seat and flipped open the top of the cardboard delivery box. "I thought so, too. That's why I was eating it."

He glanced at the back seat. A carry-on bag sat next to the pizza box. "What's with the suitcase? Are you going on vacation?"

"My job requires me to look good on TV," Avarie said. "It's hot as blazes outside and I can't afford to have sweat stains all over my blouse when I'm talking to the TV reporters, in case I end up on TV myself. So I brought a change of clothes and some makeup."

The detective nodded. "Smart."

"Florida humidity will teach any woman that her hair does not look as good after a few hours."

"I'm sure. You probably have your .45 in there, too, just in case."

"Well, yeah," Avarie said. "It can't protect me if it's at my hotel."

Sergio pulled his car onto the long asphalt drive between the acres of green grass that formed the rear entrance to the Florida State Fairgrounds, slowing down as he approached the security shack. Two uniformed Tampa Police officers stood outside the tiny building, near their squad car.

The detective lowered his window. "Hey, guys."

"Afternoon, Sergio." The closest officer waved. "You working this case, too?"

Sergio nodded. "I'm helping Harriman. Kind of a favor to the chief."

"Landed yourself in hot water again, huh?" The officer smirked. "Mark's up at the expo hall. Straight ahead. You'll see the flashing lights."

"Got it. Thanks." Sergio nodded. "You guys want some cold pizza?

"Nah." The officer patted his belly. "I'm saving my appetite for a couple of corn dogs and maybe one of those fried elephant ear pastries.

Sergio raised his eyebrows. "Oh yeah? They serving those today?"

"Sure are. I've been smelling them all morning."

As he drove away, Avarie looked at her driver. "Corn dogs and fried dough, huh? That sounds healthy."

"It's the fairgrounds." Sergio shrugged. "The rules of nutrition don't apply."

"I'm not knocking your food selection." Avarie undid her seat belt and climbed halfway into the back seat, her rear end brushing against Sergio's shoulder. "I'm wondering if they have fried Snickers bars, too."

Grinning, Sergio peered at his co-worker's firm butt. "What do we know about this Gabriella Romain?"

Avarie plopped back down into her seat, holding a piece of pizza in one hand and lifting her phone with the other. She scrolled through several open tabs. "I was checking that. We're gonna have to ask a friend or relative to grant us access to her social media accounts. There's a few public posts, but other than the Vegas wedding announcement, there's not much here that's recent. Insta, Tik Tok—it's all private."

Sergio nodded. "I'll have Max request a warrant. What else have you got?"

"There are a few mentions in the local Tampa media. Gabriella's new husband has been acquiring some big assets since he arrived in town. An old theater in Ybor City and a stately manor on Bayshore Boulevard. Apparently, he also made an unsolicited bid to buy a fruit importing company, but that fell through." She lowered the phone. "That's a lot of high-profile activity for a guy that's new to town."

"It sure is." Sergio pulled his vehicle to a stop near an array of squad cars, their emergency lights flashing in the midday sun. Sighing, he put the car in park and dropped his hands to his lap. "This guy is acting like no criminal I ever saw before."

* * * * *

Chief Clemmons ushered Schmertz and Marshall out of his office and shut the door behind them. "Are you okay, Carly?" He went to her side. "Can I get you something? A glass of water?"

The detective shook her head, squeezing her eyes shut as she pressed her hand against her stomach. "It usually passes in a second." She exhaled sharply.

"Carly, what's wrong?" The elder lawman kneeled next to Carly's chair, putting a hand on her shoulder. "Do I need to call someone? A doctor? I know there's a bug going around…"

She took a few breaths and relaxed, the pain and nausea subsiding. "Whew. That was rough." Sitting upright, Carly looked into the concerned face of the chief. "I'm sorry, sir. That was awkward for you, I'm sure."

His face stern, the police chief stood, keeping his eyes on his detective. "No, it's fine. Are you all right?"

"I've… been experiencing some discomfort." She glanced up at him, her cheeks growing warm. "Obviously. But I saw my doctor and she ran some tests. I'm kinda in the waiting stage."

Clemmons moved behind his desk, nodding. "Okay. Well, your health is private, and I don't want to cross any lines…" He sat down, placing his elbows on the desk top and putting his fingertips together, bouncing them against his chin.

"I appreciate that, sir."

"Carly," the chief said, "I'd hoped you would accept the promotion so that we could announce it on Monday and start re-assigning your cases over the weekend. There's a somewhat sensitive matter I've assigned Sergio to, and I was hoping you'd oversee him on it. Maybe keep him out of trouble, too. He listens to you."

She shook her head. "Why does everybody think he listens to me? I'm the last person he'd listen to right now."

"Well…" The chief tapped his fingers together. "I'm planning on announcing your promotion to sergeant this Monday morning—unless there's a reason I shouldn't. You worked hard for the job. You earned it."

"Sir, Tampa PD has always been fair to me," Carly said. "Now, I have to be fair to the Department." She shifted in her seat, suppressing another wince. "I really want this promotion, but I have…" She looked away, frowning. "There just… may be some limits to my ability to perform in the near future. Health-wise."

"Mm-hmm." The chief nodded. "I won't question you on that point. But I'm still offering the promotion to you. A little stomach issue isn't going to get in the way of that."

She looked down. "It's… not a *little* stomach issue, sir."

"No." The chief lowered his voice. "From the way you reacted just now, I'd guess not. But you don't have to elaborate. The law is, any—"

"Sir…" Carly blinked hard, looking up at the ceiling. "I got some lab test results from my doctor's office this morning. Right after Carmello was apprehended, when I was in the undercover van. In fact, that's probably why I took Detective Martin's head off."

"I'm sure he deserved it," Clemmons said. "The state attorney seemed to think so."

"Anyway…" Carly took a deep breath. "With all of this morning's chaos—the blown drug bust, the homicides in the warehouse, filing my after-action report, and then the text from Deshawn to come here to meet with you… I really haven't had time to process the doctor's news. I mean, the nurse seemed pretty certain on the phone, and… without getting into too much detail, this, uh… *situation*, it could impact my… this could hamper my ability to do a good job as sergeant for a while."

"I see." The elder lawman stood up, lumbering out from behind his big desk. "Carly, sometimes you are too straight-laced for your own good."

"Sir?"

He frowned, standing over her. "You've worked for the Tampa Police Department for, what? A decade? That means you're family. Whatever your health situation is, the department's got your back. If your focus really needs to be on your health—or anywhere else—then focus it there. You've been a big asset to this place, and I can't help but think that a promotion to sergeant, with the commensurate increase in pay, will be very helpful to you no matter what the circumstances are. A sergeant should handle a lot of their caseload from behind a desk, anyway, and you'll have a lot more flexibility in your work schedule to arrange doctor's appointments or whatever it is you'll need." He wagged a finger at her. "So don't worry that your health will have an impact on your job. Take the promotion, and take whatever time you need to get your health back on track."

The detective smiled, her breathing returning to normal as if a large weight had been lifted off her shoulders that she didn't realize she was carrying. "I appreciate that, sir.

"You proved yourself to be more than capable when you were serving as acting sergeant."

She lowered her head and sniffled, blinking away a gathering tear. "If it's not too much trouble, I'd still like a day or two to decide."

"Take all the time you need," Clemmons said. "And whatever this health situation is that you're dealing with, when you beat it—which you will—you can make up for any lost ground then. Okay?"

Jumping up from her chair, Carly threw her arms around the chief. "Thank you, sir."

Chuckling, Clemmons patted the detective on the back. "Now who's crossing the line?"

"I really appreciate the support, Chief." Carly stepped away, wiping her eyes. "I won't let you down."

* * * * *

Sergio and Avarie made their way across the hot asphalt walkways of the fairgrounds, toward a cluster of police cars and an ambulance with a tent canopy next to it. A throng of news crews huddled near the expo hall entrance. Reporters shouted out questions from where they had been corralled behind the yellow crime scene tape. At the back of the group was the young face of Kerri Milner.

"News people." Sergio shook his head. "They don't waste any time, do they?"

"They listen to the police band radio channels." Avarie turned and called out to the reporters. "We just got here. Let me see what's going on and I'll come back and give you an update."

Officer Mark Harriman was exiting the building as Sergio and Avarie approached. The officer clutched a thick stack of preliminary interview forms under his arm. "Sergio." Harriman beamed. "Long time no see. How'd it go with the chief?"

The detective frowned. "I fell all the way down the stairs from Homicide to the Missing Persons division." He nodded at the expo hall. "What's the situation here?"

"I hate to say it..." Harriman lowered his voice. "But between you and me, this is looking less like a missing persons case and more like a homicide." He glanced over his shoulder at the entrance doors to the big building. "I don't see how anybody could lose that much blood and stay alive. And I doubt she did it to herself."

"Yeah?" Sergio ran his fingers across the stubble on his jaw. "Show me what you're talking about."

CHAPTER 13

As Carly drove to her appointment, her phone rang with an incoming call. She tapped the screen to see who it was.

Sgt. Mona Schmertz, TPD

Carly slipped an earbud into her ear and hit the green button. "Hello?"

"Detective Sanderson," Schmertz said. "When Chief Clemmons told Lieutenant Marshall and I that he'd be promoting you on Monday, we went to his office to be the first ones to pat you on the back—and then you asked us to leave. So, by phone, congratulations."

Carly nodded. "Thank you, Sergeant Schmertz."

"Oh, call me Mona. After all, we're peers—or almost. Yeah, it'll be good to have a little more estrogen in the staff meetings. Know what I mean?"

Carly huffed.

Yes, because that's all I am. Estrogen.

"Anyway," the sergeant said, "I hope I can count on you to help make some changes around here. When will you be back in?"

Carly shifted on her seat. "Well, the chief said he'd announce my promotion on Monday, so I figured, you know... Monday."

"Oh, well, you're going to want to clean out your old desk and move into your new one, aren't you? You should come on in. I'd be happy to help you with that."

Carly stifled a chuckle.

You would? Why, because you're such a good friend? You've always been a pain in my butt, Mona.

You want something. That's why you're calling. What could it be?

"Actually," Carly said, "I've got a doctor's appointment this afternoon so I'm gonna be doing that."

"Oh, I see." The sergeant's tone turned icy. "Right off the bat, taking leave again. I guess I should've seen that coming. Some things don't change."

"Sergeant—"

"No, it's fine," Schmertz said. "You run your career the way you see fit, and I'll run mine the way it's supposed to be done. How is Sergio taking the news about your promotion?"

Carly shrugged. "I haven't spoken with him about it. I'm sure he'll be happy for me. Why wouldn't he be?"

"Men are different animals, Sanderson. You should know that by now."

Carly frowned. "I thought you liked Sergio."

"I do—because he's subordinate to me and he does top-quality work. But I haven't been sleeping with him, and you have."

Putting a hand to her head, Carly sighed. "This has been a great chat, Mona."

"I'm glad you took the time to enjoy it before you took another vacation. I guess I'll see you Monday."

"Okay, then," Carly said. "Thanks again for—"

The call ended.

"...calling." Carly picked up the phone and stared at it. "Geez."

* * * * *

Officer Harriman led Sergio and Avarie past the hundreds of empty chairs facing the vacant stage. The equipment was still in place—cages on pedestals, smoke machines, laser lights and boxes of pyrotechnics.

"This is what you want to see." Harriman climbed up the steps to the stage, stopping at the sixth cage.

Sergio followed, with Avarie trailing him, and peered down through the false bottom of the blood-strewn enclosure. A team of people in coveralls took swabs from a pool of blood and photographs of the under-stage area from all angles.

"The CSIs just got here an hour ago," Harriman said. "They were delayed."

Nodding, Sergio glanced at Harriman. "Carly's joining us later. She's been delayed, too—a meeting with the chief or something. So let's keep the interoffice case report current so she's up to speed."

One of the coveralls-cloaked technicians raised her head. "We were delayed because we had to retrieve a few dozen bullets from a storm drain at the port." She smiled. "But you wouldn't know anything about that, would you Sergio?"

"Relax, Carina," Sergio said. "Consider it job security."

The technician put her hands on her hips. "How about you chase the next suspect into a popcorn stand? Something above ground and well-lit for a change?"

Stepping away from the cage, Sergio turned to Harriman. "How do we get down there?"

"Out any exit door and walk around to the back." Harriman pointed toward the closest door. "This way."

Harriman held the door as Avarie and Sergio exited. "Preliminary interviews have been conducted with almost all of the performers and stagehands. They all basically said the same thing. The act was going along as usual, until the woman disappeared. They all claim not to know anything about her mur—well, her disappearance."

"Yeah," Sergio said. "It'd be nice if the killer would just confess when we showed up, wouldn't it?"

The trio re-entered the expo hall through a small, unmarked door. Inside, a wooden framework of beams and plywood divided the space into sections. A yellow tape ran from the exit door and through a narrow, dimly-lit passageway between the framework walls, to where the crime scene investigators were performing their duties.

Sergio stopped at the edge of the scene, putting his hand to his chin and running it across the roughness of his beard.

The pool of blood was enormous—enough for several killings. Blood splatter covered the ladder going up to the cage on stage and anything close by.

"A volunteer from the audience goes on stage, right?" Sergio squatted, pointing to the little trap door over the CSI technicians. "Then, he or she steps into the cage. When they get the prearranged signal, they come down here. Is that the deal?" He looked up at Harriman.

The younger officer nodded. "That's my understanding, Detective. Then, the volunteer follows the tape to the exit door and walks around to the other side, where we came in."

"And magically reappears," Sergio said.

"It's a lot more impressive when you see it onstage." The blonde assistant with the toned legs and honey-vinegar southern accent strutted toward Sergio, one hand on her hip, the other holding an unlit cigarette.

"Ma'am." Harriman stepped toward her. "You were told to stay upstairs."

"And yet, here I am." She glared at him, her fishnet stockings stretched tight across her firm legs, her sparkly bustier shimmering in the light. She raised her cigarette to her lips. "Anybody got a light?"

Sergio stood up, smiling at the buxom blonde. "We haven't had the pleasure of an introduction."

Harriman gestured to the woman. "Detective Sergio Martin, this is Scarlet. She's part of the magic act."

Sergio nodded. "So I gathered from the attire."

"As I mentioned," Harriman said, "we got statements from almost all the other performers and stagehands. Everyone except Scarlet. She refused to talk to us."

"No, I refused to talk to *you*." Scarlet faced Sergio. "Daddy always said, give information to a lackey and you're bound to repeat it. I prefer to give it to the head man."

"Sure," Sergio said. "But if we have someone give us their story twice, we might notice inconsistencies in it."

"All the more reason to only say it once." Scarlet looked away, towards the CSIs and the bloody concrete floor, then turned back to Sergio. "Look, sugar, none of the staff had anything to do with Mrs. Romain's murder, as they all told him."

Avarie cocked her head. "How do you know it was a murder?"

Scarlet's eyes narrowed. "Oh, I guess Mrs. Romain stubbed her toe, huh, sweetie? And there's blood everywhere because she was a hemophiliac looking for a Band-Aid." Her gaze returned to Sergio again. "A proprietary recording is made of every show, for training purposes and to help hone the act. Why don't y'all just look at that?"

CHAPTER 14

Behind a plywood partition in the far corner of the expo hall's back room, a small desk supported a stack of computer monitors. Scarlet plopped into a desk chair. Hovering over the keyboard, the performer moved the mouse to display the various angles that the act's hidden cameras captured.

Sergio, Avarie and Harriman stood behind Scarlet, peering over her shoulder.

It was almost like watching a TV show, but it required glancing from one screen to the next to get the whole act. Some cameras were fixed on the audience; some viewed the stage from different angles—from the front and from behind. A few screens were black, their cameras appearing to not have recorded anything.

One screen was labeled "remote control unit," and its lens stayed on Sinclair O'Lair at all times.

"Is this the main one to watch?" Sergio pointed to the remote-controlled camera's monitor.

"Not if y'all want to see what's really going on." Scarlet shook her head, her unlit cigarette perched between her shiny red lips. "Let's watch the show one time through, like an audience member. Then, we can watch it a second time to see what you really want to see." She leaned back in the chair and clicked a button, re-starting all of the monitors.

"We'll need copies of all this," Sergio said.

"Yeah, I figured." She sighed, clicking the mouse and starting the playback. "Let's just not have this take all week."

On the screen, the magician strutted across the wide stage, his arms outstretched.

"And now, ladies and gentlemen..." Sinclair O'Lair stopped midway across the raised wooden platform, narrowing his eyes as he smiled at the sold-out crowd. "I shall tell you the tragic story of the six sisters."

The backdrop of curtains behind him went dark, an offstage fog machine sending a thin white cloud across the floor, creating a wafting translucent carpet.

At center stage, the handsome young man lifted his chin and clasped the lapels of his tuxedo. "There once were six sisters in a small village, and they were captured by an evil queen who locked them away in cages in her dungeon."

As he spoke, his beautiful assistants walked out from the sides of the stage.

From the desk chair in the expo hall, Scarlet pointed at two of the women on the computer monitor screen. "Olive and Jade were sawed in half during the prior trick by the man in the tuxedo—Sinclair O'Lair, magician extraordinaire."

Each of the magician's scantily-clad female assistants was more stunning than the next, dressed like bawdy cabaret dancers in corsets that amplified their ample cleavage, and fishnet stockings that showed off their shapely legs. There was Scarlet, a blonde; and a brunette, a redhead, a second blonde, and a raven-haired African-American, all with thick eyelashes and long hair. Their costumes were similar but not the same. Several wore tight black leather shorts and elbow-length black gloves, while their counterparts on the stage donned black miniskirts and shiny, knee-length black boots.

The outfits seemed to serve one purpose—the same as the fog and the laser lights and the flashes of fire that had occasionally burst from handsome young Sinclair O'Lair's fingertips during the hour-long magic act: distraction. Keeping the eyes of the crowd where the master magician and his crew of attractive female assistants *wanted* their eyes focused.

And it seemed to work—on the men in the audience *and* the women.

The showman on the stage kept his eyes on the ten A.M. crowd, scanning their faces as tiny beams of bright morning sunlight peeked in from around the edges and bottoms of the exit doors. "The evil queen told the six sisters, 'All of you will remain here until your beauty has faded into old age like mine—unless one of you would agree to sacrifice herself, trading her life today so the others may go free.'"

Six cages descended from the ceiling of the state fair expo hall. O'Lair's five assistants sauntered across the stage, stopping so that one stood between each of the steel enclosures. On the tops of the cages, bundles of blue velvet lay coiled up, hovering over the long bars that comprised each enclosure's four walls.

The magician leaned forward, speaking in a stage whisper to a small boy in the first row, his lapel microphone carrying the showman's words through the sound system and out to the packed auditorium. "And the evil queen said that because... she was evil."

He gave the child an exaggerated wink. A murmur of laughter rippled through the audience.

The five shapely assistants entered the cages, one after the other, and pulled the doors shut, locking themselves inside.

The last cage, on the far-right side of the stage, remained empty.

"Believing that none of the siblings would be willing to die," Sinclair O'Lair said, "the evil queen took out a large dagger and held it up, letting the dungeon torches illuminate the sharpened metal blade." The handsome young man in the black tuxedo raised his empty hand, his face contorting with fake fear. A shake of his fingers produced a long dagger, nearly twelve inches in length, with a pointy tip that shimmered in the auditorium spotlights.

As the audience applauded, Sinclair O'Lair continued with his stage patter. "The six sisters gasped, backing away in horror."

His assistants feigned fear, moving to the back of their small cages as O'Lair gently ran a finger along the side of the shiny dagger.

He stepped toward the empty cage on the far-right side of the stage. "But the youngest sister, who was the most beautiful of them all, said, 'Please, take me, dear queen. For I believe your blade will be unable to do any harm to one that is pure of heart.'" The handsome magician returned his gaze to the crowd. "And truly, anyone offering to sacrifice themselves to save others would have the purest of hearts."

With a dramatic flourish, he twirled around and placed the long dagger in front of the sixth cage.

"The other sisters tried to protest," he said, "but the queen greedily accepted the offer. She lowered a curtain over each cage, so the other sisters would not have to watch their youngest sibling die." One by one, he pointed to each cage, and the blue velvet bundle on top of it, which remained in place.

"From the cloaked darkness of their cages," the magician shouted, "the sisters heard a scuffle, and a shriek! They managed to lift their curtains to see what had happened..." The magician shrugged his shoulders. "The sixth cage was empty, and the evil queen and their sister were gone. All that remained was the dagger."

He strolled back to the center of the stage, his five beautiful assistants still preening in their enclosures, the curtains atop each steel frame still rolled up and waiting.

"Then, from behind them, their youngest sister walked out of the darkness, smiling and unharmed. All the cages opened, and her sisters were released."

He held his hands out, peering over the crowd.

"Now, unfortunately, as you can see, we only have five assistants. Lovely as they all are, we will need the help of a volunteer from our audience to show you the tragedy of the six sisters today." He grinned, his gaze wandering over the audience. "Who would like to help us?"

Hands went up here and throughout the crowd. O'Lair's five lovely assistants exited their cages, smiling as they swayed their hips and batted their eyes, sashaying down the steps of the expo hall stage and immersing themselves in the crowd.

As the scantily-clad ladies made their way through the audience, more hands shot up—quite a few of them attached to the arms of middle-aged men.

Spotlights in the rafters zoomed back and forth over the crowd as the assistants stopped by enthusiastic would-be participants.

Onstage, Sinclair O'Lair held a hand up to his forehead, blocking the glare from the overhead stage lights. "It's hard to tell from up here, but it seems as if my lovely assistant Ms. Olive has located a volunteer for us." He pointed to his African-

American coworker, who stood in the aisle with an elderly lady clutching a cane.

Sinclair O'Lair smiled at the old woman. "Dear, we appreciate your enthusiasm, but… I see you're holding a cane. Do you think you'll be able to get around the stage unassisted? Ms. Olive and her teammates have to move pretty quick."

The elderly lady blushed and shook her head, smiling as she lowered herself back into her seat.

O'Lair feigned disappointment. "Ah, well, then. The search continues." He moved his head back and forth, stopping at another assistant. "Ms. Violet, do you have a volunteer?"

The brunette assistant put her hand on the shoulder of a rotund middle-aged man, flashing her big green eyes. The enormous man stood up and stepped into the aisle next to the gorgeous assistant.

"Excellent, sir." O'Lair said from the stage. "We appreciate your help—but… Uh, do you think you'll be okay inside the cage? It's a bit small." As the audience laughed, the magician glanced around and tugged his collar. "No, what I mean is, once those blue velvet curtains come down, it can be quite claustrophobic in the enclosure. And we have very nervous lawyers, and they'll… well, they'll do what lawyers always do. They'll mess everything up."

The portly man smiled, his cheeks turning bright red.

O'Lair rocked his head back and forth, wrinkling up his nose. "*Mayyy*be let's have our people call your people and see about participating in an event at a later date."

Nodding, the massive middle-aged man took the hint—and re-took his seat.

The spotlights roamed the audience again, landing on the buxom blonde with the firm, toned legs.

"Ah—Ms. Scarlet," Sinclair O'Lair said. "By any chance do you have a volunteer for us?"

Scarlet produced a microphone from somewhere behind her back and held it to her shiny red lips. "I think we just might."

She extended her hand to the shoulder of a stunningly beautiful woman in the crowd.

The woman was dressed in a simple t-shirt and shorts, but her statuesque figure and model-like good looks were obvious on the stage's big screen for all to see. She clutched an oversized handbag made of white cloth, almost crescent-shaped but with a flat bottom, and printed in a blue seashell pattern, with arched white handles.

Sinclair O'Lair grinned. "Madam, could we persuade you to join us this morning?" He faced the audience. "Give the young lady some encouragement, ladies and gentlemen. Let's see if we can persuade her to volunteer."

The crowd applauded, cheers and whistles filling the massive expo hall.

"Excellent, excellent." The magician beamed at the woman. "What do you say, ma'am? Will you help us out? Because there's another show in a few hours, so at some point we need to finish this one."

As the audience chuckled at the magician's banter, the beautiful young lady nodded her head.

"Terrific! Thank you!" O'Lair waved a hand at the audience. Triumphant music boomed from the sound system. "Let's give her a round of applause."

Scarlet guided the volunteer onto the stage and over to where the handsome magician stood. The spotlight beamed down on them.

Putting his hand on her arm, he leaned in close to the new recruit. "And what is your name, kind lady?"

The reply was barely audible. Scarlet moved the microphone closer to the volunteer's chin.

"My name is... Gabriella Romain."

Sinclair O'Lair smiled out at the crowd. "Well, thank you for volunteering, Gabriella. Now, we'd like you to..." He cocked his head and turned back to the woman. "Wait, did you say Gabriella Romain?"

The beautiful volunteer lowered her mouth to the microphone, peering up at him. "Yes, that's right."

O'Lair took a step back, his jaw hanging open. He recovered quickly and faced the audience again, a wide grin spreading over his face. "Ladies and gentlemen, we have a Tampa celebrity onstage. I read that Ms. Romain and her husband recently acquired the old Cuban Cigar Club and reopened its Los Amantes theater again—a multimillion dollar renovation for the fair city of Tampa!"

The crowd applauded.

Gabriella nodded, clasping her oversized cloth bag in front of her as she hunched her shoulders again. She leaned in close to Scarlet's microphone a second time. "The updated club features the kinds of burlesque acts and drag shows that were historically a staple there. My husband also purchased the Fleerman House, which is on the national register of historic places, with plans to restore it to its original elegance. Presidents have stayed at Fleerman House."

"It's also on Bayshore Boulevard," O'Lair said. "One of the priciest locations in Tampa Bay." The magician strutted around the stage. "Well, we are very lucky to have Tampa royalty with us at our early show today. Folks, you might want to check the floor around where she was sitting. If any loose bills fell out of her pockets, it's probably more money than I make doing this show in a year!"

Gabriella blushed as another round of laughter went up from the audience.

O'Lair walked back to her. "Okay, well, now we finally have six sisters. Gabriella will play the role of the beautiful young sibling that saves the day—and you certainly fit the part. You're just... gorgeous." He put his hand on his chest and shook his head, his mouth hanging open, then snapped upright and winked at the crowd. "And I'd better shut up before your husband hears me. Those Miami real estate guys don't mess around!"

The beautiful Gabriella laughed along with the audience this time, turning a deeper shade of crimson.

"Okay! On with the show!" As the master magician guided Gabriella Romain to the cage on the far-right side of the stage, the five assistants re-entered the other cages.

Gabriella gestured to her bag. "Should I put this somewhere?"

"Oh, just take it in with you," the magician said. "No one will steal anything, I promise—after all, it'll be locked in a steel cage."

The enclosure doors were pulled shut, and the showman walked back to center stage.

"And now, ladies and gentlemen..." The handsome young magician strutted across the darkened set, the spotlight following his every move. Reaching the center of the stage, he tugged at the lapels of his tuxedo. "The finale of the tragedy of the six sisters!"

The room darkened. Fog rolled across the floor. Laser beams shot out from behind the six cages, and the blue velvet curtains unfurled, hiding each enclosure's occupant from the eyes of the audience.

As soon as the curtains reached the bottoms of the cages, Sinclair O'Lair rapidly flung fireballs at each enclosure, left to right, one after the other, creating a puff of smoke as the blue velvet curtains raced toward the ceiling again.

In an instant, all the curtains had recoiled, showing the six enclosures to be empty.

As the audience applauded, O'Lair took a bow and then leaped to the edge of the stage. "But wait! There's more!"

The curtains dropped again.

Immediately, the blue velvet fabric bounded back upward, revealing that each of the five beautiful assistants had reappeared—locked back inside her original enclosure—but now adorned in elaborate, flowing ball gowns of various pastel colors, complete with a dainty matching lace umbrella.

Five, with the last cage empty.

"The maiden's older sisters are saved!" the magician shouted. "All thanks to the youngest and most pure of heart, our volunteer."

The morning audience erupted with applause as the spotlight beams zoomed to the rear of the room, landing on the exit doors.

"Ladies and gentlemen, give a big round of applause to our volunteer—Ms. Gabriella Romain!"

The music rose to a fanfare, but the expo hall doors remained shut, and confusion ensued onstage.

Sergio folded his arms across his chest as the recordings continued to play. None of the cameras were in a position to view what had happened under the stage after the volunteer went through the trap door and descended the ladder rungs. A moment after Gabriella walked off screen, the blood splatter began to fly everywhere.

On the monitors, the rest of the act milled around onstage, apparently unsure of how to proceed—until Scarlet walked to the trap door and opened it, followed by Sinclair O'Lair.

The magician dropped to his knees, jamming a fist into his gaping mouth. "Wh—what happened?"

The dramatic conclusion of the six sisters became an empty steel cage splattered in blood, a giant crimson pool spreading over the concrete floor below, and a red dagger soaking in the middle of it all.

In the backstage area, Sergio shook his head. *We're not getting any prints off that knife.*

Scarlet leaned away from the monitors, gazing up at Sergio as she crossed her shapely legs.

"Well, that's pretty much it, sugar." Lifting her cigarette back to her lips, the buxom blonde produced her lighter and fired it up, taking another long, slow drag of her cigarette. Scarlet sent a thin stream of white toward the ceiling. "Looks like the Tampa socialite scene is one member lighter this morning."

CHAPTER 15

Sergio walked toward the exit, Harriman and Avarie trailing him. "I don't know how we're going to keep this quiet," he said. "Everybody in the audience heard the volunteer say her name was Gabriella Romain." The detective pushed the expo hall doors open, squinting in the bright sunlight. "Did anybody in the crowd take a video with a smart phone?"

"No," Harriman said. "Before the show starts, all phones and devices are placed in individual security bags with a scan lock, which blocks any use of electronics. The bags are only unlocked after the performance ends."

The heat of midday rose from the asphalt, the humidity of early summer clinging to Sergio's skin like he'd stepped into the shower room at the gym. A mob of sweaty, happy people filled the walkways, on their way to eat a hot dog, lose a few bucks playing midway games, or take a ride on the world's largest relocatable Ferris wheel.

"Detective Martin!" A man shouted over the rabble.

Sergio turned to the voice. "Yeah?"

Officer Jim Rondo trotted toward him from the other side of the parking lot, sweat staining his collar and armpits. "Earlier, when we were just getting all the witnesses together from the audience, a young woman came up and said she was supposed to meet her sister. So I'm like okay, who's your sister? And she says Gabriella Romain." Rondo grimaced, holding up his notepad. "Apparently, she heard about what happened on stage from some of the audience members."

Nodding, Sergio eyed the officer. "Where is she now?

"I didn't want her getting hysterical if she heard a lot of details," Rondo said, "so I said we didn't know much at this point. She was a little worried, so we got her contact information and let her go home." He handed Sergio the notepad. "Crisalyn Hartford. It's... you know—a messy crime scene, and she seemed like a nice kid. I'd have hated for her to see her sister's body come out of there..."

"No, no." The detective held a hand up. "You're right. Probably a good idea to not have a distraught family member on scene." He looked at Rondo as he handed the pad back. "Update the case file with her information and we'll have somebody follow up with her when we know more. Thanks."

Sergio turned to the others.

"See? This is what I'm talking about. There's gonna be no way to keep a lid on this thing."

He put his hands on his hips and peered at the top of the expo hall building, checking each corner, and every light pole nearby.

There's not a security camera out here that would be close enough to see the injured woman leaving the building—or spot her killer coming inside.

But we had a similar situation this morning, didn't we? Nobody saw Carmello get into that fish warehouse.

"Mark." Sergio looked at Harriman. "Call Max Fuentes and have him get a warrant for the original recordings we just watched. We can't take copies. If any of the footage was to leak to the media, we'd have chaos on our hands."

"And your ass would be grass with the chief," Harriman said.

"And that." Sergio nodded. "But get the recordings from a few of the earlier shows, too. I wanna know if the viewing angle for the camera under the stage was different for this morning's performance."

Pointing toward the gaggle of nearby reporters, Avarie stepped away. "I'd better get over there and start handling those news crews. I'll catch up with you afterward."

As the PR rep departed, Harriman turned to Sergio. "You wanna look through the witness statements we took from the audience?"

"No." The detective shook his head. "You can let all those people go now. Whatever we're going to learn, we'll learn it from the performers and the stage recordings. You got statements from everyone but Scarlet, right? Tell me about Mr. Master Magician. What did he have to say?"

"Sinclair O'Lair?" Harriman chuckled. "Nothing useful. He just blubbered a lot. For a guy in charge of such a complicated act, he's a mess."

"He's not in charge of the act," Sergio said. "Scarlet's in charge. And we don't have a statement from her."

* * * * *

Avarie smiled as she approached the group of reporters. "Hey, everyone. Let me give you a quick update on what we know so far…"

None of the local TV stations had sent their high-profile on-air talent yet—a good sign. Most of the attendees were low-level beat reporters, assigned to do a brief fluff piece that might air at lunchtime and possibly at the five P.M. broadcast if nothing interesting happened the rest of the day.

But that can change in an instant.

Kerri Milner was the sole possible exception. She could be trusted to be discreet and accurate.

But even Kerri would have to run with a story about a confirmed murder at a popular tourist attraction.

If the local stations smelled a bigger story, they'd send their franchise players to the fairgrounds, and a feeding frenzy could begin.

So the goal is to play it cool, feed the fairgrounds reporters information as slowly as possible without making it obvious, and hopefully keep their stations' attention on the drug dealer killings from earlier.

That was its own problem, but if the fish warehouse murders could be pushed as crime-on-crime killings, the regular citizens might feel safe, and that could give it a chance to keep from boiling over into something bigger.

Avarie approached the reporters. Tiffany Tierson of Channel Thirteen stepped forward from the group, wearing a blouse that was at least two sizes too small. The borderline-inept blonde held her microphone out as her videographer hoisted his camera onto his shoulder and pointed it at Avarie.

"We understand a woman has been murdered," Tierson said. "Do you have any information on her killer?"

Avarie held her hands up. "Hold on. We have a crime scene, and we are investigating. We can't confirm that anyone has been murdered—"

The reporter moved her microphone closer to Avarie's chin. "But Ms. Fox, we've been interviewing members of the audience. People in the front row told us there was blood all over the magician's prop cage, and we overheard one of the CSI techs saying there was so much blood in the under-stage area, the victim couldn't possibly have survived."

Avarie winced. Crime scene investigators weren't supposed to talk to the media without authorization, and are instructed to be careful when they discuss the case with each other.

The PR rep tried not to let her concern show in her voice. "Those are essentially true statements—

there was blood on the cage and there was a substantial amount of additional blood under the stage." She looked the blonde reporter in the eye. "But we don't have a body, so we can't definitively say anyone was killed. I'm just going to have to ask you to be patient with our investigation."

A new, brown-haired reporter from Channel Ten moved toward Avarie. "Is it true that the victim was socialite Gabriella Romain?"

"Again, we don't have a body, so we can't—"

Kerri Milner spoke up from the rear of the group. "Ms. Fox, the woman *said* her name at the show. In front of everyone."

A jolt went through Avarie's insides.

If the news people reported that Gabriella Romain was murdered, the story would instantly grow legs it didn't need to have yet—and the fairgrounds would be teeming with news crews from all over within the hour. Audience members were probably already posting about it on social media.

From there, it would only be a matter of time before one of the reporters dug around and connected Gabriella Romain to the Chief of Police.

Then, the story could spin completely out of control.

* * * * *

Sergio returned to the office area near the expo hall stage. All of the stagehands and assistants were there except one.

Scarlet.

"I need a statement from your boss," Sergio said.

The redheaded assistant looked at him and pointed to the closed office door. "Sinclair O'Lair's in there, but he's still pretty much Jell-O."

"Not him." Sergio pulled out his notepad. "Your real boss." He glared at the assistants.

They looked at one another. The African-American assistant pointed at a side exit. "Lot K, at the very back. There's a row of big oak trees. Scarlet will be in a trailer there."

Sergio nodded. "How will I know which trailer is hers? Do they have numbers or something?"

The assistant smiled. "It's the one that looks like it belongs to a magic act."

* * * * *

Forcing a smile, Avarie worked to appear nonchalant to the reporter's question.

"Is it true that the victim was socialite Gabriella Romain?"

"The woman said her name at the show. In front of everyone."

The PR rep clasped her hands in front of herself and shrugged.

Buy some time.

Avarie cleared her throat. "I could stand up in front of an audience and say my name was Santa Claus. That doesn't make it true. The stage performers were in the middle of doing a magic act. They didn't stop to check the volunteer's ID."

The Channel Ten reporter chuckled.

Avarie glanced at the faces of the others. Kerri nodded. Another videographer lowered his camera.

Looks like they agree with me—for now.

Good.

PR 101. Deflect the thorny question and then lead the media to a different shiny object.

"The performers record their act, though." Avarie glanced back at the expo hall for effect. When she faced the reporters again, their eyes were on her.

Video of the crime scene increases the watchability of the story—and increases the value of the reporter to the station.

They want to know more, so offer it to them—if they agree to behave.

Then try to lead them away from specific names that could embarrass the Chief of Police—and by association, the entire police department. Find another shiny object.

Avarie glanced over both shoulders. "I watched the footage of the show a few minutes ago." She lowered her voice. "Certain segments might be very intriguing for your viewers. That means good ratings. But only if you hold back from making potentially devastating statements that aren't confirmed and may not be true."

She checked each face. The promise of a better visual seemed to hook the reporter from Channel Ten.

She gets it.

"Seems like you're hedging," Tiffany Tierson said.

"I don't mean to. Here's what the situation is." Avarie stepped to the blonde reporter. "A woman is missing. If we announce a name without confirmation, or say she was murdered when we don't have that evidence, we send a shock wave through her friends and family. That's not fair to her or anyone who cares about her. She could have small children." The PR rep shook her head, a light wind lifting her blonde strands and tossing them onto her cheek. "I know you all have a job to do but it's important to be accurate. Otherwise, we'll be on the air later saying you got the story wrong and we told you so before you ran it—and you'll have to explain that to your station manager."

Her message delivered, Avarie held her breath and waited to see if the reporters would take the bait.

CHAPTER 16

CARLY SLOUCHED IN THE CHAIR, massaging one hand with the other, the knot in her stomach growing as she mentally walked through her dinner with Kyle a few weeks ago.

The evening had started out civil. Unfinished business, she'd taken to calling it—her code for anything to do with her soon-to-be ex-husband and their divorce proceedings.

It was easy enough to carry on her part of a conversation with someone she'd been having conversations with for more than a decade. It was all the same and very familiar.

And yet it was very different. Oddly platonic. Sterile, at times, as if they were avoiding any topic that was deep enough to have any real meaning. Half a dozen times or more, her thoughts wandered.

That night, she thought about what Sergio was up to, or what funny comment he might make about the dinner conversation topic.

And each time, she brought herself back to the dinner with Kyle, hoping it wasn't too obvious that she'd been mentally away.

And she felt guilty every time.

Not because she wasn't allowed to think about things other than what her soon-to-be ex-husband was talking about, and not because she didn't want to be present in the moment. Not because the new man she'd allowed into her life was more exciting and more unique and more humorous than the one she'd married. But because of a vow she had taken, and because of her children. No matter how often a friend or colleague reassured her, Carly's pending divorce made her feel like a failure.

And during that dinner so many weeks ago, the one thought that came back to her head most often, she didn't have an answer to:

What am I doing?

She loved her husband. She loved him for all of their ten plus years together, and through the counseling, and the long hours when he had been away at work, and the long hours when she had been away at work. She loved him when their sons were born, and she loved him when he said he thought things weren't working.

He broke her heart that day.

She still loved him when he packed his things and moved out. It was painful and embarrassing, but she thought in some way that maybe she deserved it. Maybe she hadn't been there enough for him. Maybe her job took her away from her husband and he resented it.

Fair or not, that was his view of the situation.

So, a few weeks after he had moved out, when he called and said maybe it was a mistake, she loved that, too.

She loved the idea of a second chance with Kyle, and she loved the idea of fixing her family. It seemed her job as a wife and mother to ensure that she remains her husband's wife and her sons' mother.

But...

But she also loved the crooked smile Sergio always gave her. And she loved her work partner's sense of humor. She loved how much she and Sergio had in common, on so many levels, and how he always seemed to know just what she was thinking.

She loved how Sergio played with her boys, gracefully accepting the moniker of Uncle Sergio from them. Who really knew how things like that came about? But it had, and at times he was almost as much of a part of the family as any of the rest of them.

Except he wasn't.

He was her coworker. Her partner. Her best friend.

Then, he was her lover.

He was the guy who always had her back and the guy whose heart she smashed into a million pieces when she pushed him away.

It was necessary, she told herself.

She knew what would happen when she delivered that news to the partner she'd fallen in love with. The one that always had her back.

He'll die. Maybe not outwardly and maybe not even to himself, but I know him. He'll be devastated. But I think I have to do it.

And Sergio was crushed.

Now, although they seemed to be getting back to being just friends and coworkers, each disagreement or difference of opinion begged the question of whether there was lingering resentment.

Of course there was. From both of them. How could there not be?

Sergio probably thinks that's why I was so angry at the fish warehouse this morning.

She sighed.

We'll work through it. With this promotion, Sergio and I will see less of each other, and we will get through it.

Unless...

During the brief period where she and Sergio had allowed themselves to become more than work partners, there had been another instance of "unfinished business" to attend to with Kyle. So, she met her ex as she had half a dozen times, to go over the issues in as civil a manner as possible.

Dinner, as usual.

Civil and pragmatic, as usual.

But there was also warmth, and smiles that had become more and more rare.

And as dinner became drinks became the drive home, some of the familiar routines took shape. Relaxing on the couch. A glass of Pinot Grigio for her and another one for him. Sometimes, in the past, they'd share the same glass.

That night, two glasses seemed more appropriate. But as the evening wore on, she had finished her drink and found herself sipping from his.

Like old times.

With the handsome man she had fallen in love with a dozen years ago, and had never wanted to part with.

And as the conversation on the couch became a conversation in the bedroom, she tried to put aside the guilt.

This is my husband. I shouldn't feel guilty for doing this.

The room was the same, but different. She had changed the sheets that morning before going to work, but that only fooled one of the two participants moving in the darkness. The cologne was different. The deodorant, the shampoo. The beard stubble. The well-toned body.

Although they were roughly the same size and shape physically, Sergio and her husband were worlds apart in their mannerisms.

And as she put her hand on the back of her husband's head, and let the soft curls of his hair wind between her fingers, it all changed.

For an instant, it wasn't Kyle anymore.

The simple act of her hand at the back of his neck, the way she had done once with Sergio, changed it all. Suddenly, Sergio was there. Only for an instant, but she visualized him. How he moved. His breath on her cheek.

And the tingles that swelled within her at that moment were enough to push the guilt away and enjoy the fantasy.

She gasped, surprised and thrilled at the transformation. At that moment, the man in her bedroom was Sergio, and she let herself go. For a moment, in the darkness, she allowed the pleasure of the action to take over.

The guilt would come later.

As she lay next to her husband, both of them breathing hard, the ecstasy faded and the guilt came rushing in like a tidal wave.

But it didn't matter. She wouldn't let it matter.

As Kyle got up from the bed they'd shared as a married couple, she watched his naked form go to the kitchen for a glass of water, as he had so many times before.

But her thoughts were not on Kyle. They were on Sergio and how passionately she'd made love with him the night before.

"Ms. Sanderson?" The OB-GYN nurse stood at the door of the waiting room, a clipboard in her hand, glancing around. "Carly Sanderson? Doctor Sherwood will see you now."

Carly's thoughts came rushing back to the present.

She stood up from the waiting room chair, trying not to think about the dinner with Kyle, the night that followed, or any of the rest of it.

Not right now.

Focus on talking with Doctor Sherwood. Don't worry about Kyle or Sergio or anything else.

Then, when you're done here, you stiffen your spine, go out to your car, and make a phone call.

You tell him, plain and simple. That's the right thing to do.

Isn't it?

As Carly approached her, the young nurse held the door open, smiling cheerfully. "And how are mother and baby doing this morning?"

Carly put a hand to her abdomen, trying to smile back. "It's been a rough couple of days."

CHAPTER 17

Across a sea of grass that was covered with parked cars, a distant patch of oak trees lined the horizon. Sergio trudged over the brutally warm acreage, stopping at a mobile home painted like the billboard outside the expo hall. Sinclair O'Lair's image loomed large on the side of the bright red trailer, emblazoned with old-time gold lettering that described the master magician's act.

The detective knocked on the door. "Tampa Police Department."

A woman's voice came through the flimsy entryway. "Come in, Detective Martin."

He opened the door and stepped inside.

The lodging was filled with costumes and props, makeup and vanity mirrors and crates, strewn about as if the users had left it all in a rush to get onstage somewhere. Leggings and fishnet stockings hung over the backs of the sofa; wire cages along the walls held white rabbits and doves. Most of the rest of the space was packed with black equipment boxes, labeled in white chalk with "Drill of Death," or "Chinese Water Torture," and "Sands of the Nile."

Toward the back of what would normally be a mobile home's living room area, a colorful Asian-style dressing screen had been erected. In front of the partition sat a petite, brown-haired woman with her hair in a bun and thick reading glasses, rifling through a stack of papers as she typed on an old 10-key adding machine.

A long paper tape spiraled from the top of the ancient calculating device, dangling to the floor and jumping every time she hit the big button on the machine's keypad.

The brunette didn't look up from her work. "May I help you?"

Her dialect carried a thick New York tone, her fingers continuing nonstop over the mechanical adding machine keys, hammering away at them and filling the trailer with a sound like a miniature machine gun.

Sergio glanced around, holding up his notepad. "I'm sorry. I was looking for Scarlet, the blonde lady from the magic show. I was told she was here."

The woman stopped, glaring at him.

Sighing, she stood. "One moment." She walked around the back of the silky partition, disappearing from view. Scarlet walked out from the other side, still in her stage attire of fishnet stockings and tight bustier, puffing on her cigarette.

"Hello again, sugar."

The curvy performer slipped her toned rear end onto the arm of the couch and rested a hand on her thigh. "What would you like to talk about?"

Sergio pointed at the silk partition. "Do you mind?"

"Y'all want to peek behind the curtain, so to speak?" Shrugging, the blonde looked away. "Knock yourself out, darlin'."

He stepped to the dressing screen and leaned forward, peering behind the colorful silk wall.

No one was there.

The space was barely large enough for the brunette to have stepped into, and definitely not big enough to accommodate two women at the same time.

Sergio looked back to the buxom assistant. "Where'd she go? The brunette who was working the adding machine?"

A hint of a smile tugged at Scarlet's shiny red lips. "Magic."

"I wouldn't say that." Sergio shrugged, walking back to the couch. "But it was a good trick. How'd you manage to swap her out so fast? Is there a trap door, like in the stage show?"

"Sorry, handsome." Scarlet dropped her cigarette into a nearby Styrofoam coffee cup, extinguishing it in an inch of dark brown liquid. "A good magician never reveals her secrets."

She shifted her legs, uncrossing them and then re-crossing them the other way, and slid her hand along the top of her thigh, coming to a stop at the knee. Her foot, in its midnight black stiletto heel, bobbed up and down.

Smiling, Sergio leaned against the trailer wall. "It's a trap door, right? In the floor?"

Pouting, Scarlet stuck out her lower lip. "Do you really wanna talk about that?" She stood up from the couch and went over to him. "We have the whole trailer to ourselves."

The blonde assistant walked two fingers up the length of Sergio's arm, going from his wrist to his shoulder, and leaned in close, allowing her full red lips to hover near his ear. "I can think of a lot of other things to do." Her voice was low and soft, filled with honeyed, southern sweetness. "Can't you?"

He gazed at her, admiring the beauty of her features. The big eyes and dainty nose. The full breasts and long legs.

"They say…" Sergio whispered. "That these costumes are designed to distract. To keep the audience's attention away from where it should be."

Scarlet's breath was hot on his cheek. "Should I take mine off so you're not distracted, Detective Martin?"

"That's up to you." His eyes locked on hers. "I'm just here to get your statement."

She looked up at him. "Only a statement? That seems like a waste."

Her fingertips glided across his chest.

"But I've been in this outfit for hours now. These stockings are strangling my legs, my feet are dying in these heels, and my casual, comfortable street clothes are calling so loud someone outside might think our macaw got loose in here. So, I'm gonna change—if that's okay."

She strolled to a doorway at the back of the trailer. "This is my room. I promise not to run away."

"Don't you mean disappear?" Sergio asked.

"Hey, you're learning already." She stepped into the tiny bedroom, leaving the door open a few inches. "But trust me, sugar—if I truly wanted to hike my booty outta here and run away, y'all would never find me."

CHAPTER 18

Doctor Sherwood clasped her hands together, leaning forward and resting her elbows on the top of her desk. "Normally this is where I say congratulations, you're having a baby girl. But, I guess we're not doing that."

Carly swallowed hard, barely able to speak. "No, we aren't."

She sat alone in one of the two chairs in front of the doctor's desk and glanced at the other chair.

That's where the husband or boyfriend sits when the woman is getting good news.

Nodding, the doctor turned to her computer. "Well, the rest of the news is, based on your blood type, and the blood type you provided us for Kyle and Detective Martin, we were able to determine who the baby's father is."

Carly held her breath.

"I'm not sure which answer is good or bad," Sherwood said, "so I'll just tell you. According to the test, Sergio Martin is your baby's father."

Carly squeezed her eyes shut.

There were no good answers to the question of "Who's the father?" If the baby was Kyle's, Sergio would be crushed that she had slept with her ex while she was seeing him. If the baby was Sergio's, he was out of the picture now. It could make things even harder in her divorce proceedings with Kyle.

Uncomfortable conversations. Embarrassing questions. Kyle's new lawyer might raise issues in the custody talks.

Carly shook her head, her voice falling to a whisper. "I can't believe I let this happen."

"Well..." The doctor leaned back in her chair. "How exactly did you let it happen?"

"They say no method of birth control is a hundred percent effective." The detective slouched in her chair. "Looks like they're right."

"In any case," Doctor Sherwood said, "we need to have a serious conversation about what you're going to do." She pulled her keypad in front of her and grabbed her mouse. "Considering you've been diagnosed with cancer and need to start treatment right away, it's my obligation to tell you that the treatment will almost certainly affect the baby in a negative way." The physician glanced at Carly. "The recommendation, therefore, would be to terminate the pregnancy and proceed with the cancer treatment, in order to save your life. And if you're interested in having a baby down the road, try again when you're recovered and are cancer-free."

Carly sat still, staring at the floor, unable to speak.

Clearing her throat, the doctor turned her attention back to the computer. "About two-thirds of women exhibit no cessation of reproductive functions after completion of their cancer treatment. You're young and healthy."

Carly snorted. "People keep telling me that. It really doesn't seem like it when you've been told you have cancer." She looked at the doctor. "Nothing about me seems healthy at the moment."

"Carly..." Doctor Sherwood got up and came around to the other chair in front of her desk, sitting down and taking her patient's hand. "You're not the first woman who got pregnant during a divorce procedure, and you're not the first woman I've met with who had more than one man in her life when she found out she was pregnant. But one thing is true." She looked Carly in the eye. "Your cancer is very treatable right now. If you wait until you have the baby, it won't be. That additional time will take this very treatable cancer and move it into the realm of becoming very dangerous for you. You'll go from a very high chance of survival to a much, much less desirable position."

"I know," Carly whispered. "I know all that."

Doctor Sherwood nodded. "I understand it's a very difficult decision, but I'm not sure it's worth risking your life—which you will. You'll be knowingly choosing to put your life at risk."

"It's not that simple." The detective sighed, looking down.

"Carly, it *is* pretty simple. If you try to keep this baby, I'm going to have to recommend you not start your cancer treatment. If you wait on the treatment, you could die. And if the cancer gets bad enough during the pregnancy, you and the baby could both die." She gently squeezed Carly's hand. "That means two out of the three outcomes are bad. I don't like those odds. What do you need to think about? I know you don't want to terminate the pregnancy. But after the treatment is over, if you want to have a baby, you can try again."

"Maybe." Carly swallowed hard. "Maybe not. But… Do you remember when I first got pregnant? Before I was pregnant with my oldest. The miscarriage."

Doctor Sherwood nodded. "I remember."

"I know it's silly, but…" Carly's gaze went to the ceiling as she searched for the words. "I always thought it was a girl. I felt that way inside. And after the miscarriage, sometimes I'd be in the bank or at the grocery store, and I'd see a woman with a little girl, and I'd think to myself, she would've been about that age. And I would sit there and I would fantasize."

She sniffled.

"I'd imagine us in the park, or playing in the living room… And I thought to myself, if I ever got a second chance…" She looked at the doctor. "I love my two boys. I wouldn't trade them for anything in the world. But in the back of my head, I always thought about a girl." She lowered her eyes and put her hand on her abdomen. "And now, I have one."

Doctor Sherwood pursed her lips, her face falling. She inhaled deeply and peered at her patient.

"Again, that's not necessarily true. Avoiding the treatment could result in losing the baby and losing you as well. We don't want that."

"No, I know." Carly shook her head. "I don't have a death wish. I don't want to die. But... I have to think about what I want to do."

The doctor got up and moved back behind her desk. "By trying to carry this baby to term, you're risking a lot. At thirty-seven, pregnancy can be more difficult. You were twenty-seven when you had your previous child. That said, eventually people will notice you're pregnant—and Kyle may ask if it's his. Now, I might be old-fashioned, but..."

Doctor Sherwood's words faded into the walls of the office as Carly's thoughts drifted.

She saw herself in the park, her two boys walking with her as she carried a little pink bundle.

"...whether or not a man said he didn't want more children, the tendency is when you tell him he's about to be a father again, most are overjoyed. Not always, but very often..."

The first day of school, where she dressed her girl in a cute outfit they'd spent the weekend shopping for together. Watching movies on the couch, under a blanket, and hiding their eyes at the scary parts. Talking about the boy who said he liked her—after she told him first, of course.

Her first date. Learning to drive. Going to homecoming.

The daydreams she'd harbored for over a decade now had a chance of becoming reality. The thought warmed her insides.

Carly looked up at Sherwood. The doctor had stopped talking.

Her cheeks growing warm, the detective opened her mouth to speak.

"It's okay." A smile stretched across Sherwood's face. "Like I said, this isn't the first time I've had a patient who had a lot to consider."

Carly nodded. "I can't let go of the fact that I've been given a second chance at something. I... I don't know what I want to do."

"Well," the doctor said, "You can take some time to think about it. But don't take too long."

Carly put a hand to her abdomen. The appointment with the oncologist was first thing tomorrow morning. "No, I won't take too long."

CHAPTER 19

S ERGIO WENT TO THE PERFORMER'S CLUTTERED SOFA AND SAT DOWN. "What happened out there this morning?" He took out his notepad. "What did you see?"

"I saw what you saw," Scarlet said. "Y'all watched the monitors. I was in plain sight of two hundred and fifty audience witnesses the whole time."

"Yeah." The detective nodded. "Yeah, you were. What about before?"

"Before was like every other performance. The recordings will show that, too. The female volunteer is supposed to come up onstage, I tell her about the trap door, and tell her to use it when the curtain comes down, then go down the ladder and follow the plastic tape to the exit door. Kevin meets her there and takes her to the back of the audience, where the spotlights land on her at the end. That's it."

"Which one is Kevin?" Sergio asked.

"Big guy. Face tattoos. Kinda scary-looking."

He made a note on his pad. "But Kevin never met up with her."

"He waits there until she shows, but she never did. She wanted to get picked, though, I can tell you that."

Sergio cocked his head. "She did?"

"Yeah." The sound of dresser drawers slamming came to his ears. "I mean, they all want to go up on stage, you know? Anybody who raises their hand when we ask for volunteers, they're all hoping to become part of the act for a few minutes. But Mrs. Romain… She didn't say anything, or do anything, but I could tell she really wanted it."

"How?" The detective turned halfway toward the bedroom door. "How can you know that?"

"I can read people," Scarlet said. "It's part of what I do. A magic act isn't magic, Detective Martin. It's reading people and guiding them to do what you want, but doing it in such a way that they think it's their idea. You can learn almost everything about a person in ten seconds. Anyone. They tell you without telling you."

"Yeah? What can you read about me?"

"Oh, let's not, sugar." Scarlet said. "You seem like a nice guy, and I don't want to offend you when we were getting off to such a good start."

"I'll be okay." Sergio flipped through his notepad. "Cops develop a thick skin."

She strolled out of the bedroom, wearing blue jeans shorts that were halfway unzipped but somehow managed to stay in place on her hips, a cutoff white t-shirt and no bra, and bare feet that had recently enjoyed a pedicure. The stage makeup was gone, as was the big hair and fake eyelashes. A cute, slender blonde with round-frame glasses stood in the hallway of the trailer now, adjusting a tiny medallion on the gold chain around her neck.

"Go on," Sergio said. "Try to read me."

"Okay…" Scarlet looked him over, biting her lip. "You were a decent student in school, but never got straight A's. You went to college because you were supposed to, and you paid your own way because you don't believe in loans just like your daddy didn't—and because you didn't get a scholarship for baseball. You drive a car that your friends think you should upgrade. You became a cop because you always wanted to be one."

She plopped down on the couch next to him, tucking one leg under herself and taking his left hand.

"You work out." She smiled. "Probably at a gym, because it's more social and you like to be out among people." Her gaze went to his hand. "The lack of a wedding ring—or a tan line or skin indentation where a wedding ring would be—indicates you're not married. Now, you might be divorced, and you might be the sleazy type who's married but doesn't wear his ring so he can still be a player, but I'm guessing you never got married. You date a lot, though. Maybe too much. And…"

She let go of his hand, leaning forward and looking deep into his eyes.

"You're carrying some relationship pain from a breakup, and you tell the new girl you're over the last one, but inside you wonder if you really are. You think you're not good at relationships. But I…"

She lowered her eyes, rolling the neck chain between her fingers. "Well… honey, I think y'all just hadn't met the right woman yet, is all."

Heat rose to Sergio's cheeks. Scarlet sat upright, brandishing a smile.

"You're good at being a cop, though. And you'll obsess over this murder case until you solve it, because that's your thing. It's who you are. You believe the white knights of the world should go out and slay dragons instead of waiting for them to show up at the front door, and this job is the closest thing to that as you could find."

"Wow." Sergio grinned. "You put all that together in the short time we've been talking?"

She smirked. "Sugar, I put all that together in the first ten seconds after I met you. It's deductive reasoning—figuring out the odds. You probably do it all the time in your job, but in my line of work, knowing how people will react can be the difference between putting food on the table and being on welfare."

"Ten seconds, huh?" He shook his head. "That's impressive. In my job, I usually take a lot longer." He shifted on the sofa. "What about when you said you could make people do something they didn't want to do?"

"I said I could *guide* someone to do something but make them think it was their idea. Here, I'll give you an example." Scarlet grabbed a piece of paper from a nearby box and wrote something on it, then folded it in half and held it in her hand where he could see it. "I'll ask you some questions, and you think of the answer as quickly as you can, but don't say anything out loud until I tell you."

"Okay," Sergio said.

"What's one plus one?" She kept her eyes on his, holding the folded paper in front of herself. "Now, what's two plus two? And what's four plus four? And finally, what's eight plus eight? Okay, now answer this one out loud." She eyed the detective. "Tell me the name of a vegetable."

"Carrot."

Scarlet unfolded the paper. The word carrot was written on it.

"See, that's priming." She tossed the white scrap onto the desk. "Ain't nobody expecting a Dixie darling to be analyzing them, but by getting you to focus on a few simple math calculations, your thought process moved to simple, common answers. Doing what we just did, ninety percent of people will say carrot as their answer. If I do that enough times—make enough assessments about someone—this simple southern girl starts to appear fairly omniscient."

Sergio grinned. "And you're moving on to the next trick before they can figure out the last one. It's a game of constant distraction." The detective leaned forward, pointing at her with his pencil. "You know, the Tampa PD would be a lot better off if you'd cooperate with us on this case. Maybe even assist us a little."

Scarlet frowned, turning away. "I don't work for this side or that side, I only work for me. The expo hall being shut down during your investigation is costing me ten dollars a ticket times 250 people per show, for four shows daily. That's $10,000 a day, and I can't afford to lose $10,000 a day." She peered at Sergio over her shoulder. "Can you?"

"Nope." He made a note on his pad and got up from the couch, not looking at her. "Maybe with a little help from you—and a lot less resistance—we can figure out what happened on stage this morning, and figure it out quicker." He walked to the exit and put his hand on the knob, turning to look back at her as he opened the door. "That helps both of us. What do you think?"

Sighing, Scarlet put her elbow on the back of the sofa and rested her head on her hand. "Okay. I'll help y'all get this thing figured out." She narrowed her eyes. "But only so I can get back to business, sugar."

CHAPTER 20

THE REPORTERS SUBDUED, AVARIE DROPPED A FEW tidbits to them about what she'd seen in the videos. Nothing outside the lines; they'd have to wait for that. But she was confident that a few clips from the show—like when the firebombs were going off around the cages, or when the dagger was held up—would be a terrific appetizer to the main course she'd serve them later: actual footage of the volunteer climbing down the ladder under the stage before she disappeared.

"That," Avarie said, "would be a very watchable video. I think your bosses would agree."

And it would do so without compromising the goal of keeping you reporters from investigating too hard into the victim's name.

"After all..." The PR rep smiled. "It might make a splashy headline for some random guy to say he's Tom Richie, and then do something crazy. People might initially think, 'Oh, Tom Richie, the Governor of Florida, did that?' but a little research would show it isn't true…"

As she spoke, a man in light gray coveralls pushed a cart towards a nearby trash barrel.

"Then," Avarie said, "the guy is shown to merely be a nut case or prankster…"

The maintenance worker lifted the round top off the orange-colored barrel and placed it to the side.

"…and any reporter who accepted his statement would end up discredited by the public, as well as to their…"

The worker glanced over both shoulders and leaned over the side of the trash barrel, lowering his arm deep into the metal bin and coming out with an oversized, crescent-shaped, blue and white handbag.

Avarie gasped, her hand going to her chest.

That's the bag from the video. The victim's handbag.

"…their, uh… they'd be embarrassed to… to the, uh, their bosses at the… um…" She stepped to the side of the reporters. "Excuse me for just one second."

The man grabbed the zipper at his neckline and opened his coveralls to his waist, shoving a corner of the oversized bag inside.

Avarie raised her hand. "Hey! Hold it!"

He looked around, his eyes landing on her.

"That handbag." Avarie waved, moving toward him. "That's not yours. Hold on."

The man's gaze darted around. A few passing people looked at him.

He looked back at Avarie, his eyes wide. Turning, he ran away.

"No!" She raced after him shouting. "Stop! Drop that handbag!"

The maintenance worker clutched the bag to his chest, charging over the steaming asphalt. He zigzagged between the patrons.

"No!" Avarie sprinted after him. "Stop!"

Kerri Milner took off with her, holding her phone out as she ran.

Tiffany Tierson slapped her videographer on the arm. "Record this!"

His camera swung upward, its lens aimed at Avarie.

"Go, go, go!" Tierson shouted. "Keep up with her."

The maintenance worker cut left, disappearing behind a small tent with a collection of colorful balloons overhead.

Avarie turned the corner right behind him, her arms and legs pumping. "I'm with the Tampa Police Department! Drop that handbag!"

He knocked into a rotund woman eating an ice cream cone, sending her over sideways. Avarie dashed past the casualty, gaining on the fleeing trash collector.

He bounced into other patrons as he pushed and shoved his way through the crowd, the bag against his chest. Avarie followed in his wake, her heart pounding.

At the back of the concession stand, he threw the handbag into a pile of plastic garbage bags and made another sharp turn, heading toward the crowded midway.

Avarie gritted her teeth.

If he gets in there, I'll lose him.

He sped past the first game—a low, wooden counter with a smattering of young children on one side. The youths smiled and laughed as they tossed ping pong balls at bowls of goldfish.

Glancing over his shoulder, the maintenance worker hurled himself forward—and straight into the back of a large man holding a young woman's hand.

As the fleeing worker staggered backwards, Avarie jumped onto the empty side of the fish game countertop and launched herself through the air, landing on the back of the trash collector. The pair crashed to the ground.

"I'm with the Tampa police! Stop!"

He shoved her away, scrambling to get to his feet. Avarie thrust a hand out and snagged his collar, halfway stopping him and halfway getting herself dragged forward.

The man toppled over sideways.

Groaning, Avarie strained to maintain her grip on his coveralls. He rolled over, shoved her down on her back and reared back with his fist.

"Aah!" Avarie screamed. She squeezed her eyes shut and hunched her shoulders, thrusting her forehead into her attacker's inbound fist.

The crunch filled her ears. The impact sent a jolt through her. Yellow and green fireworks shot past her eyes, pain exploding across the top of her head.

Shrieking, the maintenance man fell backward and clutched his fist. "You broke my hand! You broke my hand!"

Avarie winced, sitting up. "You broke my head." She rubbed the top of her blonde scalp.

As the news reporters swarmed the scene, uniformed police officers arrived, grabbing the maintenance worker's arms and putting him in handcuffs.

* * * * *

Avarie sat on the grass by the midway games, dabbing her head with a napkin wrapped in ice.

Sergio slipped his hands under her armpits and hauled her to her feet. "What were you doing?"

"Catching a bad guy." She looked at her skinned-up elbows and the new holes in the knees of her jeans. "He had our victim's purse."

Harriman brought the blue and white handbag forward. "She's right, Detective. This sure looks like the handbag in the video."

Sergio glared at the maintenance worker. "Care to explain that?"

"Hey, I don't know nothing." The trash collector shrugged. "I just saw a purse in the trash and decided to check it out. It's finders keepers in this gig."

Sergio shook his head. "Why'd you run?"

"I'm on parole," the man said. "This placed is covered in cops, and when she yelled at me, I got scared."

Sighing, Sergio rubbed his brow. "Okay, take him to the squad cars and check him out. If he's clean, let him go. And secure the handbag. Have CSI go through it, then bring it straight to me." His gaze went to Avarie, his eyes narrowing. "You—this way."

He led her toward the squad cars. "You're here to do PR, remember?"

She walked fast to keep up with his pace. "Don't talk to me like I'm a child. I just... overreacted."

"Ya think?" He glanced over his shoulder at her. "At the risk of sounding like my overly-cautious friend Carly, you could've been killed. It's possible you were chasing a guy who stabbed a woman to death earlier today—remember?"

"I know." She hung her head. "I'm sorry. I thought I should... I don't know... try to help."

He stopped under the canopy next to the ambulance. "You *are* helping. You're an important part of the team. But the team only works effectively when everyone does their job. There are a dozen cops wearing body armor and carrying guns who could've chased that guy down."

One of the paramedics brought over a first aid kit.

Taking the box, Sergio opened it up. "I guess I should be happy you didn't drop him with your .45. Next time, try that flying elbow move, like Randy Savage." He glanced at her. "That's a professional wrestling maneuver."

"I know what a flying elbow drop is," Avarie said. "That's legal?"

"Not for cops." Sergio shrugged. "But you're not a cop."

"Hmm. It's always good to know a loophole."

Sergio reached into the box and took out some gauze and a bottle of antiseptic, wiping down Avarie's scraped-up elbow.

"Ow!" She recoiled.

He raised an eyebrow.

"It's still a little tender," she said. "Take it easy."

The detective eased her arm to his face and lightly blew on the wet area for a moment, then balled up the gauze and gently dabbed the sore spot. "Better?"

She swallowed hard, nodded. "Much."

"Mm-hmm." He moved to the other arm, caressing the skin with the gauze. "Did your little mad dash back there bring back any old feelings about wearing the badge?"

"Maybe a few," Avarie said. "But my knees and elbows agree with you, wishing I'd have sent the uniformed officers after him."

Chuckling, Sergio knelt down and addressed her reddened knees. "That's why we carry Band-Aids." He gazed up at her. "How's your head?"

"Good—surprisingly." She ran her fingers over her brow. "I think his fist got the worst of it."

"Well, you are pretty hard-headed." Sergio dabbed at her scratches through the holes in her pants. "And what about your adrenaline, wild child?"

"Through the roof," she said. "My heart's pounding harder than my head."

"I bet." He stood, taking her hands and turning the palms up, and wiped the dirt from them with the gauze.

Her fingers were light and soft and smooth and warm. He brushed the fabric across her hands, wiping slowly and methodically, long after any traces of dirt had been removed.

Holding Avarie's hands in his, Sergio gazed into her eyes. "The PR stuff you do is the body armor for the team. If you go down, we're all more vulnerable. Besides..." He shifted his weight from one foot to the other. "I like having you on my team. That means staying in one piece. So don't go chasing bad guys by yourself again, okay?"

Her eyes locked on his. "I promise."

He stood there, under the medical canopy, near the crowds and the noises of the midway games, all of it fading into the background, blurred out as he gazed at her.

Avarie leaned forward, pressing her warm lips to his. She slid her hand across the back of his neck and kissed him deeply, sending tension throughout his insides.

As she slowly pulled away, she looked up at him and batted her eyes, her voice as gentle as a whisper. "I'm going to go change into some clothes that aren't ripped up. Thank you for taking care of me just now."

Sergio swallowed hard, opening his mouth to speak.

"Uh, Detective?" Harriman appeared over Avarie's shoulder. "Max just radioed. He says he's at the entrance gate and has some information he needs to share with you."

Sergio dropped his hands to his sides. "Well, we, uh... should let the paramedics check Avarie's head for a concussion. My medical training stops at bandages." He balled up the gauze and patted Avarie on the shoulder. "Go get that thick noggin of yours looked at."

She smiled, turning away.

"And Avarie..."

Stopping, the beautiful PR rep peered back at him.

"Seriously," he said. "Don't do that again."

She raised her eyebrows, putting one hand on her hip. "Hmm. Which part?"

Smiling, she sashayed toward the ambulance.

As the paramedic returned to the medical aid canopy and retrieved the first aid kit, Sergio folded his arms across his chest. His eyes stayed on Avarie as she made her way across the grass, weaved through the tourists on the walkway, and disappeared behind the ambulance.

CHAPTER 21

THE PHONE RANG IN CARLY'S VEHICLE, the word "Mom" appearing on the screen. She put on her sunglasses as she pulled onto the interstate and absently tapped the phone. "Hello?"

"Honey, it's me. How late do you think you'll be tonight? There's a movie I want to go see, and I was hoping we might go together."

Her mother's words didn't register.

"Carly?"

Sighing, the detective resigned herself to the fact that the conversation was going to happen sooner or later. "Mom, are you somewhere that you can talk?"

"Why wouldn't I be?" her mother said. "I'm going to the grocery store for popcorn, in case you're free tonight. Why? What's the matter?"

"I just..." Carly shrugged, the words not coming. It was a conversation she completely wanted to avoid, but at some point it would become inevitable.

Might as well be now.

The detective glanced at her phone. "Mom, I need to talk."

"You sound worried."

Carly nodded. "I am."

"Is it about the cancer treatment?" her mother asked. "Honey, a woman your age... I looked online. There's a very high chance of getting through this. You probably won't even lose your hair. I think the statistic I saw was upwards of ninety-five percent of women recover fully when they catch the cancer early, so you're in good shape. What—"

"Mom, it's not that." Swallowing hard, Carly forced the words out. "I'm... pregnant."

The afternoon traffic on the interstate moved slowly, as tourists and residents escaped the Tampa area for a weekend in Orlando, Cocoa Beach, or The Keys, and people on the other side of the state came through Tampa on the way to the picturesque waters of Clearwater Beach or Sarasota.

Carly glanced at her phone. "Mom?"

"I heard you. I just don't know what to say." Her mother sighed. "Carly, how did this happen?"

"It happened the way it's been happening for millions of years." The detective adjusted her sunglasses. "Like you told me in high school, there's no method of birth control that's a hundred percent effective."

"Don't be snide. Do you know who... I mean, don't get mad, but I have to ask you this. Who is the father?"

Carly winced. "Mom..."

"Carly, just tell me. I don't want it to be Sergio's, but..."

"It is. It's Sergio's."

She held her breath, waiting for her mother's reaction.

"Oh, for..." Mrs. Sanderson exhaled loudly into the phone. "Lord Almighty, you can sure get yourself into a jam."

"Mother..."

"Sorry," her mother said. "I just—I'm sorry. You're not going to keep it, right? What about the cancer treatment? That can't be good for a baby, so... Well, you're not going to keep it..."

"I don't know."

"What do you mean? You aren't married to Sergio. He's a single man who's showed himself to be remarkably irresponsible. Those are your words, Carly. That's what you've been saying about him for the past four years. Don't get caught up in some swashbuckling fantasy of taming the rogue warrior. Sergio is not fit to be a father. It's not in him."

"Mom..." She took a deep breath, a sadness welling inside her. "It's a girl."

Saying the words out loud made it more real.

A girl. A baby girl.

I'm pregnant, and it's a girl.

"No," her mother said. "Don't... Honey, step back from the situation. You cannot have a baby with Sergio. You probably shouldn't even be considering having a baby at all. What did the oncologist say—Doctor Mendez? Did you tell her?"

"No." Carly shook her head. "But I will tomorrow. I told my gynecologist, Doctor Sherwood."

"And?"

"And she said the baby would probably be negatively affected by the cancer treatment." The detective pursed her lips. "Basically, she said I'd lose the baby while I was going through the treatment."

"Well, then that decides it. Look, whether or not you wanted to have another child, you *do* have cancer. Treatment is going to take the baby away, so why drag it out? Take care of it now while it's less of a problem. Before—"

"I…" Carly bit her lip. "I don't know if I want to do that."

"Have you lost your mind?" Her mother raised her voice. "I think you've gotten so stressed out about having cancer that you're not thinking clearly. You're trying to cling to something that's irrational. Where are you? Are you home? We need to talk."

Gripping the wheel, Carly glared at the phone. "I didn't want to lay all this on you, and I'm sorry I did, but I've got enough on my plate tonight. I'm going to the oncologist tomorrow. We're going to lay out a treatment schedule and discuss the options."

"Carly, there are no options. You cannot have a baby with Sergio, and if you ever had any chance of getting back together with Kyle, him finding out you got pregnant by someone else is going to throw things right onto the rocks. Believe me, a man is not just going to sit back and take that kind of news very well."

The detective took another deep breath, letting it out slowly.

"I know," Carly said. "You're right, I know."

"Then you know what you have to do. Honey, I love you and I would love another grandchild. But I don't want the possibility of a grandchild at the *very real risk* of losing the daughter I *have*. And your boys need a mother. And your husband—"

"He's not my husband." Carly frowned. "He's divorcing me, remember?"

"You aren't divorced yet. And haven't you been telling me he's been softening his tone and making overtures about coming back?"

Her cheeks growing hot, Carly shook her head. "What are overtures worth? He walked out, didn't he? He packed up his things and left."

"Well, then," her mother said, "that's all the more reason not to have the baby at all. I love you and I care about you, dear. More than anything else."

"I know, Mom. I love you, too." She loosened her grip on the steering wheel and wiped her sweaty palms on her pants leg.

This is not your mother's fault, and it's not her problem. She's trying to help you. Stop taking your frustration out on her.

Carly softened her tone. "I just need some time to think—about everything. I've got a lot of work stuff to look at tonight, too."

"Work can wait," her mother said. "Your health is more important. Take the night off and call me as soon as you finish with the oncologist tomorrow morning."

"Okay, Mom." Carly nodded, reaching for the phone. "I'll take the night off."

The women said their goodbyes and Carly ended the call.

I don't want to take the night off. Distracting myself with work might be the only thing that keeps me from going insane right now.

CHAPTER 22

Sergio approached the expo hall, passing a cadaver dog team. "Are we just starting or just finishing, guys?"

The officer patted his German Shepherd. "We're about to start, Sergio." Behind him, another officer helped a man unload a bloodhound from the back of a pickup truck.

"Okay," Sergio said. "Have you seen Max Fuentes?"

"He was inside, last I saw. In the back."

Waving, the detective entered the building, cool air sweeping over him. Max was near the office area with Mark Harriman, sitting in front of the magic act's computer array. On the monitors, the end of the six sisters disappearing woman act played out.

The young lab tech's tall, athletic build was perched on a folding chair in front of the little desk, his rolled-up sleeves allowing the display of the many colorful tattoos that adorned each of his thick arms. Max's ears held several piercings apiece, and a small gold bar hung between his nostrils. His latest hair style was bright blue, trimmed close on the left side of his head and shaved bald on the right, with a sweeping pile of curls on top.

Max leaned forward in his chair. On the screen directly in front of him, master magician Sinclair O'Lair went to the bloody cage where the volunteer had disappeared, his eyes opening wide as he looked at Scarlet. "What happened?" O'Lair moaned. "Somebody tell me what just happened!"

Sighing, Harriman stopped the playback and looked at Max. "And that gets you up to speed."

Sergio clapped the young technician on the shoulder. "Welcome aboard, amigo. Got anything for me yet?"

"Hello, sir. Actually, yes. I do have something."

"Yeah?" Sergio's eyebrows went up. "That was fast."

Max stood up and went to a computer bag on the floor.

As the technician dug around in his satchel, Sergio turned to Harriman. "Any statement from the master magician yet?"

"Nothing we didn't already see in the recording." Harriman shook his head. "His story is, he's basically a glorified stage prop. The women do all the hard stuff like getting in and out of boxes while appearing to get sawed in half. He just makes speeches and does game show moves like a model on

The Price Is Right. His so-called assistants invent all the acts for the show, too. Design, engineering, assembly—the works. He just goes to center stage with a microphone and says what they tell him to say."

"And gets all the credit." Sergio smirked. "It's his name on all the posters and signs."

Max stood up, holding his tablet. "The magician's job is to give the show some panache while guiding the audience's attention away from whatever the performers don't want you to see."

"Yeah. Distraction." Sergio nodded. "I've heard about that. But I thought the distraction came from the assistants' skimpy costumes, and the stagehands using bright laser lights or setting off smoke bombs."

The lab tech set his computer on the desk. "Everything these people do is a form of distraction. Even the magician's name isn't his. 'Master Magician Sinclair O'Lair' is a registered trademark." Max opened the tablet, showing an online registry of fictitious trade names and corporate entities. "There have been six Sinclair O'Lairs over the years—just employees, or actors, playing a role. The current O'Lair is Bernard Chaim Leibowitz, from Market Street in San Francisco."

Sergio studied the screen. "I suppose the assistants all use stage names, too?"

Mark Harriman stepped forward. "Yeah." He took out his notepad and opened it up. "According to their drivers licenses, magic assistant Olive Huskins is actually Margaret Frances Cleaves, from

Cincinnati. Jade Monrie, the brunette, is Joanna Marie Burton, from Baton Rouge…"

"Who have I been talking to?" Sergio asked.

"Katherine Tanya Jameson," Scarlet said, strutting into the office area in a sequined red jumpsuit that clung to her every curve. The outfit's gaping neckline plunged down past her ample cleavage to just below her navel. "A boring, plain name for a boring, plain girl from little ol' Magnolia, Mississippi—until the stage lights go up and she becomes…" The magician's assistant thrust her hip out and held her arms away from her sides. "The amazing Scarlet Salazar!"

Laughing, she tossed her head back, sending her long blonde locks cascading over her shoulders as she sauntered over to Sergio, her cleavage straining against the sparkling material of the jumpsuit. "Katherine, or KT, or Scarlet—we are all one and the same, sugar. But I'd prefer my friends to call me Kitty."

Sergio ran a hand across the stubble covering his jaw line. "You do, huh?"

"I would, but I don't have any friends." Scarlet strolled to the desk and hoisted herself on top of it, crossing her shapely legs. "Poor Mississippi towns are always so quaint and picturesque in movies, but in real life they can be quite cruel. That's why I ran away to join the circus."

Sergio pointed to a poster on the wall next to the little desk. The main image was of Sinclair O'Lair in his tuxedo, but the five scantily-clad assistants were featured prominently next to him.

"How did you get together with the other women in the act?"

"Oh, that?" Scarlet reached into the pocket of her skin-tight suit, pulling out a crumpled pack of cigarettes. She slipped one of the bent smokes between her lips. "This poor country girl ran away and made it all the way to Key West. I was almost eighteen, barely out of high school, with no money and no prospects, as they say... And then, there I was, watching this beautiful juggler at Mallory Square, with the sun sinking into the ocean right behind her." She took out her lighter. "She was brilliant. You could tell her act was just her, though. Solo."

Scarlet gazed up at Sergio, the unlit cigarette dangling from her lips. "It was her own business—a crappy one, yeah, with a threadbare costume and worn-out props—but... Olive didn't answer to anybody. She just juggled, did card tricks from a dog-eared deck, and made a patched-up stuffed rabbit disappear." Her voice faded, her eyes appearing to look back at a very distant, very different, time. "Nobody hit her for getting a bad grade," Scarlet whispered. "Nobody locked her out of the house for three days to go ride the crack pipe again. And nobody pretended not to see whenever one of Momma's new boyfriends stumbled into my bedroom at night."

The office area was silent, all eyes on the performer.

Scarlet flicked the lighter and raised up its flame, igniting her cigarette with trembling fingers.

"But Olive and her crappy little sunset show managed to scratch together enough money each night to make it through the next day. That's what I wanted. That's *all* I wanted. Twenty-four more precious hours as far away from Magnolia, Mississippi as I could get." The performer took a drag on her cigarette and sent a stream of smoke upwards to the ceiling. "So..." She sat upright. "When her show ended that night, I struck up a conversation. Two hours later, we had recruited the fire-eating girls from next to the snow cone stand, and an escape artist who got herself out of a straitjacket while suspended from a tightrope. We figured out an act, hired a front man..." She smiled, looking at Sergio. "And a week later I'd made enough cold calls to get us booked into the Holiday Inn at Fort Lauderdale airport. We've been on tour ever since, growing into the professional act you saw in the recordings. In ten years, we've performed in thirty-three of the fifty United States, with an occasional sidebar to Tijuana and Juarez in Mexico."

The detective kept his eyes focused on hers.

There seemed to be a pained honesty in Scarlet's words, but the story still contained the shell covering of someone who was trying a little too hard to be forthright while still holding something back. "Key West is a long jump for a kid from Mississippi with no money."

"I told you, I ran away." Scarlet took another puff of her cigarette, her voice unemotional and even. "That's what damaged people do, Detective. The more damaged they are, the farther they run. And they'll do what they have to do—*whatever* they have to do—to make sure they get away."

CHAPTER 23

Sergio rubbed his eyes as he lowered himself onto the edge of a wooden crate. From down the hall, the sounds of the cadaver dogs came to his ears. Outside, the bloodhound howled and barked.

Sighing, the detective looked at the core of the team he'd be working with until Carly joined them: Harriman, Max, Avarie—and temporarily, Scarlet.

"What do we know so far?" he asked. "I mean, what actual facts do we have?"

Harriman opened his notepad again. "We have a missing woman but no body. We have recordings of the victim going down the ladder under the stage, and so much blood down there that the CSIs say nobody could have survived the attack, but no corpse. We have drag marks that lead toward the door, ostensibly from the killer pulling the victim's body across the floor, but we have zero observational evidence that her body ever left the building. We have what is probably her purse, with some personal effects inside it. And we have two hundred and fifty witnesses that said the missing woman announced herself to be Gabriella Romain, with enough images from the stage cameras, social media, and the photo she has on record at the DMV to conclude it was her."

He flipped the notepad shut and looked at Sergio. "We also have cadaver dogs looking for a dead body and a bloodhound looking for a live one."

"Okay." Sergio stood up. "Mark, get some patrol cars over to the Romain residence on Bayshore. Maybe we'll get lucky and one of them is home, but swarm the neighborhood with cops. Interview the neighbors. Let's see if anybody saw anything noteworthy today—or ever—regarding these two. And make a note of any neighbors' video doorbells or security cameras that could have a view of the Romain property."

He turned to the lab technician, counting on his fingers as he peeled off the orders. "Max, request warrants to search the Romain house, the nightclub Teodoro bought in Ybor City, and anything else he owns or rents in the area, like storage units or warehouses. Track the locations of their phones today—Chief Clemmons can provide the numbers if you don't already have them—and look at any calls they made in, say, the last two weeks. I want to hear from the lab as soon as they get a blood screen on the puddle downstairs, so we can check it against any of

Gabriella's hair or other DNA samples we pull from the purse or residence."

The two men picked up their phones and started making calls.

"Mark," Sergio said, "I need to borrow a radio."

Harriman unclipped his radio from his belt and handed it to the detective.

Sergio's gaze went to Avarie. "How much cooperation can we expect from the reporters outside?"

She shook her head. "Some, but not a lot. They got most of what they needed from people in the audience. They're waiting on us—for now. But that won't last long."

"Okay. You work on keeping them contained while I sit here and try not to get a headache figuring out how a dead woman got out of this building without leaving a trace of how she did it." He put his hands to his face, exhaling a long, slow breath. "If Gabriella is dead, she had help getting out of here. If she's alive... I don't know. She gave everyone the slip while leaving all her blood behind. How do you do that?" He lowered his hands and looked at Scarlet. "You're the magician. How would you do something like that?"

Nodding, Scarlet leaned forward, resting an elbow on her knee. Her cleavage pressed forward against the shiny sequins.

Sergio managed to keep his attention on her eyes.

"Distraction." The magician's assistant jabbed the air with her cigarette. "I get you to look *here*, while the body goes out over *there*. Olympic gymnasts spray their butts with adhesive and magician's assistants spray it on our boobs—so everyone, men and women, are involuntarily looking at our low-cut costumes and considering the possibility that at any moment something just might come spilling out. It never does, but it's hard not to watch, because you don't know the secret." She sat up and looked at Harriman. "Whoever committed this murder would need to know where to go. And you've accounted for all of the performers and stagehands in the act—right?"

Harriman nodded, his phone pressed against his ear.

"Where?" Sergio asked. "If you had to get someone out, where would they have to go?"

"Under the stage would be easiest," Scarlet said. "Dead or alive. It's basically a big hollow area. There's plenty of space between the framing supports to go from the back area to the front of the stage, near where the audience sits—if a person knew to do it. The front of this stage is just black bunting material. But if the victim tried to get out that way, in her condition, there'd be a blood trail. A big one."

Sergio nodded. "And we didn't have that, so let's say she didn't walk out." He put his hands on his hips, staring at the ground as he paced back and forth. "Then someone killed her and took her out of here. And they did it with everyone in the place watching. Who could do that?"

Scarlet smiled. "Someone you notice, but don't take any notice *of*, sugar."

"Who's that?" Sergio asked.

Scarlet glanced at Avarie. "How are your knees, sweetie?"

"What..." Avarie cocked her head. "The garbage guy?"

"Why not? Or a guy dressed like a maintenance worker." Scarlet slid off the desk and strutted toward the PR rep. "The last time y'all went to a movie, did you pay attention to how the trash got emptied? Or who tore your ticket stub? You saw the people, but could you pick them out of a lineup sixty seconds later?"

Avarie opened her mouth, but no words came out.

"Same thing, in reverse," Scarlet said. "Someone dressed as a maintenance worker could easily get near the stage from the audience and sneak underneath the bunting. From there, the killer has access to the back area where the ladder was."

Avarie nodded. "If they did it when there was a distraction, like when the smoke bombs are exploding on the stage, or when the sexy assistants go into the audience to look for a volunteer..."

Scarlet smiled and looked at Sergio. "She's smart. I like her."

"Okay." Sergio ran a hand through his hair. "Gabriella's killer sneaks under the stage when Sinclair O'Lair has the spotlights trained on the assistants as they're interviewing potential volunteers. The killer can't sneak in the back door, because your guy is waiting there. Scary-looking Kevin. He'd have seen that."

"The guy I tackled was pushing a big cart," Avarie said. "A body could easily fit into one of those."

Sergio continued pacing. "He kills her by the ladder, drags her to a bag or something he's got waiting, so the blood trail—and the evidence trail—stops. He moves the body from underneath, between the framing supports, until he's near the front of the stage, but he's entirely hidden from sight. The cameras aren't focused there, the audience can't see him, and neither can the performers. After that, it's just a few feet with it to the side door."

"But this was a morning show." Scarlet shook her head. "The stage area is darkened, and it was bright outside. Lots of people in the audience would have noticed a side door opening. Our cameras would have spotted it, too."

Harriman raised a hand, his phone still pressed to his cheek. "Hey, I'm sorry. Can you hold on one second for me, please?" He lowered his phone and covered it with his hand. "I've watched that recording three times. No doors opened, that's for sure."

Sergio looked around the office area. "Then... the killer got her out when he was still under the stage."

"How?" Avarie asked.

The detective clutched the borrowed walkie talkie and approached the access door to the performing area. "Scarlet, how big is your stage?"

He pushed open the door and walked through without waiting for her answer. His teammates scurried to follow as the detective approached the rear of the elevated performing area, and the thick, black curtain that kept the audience from seeing the props there.

Scarlet joined him first, taking the detective's arm as she pointed to the stage floor. "The part of the stage that's visible to the audience is twenty feet, front to back, with another fifteen behind the rear curtain. It's seventy-five feet across, with about ten of that on each side obscured by the side baffles."

Sergio went up the steps at the back of the stage and pushed through the heavy black curtain, walking out onto the expo hall's main stage. He scanned the empty seats and the dark walls of the expo hall's interior.

His gaze landed on the little illuminated signs that said Exit.

"There." His words echoed off the empty auditorium. "That's it." He walked to the front edge of the stage and pointed at the emergency exit closest to the stage. "These emergency doors aren't more than forty feet apart—that'll be a construction standard set by the fire code. And this one's about ten feet from the stage."

Turning, he viewed the space to the curtain. "There's another emergency exit we can't see, between here and the rear of the stage."

He walked between the thick curtains of the side baffles, pushing the velvet rows aside until he arrived at the hidden exit.

Sergio put his hands on his hips, smiling. "The killer didn't have to worry about the outside light being visible. You did it for him. These cloth baffles blocked any light from getting through when the door opened, and even if it didn't, there were enough flashes and bangs going off to not catch anyone's attention."

"Detective?" A CSI technician walked through the door of the audience section of the auditorium, bright light filling the hall. He moved past the rows of empty seats, carrying a large evidence bag. "Here's the handbag we recovered from the maintenance worker, Sergio. We checked it for prints and inventoried everything inside."

"And what was inside, Dave?"

"A wallet with Gabriella Romain's driver's license and credit cards in it. A smart phone, some makeup and a hairbrush… and sixteen thousand dollars in cash strapped to her passport with a rubber band." He lifted the evidence bag and set it down on the stage floor. "Everything somebody would need to go on a nice little trip."

Squatting in front of the blue and white handbag, Sergio ran his hand over his chin stubble. "No, it's everything you'd leave behind if you were killed before you could make that trip."

CHAPTER 24

THE DETECTIVE RUSHED ACROSS THE STAGE, TO THE set of heavy, cloth baffles on the other side. An exit door was hidden there as well.

Lifting his borrowed radio to his cheek, he pressed the red transmit button. "All canine units, this is Detective Martin. Meet me inside the expo hall, in the back. Bring the dogs."

As Sergio went back to the office area, the radio squawked with the canine unit officers' affirmative replies.

"Listen," Avarie said. "It's time for the reporters' afternoon feeding. I need to give them something."

"Yeah, okay. Go." Sergio peered up from the floor and looked at her. "Give them something, but don't really give them anything, okay?"

She smiled, walking away. "That's my specialty."

Breezing past Max, Scarlet strolled to the computer, fluffing her hair and adjusting her red-sequined sleeves. She turned to Sergio. "You know, Detective... if your murderer was smart enough to use that hidden door to escape with the body, he probably used it to get into the expo hall, too."

"That's why he wasn't on the recordings." Sergio nodded, leaning against the wall. "But the only way he'd know exactly when your volunteer would be under the stage was if he was watching from the audience—unless he hacked your cameras."

Scarlet shook her head. "That system is hard wired and closed-circuit, honey. The only one watching the screens is me, after the show, with a big ol' glass of Jack Daniels. But if the killer had seen the Six Sisters piece before, he could figure out how it works. A quick internet search would tell him that most magicians use a trap door in a disappearing act. He'd know she was under the raised stage." Scarlet looked up. "So, if he was watching her, do y'all think he could have been stalking her?"

"Maybe." Sergio crossed his arms and exhaled. "Let us look at the recordings for all the shows you did since the act came to Tampa—however many there are. We need to see if there are any repeat faces in the audience."

Whistling, Scarlet pointed to her monitors. "That's an hour-long show, four shows a day, shot from multiple cameras. It'll take somebody a week to watch all that footage."

Sergio glanced at his lab technician. "Max?"

"It'll definitely take a while, sir." Max lowered his phone. "But we can request volunteers from the criminal justice majors at the local colleges. That would help speed things up. And there's some new facial recognition software I've been dying to try…"

Sergio nodded. "Then, Merry Christmas. How fast can you get it up and running?"

"Well…" The technician rocked his head back and forth. "If I call the professors now, and they email their students this evening… Maybe by tomorrow morning?"

"Good—but sooner is better. If any of them can start tonight, I'll personally write them a letter of recommendation. What's the status on the warrant for the Romain residence?"

"We should have that within the hour, sir."

"Okay. Thanks." Sergio paced back and forth, arms crossed, staring at the floor as his fingers idly massaged his chin.

The sound of huffing dogs and canine nails scratching smooth concrete came down the hallway. The canine officers arrived with their partners—one bloodhound, one German Shepherd.

"I know it's early, guys," Sergio said, "but what's the word from your four-legged investigators?"

The German Shepherd's handler rubbed the cadaver dog's big furry neck. "No hits from Tino, Detective, and we've made two passes. Mrs. Romain was very likely still clinging to life when she left the building."

"Yeah." Sergio sighed. "No surprise there after what we just learned. Her attacker possibly stabbed her, wrapped her in something, and took her out through a stage door—and he did it fast. We're thinking he may have put the victim into one of those canvas trash carts." He looked at the other officer. "Now, if he did, is your bloodhound's nose sensitive enough to identify Gabriella Romain's scent from the handbag and follow that trash cart to wherever her attacker took it?"

The handler's eyes widened. "That's a tall order, but me and Missy will give it a go. Which door?"

"This way." Sergio went toward the exit door behind the right side of the stage.

The dogs and their partners followed, the bloodhound leading the way. Missy strained against her leash, whimpering louder and louder as she neared the exit door.

"She's hit on to the scent, Detective." Her handler beamed. "The woman definitely went this way."

At the door, Missy became frantic. She barked and howled, clawing at the exit.

Sergio pushed the door open.

The bloodhound raced outside, sniffing the asphalt as she ran in circles. A row of crime scene tape fluttered in the breeze, encircling the large expo hall and a dozen yards on every side.

After a few passes, Missy's barking became quieter. She slowed her pace, going back and forth across the doorway and whimpering.

"That looks like a no." Sergio grimaced, looking at the handler. "Too much traffic out here for Missy to follow the scent?"

The handler hauled in the leash line. "Well, sir, my guess is—how do I put this? Missy's reaction indicates that the victim was no longer making contact with the ground at this point." He looked out over the mobs of people, squinting in the bright afternoon light. "If she went into a cart, she was probably in it by here. Now, all those trash carts are gonna make their rounds and then go to a central location to be emptied. The sanitation fellas are probably hourly employees, with designated routes. If you can locate the dumping location, me and Missy can wait there—and I'll have her sniff the carts as they come by."

Sergio exhaled, staring into the crowd. Trash barrels appeared near every concession stand and midway game. They were under every light pole and every vendor kiosk.

He looked at Missy's handler. "Can we chase down the carts *on* their routes and locate our victim faster?"

The officer shrugged. "We can try..."

"Then let's try," Sergio said "Talk to Mrs. Diaz in Guest Relations and get the routes. Worst case, you'll have to stay here until the event closes tonight. But if Missy hits on anything—and I mean anything—you lock it down and call me. I don't care what time it is, you call. Okay?"

The handler nodded, reeling in his bloodhound. "You got it, Detective."

* * * * *

Sitting on the desk in the office area with her legs crossed, Scarlet's eyes followed Sergio as he paced back and forth.

He checked the time on his phone and shook his head.

Sighing, Scarlet slid off the desk and sauntered over to him. "Can I get you an ice-cold Coca-Cola from the concession stand, darlin'?"

"No." Sergio stared at the floor, rubbing his chin. "Thank you."

Scarlet put her hands on her hips. "Maybe a glass of Jack Daniels, then?"

The detective stopped pacing and looked up at her. "I'm sorry. I'm just… a little tired. I was up all night planning a drug bust before I came here."

"I understand." Scarlet smiled. "You've got a lot on your mind. But Detective Martin, if you don't ease up, you might give yourself a heart attack right here."

He nodded and brought his hands to his face, rubbing his eyes. "Yeah, okay."

"Okay. Well, try to relax a little." Scarlet pointed a finger and wrote on the air. "Detective Martin. Detective *Sergio* Martin." She shook her head, looking at him. "That's a mouthful. How about I call you… Serge? Or Marty?"

The detective winced. "Not Marty. Let's just stick with Detective."

"Okay—for now." She sashayed back to the desk. "But I have to ask… why the rush? Y'all been acting like we need to find this woman today. She's dead, sugar. Nobody loses that much blood and survives."

Sergio took a deep breath and let it out slowly. "Most missing persons cases are solved with information they collect in the first forty-eight hours. Before people's memories of the events start to fade. Before the abductor drags the victim into the woods to make sure she never becomes a witness testifying against him in court. Before the wind and sun and rain obscure the identity of the corpse. Before he gets out of town."

Scarlet cocked her head and peered at him, her sequins twinkling in the fluorescent light of the backstage area. "That's not your only reason why." She lowered her voice. "Did you… lose someone once in that way? A family member?"

The detective raised his tired eyes to view her.

Scarlet was every bit as sharp as she let on, picking up on subtle context clues and reading him the way she did in the trailer. Each question he asked gave her information. She seemed to effortlessly analyze every detail he let slip and every inflection he allowed. The performer's honey-dipped drawl made even her sharpest, most probing personal questions seem soft and generous.

Scarlet produced another cigarette from somewhere in her skin-tight ensemble, along with a stainless-steel lighter. As she placed the filtered tip between her lips, the detective walked over to her.

Sergio took the lighter and flipped open the top. He thrust his thumb downward over the metal roller, igniting the wick. Raising the flame up to Scarlet's cigarette, he kept it there until the tip glowed.

"This woman has a family." Sergio closed the lighter top and handed it back to Scarlet. "Right now, they're scared to answer the phone for fear that it's a cop like me on the other end of the line, giving them the worst news anyone can get." He turned away, sliding his hands into his pockets. "If I work fast, maybe they don't have to get that news. Worst case, the family doesn't suffer any longer than they have to. Forty-eight hours. That'll seem like a lifetime to them."

"Why, Detective Martin." Scarlet's face fell, her voice soft and low. "I believe you did lose a family member that way. I apologize for my insensitive remarks."

Sergio looked at her then looked away again. "I'm just saying, if there's a chance Gabriella Romain is alive, then the clock is running."

CHAPTER 25

Sergio leaned against the wall in the office area, stroking his jaw as the clues and tiny fragments of information on the case swirled in his mind like a Cajun cauldron cooking gumbo. Max worked at his computer as Harriman continued making phone calls. Scarlet lit another cigarette as she rested on a crate, her sequined legs crossed and her top foot bouncing rhythmically.

Max's phone rang. He answered it, then held it out to Sergio. "Detective Sanderson calling for you, sir."

Sergio took the phone. "Hey, Carly, I'm sorry. I got a replacement phone and I'm not getting my calls."

"That explains a lot," Carly said. "I'm supposed to join you, but I had a doctor's appointment first."

"Oh, yeah." Sergio nodded. "I heard there was a bug going around. Carina said a couple of their CSIs are out sick. She's working a double shift."

"Uh, well... I'm probably going to go home and get some rest. I've been reading the status reports. You're doing everything I would do."

Sergio grinned. "Because I ask, 'What would Carly do?' and then I do that."

"Uh huh." She chuckled. "Anyway, give me the new number and I'll check in later if I'm up to it. Sorry to leave you hanging."

"Hey, no worries. I've got your b...Uh, we—we've got... we're on it. Here's my new phone contact." He lifted the temporary phone and read off the number.

"Okay," Carly said. "Thanks."

"Sure." Sergio nodded, putting the temporary phone in his pocket. "Feel better soon."

As he ended the call, Avarie re-entered the office area, her face grim.

"What?" Sergio looked over at her. "What is it?"

The PR rep shook her head as she approached the desk. "Those news reporters are getting antsy. They missed their noon filing cutoff and they want to make sure they have a story ready for the five o'clock broadcast. But their stations have been cutting to them for live drops, and they're all starting to speculate that we're stalling. I told them to stand by for something good."

The detective cocked his head. "Which is what?"

"I'm going to give them a clip of Gabriella Romain." Avarie pursed her lips, looking at him. "One from the camera under the stage that shows her coming down the ladder right before she got killed."

Sergio winced. "Not that. They'll tell the public who she is, and the Chief will go bonkers."

"The reporters already have Gabriella's name," Avarie said. "The audience members they interviewed gave it to them—and those people have been posting all over social media using it. She'll be trending soon."

Sergio put his hand to his forehead. "Crap."

The PR expert stepped toward him. "You have to trust me on this. We can use the attention to our advantage. We ride that horse. We ask the news crews and the public to help us with any tips they might have. Did anyone see her today, what was she wearing—that sort of thing. And we set up another tip line so it looks like we want the name out there, just like we did at Hillmont Day School. Like we aren't afraid of her name being known."

Max looked up from his computer. "Sergio, I can cut the clip so it doesn't show any blood or evidence. And since Gabriella's name is already out there, maybe it doesn't matter."

"But then we can ask people to help." Avarie peered at Sergio. "It turns the slant of the news stories from TPD hiding something, to sympathy."

Sergio frowned. "Have you met the Chief? He doesn't want sympathy. He wants the story contained. That's why—"

"There's one other card to play." Scarlet blew a stream of smoke toward the ceiling and turned to Sergio, pointing. "You."

She crushed her cigarette against the wooded box and let it drop to the floor as she slid off the wooden box. "Leave the scene like you have a hot lead, Detective. The news crews will want to follow you, which takes them away from the story here."

Sergio took a deep breath, stroking his chin. "I could go home and take a real shower to wake up. I'm starting to smell like fish again anyway."

"Well, it's not a terrible plan." Avarie nodded. "Go out a back door and act like you don't want to be noticed—but do it where the reporters can see you."

Scarlet smiled. "Maybe someone could accidentally spot you leaving and call out as you go to your car. I'm available." She put her hands on her hips and slinked across the concrete floor to Sergio. "I'll go out and talk to the reporters—making good on Ms. Fox's promise to deliver something special to them for being so patient. If I was out there speaking with the news crews, I could look over at just the right time."

"No." Avarie held her hand up. "I—"

"Deal." Sergio pushed himself off the wall, grinning. "Just don't say anything we haven't authorized. Don't even say it's a murder. Tell them, the police suspect *this*, the police think *that*—but no hard facts except that we're here and we're investigating everything fully."

"So in other words," Scarlet said, "use some distraction."

"Yep." He faced Avarie. "We'll keep your suggestion in our pocket for now." Turning back to Scarlet, he looked her over. "Yeah, that outfit will get their attention. Get out there. In five minutes, I walk out the side door."

He looked at his team members, then returned his attention to the sexy performer. "And when you're done out there, don't leave town."

Scarlet winked at him. "Not a chance, sugar." She walked toward the exit, with Avarie following her.

"Uh, Avarie," Sergio said. "Why don't you stay behind?"

The PR rep turned around, her mouth hanging open.

"Let Scarlet go alone." Sergio rubbed his chin. "It'll seem less… authorized that way. Mark, after I leave, go out and interrupt Scarlet like you don't want her speaking to the media. The news crews that don't try to follow me can speculate on why we're shutting her down."

"That'll only buy a few hours, at best," Harriman said.

"It's better than nothing." Sergio patted his pockets for his car keys. "Maybe the drive home will give me a chance to clear my head. We need a break in this case. And we need it soon."

As soon as the exit door closed behind Scarlet, Sergio set a timer on his phone for five minutes.

At the four-minute mark, he tapped Avarie on the shoulder. "Let's go."

She frowned, her face a puzzle. "I thought I was staying behind."

"Change of plans." He headed for the door. "Besides, your car is at my place, remember?"

* * * * *

Carly drove toward her house, stopping at the grocery deli counter for something ready-made to eat for dinner. As she waited in line, she peered through the glass displaying the hot food.

Rice. Beans. Mashed potatoes. Green beans. Cauliflower.

Nothing sounded good.

A young girl ran toward the glass. "Poppy chickie, Daddy?" She turned around, facing a handsome young man who was following her.

He scooped the child up in his arms. "You want what?"

She pointed to the far side of the hot food display. "Poppy chickie."

Carly leaned around the lady in front of her. In the display case, she spotted a stainless-steel container of tiny chicken nuggets with a small sign above it that said Popcorn Chicken.

Carly smiled.

Poppy chickie.

As the young man carried his daughter to the end of the waiting line—promising her some poppy chickie if her mother approved when she came over from the vegetable section—Carly imagined herself with the child.

They strolled hand-in-hand through the store, picking out Oreos and microwave popcorn, placing each item into the cart until the little girl tired and Carly had to lift her into the shopping cart.

A man's voice came from behind them. "How are my girls?"

She knew the voice. She'd known it for years.

"Daddy!" The child jumped up and down in the grocery cart, holding her arms out to her father.

"Hi, baby!" Sergio scooped her up, swinging her around in the aisle. He smiled at Carly. "And how are you, gorgeous?"

Then, the three of them were at the beach. Carly and Sergio each held onto one of the little girl's hands as they walked, periodically lifting her into the air to swing forward in a giant step.

"One, two, three—go!" They laughed, hauling her into the air and setting her down a few feet later.

The girl giggled. "Again!"

Carly smiled, letting the daydream play on. Sergio picked their baby up and swung her around again.

Then, the daydream turned.

Sergio held his gun to the side of his face, barrel aimed into the air, as he stood outside an old warehouse.

Carly knew the scene. He'd gone running in without backup, into a mob of drug dealers.

Angry, armed drug dealers.

This time, Sergio didn't talk them into surrendering. He didn't get a citation. He didn't get interviewed by the news.

As his little girl chased after him, Carly screamed and rushed forward, grabbing their child as the gunshots filled the air.

"May I help you, ma'am?"

Shuddering, Carly returned to the deli counter at the grocery store.

The clerk smiled at her. "What can I get for you tonight, ma'am?"

Carly backed away, her jaw hanging open. "I'm... I lost my appetite. Sorry."

She turned, almost running into the little girl and the young father, as they awaited their poppy chickie.

The child's face was angelic. Youthful and innocent. Beautiful.

The echo of the daydream's gunshots rang in Carly's ears.

Her heart racing, Carly shook her head.

Sergio will get himself killed before he ever meets his child.

"Excuse me." She stepped out of line and around the man and his child, rushing for the exit.

* * * * *

As he drove along the highway, Sergio clenched and unclenched his jaw.

Something's wrong with this picture—but what?

Where's Teodoro? On his way back to Miami?

Why was Gabriella up on that stage in the first place?

He put on his sunglasses to block out the afternoon sunlight.

Ugh, it's already afternoon. I'd better call my mom and tell her I can't make the shopping excursion with her and Mina tonight.

Sighing, he took out his phone and entered her number.

This ought to be fun.

His mother's voice came over the line. "Hello? Who is this?"

"Mom, it's Sergio. I can't meet you and Mina tonight. I—"

"Sergio. Good. I need you to meet us earlier. Mina wants to go to Party City now, too."

The detective shook his head. "Mom, I'm telling you that I can't come at all. I got called in to work an urgent case."

"Yes, you can come," his mother said. "My son needs to be here for his sister. She only graduates once, and I want a nice party for her."

"Right, but I'm a little busy with my actual *job*, Mom."

"So busy you can't help your sister?" Mrs. Martin gasped. "It's a sin!"

"Why does everything you don't like qualify as a sin? I have to work. Just… Look, Mina has my credit card. Just…" He scrunched his face up. "Tell her to get whatever she wants."

"Okay," she said. "I tell her. But you don't work on the night of her party, or—"

"Or it's a sin. Got it. I'll be there, Mom. I promise. Now let me get back to work."

He ended the call and glanced at Avarie as she scrolled through her own phone. The PR rep looked at him out of the corner of her eye, then dropped her hands to her lap and turned to the window.

Exhaling sharply, she turned back to him. "You know, you're spending a lot of time with Scarlet Salazar."

"Am I?" Sergio propped an elbow up onto the car door and put his hand to his beard stubble. "I guess I didn't notice."

"Well, I did." Avarie folded her arms across her abdomen. "Be careful of that one. She's playing you. Her idea of helping us was to get herself in front of the news cameras and promote her act—by way of her cleavage. It's like she doesn't own a top that closes."

"No, she offered to help us, and she's basically an expert in her field. Give me one good reason I shouldn't work with her."

Avarie snorted. "I can think of two very big reasons."

"Aw, c'mon." He glanced at her. "I'm not like that."

"Every man is like that." Huffing, Avarie turned to the window.

"Look," Sergio said. "People who live in the spotlight get that way—flirty and outrageous, always looking for attention." He peered at his passenger. "It's part of the show biz package. An act."

Avarie turned her body a little more toward the window.

Pursing his lips, the detective sighed and returned his attention to the road, taking the next turn and heading to his condo.

* * * * *

Avarie was silent the rest of the drive. In the parking lot of the condo, Sergio parked his car, turned off the engine, and turned to her.

Avarie opened the passenger door and exited the vehicle.

He climbed out of the car, resting his arms across the roof. "Was it something I said?"

"Nope." Avarie got into her car. "We're good."

"We are?" he said. "You're good?"

"I'm fine." She slammed her door and started the car.

As Avarie drove away, Sergio lowered his head onto his outstretched arms. "Yeah. Everything's just perfect."

Upstairs, the detective pushed open his unlocked condo door to find Big Brass on the couch. The former drug dealer sipped a beer and tossed a potato chip into his mouth from a bag by his side, a large bouquet of flowers resting on the coffee table next to his feet. On the television, the Tampa Bay Rays baseball game was in the middle of the first inning.

"Make yourself at home." Shaking his head, Sergio entered his residence. "Who are the flowers for?"

"You. A gift from Carmello for saving his life this morning." Lavonte took another sip of beer and rested the bottle on his belly. "They were here when I got here, so I brought 'em in. There's a card."

"Saving his life?" Sergio frowned. "What's he been smoking?"

He plucked a tiny envelope from a pitchfork-shaped plastic rod that stuck out from the bundle of lilies and carnations. Inside was a typed note, on the florist's stationery.

Detective Martin,

Thank you for attacking me for no reason this morning. If you hadn't done so, I would have been on time for my bible study meeting in that fish warehouse, and I'd have been killed. You saved my life, and I won't forget it.

With eternal gratitude,

Carmello

Sergio tossed the card onto the coffee table. "What a load of crap. Bible study? He killed everybody in that fish warehouse, and now he thinks he can rub my nose in it because our cowardly lion State Attorney let him go. Sunny LaPierre has an even smaller backbone than her worthless predecessor."

Lavonte sat up. "Hey, it may be a load of crap, but it's also a message."

Sergio unbuttoned his shirt as he headed to the master bathroom. "I have exactly zero interest in any messages from that guy."

"Lilies and carnations, bro. Death flowers. I looked it up on the internet." Lavonte picked up the card. "Your death, brother. Ain't you worried? I think he might be getting ready to put a hit on you."

Sergio shook his head. "I can't think of anything dumber than sending flowers—delivered through a florist—to somebody you then turn around and kill. He'd be the first suspect, same as if he killed you after saying he should have."

"What?" Big Brass sat upright, his jaw dropping. "Carmello said that?"

Sergio chuckled, pulling his shirt off. "He might have mentioned it this morning, yeah."

"And you didn't think to tell me until now?" Lavonte stood up, going to the window. Lifting the edge of the blinds, he peeked outside.

"Chill," Sergio said. "Even Carmello's not crazy enough to follow through on a threat he said out loud to a cop. That'd be delusional. You're safe. We both are." He headed back down the hallway. "Now, if you'll excuse me, I need a shower."

"Go for it, brother," Lavonte said. "But I'm gonna keep eyes open in the back of my head, son. And you should, too. And before you forget, I need my Rolex back."

Sergio stopped and looked over his shoulder. "Before I get killed by Carmello?"

"No. No, no, no." Big Brass held his hands up. "You've convinced me that the entire Tampa Police Force would rally and swarm Carmello like he stepped on an angry beehive if he even thought about laying a finger on either one of us." The big man plopped back down on the couch. "But if you're wrong, it don't serve a brother to try and lay a claim to a gold watch sitting in a dead man's condo."

* * * * *

The shower refreshed the tired detective, clearing his head as he'd hoped. Energized, he threw on a clean pair of jeans and a fresh dress shirt. Plucking the borrowed Rolex off his nightstand, he carried it into the living room as he buttoned his shirt. Sergio held the wristwatch out to Big Brass. "Here."

"Thanks." Lavonte put the Rolex on his wrist and looked toward the kitchen. "You gonna eat?"

"Probably." Sergio tucked in his shirt, glancing around for his car keys.

Big Brass picked up the florist's card and peered at it again. "Boy, I still say, that's a bold statement from Carmello. Dude be messing with people's heads." He set the card back down. "What are we having for dinner?"

"We aren't." Sergio went into the kitchen. "I have to get back to work. I can't babysit your irrational fears of assassination."

"Wow, that's some kinda gratitude." Lavonte reclined on the couch and put his feet back on the coffee table. "I saved your life, and you won't even buy me dinner. Let's go watch the Rays game at Kojack's and eat some ribs."

"I can't. I'm still on a case and Kojack's is in the wrong direction." Opening the refrigerator, the detective reached past a lonely bottle of mustard and an empty cardboard beer container, to a solo can of Coca-Cola in the back. "But you're as delusional as Carmello." He popped open the Coke and took a few long gulps, wincing as the bubbles burned his throat. "And how exactly did you save my life?"

"Think about it," Big Brass said. "You said I was late for our meeting this morning. If I had been on time, we'd have walked into a hail of bullets and we'd both be dead." He took another sip of beer. "You're alive because of my complete lack of adherence to rigid appointment times."

Sergio leaned against the kitchen doorway, holding his soda. "Okay. I guess that's worth some ribs." He dug into his wallet and handed Lavonte twenty dollars.

"That's what I'm talking about!" Smiling, Big Brass clutched the bill to his chest with one hand and raised his beer to his mouth with the other. "Come with me—and not because I'm scared. I don't like eating alone."

Waving a hand, Sergio went back to the bedroom to locate his shoes. "I guarantee you won't be alone. At this hour, the place will be packed. Share your table with somebody in line and make a new friend."

"On Bayshore? Them snooty folks prefer not to sit down with someone like me."

Dropping to the edge of the bed, Sergio pulled his shoes on. "Then maybe you should shower more often." He stood, breezing past his guest on his way to the front door. "Gotta run. Lock up when you leave."

His gaze remaining on the TV, Lavonte held up the twenty-dollar bill. "I'm accepting this as a partial expression of your gratitude. Twenty dollars will buy dinner but not drinks. I'm gonna come get another fin off you later."

As he descended the condo steps, Sergio's phone buzzed in his pocket. He dug it out as he went to his car, glancing at the screen.

Max.

The detective pressed the green button and held the phone to his ear, sliding into the driver's seat of his vehicle. "Hey, Max. What do you have for me?"

"Sir, I think we've spotted Gabriella's husband at the fairgrounds this morning."

"What!" Sergio grinned. He started the car. "How did we get that?"

"I did a social media search," Max said. "I used tags like fairgrounds, magic act, Romain... Anyway, a ton of public posts came up. In one of them, I spotted a woman taking a video of her kids. The expo hall was in the background, right about the time the murder happened—and a man who looks like Teodoro Romain was visible hanging around the building's side exit."

"That's great work, Max." Sergio drove his car onto the main road. "Can you send it to me?"

"Yes, sir. I'm sending it now."

Sergio chewed his lip, steering through traffic until he found an empty parking lot to pull into. Taking a spot near the front of a drycleaners, he lifted his phone and clicked the image Max had sent.

A woman offscreen shouted directions to two rambunctious children in front of the expo hall. "We might see the noon magic show if these two behave. Hold still and wave to Grandma!"

The video stopped at that point. Sergio replayed it, zooming in on the background.

As the clip played again, a man was clearly visible by the side exit doors of the building.

A jolt went through Sergio's insides.

Even from the somewhat over-enlarged, pixilated image, the man appeared to be handsome, and walked with an athletic stride.

The same as he'd seen in the video from the Miami café. Same build. Same hair style. Same swagger.

Teodoro.

The detective exhaled sharply and played the video again. As the squirming children waved to the camera, the corner of a trash cart appeared behind the boy's head, right next to the man by the side exit door.

Sergio lowered his phone into his lap, staring off into the setting sun.

He was there.

The arrogant SOB let himself get caught on video.

"Detective?" Max's voice brought Sergio back to the present. "Mark Harriman has dispatched another squad car to the Romain household. Should I head over there?"

"Uh…" Sergio rubbed his chin. "We need the warrants and the dog searches wrapped up first. What's the status on those?"

"Nothing yet on either," Max said. "I doubt the dog handlers will have anything before closing time. I can buzz the warrant judge's on-call clerk again and ask for a priority status."

Sergio nodded. "Do that. Tell them I'm on my way to the Romain residence with fifty cops, and I want that warrant there before we arrive."

"Will that work?"

"Maybe." Sergio shrugged. "Judges are elected. Nobody wants to piss off fifty voters."

CHAPTER 26

THE ROMAIN RESIDENCE ON Tampa's affluent Bayshore Boulevard could have been a small resort on almost any other street in town.

Sergio parked on the side of the home, among the dozen or so squad cars that filled the street, and trotted toward the property.

A sprawling, two-story Spanish-style manor, the Romain estate was an elegant throwback to America's gilded age. With a green tile roof and a low, manicured hedge tucked up against its century-old foundation, the home announced its *nouveau riche* owners to the world. High, arched-top windows lined the exterior of the stucco residence, like sentries guarding a king's castle; limestone block quoins decorated the outer corners of the home. Two guest houses rested behind the massive main residence, along with a pool, a pool house, and several ornate terraces. Palm trees lined the edges of the property, looming over an emerald green, golf course-like lawn.

The master balcony was the centerpiece of the majestic estate's front elevation, rimmed with a row of thick limestone balustrades that supported a wide, tiled railing, and giving the homeowners a sweeping view of the bay.

The streetlights from Bayshore Boulevard cast enough illumination on the massive house to see without flashlights. Uniformed officers came and went, stringing crime scene tape around the perimeter and stockpiling evidence markers by the door.

On the front walkway, Sergio stopped a young officer with M. Correy engraved on her name badge. "You're... Madison, right?"

"That's right." She nodded. "You spoke at our training session last month."

"Yeah. Did I miss something, Madison? Are we inside the house, with an active crime scene?"

"We've been waiting for you, Detective," Officer Correy said. "But Harriman thought it'd be a good idea to string the tape and make a show of placing evidence markers. He figured that would raise the attention of the neighbors and they'd be more likely to talk to us."

Sergio nodded. "It would work on me, that's for sure." He proceeded past the security alarm warning signs, toward the entry.

Avarie's voice floated across the lawn. "Hey, that's new, isn't it?"

About fifty feet away, the PR rep stood on the lush green grass, leaning over and smiling at the forearm of a tall man with his back to Sergio. As he stood up, the male became more visible in the light—bright blue curls topped his head, with his hair trimmed close on one side and shaved bald on the other.

Sergio chewed his lip.

Max.

A section of the lab tech's muscular arm glistened with the face of a blue-green alien from beneath a rolled-up shirt sleeve.

"Yeah," he said. "Got it yesterday, so I'm still doing the Lubriderm thing."

"I love the color, Max. It's the same as the first body ink I ever got. Check it out." Avarie hooked a thumb into her jeans and pulled them down over the side of her hip, revealing a teal butterfly the size of a postage stamp. "I was nineteen, expressing my wild side."

Max chuckled. "Is every girl's first tattoo of a butterfly?"

"I know, right?" Avarie hiked her jeans back up. As she adjusted her waistline, her eyes met Sergio's. She paused momentarily, then looked back at Max. "Like I said—the mark of every nineteen-year-old's rebellious stage."

They laughed, the last embers of the setting sun casting a dark blue haze onto the blackening canvas of the sky behind them.

Frowning, Sergio walked up to the front door, addressing the officer there and a gray-haired man in a polo shirt embroidered with Red's 24-Hour Lock and Key on the front. Next to him, on the ornate door frame, was a video doorbell.

The detective spoke louder than necessary, to be heard out on the lawn. "Do we have a search warrant for these premises?"

Nodding, the young officer handed over the paperwork.

Sergio took it and looked at the locksmith. "Then open this door and let's get to work."

A blast of cool air scented with the aroma of fresh flowers greeted Sergio as the front door swung open. With the officer from the entry at his side, the detective walked in and gazed past the decorative foyer and into a massive white living room.

Two milky linen loveseats faced each other from the sides of a glass-topped coffee table, with a long, red-patterned sofa behind it. The cushions on the chairs matched the fabric of the sofa and drapes; three short stools stood in front of the coffee table, boxing it in. On each side of the couch were matching round tables cluttered with marble busts of Greek heroes, vases of fresh flowers, and a tall lamp. The steep, chalk-colored walls of the room were decorated with oil painting scenes of the Greek countryside, hung from wires attached to a hanging rail a few feet over the top, the way it was done in ancient European palaces.

The detective walked across the herringbone wood floor to the square coffee table, putting his hands on his hips.

The security alarm never made a warning tone when we entered. The video doorbell didn't activate when the door opened.

Why?

He glanced around.

They've got a lot of construction people coming and going. Turning the alarm on and off for each tradesperson would be a pain... Same with the video doorbell. No point in getting fifty notifications about painters and plaster repair guys walking back and forth to their trucks.

But having it all turned off when your wife goes missing is pretty handy, too. No record of you leaving before the murder and coming back afterward. You could say you were here the whole time, and your video doorbell wouldn't undermine your alibi.

The young officer next to Sergio looked around, his mouth hanging open. "This house is amazing. You could have a basketball game in this living room. And what a view of the bay." He looked at the detective. "Does it bother you to think you'll probably never own a house like this?"

"Nope." Sergio shook his head. "I've been in houses like this a few times, and it was never for a good reason."

Other uniformed officers commenced the process of checking the rooms of the house; CSIs took photographs. Doorways to other rooms revealed painter's scaffolds, canvas tarps, and workers' buckets.

Avarie walked into the living room. "What a dump." She smirked, glancing around at the opulent fixtures. "Apparently, this place is still a work in progress."

Sergio looked past the PR rep to a large, marble fireplace—and the huge oil portrait of Gabriella Romain hanging above it.

The painting depicted Teodoro's new wife on a balcony with her back to the artist, dressed in a short, strapless blue dress that complimented her slender figure. Gabriella Romain's light brown hair was visible from under the edge of a wide-brimmed sun hat, her arms stretching out from her sides as they rested on the balcony's thick limestone railing. Only the side of her face was visible, and not even all of that, but it was a clear match for the lady they'd seen in the magic act's recordings and the one identified through social media. A large red ring graced the middle finger of her right hand, displaying the letter V in gold.

The artist had captured Gabriella's beauty and elegant appearance, but the woman in the portrait seemed sad as she gazed out over the calm span of water, toward a cloudy horizon.

"That's here." Avarie pointed to the painting. "That's the master balcony, upstairs." She looked at Sergio. "I checked out this house on the internet while we were waiting for you."

The detective walked toward the portrait. "What do you think she's looking at?"

"That painting's not very old." Avarie scrolled through her phone, stopping at a real estate listing for the house. "The pictures online are dated three weeks ago, and in those, the master balcony railing is made of glass and steel. Now, it's stone."

Sergio nodded. "It's also new because Teodoro Romain hasn't known Gabriella very long.

It was a whirlwind romance." He glanced at Avarie. "That balcony is upstairs?"

She nodded.

"Care to join me in the bedroom, then?" He gestured to a wide staircase that curved upwards and away from the base of the marble fireplace, disappearing behind the wall holding Gabriella's portrait.

"Sure," Avarie said.

They ascended the stairs together, passing uniformed officers scurrying up and down along the way.

The Romain sleeping quarters were much more modern and austere than the ostentatious living room. The master suite contained only a king-size bed, his and hers dressers, and a large mirror, all in a Scandinavian wood design that was sleek and functional. The bed was unmade, and cluttered with a man's clothing. The tops of the two dressers were a study in contrasts. One contained only a large, half-empty bottle of Clive Christian's "Imperial Majesty" cologne. The other dresser top was overflowing with framed pictures of the home's young occupants at clubs and casual events. Earrings, bracelets and other jewelry lay strewn among the many pictures. A ladies' large cocktail ring rested near the back corner of the crowded surface, encrusted in rubies and displaying the letter V in gold. It was an older piece, the kind that went in and out of fashion with elderly women of means, but the ring's rubies had maintained their sparkle over the years—and was a match for the one in the portrait downstairs.

Avarie leaned close to the cluttered dresser's many framed pictures. "Teodoro sure photographs well. They both do—or, did." She looked up at Sergio. "What a shame, you know? She had her whole life ahead of her."

Sergio walked past the bed to a wall of glass doors with white sheer curtains. On the other side was the balcony from the portrait. "He was dangerous. She probably knew that from her uncle."

"Maybe that's what attracted her to him." Avarie walked over to the detective. "It's strange what attracts people to one another."

He pulled a latex glove from his pocket and put it on, holding out his index finger to the large wooden handle of the sliding glass doors. With very little pressure, the door slid open.

The air of the hot, humid night washed over him.

"It's always nice when a sliding door actually slides." Sergio reached up, pushing aside the billowing, see-through curtain. "Mine practically need two people to get them open."

He held the sheers back and let Avarie step onto the balcony first, following her. The bay was nearly dark, lapping at the base of the rocky shoreline beneath Bayshore Boulevard's famed four-mile-long sidewalk.

Spectators had gathered on the grass median of the divided street, their faces reflecting the flashing lights of the police cars surrounding the Romain property. Rollerbladers, dog walkers, joggers; none seemed to be able to resist the hint of scandal that came when emergency vehicles appeared at a rich person's house.

"Nice view," Avarie said, "but it's a little hot out here for me."

"Definitely." Sergio took a small flashlight from his pocket and passed the beam across the balcony's floor and railing. The area appeared to have been recently cleaned. Squatting, he inspected the surface area between the thick, stone balustrades. "Uh, Avarie… try to exercise a little more professionalism when you're on my crime scene, would you?"

"Huh?" she said. "What are you talking about?"

"Well…" Sergio shrugged, illuminating a tiny bit of dust on the balcony. "I hardly think pulling your pants down in front of fellow employees is a—"

"How'd it feel when you saw us?" Avarie said. "Me and Max, comparing tattoos."

"Hmm?" Sergio looked up at her. "I… didn't feel any particular way about it. You're—"

"You're lying." She turned away, the wind pulling at her hair.

Sergio shrugged. "You're both adults…"

"Still lying."

Sighing, he rose to his feet. "Okay. I wasn't crazy about it, but if you want to play show and tell on the front lawn, I'm not in a position to—"

"I don't."

He cocked his head, his mouth hanging open. "What?"

Avarie turned to face him. The hot breeze from the bay pushed strands of hair over her cheek and mouth. "I don't. I don't want to do that. You think I get off on showing Max my tattoos? I was showing you what it felt like to me when Scarlet Slutazar was pushing her big fake boobs in your face."

Sergio chuckled. "She didn't push them into my face."

"No?" Frowning, Avarie crossed her arms. "She pushed them everywhere else."

The detective held his hands out. "Let's not do this, okay? Let's just... focus on the job."

"Fine." She turned away a second time.

Sergio winced. "There's that word again."

"Just don't expect me to not have a reaction when you're being mean to me."

He recoiled. "I—wasn't being mean."

"You know what I'm saying." Wheeling around, she jabbed a finger into his chest. "We only went on one date, so we're not boyfriend-girlfriend, but don't flirt with someone right in front of me. It's rude. And it's disrespectful."

"Scarlet? You think I was flirting with Scarlet?"

"Are there so many women you're actively flirting with that you've lost track? Yes, Scarlet. She's just playing you."

"Did it ever occur to you that I might be playing her?" Sergio said. "Going along, letting her think she's got me wrapped around her finger, so she'll relax—and maybe make a mistake?"

Avarie narrowed her eyes, her tone softening. "Is that what you're doing?"

"I told you, I think Scarlet knows more than she's letting on." The detective rubbed his chin. "A lot of times, a killer will volunteer to help with a case so they can steer it off track. Letting Scarlet feel confident and in control might cause her to become a little arrogant—and then she'll screw up."

He gazed into Avarie's eyes. The hot breeze caught her blonde locks, lifting them to dance around her shoulders. Sergio lowered his voice. "Avarie, you said you knew I was on the rebound and that we'd take it slow."

"Yeah, but..." She shrugged, biting her lip. "...any slower and we'd be going in reverse."

He smiled. "Maybe I think some things are worth waiting for."

"Detective?" Officer Correy appeared at the bedroom door. She was breathing hard. "We could use your help with a situation downstairs."

"Let me go!" A woman screeched. "My daughter's been killed, and that Miami mobster did it! I just know it!"

CHAPTER 27

A HEAVYSET WOMAN IN THE LIVING ROOM STRUGGLED AGAINST the two uniformed officers restraining her.

"Let me go!" She shouted, her face red. "My brother is Cass Clemmons, the Chief of Police!" She twisted and pushed, but the officers maintained their grip on her arms.

Groaning, Sergio raced down the stairs. "Ma'am, I'm Detective Sergio Martin. Chief Clemmons put me in charge of this case, and you really shouldn't—"

"Detective Martin?" She scowled at Sergio. "You're the one I keep calling. Cass gave me your number. Don't you answer your phone? I've been leaving messages since this morning!"

"Oh, I'm sorry—I just got a new phone and you're probably calling the old one." He glanced at the officers and nodded. They released her arms.

Mark Harriman entered the living room. "She just ran right by us, Detective." He glanced at the woman. "Ma'am, this is an active investigation scene."

Sergio faced Gabriella's mother. "He's right, Ms…"

"I'm Joanna Clemmons-Hartford." She huffed, opening her purse and pulling out her wallet. She handed Sergio her drivers license and a business card from the chief. On the back was written, *Please show my sister Joanna Hartford every courtesy*, and it was signed by Chief Clemmons.

Sergio recognized the chief's signature. The detective had come across one of Clemmons' courtesy cards before. The chief didn't use them to get people close to him out of trouble with the law; it was merely a way of indicating the holder was who they said they were.

It may have also been a way to ensure that an overly aggressive officer didn't go too far.

The last time Sergio heard about a courtesy card being shown was when the chief's twenty-five-year-old son was pulled over for a DUI. The kid had never been in trouble before, but the breathalyzer showed he was more than twice the legal limit.

Clemmons was called, arriving on the scene within minutes. He thanked the officers present, then sadly insisted his son be arrested and booked.

"Well, Ms. Hartford…" Sergio handed the ID and business card back to the woman. "As officer

Harriman indicated, it's an active investigation scene. You being in the residence could contaminate valuable evidence that we need to help your daughter."

"Have you found her?" Ms. Hartford asked. "Is she hurt?"

Sergio held his hands up. "Ma'am, I can't really give you any—"

"Is she..." Tears formed in the woman's eyes. "Can you just tell me if my daughter is alive?"

Sergio bit his lip, a knot forming in his abdomen.

He didn't know.

The detective couldn't say for sure that Gabriella Romain was dead, and he couldn't report that she was alive. The circumstances of the case dictated that he acknowledge the evidence.

We have a lot of blood at the crime scene.

No one could lose that much blood and remain alive.

But even though the lab has yet to confirm that the blood was your daughter's, we are unaware of anyone else on the ladder under the stage...

He could state the truth. The facts.

He could lay out the undisputed evidence and Joanna Hartford would come to the conclusion that most of the officers working the case had already come to. The same conclusion the canine unit officers had reached when the cadaver dog was ordered on site with a bloodhound. The same conclusion a loose-lipped CSI had inadvertently given to reporters.

Gabriella Romain appears to be deceased.

That was not an incorrect statement, and it was what the evidence suggested. People who are alive tend to be able to be reached. They reply to a text or use a credit card at a gas station or grocery store. They post on social media.

Gabriella Romain had done none of those things.

Instead, she walked onto a stage and disappeared into a room that was later covered in blood. She left behind all her personal belongings—phone, wallet, makeup—the things people take with them if they are alive and well.

Gabriella Romain appears to be deceased.

That was what the evidence suggested. That's what he could tell Gabriella's mother.

But he couldn't.

He could not take away the last remaining hope a mother had for the safety of her child.

As the mascara streamed down Ms. Hartford's cheeks, she lifted a hand to her nose. Sniffling, she burst into sobs.

Sergio held his hands out, letting the distraught woman fall into his arms. She cried, pressing her face against his shoulder.

"My baby. My baby."

The detective closed his eyes and patted the grieving mother on the back, a task he had performed too many times in his job as a police officer. The faces were different, but they were the same. Each was etched in pain, their souls destroyed, their mouths curling in agony. Old, young, mother, father, sister, brother… Words could not describe the devastation the news of the death of a loved one imparted into their family members. It was a one-way door into a world they never wanted to enter and from which they would never fully return.

That, he knew all too well.

"Sergio, take your cousin to her room."

His father was a large man. Powerful and strong, from a life spent working with his hands. But when he issued that simple instruction to his young son, Sergio's father changed. Mr. Martin stood in the doorway, staring at the police officer who had come to deliver the news, and before the officer said a word, Sergio's father made the request of his son—and choked on his words in the process.

And the boy knew.

"Cousin" Stevie was gone. His little cousin Gina would never see her father again.

The hollowness that entered his body that day—that minute—and certainly that of Gina and her family, never really left.

Gabriella Romain appears to be deceased.

The words were inadequate.

And as the deliverer of such words, Sergio was inadequate.

The endless night would turn into a series of days that blurred into one another as the parent processed the information. There would be no more smiles from their child, no more hugs. None of it existed anymore as part of a person who was a continuation of that life. It was all now a memory, in a framed picture on the piano, or in a video on the phone, but not in a physical reality with soft skin and bright eyes, that had been a small child that gave warm hugs and loved to be hugged, and got tucked into her first big girl bed one night and then came crawling into her mother's bed a few hours later when an evening rain turned into a scary thunderstorm.

The smiling face looking out from framed pictures, first from a crib, then with Grandma as she learned to walk, then with Dad as she rode a two-wheeler for the first time, then at her fifth birthday party, surrounded by friends. When she was thirteen and finally got her braces off. Her sweet sixteen. Her first day at college.

None of it continued. The smiles in those pictures had evoked smiles in return, and now they would only elicit sorrow and tears.

Sergio knew the pain.

Gabriella Romain appears to be deceased.

And he would not put that pain into another human being if he didn't have to.

Swallowing hard, the detective closed his eyes and put his mouth close to the ear of Gabriella's mother. "Ma'am, I… want you to listen very carefully to what I'm about to say."

He took a deep breath.

"The evidence suggests a certain outcome. But we aren't finished, so that outcome may change. If your daughter is alive, I will find her. Don't you lose hope. Don't. Because I won't. Okay?"

Leaning back, he gazed at Ms. Hartford's face. "I'm gonna promise you something, and I want you to promise me something in return. Until I come to you, face-to-face, and tell you that your daughter is not alive, don't you believe it. Not from a news report, not from any other cop, not even from your own brother—even if he is the Chief of Police." He put his hands on her shoulders, a lump forming in his throat. "Only when you look in my eyes, and I tell you those words, do you stop carrying the hope that's burning inside you. I'm not going to stop until I find out the truth of what happened. That's my promise to you. You need to promise me that you won't give up on her unless you see me face-to-face and I deliver that information to you personally. Can you promise me that?"

Ms. Hartford nodded, wiping her nose. "I promise."

"Well…" Raising his shoulder to his cheek, Sergio wiped a tear from his eye. "I'm not telling you that right now, so how about we both stop crying?"

He chuckled, and a smile found its way onto Gabriella's mother's face.

"Okay," she said.

The detective guided Ms. Hartford to the living room couch and sat down with her. "Actually, there might be things you can do to help us with the case. Let's focus on that. Let's stay productive."

"Yes, please. That would be…" She shook her head. "I'm going crazy with worry. I know how Gabriella and Teodoro have been fighting, and I know his reputation in Miami."

"They were fighting a lot?" Sergio pursed his lips. "Well, let's talk about that."

"Your people should know." Clasping her hands in her lap, Ms. Hartford shrugged. "The police were called out here on a regular basis. It was an embarrassment to Cass, her being his niece and all, but that psycho Miami mobster would fly into a rage all the time, at anything Gabriella did that he disliked. If she wore the wrong kind of shoes when they were going out, or if she took too long to get back from shopping… There were constant shouting matches—she'd call me, and he'd be screaming in the background…"

Sergio kept his eyes on Ms. Hartford. "Mark?"

"I'm on it," Harriman said. "I'll pull the run sheets for whoever came out here, times and dates. A few of the officers outside were saying they'd been here."

"Bring them in." Sergio looked around. "And where's Max?"

The lab technician stepped forward. "Yes, sir?"

Sergio rubbed his chin. "Do we still have the evidence we collected from the fairgrounds this morning? The items from that big blue and white bag?"

"Yes, sir." Max hooked a thumb over his shoulder. "It's in the evidence van, outside."

"Please go get it and bring it here."

"Yes, sir."

Max departed.

"Evidence?" Ms. Hartford said. "How can I help with that? I'm not a police officer, I answer phones at an accounting firm."

"Well…" The detective leaned forward, resting his elbows on his knees. "My mother and sister are very close. They talk almost every day."

Ms. Hartford nodded. "So did Gabriella and I. We spoke all the time."

"Right," Sergio said. "Because you're a good mom. Now, as it happens, my mother and my sister are so close, my mother knows things that nobody else knows."

"Well, I…" Ms. Hartford's cheeks turned red. "I'm her mother. She trusts me."

Max returned, carrying a plastic bin. He set it at Sergio's feet and opened it up.

"Gabriella trusts you like any good daughter would trust her mother, if they're really close." Sergio reached inside the bin. "So, Ms. Hartford, I'm willing to bet that you know the access code to this."

He pulled out Gabriella's smart phone and handed it to her mother.

CHAPTER 28

M<small>AX SAT BY</small> Ms. Hartford on the couch as she held down the buttons on the sides of the phone until it powered up.

"Be careful here, ma'am," Max said. "If we enter the wrong code too many times, the phone will lock us out."

Snorting, Gabriella's mother entered 737737.

The phone came to life.

She handed the device back to Max, turning her nose up. "The code is Pepper, the name of our family dog when Gabby was little."

"I'm sorry I ever doubted you." Max scrolled through the pages and pages of apps on the phone. "With your permission, I'd like to open some of the personal applications on this device. Her call log can show any incoming and outgoing calls, missed calls, and voicemail messages… but Gabriella might have an app that compiles her purchases, or one that tracks her phone and shows where she's been with it."

"Teodoro had her install that." Ms. Hartford nodded, peering over Max's arm, to the screen. "The tracking one. I don't know what it's called, but she has something that does that. She told me. He wanted to keep tabs on her."

As the lab tech studied Gabriella's phone, Mark Harriman returned with two other officers. "Detective, I collected the run report you asked for. TPD has been called to the Romain residence nine times in three weeks." He gestured to the officers by his side. "Trent Ferrar and Pete Burnside were each out here. Trent came out multiple times."

Sergio stood to address the officers. "Did either of you know the Romains personally?"

Neither did.

"Just luck of the draw," Officer Ferrar said. "I happened to be on duty in the area when the call came in. Domestic dispute, each time."

Sergio nodded. "How many times?"

"Three, for me," Ferrer said.

Burnside clasped his hands in front of himself. "Just once, sir."

"And the rest were by individual officers." Harriman looked at Sergio. "I can call downtown and bring them here if you want."

"Let's start with these two." He peered at Ferrar. "You said you were here three times. What did you see?"

The officer glanced toward Ms. Hartford, then brought his gaze back to Sergio.

"Right." Sergio nodded. "Let's talk…"

"There's a big patio just outside the rear door." Avarie moved toward the front entry, pointing to a set of large sliding glass doors at the far side of the living room. "Some news crews have shown up. I'm gonna go deal with them."

Sergio looked at Ferrar and nodded at the sliding glass doors. "You, come with me. You..." He glanced at Burnside. "Just wait in here for a moment."

The Romain's lower set of sliding glass doors opened as easily as the ones in the bedroom.

Sergio shook his head, stepping over the threshold. "I've gotta find out who they use for these and have them come do my place."

"It won't be cheap, I can tell you that." Ferrar took a few steps onto the patio. "Everything here cost a ton."

"Yeah." Sergio looked up at the estate's tall exterior walls. "Probably."

The officer stopped and turned to Sergio. "So, I was going to say, each time I came out here, the husband and wife were going at it, screaming at the top of their lungs, according to the neighbors."

"What? Neighbors?" Sergio peered at the estate's exterior. "How'd anybody hear through these walls? The closest house is half an acre away, and this place is a fortress."

"The first time I responded," Ferrar said, "the homeowners were arguing out on the front balcony. When I came two days ago, they were in the living room, with the doors and windows open. When I was coming up the walkway, I could hear them yelling from out on the street."

"What were they yelling about?"

"Well, they *said* it was about her shoes." Officer Ferrar shook his head. "Mr. Romain said he lost his temper when he saw how much his wife spent on shoes. Her statement was essentially the same. But sir... from outside, he was calling her a puta—that's a slut, in Spanish."

Sergio nodded. "Yeah, I know the word."

"He said a lot of other Spanish words," Ferrar said. "Yelled them, I guess. Cursing and swearing. You're a this, you're a that. There was no evidence of anything physical. No bruises, no broken dishes or anything. In fact, the house was immaculate each time. Since we tend to show a little deference to this area, I issued them a warning and I left. Then, when I was here the last time..." He shrugged. "I was sitting in my car writing the report, and let's just say I observed sounds that would commonly be associated with two consenting adults very much enjoying each other's company."

"All passion, in both directions." Snorting, Sergio glanced at the house. "They're either fighting or making love."

"Yes, sir."

Turning back to Ferrar, Sergio rubbed his beard stubble. "Did you do a sweep of the house?"

"Only the main area—where we were tonight." The officer pointed toward the house. "The living room, the front entry, a look into the big dining room off the kitchen. The place was spotless each time, and nobody else appeared to be present."

"Mm-hmm." Sergio nodded again. "Did you see the big portrait of Mrs. Romain? The one over the fireplace?"

"I... saw it tonight, when I walked in." Ferrar cocked his head and frowned. "Not any of the other times I was here, no."

"And your last visit, that was about two days ago. So the portrait is new."

"Yes, sir." The officer put his hands on his hips, looking down. "He looked like such a nice guy. Then he screams at his wife all night, finally kills her, and hangs up her portrait as a trophy. What a sicko."

"Okay. Thanks for the info." Sergio patted the officer on the shoulder. "Go on back and check in with Harriman."

"Thank you, Detective." He started away.

"Oh—why the dining room?"

Officer Ferrar stopped and turned around. "What, Detective?"

"You said you looked into the dining room," Sergio said. "Why?"

"Oh. They were eating." Ferrar peered back toward the residence, gesturing to the sliding glass doors. Beyond them, the walls of the kitchen and dining room were visible. "The lights were on in the dining room and there were serving dishes on the table, two places with some leftover food on them, an open bottle of wine and two glasses." He grinned. "Smelled good, too. Roast pork, I think."

"Okay." The detective sighed. "Thanks."

Ferrar left. Sergio stood in the middle of the terrace, staring up at the house.

The neighbors could hear them yelling. Ferrar heard them when he was walking up to the house.

He went to the sliding glass doors and slid them open, going past Max and Ms. Hartford to the stairs.

"Oh, Detective," Max said. "There's something here that might interest you."

"One sec, Max." Sergio scampered up the long, curved staircase, to the master bedroom. He stopped at the sliding glass doors and peered over the spacious balcony.

Across the lawn, Avarie stood in front of several reporters and cameras, gesturing with her hands and nodding her head.

Without opening the door, Sergio called out to her. "Avarie! Wrap it up!"

She continued speaking to the reporters.

"Avarie!" Sergio shouted. "No more press updates for now!"

The PR rep appeared to continue her discussion with the media, never even glancing in his direction.

He opened the sliding glass door and stepped back to the middle of the room. "Avarie!" he yelled. "Where are you?"

Nothing.

He raised his voice even louder. "Avarie, where are you? I need—"

Avarie wheeled around and looked at the house. She put her hand to her forehead, gazing at the balcony. "What?"

Smiling, Sergio walked out into the warm, night air. "Nothing." He waved a hand. "Sorry, I thought you were someplace else. Please go on. Sorry about the interruption, everybody."

As she turned back to the reporters, Sergio went back inside and shut the sliding door. He exited the bedroom, slipping his hands into his pockets as he went back downstairs.

"Sir." Max walked toward him, balancing his computer in one hand and Gabriella's phone in the other. "This phone is a wealth of information. We found the tracking app. It shows where Gabriella was, but she could see where Teodoro was, too. It shows his number, and he was at the fairgrounds during the show. He called Gabriella at ten twenty-eight and again at ten twenty-nine."

"That's during the show," Sergio said. "The performance started at ten."

"Right." Max nodded. "But she didn't answer. I cross checked his number against the fairground cell tower report, and his phone communicated with the tower at those times. He was definitely there, sir."

"He was watching her."

"There are also some saved messages where he yells at her. One is from this morning. I didn't play them in front of Ms. Hartford, but you should give it a listen."

"Over here." Sergio headed toward the kitchen, and the long, elegant dining room adjacent to it. Mark Harriman joined the two men.

The spacious dining table appeared to be host to an interrupted meal. A lone plate was piled high with yellow rice and black beans, with a generous helping of shredded pork. The food appeared to have been at least partially eaten: the portions were scattered about, the fork was resting on the plate, and the napkin had been crumpled. A stemmed, crystal glass contained a tiny amount of water, with the slightest smudge of a lip mark on the rim.

There were no other plates or place settings on the table.

Sergio glanced at the phone in Max's hand. "Do it."

The lab tech raised the phone to Sergio and tapped the screen.

Teodoro's voice held the same controlled hostility he showed in the Miami café. "Listen, you disrespectful little *puta*. When I say don't go to the fairgrounds, you do not go to the fairgrounds. You call me when you get this message, do you hear me? I will not tolerate this disrespect. You call me, and you come straight home. And if you don't, I'm going to... you'll be sorry."

Max sighed, swiping a finger across the screen. "Then there's this. A video she recorded from the other night."

He set the phone on the edge of the dining room table and tapped the screen again.

The video began with a close up of a woman's hand. A moment later, the hand pulled away, showing Gabriella's face, looking into the phone and trying to balance it against something. Behind her was the Romain living room.

Teodoro stormed into the opulent white room, pacing back and forth in front of the red patterned sofa and cursing in Spanish. As Gabriella walked toward him, he threw his hands in the air and ranted, his voice growing louder.

"Puta!" Teodoro's face was red, his dark hair disheveled. "You disrespect me! You are a child, with no restraint." He glared at her, pointing his finger. "You will learn to be obedient. You will learn, or…" He pounded the back of the loveseat, spit flying from his mouth. "I will end you!"

"I hate you!" Gabriella clutched her fists at her sides, leaning forward. "You're nothing but a—a cheap criminal from Miami. If it wasn't for your brother—"

"That's it!" He came toward her. "Not another word!"

"Or what?" She put her hands on her hips. "Big man! Do you hit women now? I'm not afraid of you."

His eyes narrowed. "Then you are even dumber than I thought, because you should be afraid of me."

"Then, do something! Do it, you—"

"Shut up!" He ran at her. "I will kill you!"

Gabriella leaped backward, raising her arms. She crashed into the phone, knocking it from its perch.

The video ended.

"Holy crap." Avarie stood in the doorway, her mouth hanging open. "He threatened to kill her on the night before she died."

"I guess that's it." Sergio frowned and rubbed his eyes. "Mark, put out an APB for Teodoro Romain. Include that he's a suspect in the disappearance and possible murder of Gabriella Romain, maiden name Hartford, and that he is to be considered armed and dangerous."

As Harriman left the room, Avarie stepped to Sergio's side. "You know those reporters are going to be all over that APB as soon as it goes out."

"Yep." Sergio nodded. "No choice."

She exhaled sharply. "Sergio, the chief—"

"Won't be happy." He shrugged. "Too bad. Showing restraint is gonna cost us this case. That's the priority, not how the department or the chief looks." He walked to the kitchen, peering at a wall calendar with writing on it. "Trying to keep a lid on this thing was never a good decision. Now, we'll all just have to deal with it."

"Clemmons is going to explode."

"I'll deal with the chief," Sergio said. "You'll really need to deal with those reporters now. Sorry."

She nodded. "It's going to get ugly, but I'll do my best."

"Detective Martin!" A breathless officer raced into the dining room. "Sir, you're going to want to see this."

"Now what?" Sergio mumbled. He turned away from the calendar and looked at the officer. "What did you find?"

"Teodoro, sir. He's dead."

CHAPTER 29

THE OFFICER GUIDED SERGIO AND AVARIE ACROSS THE front yard down to the street, toward the limestone railing that separated Bayshore Boulevard from the dark water below.

The dead man lay face-down on the front of a small aluminum boat, in a t-shirt and swim trunks, his arms hanging over the sides and his hands immersed in the salt water of the bay. Gentle waves rocked the tiny vessel, bumping it into the huge rocks that lined the water's edge.

Two uniformed officers held the boat in place as the beam from Mark Harriman's flashlight swept over the body. He looked up at Sergio from the rocks. "One of the joggers noticed this dinghy here, and that the guy wasn't moving. The wallet says it's Teodoro Vance Romain, from this address."

"Okay." Sergio nodded. "I'm coming down."

The detective descended a set of concrete steps a dozen yards away and climbed over the slippery boulders that made up the shoreline. The big stones had been piled along the bay's edge decades ago, protecting the boulevard—and the expensive properties on the other side—from erosion.

At the dinghy, he put his hands on his hips to catch his breath. "Who made the ID?"

"Me." Harriman gestured with a latex glove-covered hand, to an evidence container resting on a body bag. A wallet was visible inside. "Checked for a pulse, too. The body's cold and stiff, so he's been here for a while. I called the medical examiner's office for you. Someone is on the way."

Sergio wiped the sweat from his forehead and opened an internet browser on his phone, searching "Tide table, Tampa, Florida."

How did this guy go unnoticed until now, if he's been dead "for a while?" Cold and stiff could mean he died before sunset.

A local fishing website showed the peak tide was about an hour ago.

And how did this dinghy manage to stay here, unmoored?

"Detective," Harriman said, "have a look at this."

The three officers lifted the corpse from the aluminum boat and lowered it onto the body bag, while a fourth secured the dinghy with a rope to prevent it from drifting away. The dead man's face was scratched and marred, his mouth covered in white foam. The corpse's hands were pale and bloated from soaking in the salt water.

Sergio sighed.

That oughta make the coroner's job fun. It'll be days before those swollen fingers give up any prints.

He moved his flashlight beam to the front of the dinghy. The sides came to a point, like the tip of a canoe, where the man's face had been. The flat surface there was covered in white foam as well.

He peered up at the limestone railing, where Avarie still stood. The nearby streetlights lit up her blonde hair. "Avarie, do me a favor and ask the CSIs to take photos of the Romain dining room, and then bag up the food on the table. Heck, bag up everything in the fridge, too."

She nodded and disappeared from the railing.

Squatting, Sergio raised his flashlight and moved the beam across the bow of the little boat, where the registration numbers identified it as FL 15239 RR, with the name "Sea Pass" painted in blue. He followed the side of the line to the rear. The little vessel seemed new, and well cared for. Clean. A small motor stood up from the stern, water lapping its shiny, raised propeller blades.

A fishing rod lay on the floor of the boat, with a hook and some cut fish for bait. Near the stern, a tackle box was visible.

He lowered himself onto one of the smoother rocks, staring out over the dark water. In the distance, the lights of Davis Island flickered in the haze. Sighing, Sergio lifted his hands to rub his tired eyes.

None of this makes any sense.

He took out his phone to call Max, to have him run a check on the dinghy's ownership.

It'll come back as registered to Teodoro, which won't help me at all...

But there's a chance the dinghy is registered to someone else.

And maybe that person will lead to me figuring out what's going on.

On the fifth ring, Max answered his phone. "Yes, sir?"

"Max, I need you to verify the dinghy's ownership. If it belongs to a bigger boat, there'll be a registration and a name."

"Will do, sir."

"And Max—tell everyone up at the house to be aware that Gabriella's mother is present. Ms. Hartford just lost her son in law, and we don't need anyone saying anything irreverent in her presence."

"Uh, well..." The lab tech cleared his throat. "That's not going to be a problem. Ms. Hartford left."

Sergio recoiled, pressing his phone to his ear. "What?"

"Yeah," Max said. "She overheard someone talking about Teodoro's body being found, and she bolted. Said if we wanted anything else from her, to get a warrant. I guess she's worried we'll try to pin Teodoro's death on her daughter."

"Great." Sergio scowled. "What moron did she overhear talking about that?"

"Uh... She overheard you, sir."

Stifling a groan, Sergio lowered the phone and squeezed his eyes shut.

* * * * *

"Hey, guy." Avarie held her hands out at her sides, balancing as she stepped from rock to rock toward Sergio. "Whatcha thinking?" She eased herself onto the rock next to him.

The detective shrugged. "Just kinda... compiling."

"Well, this is a good place for that," Avarie said. "It's pretty. Although it's a little hot. And the seating is very uncomfortable. And the dead guy ruins the ambiance."

The Sea Pass tugged on its tether, its stern side scraping against the rocks.

"Chief Clemmons called me. Apparently, Kerri Milner posted a video of me from when I was chasing down that maintenance guy at the fair, and it's blowing up. Clemmons wasn't happy. I..." She chuckled. "I told him I was doing my job and keeping the Romain case out of the headlines."

Sergio peered over his shoulder at her. "Did he buy it?"

"Maybe. We'll know if I'm told not to report for work on Monday."

"Yeah." The detective gazed out over the dark water. "There's a lot of that going around."

"Carly's getting promoted to Sergeant." Avarie lowered her voice. "He told me they're going to hold a press conference to announce it, and he wants me to write something up."

Sergio nodded. "Well, good—and it's about time, too. She earned it, after being Acting Sergeant under that scumbag Lieutenant Davis for so long. She's probably out celebrating." He sighed, shaking his head. "You know, I like the chief a lot, but he coulda acted on that clown Davis a lot sooner."

"I think Chief Clemmons likes you a lot, too. He said I could learn a lot from you."

"He's right about that." Sergio gave her a smile. "But let's see how he feels if I don't solve this case."

"How do you like this Teodoro guy, anyway?" Avarie pursed her lips looking back toward the Romain house. "I hope he choked to death on his dinner. Arrogant bastard killed his wife, then came home, cooked dinner, and went out for a fun little fishing trip? What a freaking psycho."

Sergio cocked his head. "Cooked? I didn't see any signs of cooking. He had yellow rice and roast pork. There weren't any pots or pans in the sink."

"Okay, he's a neat freak and put them in the dishwasher. So what? Or maybe they had a personal chef do the cooking. He's rich enough."

"Detective?" A uniformed officer waved at Sergio from the other side of the limestone railing. "The coroner's here. We're going to bring the body up now."

"Okay, let's do it." Sergio turned to Avarie. "I think you're on to something. Wanna bet he didn't cook?"

She furrowed her brow. "How will we know?"

"Pots and pans in the dishwasher, you win. Carryout bag in the trash, or Tupperware in the fridge with rice and beans in it, I win."

"You're on." She stuck her hand out at him. "What's the bet?"

Sergio stared at her outstretched hand. The smooth skin, almost unblemished; the French manicured nails, polished and shiny.

Teodoro's hands were in the water.

A smile stretched across Avarie's face. "Losing your confidence, old man?"

Sergio stood up, brushing the wet sand from his butt. "No—and don't call me old. It's bad for my ego. The bet is a dollar."

"What!" Avarie said. "That's no bet."

"I don't want to inflict financial damage on a co-worker." He stepped toward the dinghy as several paramedics approached.

"Dinner," Avarie said. "Loser pays and winner picks the restaurant. And when I win, it'll be a very expensive restaurant."

He narrowed his eyes. "And here I thought you were a hot wings and beer girl."

"I am, but not all the time." Avarie's grin grew larger. "I could be out of a job soon. Is it a bet?"

Nodding, the detective extended his arm. "You're on."

They shook hands as the paramedics worked their way over the rocks, nearing the corpse.

Sergio took a deep breath and rubbed his eyes. "Wanna help lift a dead guy in a body bag?"

"I do not." Avarie shook her head, her smile disappearing as her gaze went to the dead man. "In fact, I think I hear the reporters calling for me to give them an update." She slid off her rock and started the climb back toward the staircase.

"Okay," Sergio said. "But don't wander far."

Stopping, Avarie looked back at him. "Why?"

"Because right after I help move this guy…" Sergio hooked a thumb over his shoulder at the corpse. "You and I are checking Teodoro's fridge for yellow rice in a Tupperware container."

* * * * *

The paramedics' second unit engaged a winch motor and lowered a stretcher over the side of the limestone railing. Sergio and the first group hoisted the body bag onto it. As the winch raised the corpse, Sergio climbed over the rocks and went back to the barnacle-covered lower platform of the staircase. He ascended the wet steps and walked to the coroner's van. A stocky woman in a white lab coat scribbled frantically on a clipboard as she sat behind the wheel.

"Evening, Doc," he said.

Doctor Shira Shapiro looked up from her work, her ice-blue eyes peering at him from behind her reading glasses.

"Sergio." She frowned, tucking her well-chewed pencil into the black hair covering her ear. "I should have known you're responsible for dragging me out here. Nobody else would have the nerve to request an emergency autopsy in the middle of the night."

"Hey, we just asked for the best coroner the city of Tampa has, and they summoned you." The detective opened the doctor's door for her. "Get a look at the body yet?"

"No." She dropped her clipboard onto the seat next to her and picked up another one, sighing as she swung her legs out of the vehicle. "I was knee-deep in hosting a party at the morgue. Or as we call it, catching up on reports. What's the story?"

"Dead guy in a boat," Sergio said. "Victim's hands were soaking in the water, and his face was scraped up." He shoved his hands in his pockets, peering at her. "I need a time of death, ASAP."

"Of course you do." Doctor Shapiro shook her head. "When do you ever not *need* everything ASAP?" She tucked the clipboard under her arm and walked toward the stretcher with the body bag on it, Sergio by her side.

"How fast can you do it?" he asked. "Can you check the liver temperature here, on site?"

"I can, but why would I?" Shapiro glared at him. "What's the rush? You late for a date?"

Sergio stopped walking and put his hand on her arm, lowering his voice. "Shira, the victim in the boat appears to be Teodoro Romain. He was our best chance of locating his wife, who disappeared from the fairgrounds this morning. She's..." He glanced over both shoulders. "She's the niece of Chief Clemmons, Doc—Gabriella Romain. The more I know about our dead boater, the faster I might be able to find Gabriella."

The doctor scrunched up her face. "I get the feeling you're not telling me everything, but okay. I'll have it for you in a few minutes. Where will you be?"

"In the kitchen, checking the contents of the refrigerator. And I'll need a rush on the tox screen, too, please Doc."

"Well, why wouldn't you?" She turned toward the stretcher, walking away while she pulled out her clipboard. "It's not like I have other cases. Anything else? Want me to wash your car while you're out?"

Sergio grinned. "Would you?"

The doctor faced him, scowling.

He held his hands up. "Just the time of death, please. And the tox screen—for now. Thanks! I owe you one."

"Again with this 'I owe you one' nonsense. You can show your appreciation at the holidays with a nice gift." She put her hand on her hip. "Like you didn't do last year, you schmuck."

The detective frowned. "I... got you a nice bottle of wine."

"Oy, but it wasn't kosher." She wagged a finger at him. "I ended up giving it to the *shicksa* next door."

"Kosher wine? There is such a thing?" He put a hand on the back of his neck. "Well, it's the thought that counts, right?"

She nodded. "And just what were you thinking, *bubbeleh*?"

"I... was thinking I'd spend twice as much on you this year, but I'd also check the Wine Spectator website first, so I get an acceptable vintage for my very good friend who does so many favors for me."

"Uh-huh." She turned back to the stretcher again. "Goodbye, Sergio."

"Thanks, Doc." Smiling, he walked backwards for a few steps until he was sure the coroner was finished with him, then trotted across the lawn toward the front door of the Romain residence.

* * * * *

Carly sat on her living room couch, her computer on her lap, open to the latest Romain case file update.

And her thoughts were a million miles away.

He deserves to know. Sergio has a child on the way. He should know that.

And then what? The next time he has to make a split-second decision, he hesitates because he thinks about her? He changes his ways? Hesitating in the wrong situation can get you killed faster than anything else.

She squirmed on the couch, putting a hand to her abdomen.

Or he doesn't change his ways. Then, he goes into another warehouse and ends up dead anyway.

She shook her head.

I shouldn't tell him. I should keep my mouth shut and let everyone think it's Kyle's from our moment after dinner. Everyone would believe that, and it would be the easiest on the family. The boys, Kyle...

Everyone but me.

Unless I tell Kyle that the new baby isn't from our recent night together. Then, the strain between us grows, and the divorce gets worse, and the boys are confused and hurt—on top of being fearful about what the cancer is doing to me.

No, that's not the way.

Groaning, the detective grabbed a throw pillow and curled up around it.

And if I let everyone believe Kyle is the father, then Sergio would be crushed. Every time I saw Sergio, he'd think I had cheated on him, and I'd know I had lied to him—that every day, all the time, I was perpetuating a lie. How is that right?

If we managed to get past that, there'd be a sweet little girl who called him Uncle—and was actually his child.

What would the next woman in his life think about him having a child? When he decides to settle down, it would only complicate things for him and his future family. He wouldn't want that. But is that my decision to make?

She put her hands to her forehead, sitting up and staring across the empty living room, to the staircase that led to her children's rooms upstairs.

He'd want to know the child was his. He deserves to know that a child of his blood is running around out there, and he'd want a relationship with her. He loves kids, so he'd love her—and I'd be taking that away from him.

How can that be the right thing? It isn't fair. If someone took my knowledge of my children away from me, I'd go bonkers. But I'd do that to him?

Exhaling sharply, Carly collapsed back onto the couch and put the pillow over her eyes.

No matter what happens, someone gets hurt or their life is potentially ruined.

What am I going to do?

* * * * *

Sergio inspected the plastic containers in Teodoro's refrigerator. Copious amounts of yellow rice and roast pork were clearly visible inside the opaque canisters with their colorful lids. Stepping away, he opened cabinet drawers until he located one with flatware and took out a fork, raking it over the rice on the dinner table. It was hard and dry. Same with the pork.

"He didn't cook this." Sergio frowned. "At least, not today."

Sighing, Avarie crossed her arms and leaned against the kitchen room wall. "I guess dinner's on me. Remember, I'm on a budget."

"Check this out." He walked to the wall calendar hanging next to her, and leaned in close, reading the appointments. "The upcoming days are filled. Tuesday, five-thirty, Doctor Freeman. Wednesday, seven A.M., Mike from Terrace Builders. The whole calendar's filled with appointments, meetings with contractors..." He looked at Avarie. "Why would you write all this down and hang it on your wall? Most people keep their appointments on their computers." He turned back to the checkerboard of scheduled boxes. Doctor Freeman was a regular weekly appointment for the rest of the month.

Psychiatrist? Marriage counselor?

Gabriella didn't look pregnant in the video, but even if she was, weekly appointments with an obstetrician don't usually start until the eighth month or so...

She hadn't known Teodoro that long. Was Gabriella pregnant by another guy and Teodoro found out? That might explain him calling her all those names.

And the fighting.

It's certainly been the motive for a murder in other cases...

The smooth, cursive handwriting with wide, round lettering had probably been written by Gabriella. The handwriting with sharper edges—which was much less legible—probably belonged to Teodoro. Numerous dates on the calendar had been filled in for the next few weeks, sometimes several in a day.

Sergio shook his head. "Only my mom writes stuff on a calendar this way."

"Why does your mom do it?" Avarie said.

He shrugged, his eyes scanning the appointments for the month of May. "Habit, probably. And so my sister and I know what's up when I go over there. My mom sure never looks at it. Her calendar's almost always on the wrong month when I show up."

"So, your mom does it for you and your sister."

"Yeah, I guess so." The detective stood up. "But we aren't over there enough for it to matter. And the Romains aren't as old as my mom. So the question is, why do they do it?"

He lifted the current page to see the next month, June. It was blank. So was July.

The detective rubbed his jaw.

Well, we're still in early May. Maybe they haven't gotten too booked up for the rest of the summer yet.

Avarie stepped out of the kitchen and into the living room, peering up at the portrait of Gabriella over the fireplace. "What do you think of this portrait?"

He released the pages of the calendar, letting them fall back into place. "Well, like you said—it's not my style." Sergio walked across the thick white rug, staring up at Gabriella's oil-painted image. "But it's pretty, and Gabriella's pretty in it."

"Did you see that rock on her finger?" Avarie pointed to the ruby-colored ring decorating Gabriella's hand. "You don't paint that into a portrait unless it's significant. It's upstairs, on her dresser. There's probably a sentimental attachment or it's a family heirloom or something."

"I did see it," Sergio said. "Also not my style. But it's big. Probably has a lot of value. Wonder what the V stands for. Vance? Teodoro's middle name?"

"Oh, gross. He forced her to wear it like a cattle brand? And then he commissioned a portrait and put it in there, where she'd have to look up and see it every night... what a..." She shook her head, grimacing. "Cruel. That's what it is. Teodoro was a cruel man."

The detective nodded. "Why do you think it was Teodoro who commissioned the portrait?"

"It's of *her*." Avarie folded her arms across her chest. "People don't commission oil portraits of themselves unless they're a gilded age business tycoon. This was more like... like a possession. Like he was saying, 'Look what I have.' Just like with this big house and his fancy nightclub. He's saying, 'Look at me, look at my money, look at this beautiful woman I now have...' And then he killed her. It's twisted."

Sighing, Sergio slipped his hands into his pockets and stared at the rug. "It sure looks that way. I hate to go back to the chief with a story like that, but he must have suspected." He glanced up at Avarie. "What about the fighting? The neighbors heard it."

"Yeah," she said. "Because the windows and doors were open. A violent thug goes and takes his rage out on—"

"This is the hottest summer we've had in years," Sergio said. "It's still ninety degrees at ten P.M. You were on that balcony upstairs. It's an oven out there." He glanced around the living room, pointing at the tall windows. "Having all these big windows open in this heat? In a house like this?" He shook his head. "No way. And it was freezing in here when we walked in the front door. The Romains like a cool household."

Harriman came into the living room, his phone ringing on his hip. He grabbed it and held it to his cheek. "Officer Mark Harriman here. Yes?" Harriman glanced at Sergio. "Oh, sorry Doc. He lost his phone this morning. I can give him a message if you'd like."

He stood silent for a moment, nodding. Then his face fell.

"I'll give him the message," Harriman said. "Thank you, Doctor Shapiro." He lowered the phone. "Looks like Teodoro's off the hook for Gabriella's murder. He has an alibi."

Avarie turned to him. "What? How?"

"Because..." Harriman sighed. "Gabriella died at approximately ten thirty this morning, and

Doctor Shapiro estimates Teodoro's time of death to be eight AM. Maybe as early as seven, but no later than nine."

Avarie's jaw dropped. "He... was already dead when she was murdered."

Groaning, Sergio put a hand to his forehead. "That's a pretty good alibi."

CHAPTER 30

Sergio put his hands on his hips and paced back and forth across the Romain living room. "Let's start over. We have a missing woman at the fairgrounds, so we check the stage at the expo hall. Someone smuggled the body out. Do we have a final report from the canine units?"

"Not yet." Harriman shook his head. "But we should know something soon. I'll call them." He lifted his phone.

"Okay." Sergio continued pacing and took a deep breath. "Meanwhile, the phone records and a random tourist's video place the husband at the scene. Gabriella's messages suggest Teodoro killed her, but he was murdered before he got the chance."

Avarie cocked her head. "Murdered? Do we know that for sure?"

"Pretty much," Sergio said. "Nobody lays in a boat, foaming at the mouth, for no reason. So... Teodoro didn't kill his wife. Who did?"

"Is it possible that *she* killed *him*?" Avarie asked.

"Maybe." Sergio shrugged. "We don't have her body yet. Until we do, it's technically possible Gabriella's still walking around."

"What?" Harriman scowled. "After losing all that blood? Come on. You don't believe that."

The detective wheeled around, pointing at his friend. "I believe what the evidence shows. And it doesn't show a dead body for Gabriella Romain."

"Doesn't it?" Harriman glared at Sergio. "Unless she's a zombie, she's cold and stiff somewhere. We just don't know where. Probably in an abandoned trash cart in some dark corner of the fairgrounds." He softened his tone. "Look, I know you don't like delivering bad news to relatives of the deceased. Nobody does. But at some point—"

"No." Sergio shook his head. "We don't have a body, so we can't confirm Gabriella's dead."

"Sergio—"

"That's the end of the conversation!" He frowned, taking a deep breath, and holding his hands out. He lowered his head. "I... I'm not saying she's alive, Mark. We're operating as though she's dead because that makes the most sense. But we go where the evidence leads—wherever it leads."

Avarie shifted her weight from one foot to the other. "Well, then... Is it possible that Teodoro killed her and then died? I mean, that food on the dining room table's dry as sand. Maybe it wasn't dinner. Maybe it was breakfast."

"Nope," Sergio said. "The coroner's report says Teodoro died before Gabriella even disappeared." He ran his hands through his hair. "We've checked the house. We've checked the fairgrounds stage…"

"I have a call into the Tampa Yacht Club harbor master," Max said. "The dinghy's registration number shows it was purchased there."

Sergio looked at Harriman. "Who's checking the nightclub Teodoro bought? The old Cuban Cigar Club?"

"Nobody right now," Harriman said. "I had Krantz and Mulhauser assigned to go check it out after we secured the scene here, but Mulhauser went home sick with some kind of bug."

"Krantz?" Sergio asked.

"Still working here." Harriman held his phone away from his face and checked the screen. A text message appeared. He pursed his lips. "And… the chief just pulled back our extra uniformed officers."

"When?" Sergio frowned. "He didn't tell me that."

"Just now. By text." Sighing, Harriman held the screen out to Sergio. "He says we're spread too thin in other areas. Probably doesn't want it to look like his niece is getting special treatment."

Sergio nodded. "Especially when she is. Okay, I'll go check the club myself." He pulled his car keys from his pocket. "I know some people down there. Maybe they know something."

"Christina Padrón?" Harriman asked.

"Among others." The detective headed for the exit.

"Okay. I'll stay on here and give you updates. Looks like it's gonna be a long night."

"*Another* long night." Sergio stopped, turning back to his friend and extending a hand. "Thanks, Mark."

Nodding, Harriman shook hands. "It's tough being in charge. I get it."

Avarie followed Sergio outside as he walked toward his vehicle. "Don't you think you should take a break and get some rest? You're pushing too hard."

He shook his head, walking past the patrol cars. "I'm not pushing hard enough. If it was your mother or your sister, you wouldn't sleep. You wouldn't appreciate it if the cop in charge begged off for a nap."

"It's the middle of the night."

"Perfect. That's when the clubs are busiest." He pressed the key fob, unlocking his car.

"Okay, then." Avarie opened the passenger door. "I'm coming with you."

"What?" He peered over the roof at her. "That's not…"

"I'm coming," she said. "I can't do my job if I'm not where the action is. And something tells me you'll be where the action is."

"Okay, sure." He slid behind the steering wheel. "Just… don't tackle anybody. These club owners tend to play rough."

Sergio maneuvered his car away from the Romain residence and onto the interstate that would take him to Ybor City, a subsection of Tampa known for its nightclubs, night life, and the occasional bawdy parade. The area had a rich and colorful history, not unlike New Orleans' French Quarter. Tourists visiting Ybor were as likely to encounter a roving rooster as they were a drag queen or a drug dealer, but as long as they stayed within a block or two of Seventh Avenue, they were usually safe until the wee hours of the night.

The detective squeezed his eyes shut and then opened them wide, blinking hard several times.

Avarie frowned at him as he did.

"I'm fine," Sergio said. "I've pulled all-nighters before, you know."

"You're a crappy driver when you're fully awake." She faced the windshield. "Maybe I should drive."

He glanced at her. "Do you know how to get to Ybor City from here?"

"No." She held up her phone. "This probably does, though."

Nodding, he made a gentle lane change. "We'll be there in five minutes. I can stay awake that long, so you get to remain a passenger."

"Just enough time for me to update my life insurance. Try to stay on the road this time. My mom expects me to take care of her in her old age."

Sergio exited the highway and cruised down one of Tampa's old, brick-paved streets. A few blocks away, the bright lights of Ybor City threw a white haze over the dark rooftops.

He propped an elbow on the door and rubbed his chin stubble. "Teodoro was dead two hours before Gabriella disappeared. He obviously didn't kill her. So who did?"

"That's the million-dollar question, isn't it?" Avarie said. "You think someone at the nightclub will know something?"

Sergio smiled. "I'd almost bet my badge on it."

"Who?" She turned to him, tucking a leg under herself and resting her hands on her shin. "I've waited tables before. Bartenders and servers mostly deal in gossip. Who's working in a club that would know that sort of thing?"

"Some people are just wired to be in the know." He guided the car across the bumpy brick pavers and into an empty parking spot. "My contact at the club is one of those people."

* * * * *

Music blared from the Cuban Cigar Club, its marquee announcing the long-awaited re-opening of its famed Los Amantes theater. Purple neon rimmed each tall window of the ancient building, with small spotlights swirling from its rooftop and from the sidewalk in front of the venue. Posters in Spanish showed curvy, mocha-skinned dancers wearing skimpy outfits and long feather boas, under the headline of Christina Padrón and Her Lavender Ladies.

The club's massive bouncer let them in without paying a cover, lifting the velvet rope as they approached. "It's almost time for last call, *señor*. Have a good night." He chuckled as Avarie passed. "You, too, ma'am."

The main hallway of the club was a mix of half-drunk patrons, holding up the walls as they attempted to secure romantic companionship for the rest of the late night, and well-dressed men who were mostly speaking Spanish to one another. To the left, the crowded Los Amantes theater showcased the curvaceous, scantily-clad dancers, performing a sexy and suggestive song and dance routine to the delight of the packed male audience.

The music rose to a fanfare, and the crowd burst into applause. The dancers sauntered offstage behind a thick purple curtain.

Sergio took Avarie's hand and pushed through the wall of people in the theater. "Stay with me." He shouted to be heard over the noise. "I can't afford to lose you in here."

"Why?" She looked around, her eyes wide. "Is it not safe? Why did the guy at the door laugh when I came in?"

"It's safe," he said. "But guys who've been drinking can get a little crazy this time of night. You're probably the only blonde in this whole club—and maybe the only girl—so that's gonna draw some attention. We're trying to stay under the radar."

"I know how to deal with a drunk guy."

"I'm sure you do. But in this place, there's a lot of—"

"Sir G!" A curvy African-American with hair piled high approached them, hips swinging through a skin-tight purple sequined dress that rode high on the thigh. Arms, wrapped in elbow-length purple gloves, enveloped the detective. "Honey! You are still as fine as you were in high school." The dancer released Sergio and looked him up and down. "You look absolutely yummy tonight. If you ever get an itch to walk on the wild side, you have my number."

Sergio smiled. "Well, Chrissy, I'll admit you're better-looking than some of the girls I've taken home, but I'll have to pass. Besides, I'm Catholic."

The performer wagged a finger. "Honey, I've been under the robes of a randy priest or two—and a few of their bosses!"

"Ha. No." Sergio chuckled, looking down. "I just meant if my mom found out, she might run to church to pray for me and never come out again."

Chrissy nodded. "Your momma always was a bit old-fashioned. But if she locked herself away in a church twenty-four-seven, that would be the end of fried shrimp on Wednesdays, and we can't allow that." The dancer looked at Avarie, smiling. "And who is your exceptionally gorgeous lady friend?"

Avarie blushed.

"Avarie Fox," Sergio said, "meet my friend Christopher Perez—professionally known as Christina Padrón."

Chrissy extended a hand to Avarie. "Mucho gusto." The performer's hand enveloped Avarie's. "Avarie Fox? Or foxy Avarie?"

The PR rep's mouth hung open. "Wow, you're a… I mean, you are really beautiful. In that dress, I'd have never guessed that you're really a…"

"It's okay, baby. It may be a man's world, but a girl's gotta do what she's gotta do—and a dancer's gotta dance. So I tuck up my equipment and shoehorn myself into this dress." Chrissy looked at Sergio. "Are you here for the show? I'm on next."

"Got a minute to talk first?" Sergio asked. "I need some info on the club's new owner."

The dancer frowned, glancing over both shoulders. "Gossiping publicly so early on in his tenure isn't the best idea. Meet me in the alley after my show."

"You got it." Sergio nodded. "Thanks."

"Carlos." Chrissy waved at a handsome, muscular server. "A table for my friends. Up front, where I can fawn over the two of them."

"No, no, no." Sergio waved a hand. "In the back, please, Carlos." He grinned at Chrissy. "I've seen your act before. I can't afford to end up on stage tonight."

Sighing, Crissy stuck out a lip in an exaggerated pout. "Okay. Put them in the back, honey."

Carlos nodded. "You got it, *querida*." His accent was thick with Cuban-American flavor. He glanced at Sergio. "Come with me, please, *señor*."

Carlos plucked a small, round table from a dark doorway and carried it through the packed house to the back of the room. Another well-built male server brought two chairs.

As Avarie and Sergio sat down, the house lights dimmed and the emcee walked to the microphone at the center of the stage.

The Cuban Cigar Club's drag show in its Los Amantes theater was a series of semi-interactive acts. The slender, slinky male dancers, with their femme fatale hairstyles and pushup dresses, sang and danced several numbers, routinely hauling an unsuspecting member of the audience on stage as part of the grand finale. Sometimes the unwitting participant was placed in a chair at the center of the stage and treated to bawdy lap dances; occasionally he was prompted to join a kick line. More often than not, at some point the dance troupe members enticed him to remove his shirt as they ran their hands over his chest and made suggestive comments into their microphones—to the delight of the crowd.

The best participants seemed to be those that were least aware of what Christina Padrón and Her Lavender Ladies did in their act. They selected the straightest-looking man in the room, or the whitest, and hauled him on stage to have their way with him as his friends laughed and cheered.

The Lavender Ladies had headlined the Cuban Cigar Club for a decade, only ceasing performances when the club shut down a few years ago. Chrissy took the show on the road, and when Teodoro Romain's new money came in, the Lavender Ladies were back in business locally.

As the crowd applauded the entrance of Chrissy's purple-dressed dancers, a handsome server stopped at Sergio and Avarie's table. He placed two cocktail napkins on the small, circular surface and handed Sergio a drink menu. "What would you folks like to drink?"

On stage, Chrissy Padrón belted out a pop song in Spanish.

The Lavender Ladies all dressed alike—in skin-tight purple dresses—and so did the Cuban Cigar Club's wait staff. Each server in the theater was an attractive young man, with dark hair and dark eyes, dressed in crisp black pants and a starched black shirt that barely restrained their bulging muscles.

Sergio leaned back in his chair, stifling a yawn as he set the beverage placard face-down on the table. "Cuban coffee, for me, please—and maybe a couple of guava *pasteles*, if you still have any."

"Very good, sir." The waiter peered at Avarie. "And for you, ma'am?"

"Uh… coffee, too, I guess." Avarie glanced toward the crowded hallway. "Is there a ladies' room?"

The muscular server smiled. As he walked away, he broke into a giggle.

Avarie frowned. "I'm starting to not like this place."

Sergio rubbed his eyes with one hand and patted Avarie's arm with the other. "It's just their way." He nodded toward the crowded theater. "They like you, trust me."

She scrunched her face up. "How can you tell?"

"Because you're the prettiest girl here. They're acting that way because they're jealous—in a good way."

"Me?" She sat upright, glancing at him out of the corner of her eye. "I'm the prettiest girl here?"

He nodded. "Without a doubt."

She beamed at him, then slowly turned her chin up and narrowed her eyes. "Hold on. Are you saying that's what *they* think, or is that what *you* think? Or…" She looked around. "Wait, am I the only girl in here?"

A smile tugging at the corners of his mouth, Sergio focused his attention on the stage. "Let's watch the show."

CHAPTER 31

The narrow, brick-paved passage behind the Cuban Cigar Club was clean, by back alley standards. A large dumpster overflowed with discarded food and trash; stacks of wooden crates lined the rear wall. A steel drum labeled "recycled cooking oil" gave off the aroma of French fries.

The steel exit door slammed shut behind Sergio as he guided Avarie into the alley. Bright streetlights illuminated the tight quarters.

"That was quite a show." Avarie shook her head. "And those pastries—oh, my gosh. They were so good. I wish I could have gotten another one, but our waiter wouldn't look at me."

Sergio chuckled. "That's because you were signaling to the wrong waiter. It's an easy mistake since they all dress alike and have dark hair. Our guy was the one with the little mustache."

"As opposed to the big mustaches on all the other ones?" She shrugged. "They should wear nametags or something so people can tell them apart. And how about those dancers? It's hard to believe they're guys. Some of them were really pretty. And they had great bodies."

Sergio sucked in a deep breath of the hot night air. "I guess that's the allure of this place, I don't know. Los Amantes has been a Tampa fixture for as long as I can remember."

The high-pitched, tinkling noise of a rolling wine bottle echoed over the brick street. Avarie turned to the sound. In the distance, a man wearing a t-shirt and flip flops staggered toward the street corner, a green Bordeaux bottle slowly bounced over the ancient surface of the alleyway.

She turned back to Sergio, pushing a lock of hair from her cheek. "So, how do you and Chrissy know each other? Do you come here a lot?"

Smiling, the detective shook his head. "We went to high school together."

"That must have been interesting." She grinned. "My imagination is reeling."

The door opened, and Chrissy stepped out, now dressed in tight capri jeans and a cropped t-shirt, but still just as slinky and alluring as the performer had been on stage. "Hey, baby. Let's talk fast." Chrissy walked toward Sergio, smiling. "I have a new admirer waiting in my dressing room, and he wants to take me to Thirsty Turtle—any chance you'd care to join us?"

Sergio held his hands up. "I can't go to an after-hours bottle club right now. I'm still working."

"So am I," Chrissy said, "but there's always time for some fun." The performer turned to Avarie. "Has Sir G gotten around to telling you how we met?"

Avarie grinned. "He was just about to, I think. But maybe not. He seems a bit reluctant to divulge much on that point."

Chrissy glanced at the detective. "Yeah. He would. Then I shall do the honors. It was the first day of high school—"

"It wasn't the first day," Sergio said.

"Who's telling this story?" Chrissy frowned, lifting his chin. "You had your chance."

Avarie looked at Sergio. "Don't be rude. Let your friend speak."

Holding his hands up again, the detective nodded and took a few steps away.

"Anyway..." The dancer clasped his hands in front of himself. "My dad took a new job in the middle of my first year of high school, so I had to transfer schools. I was somewhat flamboyant in those days—as you might imagine—and a couple of very mean, very sexually closed-minded boys backed me into a corner in the hallway after lunch. They were going to explain with their fists what they thought about my choice of clothing and mannerisms, when your man Sergio got in their way."

Avarie smiled at Sergio. "You beat them up?"

"Oh, no." He chuckled. "I got the crap kicked out of me."

"But he saved me." Chrissy beamed, placing a hand on his chest. "He told them to leave me alone, and so two of the teenage miscreants grabbed Sergio's arms and the third deviant punched him in the gut until he couldn't stand up anymore. After a dozen punches, they dropped him to the floor in a heap."

"It wasn't a dozen." Sergio shook his head. "It was more like three."

Chrissy waved a hand. "In my version, it was a dozen. So, they dropped him. But he got back up, and he told them again to piss off and leave the new kid alone."

"Oh, no." Avarie faked a gasp.

"Oh, yes." The performer walked into the alleyway, holding his hands away from his sides. "So, they came back for round two. And they hammered him again. And this time, when they were done working his midsection, they slammed him down on the ground. But he got back up again." Chrissy glanced at Sergio. "And he told them to piss off once more. So they came back again. He kept getting knocked down, but he kept getting back up. Those adolescent antagonists lit into Sergio four or five times, but he wouldn't stay down. My man pulled himself up after each round of attacks, clinging to the hallway lockers and just staring down those big teenage terrors. And he could barely breathe, but he managed to stay upright. The leader of the pack looked at Sergio and said, 'Haven't you had enough?' and Sir G says, 'Nope. You're gonna have to kill me.' Well, those boys didn't have anything to say to that. They didn't say a word. And my man is holding his abdomen, pointing at them, saying. 'Okay. I took your best shots, and I'm still here. That proves I'm tougher than you. Now it's my turn to swing.' He took one step, and they started backing away. Sergio says, "Yeah, that's what I thought. But I'm gonna be here tomorrow, and the day after that, and the day after that, so you need to know—if I ever catch one of you picking on someone again, I'll be the one doing the hitting, and you *won't* get up. Understand?' He was a sight to see that day."

"Wow." Avarie's mouth hung open. She looked at Sergio. "They just walked away?"

The detective shrugged. "I think their arms finally got tired from punching me."

"Quite the hero." Avarie smiled. "In a roundabout way."

Sergio slid his hands into his pockets and looked away. "The baseball coach said, if any of his players got in a fight at school, they were off the team." He glanced at Avarie. "So I didn't fight. Coach didn't say anything about getting beat up."

"He saved me that day," Chrissy said. "Nobody bothered me from then on. Sergio could barely move at baseball tryouts that afternoon. There were scouts there that day, too, so helping me probably ending up costing him a scholarship." He walked to Sergio and put his hand on the detective's shoulder. "Sir G was a chivalrous, young macho stud, an athlete on the baseball team, with all the pretty schoolgirls getting googley-eyed over him, but he invited a swishy little ol' black boy like me over to his mama's house for fried shrimp that night."

"Well…" Sergio shrugged. "She always makes too much food."

"Modest." Chrissy gazed at Avarie. "That's your man. He hasn't changed one bit." He patted Sergio on the back. "A knight in shining armor, still watching out for the weaker folk and pulling all the pretty girls—darn it. And speaking of dinner at your mother's house, how are your mother and sister these days? I haven't seen Mina in ages."

"They're good," Sergio said. "How's the boys in the band?"

"Bah. I think these younger kids are soft." The dancer crossed his arms under his surgically-enhanced cleavage. "Back in the day, we used to tuck and roll, put on a show, flirt with the audience to sell drinks…" He shook his head. "These new boys want to be on stage and then be on social media. They're building a following, but they're not selling drinks and that's bad for business." He glanced at Sergio. "But you didn't come here to talk about that. What's up?"

The detective looked up and down the alley, lowering his voice. "What can you tell me about the new owner?"

"Mr. Romain?" Chrissy shrugged, placing a hand to his throat. "Honey, all I can tell you is, he is one fine looking man. I hope he's the type of owner that likes to do a lot of hands-on management, if you know what I mean. I could stand a face-to-face review."

Wincing, Sergio cocked his head. "You'll have to hold off on that until they get new management. Teodoro's dead."

Chrissy gasped. "What!"

"Found the body at his house," Sergio said. "Coroner says he died this morning."

"How terrible." The dancer placed his hands over his eyes and lowered his head. "Oh, what is going on with this world?"

"I think it smells like Miami." Sergio glanced at the club performer. "What do you think?"

Chrissy took a deep breath and looked down the alleyway. His eyes glimmered in the streetlight, welling with tears. "Well, there's been a lot of out-of-towners coming by lately. Tough-looking boys, like the ones that run *Calle Ocho* down in Miami, and all speaking Spanish."

"Meeting with Teodoro?" Sergio asked.

Chrissy nodded.

"Anyone you'd recognize if you saw them again?"

"Maybe." The dancer sniffled, wiping his eyes. "Those guys are scary. Hard, mean... There's some in every club. If a place makes money, some tough guy comes knocking, looking to take over the booze supplier's contract or set up a drug dealing franchise in the bathroom. If that works, and the club does well enough, they've got their toe in the door." He sighed, blinking hard and looking up at the sky. "Eventually, their boss comes by and tries to push the owner out. Maybe that's what happened. Teodoro didn't look like a hard man, though. I mean, he looked tough enough, don't get me wrong, but he... had a kind side." Chrissy shook his head. "In the nightclub business, a lot of owners mess with their employees—boys or girls. Takin' them in the back room, trying to take advantage of a dancer or some poor waitress who's desperate to keep her job. Teodoro wasn't that way." He looked at his friend. "Like I said, he had a kind side to him."

"You could see that?" Sergio asked. "I thought you didn't know much about him."

"I... have that kind of eye."

"Yeah, I'll bet you do." Nodding, Sergio looked around again. The alley was clear, but it wouldn't stay that way. Last call meant squaring up the bar bill and paying the table checks. Once that was done, the club would empty out and the alley might get some foot traffic.

The detective peered at the dancer, the same delicate kid from high school who never stood a chance if things went bad. Chrissy was scared. New management might mean difficult times ahead.

But that was down the road. Right now, there was a murder to solve.

"Chrissy, was Teodoro soft enough to get himself killed?"

The detective's friend shrugged. "Maybe."

"Okay." Sighing, Sergio clamped his hand onto Chrissy's shoulder and gave him a squeeze. "Keep an eye open for me. Next time those guys come around, give me a call."

The dancer chuckled, wiping his eye with the back of his hand. "I always keep an eye open for you. It just never does me any good."

* * * * *

In the car, Sergio gripped the wheel, his eyes on the road and his head throbbing.

Who killed Gabriella and Teodoro? The same person? Different people?

Where is Gabriella's body? And why did her mom take off when she learned Teodoro was murdered?

How did that dinghy get across from the Romain residence and just stay there like that?

He clenched his teeth, drumming the wheel.

Is some Miami muscle behind all this, getting rid of the Romains so a new boss can set up shop?

Why don't I have a blood test from the fairground crime scene yet? Why haven't I heard from the canine units? What's going on with the—

"Hey," Avarie said. "You seem stressed. Maybe we should call it a night."

He glanced at her in the passenger seat. "I... can't." He shook his head. "I..."

"People understand." Her voice was soft and soothing. "Even grieving parents. They don't expect you to work yourself into a coma. You have to loosen up. At some stage, you reach a point of diminishing returns."

He nodded but kept his eyes on the road.

Avarie pursed her lips. Turning to the window, she kneaded her fingers. "Your friend was nice. Chrissy."

"Yeah," Sergio said. "He's a good guy in a tough business."

"What was it he called you?" She faced forward, peering at him out of the corner of her eye. "Sirgy? Or is it surge-y?"

"He said Sir G."

"Sirgy sounds better." Avarie smiled. "It's cute. And sexy."

"It's not." Sergio wiped his hand across his forehead. "But I'm too tired to argue with you."

"Sirgy. Yeah, I like that. I think I'm gonna call you that from now on."

"Please don't."

She tucked a leg under herself and leaned over, whispering in his ear. "Sirgy."

The detective winced, letting out a long, slow groan. "Just… don't call me that around the guys."

CHAPTER 32

Scrolling on her phone, Avarie glanced out of the car toward the passing street signs. The darkness of pre-dawn still colored the sky. She sat up and turned to Sergio, the glow of the dashboard illuminating him. "What are we doing, driving back to the Romain house?"

"I have to." He blinked hard and shook his head. His eyes were dry, his head nearing the fogginess that an extended late night brings when it turns to early morning. "The building blocks just aren't lining up. There's gotta be something at the house that we overlooked. I don't know what, but either at the house, the fairgrounds… I know there's something I missed."

Avarie crossed her arms over her chest and scowled. "Well, there were fifty cops at the Romain residence. I'm sure one of them saw whatever it was you think you missed. This forty-eight-hour deadline seems kinda arbitrary, and it's impeding your ability to—"

"You don't get it." Sergio gripped the wheel and pulled the car to the side of the road. Taking a deep breath, he let it out slowly and looked her in the eyes. "Avarie, it's not like all the clues are just sitting there like fresh-grown daisies for two days, waiting for someone to come along and pick them." The lack of sleep now added a raspy tint to his words. "All leads are strongest right when a murder happens—the killer is there and the crime scene is untarnished. But it's not like everything stays pristine until forty-seven hours and fifty-nine minutes later, and then suddenly, poof, all the leads turn to crap." He held his hands out, glancing at the ceiling. "It's… it's like you said—diminishing returns. With each passing hour, the crime scene gets weaker. The likelihood of finding Gabriella dropped a lot by yesterday afternoon. Right now, the killer could be obfuscating the location where he took her. A rookie cop could walk through some important trace evidence."

Sighing, he lowered his voice, the dark clouds of defeat gathering on his mental horizon. "The probability of success keeps dropping exponentially. By hour forty-seven, it's almost nonexistent. That's what I'm up against. In a little while, half of those arbitrary forty-eight hours will be gone—and more than half of my chances to find Gabriella go away with it." His gaze went to the floor. "I've delivered the bad news to a mother before. It's part of the job. But… if I can keep going even when it feels like I've got nothing left, because doing that might avert the worst outcome..." He looked up, shrugging. "Then I have to do it, don't I?"

"I guess you do." Avarie's voice was low and even, her eyes fixed on his. She reached out and took his hand. "And I'm with you. I am. But if you're so tired that you're missing things, then... are you really doing any good?"

Grimacing, the detective leaned forward and rested his forehead on the steering wheel. He gently squeezed Avarie's fingers, the softness of her skin creating a stark contrast to the reality of the situation they were investigating. A warm, delicate human touch versus the cold body of Teodoro Romain, laying in the morgue, and the lifeless corpse of his beautiful young wife, alone and abandoned like trash somewhere.

And what if the deaths don't stop there?

"Am I doing any good right now? I don't know." Sergio sat upright, peering at her. "After we revisit the Romain house, I'll peel off for four or five hours and get some sleep."

Avarie pursed her lips. "I won't tell you how to run your investigation. If you can keep going, then keep going. I can, but I didn't stay up all night working on a drug bust yesterday—and you did." Leaning forward, she gazed into his eyes. "What's it been now, about two straight days without sleep for you? More? You've gotta be running on fumes."

"Yeah. You're right." Sergio looked down, nodding. "I'll take a break and get some sleep after we check back in at the house, okay?"

"You know how to do this job," Avarie said softly. "I'm just trying to help."

* * * * *

Sergio parked on the street adjacent to the Romain house. The number of squad cars had diminished substantially since he left, but he knew Mark Harriman would still be inside.

In the glimmer of the coming dawn, Sergio spied several uniformed officers standing at a cooler full of water bottles and ice. As Avarie walked across the lawn toward the main entry, Sergio walked up to the cooler. He grabbed two bottles of water, opened them, and squirted one into his eyes while he poured the other over his head.

"Whoa!" The icy shock was like a cold slap in the face, sending a jolt through his insides and raising goosebumps along his spine. Heart racing, he groaned, continuing until both bottles were empty.

Officer Correy smiled, pointing toward the main house. "There's a pool shower just off the main terrace, Sergio. That might be easier than a sidewalk bath."

"Holy cow!" Sergio gasped. "Whew! That's better than two cups of Cuban coffee." The detective shook his head, sending water droplets in all directions. Winking, he tossed the empty bottles at the cooler, water stains dotting the top of his shirt. "Back to work."

Revived for the moment, he jogged across the lawn in the brimming daybreak, toward Avarie and the Romain front door.

"Ms. Fox," Officer Correy said, "is that some sort of Public Relations exercise?"

Avarie hunched her shoulders as Sergio went past. "I don't know what that was, but I don't wanna try it."

Inside the mansion, Sergio located Mark Harriman in the living room.

His face was grim.

"Welcome back," Harriman said. The bags under his eyes reflected the early hour. "I've got some bad news."

Sergio put his hands on his hips, exhaling slowly. "That figures." He wiped a trickle of water from his forehead as he looked up at the portrait over the fireplace—Gabriella, standing on her balcony, her back to the viewer; her short, strapless blue dress a warm light against the blackness gathering on the horizon.

I know how she feels, looking out and only seeing dark clouds coming.

"Okay." He glanced at his friend. "Let's hear it."

Nodding, Harriman opened his notepad. Avarie stepped into the living room and stood next to Sergio. On the terrace, Max held his computer in one hand and pushed open the sliding glass doors with the other, coming inside as the first rays of golden sunlight illuminated the pool house behind him.

"We finally heard back from the canine units at the fairgrounds." Harriman flipped through the pages of his pad. "Their dogs didn't find Gabriella Romain. Those rolling trash carts all have a county government ID number on them, so the dog handlers waited to report until they had checked each one. Nothing." He looked at Sergio. "Gabriella Romain didn't go out of the expo hall in a trash cart. According to the dog handlers, she wasn't dead when she left the scene, either."

Sergio cocked his head. "How's that?"

"Cadaver dogs pick up on changes that happen to a body. They can tell if the scent they're tracking has changed from living to dead—within something like two minutes of death occurring. So, if Gabriella left the expo hall, she left some other way. But she didn't die on the scene."

"Oh, she left all right." Sergio paced back and forth across the living room. "The dogs didn't find her inside the expo hall when they looked."

Max cleared his throat. "So, sir…" Lifting his computer, the lab tech peered at his screen. "I checked every hospital, emergency room, walk in clinic, veterinarian… dentist's office, you name it. None of them has reported a woman with knife wounds within eight hours of Gabriella's disappearance." He looked at Sergio. "The CSIs said that based on the blood loss at the scene, Gabriella suffered major wounds and would have bled out within minutes, possibly staying alive for an hour if she had immediate medical attention—which she didn't."

Sergio nodded, not slowing down his pacing. "So our trail is cold as far as Gabriella's body—again." He glanced at Max. "What else? The look on your face tells me there's more."

Max nodded. "Gabriella's blood at the scene had deteriorated."

"Yeah? So?" The detective stopped and stared at him. "Blood starts deteriorating as soon as it leaves the body."

"Not like this, apparently," Max said. "Doctor Shapiro indicated that Gabriella's blood had deteriorated substantially. Like it had been there for days."

Sergio winced. "Because it was hot that day? Or…"

"She didn't give a reason." The lab tech's eyes returned to his screen. "She just said the blood had deteriorated substantially, far in excess of what would normally be expected. She's running further tests. The good news is, the dinghy checks out to a yacht, with Teodoro Vance Romain listed as the owner."

"A yacht, huh?" Sergio leaned over, peering at Max's computer. "That's interesting."

The email from the harbor master at the Tampa Yacht Club listed the dingy as "Sea Pass," Florida registration FL 15239 RR, and the yacht as "Sea Boss," registration number FL 15238 RR.

Max tapped the screen. "The sequential registration numbers mean Teodoro registered both vessels the same day, probably because they were purchased on the same day."

Sergio nodded, reading on. The harbor master had attached a copy of the sales tax receipt, showing the purchase was for a seventy-five-foot Sunseeker yacht, built in 2017, that sold for three million dollars just a few weeks ago.

Exhaling, the detective's gaze drifted toward the ceiling.

Boats and dead bodies go together when mobsters are involved. They think they can use a big body of water like a dumping ground, never considering that the remains might bloat and float, get spotted by a fishing boat or the Coast Guard, and land the not-so-smart mobsters in prison.

We need to get those cadaver dogs down to Teodoro's yacht.

"According to the harbor master…" Max turned his computer back around. "The yacht has only ever left the marina a few times. The prior owner was some old guy who liked to throw parties on it with Tampa's big wigs and a bunch of pretty models he'd hire, and the harbor master thinks Teodoro may have been at one of those parties. Maybe that's where he met Gabriella."

"We've requested a warrant," Harriman said. "I'll have some officers serve it to the harbor master so we can inspect the yacht for evidence."

"Good. Yeah, that's real good." Sergio paced the floor again, running his hand across his beard stubble. "But the blood at the scene—it was far in excess. Far in excess." He stopped once more, looking at Max. "Doctor Shapiro said the blood at the fairgrounds crime scene was deteriorated *far in excess* of what would be expected. Why? The understage area was a little warmer than the audience section of the expo hall, but that's no big deal. It wasn't as hot there as it was outside. Why'd the blood show as deteriorated like that?"

Max looked back at Sergio, his mouth hanging open.

"No, no. I'm not asking *you*, Max." Sergio waved a hand. "I'm thinking out loud, asking... the world, I guess. But that's bothering me. It's out of place, so it could be important." He turned to Avarie, pointing at her, then Harriman, then Max. "All of you, think about anything that struck you as odd when you first saw it. Big or small, anything that seemed out of place when you first noticed it. A detail, a comment, a... a stage prop, anything—aside from a dead woman we can't find and the husband who killed her after he was already dead."

"Zombies?" Max grinned.

Sergio scowled at him.

"Sorry." He lowered his face back to the computer screen. "I also checked the beneficiaries on Gabriella's insurance. Teodoro took out a five-million-dollar policy on her a week ago, but Gabriella's mother and sister are listed as the beneficiaries. And get this. He also took out a matching policy on himself—same amount, same beneficiaries."

"Gabriella's mother and sister are the beneficiaries to both policies?" Sergio asked.

"Yes, sir. Maybe that's why the mom left in such a hurry after opening Gabriella's phone and using the videos to point us at him."

"You think?" Avarie asked.

"Could be." Sergio nodded, rubbing his chin. "Murderers come in all shapes and sizes, just like PR reps."

"They'd be in for a big payday, too." Avarie moved next to Sergio and crossed her arms over her chest. "Except it's obviously murder in both cases.

Gabriella was stabbed and Teodoro was poisoned. The insurance company won't have to pay out."

"Hey." Sergio gently elbowed her. "Don't get ahead of the class."

"Doctor Shapiro said Teodoro was poisoned with strychnine." Max looked up from his screen. "It's a rat poison. The rice and pork were loaded with it. Sent him into painful spasms and eventually shut down his beathing."

Massaging his neck, Sergio began pacing again. "That explains the foaming at the mouth. The question is, who did it?"

"Gabriella, right?" Avarie held her hands out. "She certainly had the motive and the opportunity. He's threatening her. The cops have been called out to their house half a dozen times by neighbors for domestic disputes. She's had enough. Maybe she cooked his favorite dinner, and they both ate—and then she laced the leftovers with poison and took off, figuring he'd probably eat some of it the next day and go belly up. She plans to meet her sister at the expo hall and get away—remember the stuff in her bag? That big wad of cash and the passport? She wanted to say goodbye to her sister before she ran. But Teodoro found her first—probably because he was tracking her phone—so she had to change her plans on the fly." Avarie hunched over, holding her hands up in front of her. "She can see his phone, too—so when he called, Gabriella saw he was right there in the expo hall with her. There's no way he'd kill her in front of all those witnesses, but as soon as she leaves the hall, she's history—and she knows it." Smiling, the PR rep tapped the side of her head. "Our girl is smart, though. Instead of encountering Teodoro, she volunteers to go onstage so she can sneak out of the expo hall from underneath during the Six Sisters trick. But he got under the stage during the smoke bombs and..." Avarie sighed, her shoulders sagging. "And he killed her.

She looked around. The men were silent, their eyes focused on her.

Swallowing hard, she shook her head. "He went home, fixed himself a little snack from last night's leftovers, and died. Her plan almost worked. A few more minutes and she'd have gotten away."

The corners of her eyes glimmered in the morning light, Avarie's gaze going toward the floor. "How terrible. Can you imagine?" She looked up at Sergio. "You see your *killer*—your new husband, the man you were in love with, the man you just married... and he's forty feet away, but he's not smiling at you the way he used to, the way that made your heart skip a beat. He's there to hurt you, like he said he would. You suddenly realize, *he is here to kill me*." She exhaled sharply, her face turning to a grimace. "And you're only safe because you're surrounded by complete strangers. That as soon as the show ends, he's coming for you. He brought a reputation with him from Miami. He knows how to make people go away—in ugly, awful ways."

She raised her eyes, as if watching Gabriella at the expo hall, staring at her killer a few feet away.

"You see him," Avarie said, "see the rage in his eyes... Gabriella must have been scared out of her mind. She knows that it's all over, that her death is minutes away. She must have been terrified."

Crossing her arms, she put a hand to her mouth and walked toward the sliding glass doors, staring out at the morning sky.

Harriman took a deep breath and shook his head. "Except he didn't come home and eat. He was already dead. And how did he get from the fairgrounds and into the dinghy?"

"He must've been out of his mind." Max nodded. "Thinking he could kill her like that? I mean, even if he waited until she left the expo hall, a lot of people saw her there. He might as well have killed her in front of all those witnesses. It's almost the same thing."

Slipping his hands into his pockets, Sergio stared up at the portrait of Gabriella.

"Wait!" Avarie gasped. She turned around and faced them. "He *did* do it in front of all the witnesses." Putting her hands to her forehead, the PR rep walked back toward the team, a wide grin spread across her face. "That's exactly what happened!"

Sergio narrowed his eyes and gave her a half smile. "Ms. Fox, is there something you'd like to share with the group?"

"Yep." She nodded, pounding her fist into her hand. "But first we need to watch the video of the magic show again."

CHAPTER 33

Max groaned as he placed his computer on the edge of the coffee table. "I've seen these videos five times."

"Six times for me," Harriman said.

"Well…" Sergio stepped behind Max, peering at the screen. "We're all watching them again."

The others huddled around, staring at Max's computer as he clicked various files. "I can bring them all up, but the images are going to be pretty small."

The lab tech opened file after file, reducing each video to a small square and lining them up in rows. After he moved the ninth one into place on the screen, he turned to Avarie.

"Which camera view do you want to focus on, Ms. Fox?"

"Start with when Gabriella goes into the cage," Avarie said. "Then, go backwards until she first comes on screen."

Nodding, Max clicked a video file and slid his cursor across the progress bar until Gabriella set her bag down and stepped into the sixth cage on the expo hall stage.

"Perfect," Avarie said. "Now, can you set all the other videos to that moment and have them play in reverse?"

"Yep." Nodding, Max opened his video editing software, lining up the files. He enlarged each one, synchronized it via the time and date stamp to the moment when Gabriella entered the cage, then went on to the next file. When all the videos were showing the same time, Max clicked the video mixer display and let it fill the screen. The camera angles were arranged on the top of the screen in a row, with a big dark area below them.

Max pointed to the blank space. "Whichever camera angle I select will appear here. So just tell me which one you want."

"Start with Gabriella," Avarie said, "and play them all backwards—at the same time, if you can."

Max clicked the keyboard a few times. "I can do that." With one more click, the videos simultaneously played their data, in reverse.

On screen Gabriella moved backwards *out* of the cage instead of walking into it, then bent down and picked *up* her large blue and white bag instead of setting it down, which is what she had actually done. She held it with both hands, then walked backwards away from the cage.

The recordings continued playing, everything on screen moving in reverse.

"Okay," Max said. "Now she'll be with Sinclair O'Lair's camera for a bit, then she'll be visible on the camera viewing the left side of the audience."

"Good." Avarie leaned forward. "Make Sinclair O'Lair big while she's talking to him, then when she moves out of frame for that camera, make the audience view big."

Max enlarged the different screens as directed. Gabriella chatted with O'Lair briefly, then walked backwards out of view. She reappeared on one of the audience cameras as she and Scarlet walked in reverse to Gabriella's seat in the crowd.

Avarie bit her lip. "Okay, we're almost to the important part."

"Do you want me to stop the playback?" Max asked.

"Not yet." She put her hands on his shoulders, leaning closer to the little screen. "The two women talk, and then I want to watch Scarlet go over to Gabriella. When she first sees her volunteering to come up on stage."

The video continued in reverse. After a moment, Scarlet walked away backwards, and Gabriella sat down. The camera moved along with the magician's assistant until Gabriella was out of frame.

"There." Avarie pointed to the screen, smiling. "Did you see it?"

Harriman blinked hard, shaking his head. "I didn't see anything." He leaned closer. "What am I looking for?"

"I'm not sure I saw..." Max shrugged. "I mean, maybe I saw something. But maybe not."

Narrowing his eyes, Sergio crossed his arms over his chest. His focus remained on the screen.

"Play it forward," Avarie said.

On the computer, Scarlet walked through the cheering crowd, the hopeful volunteers waving their arms as she passed. Gabriella rose up from her seat as the scantily-clad magician's assistant approached, smiling and clutching her bag as she turned to face her.

"Stop," Avarie said. She looked at the men. "See?"

Harriman shrugged, his mouth hanging open. Max stared at the screen.

"Gabriella just stands up." Avarie pointed to the computer. "All the other people who wanted to be volunteers, they're waving and shouting. Not Gabriella. She stands up like she already knew she was going onstage."

"She doesn't look scared," Max said. "Check out her expression. She doesn't look like a woman who just saw her insane mobster husband. She doesn't even look apprehensive about going onstage in front of hundreds of people."

Avarie nodded. "Another thing—she did a little infomercial before she joined the act. Play that, when Scarlet goes over to her and Sinclair O'Lair does his mini interview."

Max slid the mixer guide to the point where O'Lair was onstage with Gabriella and Scarlet. The magician mentioned reading about the beautiful young socialite, and the recent purchase by her husband of the Cuban Cigar Club.

Gabriella leaned in close to Scarlet's microphone, acknowledging the club—and continuing. "My husband also purchased the Fleerman House, which is on the national register of historic places, with plans to restore it to its original elegance. Presidents have stayed at Fleerman House."

"Look at her," Max said. "Gabriella's laughing and smiling. She's not nervous at all."

Avarie nodded. "She's not nervous because she knew she was going on stage before she ever set foot in the expo hall."

DAN ALATORRE

CHAPTER 34

Avarie narrowed her eyes and faced Sergio. "If Gabriella knew she was going onstage before she was ever selected, your trampy friend Scarlet knew, too. We need to go back and talk to her."

Sergio raked his fingers across his jaw.

"I gotta admit…" Max leaned back from the screen, sighing. "They sure seemed to act like they wanted everyone to know it was Tampa socialite Gabriella Romain going up on that stage."

"No." Avarie shook her head. "Only Gabriella acted that way. Sinclair O'Lair's reaction seems genuine enough—unless he's an award-winning actor."

"He's not." Sergio huffed. "Not based on the lump of Jell-O that was crying on the floor of the backstage office yesterday." He glanced at Avarie.

"What about Scarlet? What do you think of her reaction?"

The PR rep narrowed her eyes. "Oh, she knew. She had to know. Those volunteers don't just get to—"

"Let's not go from memory." Sergio held up a finger. "Look at the screen and tell me what you see."

Max leaned over and pressed a button on his computer, playing the recording again.

Scarlet barely glanced in Gabriella's direction before walking over to her.

"It's like they're old friends," Avarie said.

"Well…" Sergio studied the screen. "They may not be friends, but Scarlet doesn't look anywhere else. She goes straight to Gabriella." He straightened up and took out his phone. "Let's get a little supervisory input." Swiping a finger across the screen, he entered a number and pressed send.

"Hey." Carly's voice didn't sound groggy, like she'd just woken up; she seemed alert and wide awake already, despite the relatively early hour. "Calling to give me an update on the case?"

"Sorry, Sergeant, I'm not. But—"

"Uh…" Carly lowered her voice. "I'm not officially a sergeant yet."

"Maybe not." Sergio grinned. "But referring to you as Unofficial Sergeant would be too awkward. You feeling any better, or is that bug still trying to take you down?"

"Let's just say I'm not going to be worth much to the investigation today. Maybe for a few days."

"What? No!" He made an exaggerated grimace. "I can't run the case by myself."

"Of course you can."

"Well, yeah. But it won't be as fun."

Carly sighed. "Sergio..."

"Okay, okay," he said. "Get some rest. I'll just bug you a hundred times a day, like old times."

"Oof. A hundred?"

"Yeah, you're right." Sergio shrugged. "Two hundred is probably more likely."

"I was thinking ten calls might be a lot. I'm not really feeling my best at the moment."

"Okay, we'll start at ten and go from there—and this one doesn't count. I'm gonna put you on speaker so the whole team can hear us." He set his phone on the coffee table and pressed the speakerphone button. "I want your thoughts on something. You're up to speed on the case notes. We think there might be a connection between Gabriella Romain and Scarlet Salazar. Max is going to send you a video of all the camera angles from the expo hall, playing simultaneously. It appears as if Scarlet walks over to Gabriella without even looking at her."

"Okay," Carly said. "Send it, Max."

The lab tech hit a button on his keyboard.

"Okay... I'm receiving a file..." A rustling noise came over the line. "Max, do I just open it and click play?"

The lab tech nodded. "Yes, ma'am."

The rest of the team stood in silence, all eyes on Sergio's phone.

"It's playing," Carly said. "And... Scarlet goes right up to her. That's a good catch, whoever noticed it."

Sergio nudged Avarie. The PR rep beamed.

"So." Avarie leaned toward the phone and raised her voice a little. "The volunteer thing was pre-arranged. Which probably means Gabriella's sister knew all about it, too. She said they were supposed to meet for lunch. That's pretty convenient."

Max nodded again. "And maybe their mother knew, too." He glanced at Sergio. "Should we split up and re-interview them all right now?"

"Definitely." Sergio turned away, pacing back and forth in the living room. "Mark, your guy met the sister first—Crisalyn Hartford. You go to talk to her." He glanced at his lab tech. "Max, the mother seemed to like you, so you'll interview her."

"Joanna Clemmons-Hartford." Max nodded. "Got it."

"And both of you..." Sergio pointed at both men. "Be sure to mention the insurance policies—and assess their reactions. I'll re-interview Scarlet."

Avarie rolled her eyes. "Of course you will."

"There's a reason I want to be the one to talk to her," Sergio said.

Scowling, Avarie lowered her voice. "I bet there is. Two very big reasons."

The detective sighed. "Okay, why don't you come with me? You can make sure everything stays kosher." He tapped his phone screen to check the time, then peered at Harriman and Max. "At this hour, they're all probably at home—so don't call them first. I want them caught off guard, at their home, surrounded by their security blankets when we..."

"Wait," Carly said. "Sergio, it'd be better if one person did all three interviews. I agree that we need to show up unannounced. That's key. But having one person do all three interviews would let us ask them all the same questions—and see who gives a different answer." She exhaled into the phone. "We just need to put some sort of a... a *smokescreen* in place, so they don't call each other the moment you leave. We have to make sure they can't coordinate their stories."

Sergio put one hand on his hip and pointed into the air with the other. "What if we do a leave-behind?" His finger drew on an imaginary chalk board. "I take Max with me when I do the interview with the mother, and then I have him stay with her while I go talk to the sister. And then I do the sister's interview with Mark, and have him stay there while I go to Scarlet."

"Hmm. I don't know," Carly said. "How does that keep them from warning the next person after you leave? Max can't forbid Ms. Hartford from using her phone, and he can't drag out the interview with her for hours while you drive across town and visit the next person."

"Yeah." Sergio rubbed his chin stubble. "Yeah, I take your point." The dryness returned to his eyes. He inhaled deeply and paced around the room again.

"What if…" Avarie looked at Sergio. "What if we just say Teodoro was listening on their calls, somehow?"

Frowning, Sergio held a hand up. "At this point, we have to assume they all know Teodoro is dead."

"Okay…" She grabbed a lock of her hair and twisted it between her fingertips. "What if we could say we discovered that Teodoro had set up a phone tapping system on their phones, and that as part of our investigation we now have to look at all that? Our people would still be listening in, temporarily, until we can get the thing disabled…"

Max shrugged, looking over at Sergio. "In an organized crime case, the standard operating procedure would be to tap the main suspect's phone—in this case, Teodoro's—and then get warrants to tap the phones of other people he talked to, as a way to build a case. The family members don't know we didn't do that."

Sergio grinned. "They don't, do they? We can say their phones were swept up in the tapping, so we're kinda doing them a public service by letting them know. Say it like a joke—Hey, be careful who you call because you're still being recorded."

"Just telling them will be enough," Carly said. "If any of them played a role in setting up the meeting between Gabriella and Scarlet, they're smart enough to connect the dots when we tell them their phones are being listened to by the police. They won't be making any calls."

Sergio clapped his hands together. "Okay, so that's the plan. Thanks, Carly."

"You're welcome. Keep me posted."

"Will do." Sergio hit the red button on his phone, ending the call. He turned to Harriman, running a hand over his beard stubble. "Mark, I have another idea, too—something I want to try. You stay here on site, and while I'm doing the interviews, you bring in as many uniformed officers as you can. What I want to do, is—"

"Can't," Mark said. "The chief already cut the number of personnel he wants out here."

The detective shrugged. "Then call Carly back and have her make the request for additional people. Clemmons is unlikely to turn down the decision of his top cop when he's in the middle of promoting her." He pointed at the large windows at the front of the residence, and to the street beyond. "With the extra people, I want you to line the perimeter of the house." His outstretched hand moved along the tree line and the sidewalks that bordered the Romain estate. "Make it look like we're guarding Fort Knox in here. And let it slip to our friends in the media that a valuable piece of evidence has gone missing." He glanced at his friend. "Actually... no. Leak to the reporters that we've learned of a valuable piece of evidence that *exists* which could link the killer to the bodies." A smile crept across Sergio's face. "Or better yet, don't say it's the killer. Say it's a key person of interest. The evidence links *a key person of interest* to the events at the fairgrounds, and to the body discovered here at the residence."

Harriman made a note on his pad. "I'm not sure I like this. What's the valuable piece of evidence?"

"Don't get into that." Waving his hand, Sergio moved toward the entry door of the estate. "In fact, tell them you're calling people to the boat and the club and fairgrounds to look for it. And any of Teodoro's leased warehouses. All that." He pulled his car keys from his pocket, twirling them around his index finger. "But set up a wall of cops around this house. Nobody gets in or out without my express authorization. I'll take the hit with Clemmons."

The detective headed for the door. Avarie followed him.

"But…" Harriman shook his head. "We don't have anything like that. Why bluff? I mean, we have some good leads to follow."

"It's hot out here, so make sure the additional people have plenty of water." Sergio stopped at the front door, his hand on the knob. "In fact, bring in a bunch of nice catering trays from Kojack's and Publix. Ribs, potato salad, soft drinks, Gatorade—the works."

Harriman winced. "You've gone without sleep for too long, friend. Any officers who get reassigned to this location will talk to their friends and say they're just sitting around eating ribs. That's gonna get back to Clemmons, and he'll shut it all down. After he removes your head from your body."

"Yep." Sergio chuckled. "He'll probably even come here himself to shut down my irresponsible spending, especially if I stop taking his calls. So be prepared for that."

Sighing, Harriman looked away. "Oh, I see. You're trying to get fired."

"Let's hope not." Sergio glanced toward the street. "But later, when Clemmons orders all the extra cops to leave the premises, just do it. Have everybody leave at once—and make sure our media friends see it happen."

"You're rolling some big dice, you know."

Sergio opened the front door and stepped back, allowing Avarie to exit the home first. Hot air washed over him like he'd entered a low-grade steam bath. "It'll be okay," the detective said. "I think."

"Terrific." Harriman winced. The tall palm trees edging the estate swayed in the distance, the bright morning sunlight sparkling as it bounced off the waters of the bay. "When do I get to know what you're up to?"

The detective walked outside. "As soon as I figure it out myself."

DAN ALATORRE

CHAPTER 35

A<small>VARIE BUCKLED HER SEAT BELT.</small> "Is it okay to admit I don't know what's going on?" She looked at Sergio as he started the car. "You're the big detective, and I understand why we're redoing the three interviews, but why are you bringing a bunch of cops to the Romain residence on Sunday morning when they're just going to get sent home Sunday afternoon—if they're allowed to come at all?"

Sergio blinked hard and lifted a hand to rub his dry eyes. "Big detective, huh?" He pulled his car onto Bayshore Boulevard. The early morning traffic barely consisted of more than half a dozen cars. "I'm just turning up the pressure on three people who seem to know more than they're telling me. At least one will crack, or let something slip. That's all I need."

"Again, that's the interview part." Avarie held her hands out. "What about the part where I'm an accessory to intentionally pissing off the Chief of Police?" She glared at Sergio. "I don't need to lose my consulting gig."

"Yeah, that would be bad." He grinned. "Try to make sure that doesn't happen."

Sighing, Avarie turned to the window. The well-kept estates of Bayshore Boulevard went by, turning to an interstate on-ramp and then an eventual exit. The houses outside her window became progressively smaller and less unique. Cookie-cutter homes on treeless lots, with postage-stamp sized yards. The only difference between one house and the next was the shade of beige they had been painted.

Pulling into a subdivision, Sergio looked around. The street and sidewalks were clean, and most of the lawns had been mowed recently. In one of the small yards, a Big Wheel tricycle rested near the front porch. At another house, a Frisbee was visible on the corner of the roof. Despite the heat, the grass around the little homes looked thick and green.

He maneuvered his car to the side of the road and stopped.

"What's up?" Avarie sat upright in her seat. "Which house are we going to?"

"Crisalyn lives on this street." Sergio rested his hand on the steering wheel, pointing at an almost-yellow house with white trim at the end of the road. "So, we'll start with her. The mother's house is about a block away."

Avarie nodded. "What's the plan for the interview?"

Opening his phone, the detective scrolled through his texts, searching for the one from Max that would confirm Crisalyn's exact address. "I'm going to ask shocking questions and see who acts shocked."

Cringing, Avarie looked out at the houses. "That's kinda harsh for a family that may have just had a loved one die."

"It is." He narrowed his eyes, gazing at Crisalyn's home. "But one of them is lying, and the number one reason people lie in a murder investigation is because they were in on it."

"Whoa." Avarie looked at him. "You think Ms. Hartford or Crisalyn were involved in killing Gabriella? Why, to collect the insurance money?"

Sergio shrugged. "Look, I don't like the idea of a mom killing her own daughter, but it does happen." He leaned forward, resting his forearms on the wheel. "I can understand a mom protecting her daughter, though. Even if her other daughter was responsible for the murder."

"What!" The PR rep's jaw dropped. "The sister? Mrs. Hartford is protecting Crisalyn? From what? Crisalyn didn't do anything."

"Maybe she did," Sergio said. "Crisalyn could have killed Gabriella for the insurance money. She and her mother were both listed as beneficiaries."

"I just…" Exhaling, Avarie shook her head. "My brain wants to think better of sisters and mothers."

"Yeah?" He turned to her, sliding his elbow onto the back of the seat. "I know a young woman who jumped through a lot of hoops to get rid of the heir to the throne in her rich Tampa family. So keep that in mind."

Avarie shook her head. "*You* don't think Crisalyn killed Gabriella. I don't believe that."

"You think you know me that well, huh?" A smile tugged at the corners of Sergio's mouth. "You can tell what I'm thinking?"

"I'm getting there." The PR rep wagged a finger at the detective. "You don't think Crisalyn killed her sister. You've hardly mentioned her until now."

He let the smile spread across his face. It was hard not to.

Avarie was right. He didn't think Crisalyn killed her sister. Not really. But until he figured out why the sister would lie, she needed to stay on his radar screen. They all did.

He glanced at the PR rep as she scrolled through her phone.

He liked working with Avarie. She was smart, and she seemed to be trying hard to understand what made him tick. As Carly pointed out, it was a good catch that Avarie had made while re-watching the video recordings, noticing that Gabriella seemed to have already been selected to participate in the magic act before ever being noticed by the performers. That observation opened additional pertinent avenues to investigate, and it demonstrated Avarie's abilities again. On a different investigation, she had suggested intentionally upsetting a suspected psychopath during an intense interview, in the hopes of generating an unhinged reaction—which is exactly what happened. It practically sealed the case.

On their current investigation, Avarie had already put up with a long night of chasing around town, when she easily could have gone home to get some sleep. A lot of other people would have taken a break, especially a PR person. But she didn't. Her *job* didn't require working nonstop around the clock, but the *case* needed it, so she did it. He respected that kind of determination.

But most of all, she was becoming part of the team. Sergio's work seemed easier when Avarie was around, and on more than one occasion she had mentioned looking into getting reinstated as a cop. She picked up on things quickly, like Max, but she was open and honest enough to admit when she didn't understand something. Her ego didn't get in the way of the investigation. She worked hard but didn't hesitate to suggest going to have a beer—or a pitcher—after a long day.

She'd already been helpful on so many cases that he hadn't considered that she was a contract worker in the PR department, and that one day her contract would expire.

"I don't need to lose my consulting gig."

As she sat across from him, her blonde hair framing her face, he let the thought actually sink in.

Avarie could go away one day.

There were so many reasons that shouldn't matter, but it did. And it caused an uneasy feeling in him.

He gazed at her in the soft morning light as she read her phone. He didn't want her to go away.

For work reasons, and for other reasons.

She's a co-worker.

No, she's a contract employee. And you aren't her supervisor anyway, so who cares?

She's too young for you.

But she said she wasn't. And she asked you out. And you had a good time. You always have a good time with her.

You can't keep asking her to be assigned to your cases.

Why not? You always draw the high-profile cases, and she's in charge of making the department look good. Even the chief admits that. So what's the problem?

Simple. It was too soon.

Avarie had come along at the wrong time.

She was beautiful. She was smart and funny. She had a great figure and a face that any man would dream about. She didn't take any crap from Sergio, and she had a sarcastic sense of humor that he enjoyed.

As soon as he left her company, he found himself looking forward to the next time he'd be with her again. There was a comfortableness in Sergio when Avarie was around.

He had been put on waivers by Carly, after getting so close that he let himself fall in love, and the rejection hurt. A lot. His guard was up.

And how is what happened with Carly any fault of Avarie's, exactly?

There could be a future with this woman.

A future. He hadn't considered that for a long time, either. With Carly, there was her sons' never-ending school schedules, plus baseball and soccer and theatrical plays... Coordinating a rare night of "alone time" when Carly's mother took the boys for an overnight visit or when it was Kyle's week with them. And there were her divorce proceedings with Kyle, which, even though they seemed to be getting smoother, had been a near-constant headache for Carly—and therefore, for Sergio.

There was a solid relationship with Carly that had been built over years, but it had gone south after Carly decided to end it, and the wounds were too fresh to just start over with someone new.

At least, that's what he told himself so he didn't have to consider the subject in greater detail.

Because even though the timing sucked, if he had to make a list of all the characteristics he wished a woman would have, Avarie had all of them.

That might have been what scared him the most.

"What are you thinking about?"

Avarie's words brought Sergio out of his thought bubble. Her voice was soft and gentle. "Detective, you look like you're a little boy who got lost in the woods." Avarie's warm blue eyes met his. "Are you thinking about the potential damage you're about to inflict on this poor woman?"

Sergio's breath caught in his throat as he looked at the stunning PR rep.

She means Crisalyn Hartford, not Avarie Fox.

But she's not wrong, either way.

"I, uh..." The detective shrugged, gripping the steering wheel with sweaty palms. "Yeah, I'm thinking about... potential damage—like you said."

"Then just be thoughtful." Avarie looked toward the little house. "If your intentions are good, there's a way to get what you want. Things don't necessarily have to go badly." Slowly, she returned her gaze to him. "Right?"

Taking a deep breath, he nodded. "I guess I might just have to find out."

CHAPTER 36

Doctor Mendez entered the examining room, carrying an open file folder in one hand and a laptop in the other. "Good morning."

"Good morning." Carly squirmed on the examining table cushion. The doctor's office was cold and the examining table was particularly uncomfortable, for some reason, even though she was fully clothed. She managed a smile. "Thank you for seeing me so early—and on a Sunday."

"Oh, of course. We do this all the time." Doctor Mendez sat on a short, round stool, wheeling herself up to the counter and opening Carly's file. "You're in a good situation, all things considered. We caught the cancer early. That means it's still very treatable and the survival rate is very high if we start treatment right away, so today we'll be going over your treatment schedule."

"Um, well..." Carly adjusted the collar of her shirt. Stiffness had settled over her neck and shoulders, down her back, to the base of her spine. "I have a few questions."

"Oh, of course." The doctor set the folder aside and leaned forward. "Please, go right ahead."

"Well, essentially it's just one question." Carly massaged her ice-cold hands. "What happens if we were to delay the start of the treatment for nine months?"

The doctor recoiled, her face turning grim. She nodded slowly and looked at Carly. "Yes, my staff mentioned that you'd had some concerns because you're pregnant." She cleared her throat and sat up straight. "Well, at this early stage, there's no way to know how the cancer could grow, if it grows at all. It's possible that you could go nine months without any substantial health risks."

Carly's shoulders relaxed. She let out a breath.

"But that's not likely. You're already experiencing abdominal pain and nausea, an indication that we don't have nine months to play with. It's my professional opinion that you start treatment immediately and take your best shot at beating the cancer right now."

A knot formed in Carly's stomach. "But I'm pregnant. It's important for me to consider the baby."

The doctor nodded. "I understand. My job is to get rid of the cancer that, left unattended, will very likely spread throughout your lymph nodes and into your bloodstream, and kill you. Now, I know you have a family—a husband and two children..."

"We're separated," Carly said. "But yes, I have a family. Two boys."

Doctor Mendez shook her head, her voice soft. "I'm not here to talk you into anything. This is a decision you have to make. My job is to give you the best professional advice I can, and that advice is to start treatment as soon as possible."

"But then I could lose the baby."

"That's correct," the doctor said. "It would be my suggestion to terminate the pregnancy so we aren't battling additional factors while we try to eradicate the cancer. If you were to start treatment, and were to have a miscarriage, or if the fetus were to pass away as a result of your weakened system, then you would be weaker, too, and less able to fight the cancer. In your situation, trying to keep the baby makes you more vulnerable overall, and delaying treatment would almost certainly put you at an untenable risk."

Carly kneaded her fingers, her gaze searching the walls of the examination room.

"The cancer isn't going to go away on its own," Mendez said. "It's very likely to continue to grow, and then we won't have a lot of choices. It's entirely possible you try to keep the baby and in three months the cancer has caused it to no longer be viable—and drawn you into such a weakened state that you lose the baby outright and succumb to the cancer yourself. That is what you need to consider. As your doctor, my advice is to terminate the pregnancy and start treatment right away." She opened the folder again. "We'd like to have you come in this Wednesday for the initial application of chemotherapy, and then—"

"Do you think the treatment will hurt my baby? I mean, if I decide to keep it—*her*—if I decide to keep her?"

Doctor Mendez lowered the folder and clasped her hands in front of herself, leaning forward. Her voice was low and calm, her eyes sad.

"Yes. I do." The doctor gazed at Carly. "I think starting the treatment will cost you your baby and I believe waiting to start treatment will cost you your life."

Carly slouched on the examination table, the breath going out of her. She lowered her head and put her hands to her face, fighting to not be overwhelmed.

The little girl in the daydream, holding hands with her parents on the beach, now stood alone in a fog, waving at Carly from a distance. "Bye-bye, Mommy, bye-bye."

Her breath caught in her throat, a deep sadness welling up inside her.

Doctor Mendez put her hand on Carly's arm, her voice falling to a whisper. "You're facing a very difficult decision, and there are no good options. I'd like to keep you, the patient in front of me, alive for the children she already has. You do not need to risk your life, and that is what you would be doing if you delay treatment. But it sounds like you've already made up your mind."

Carly shook her head, blinking hard to keep the tears from coming. "I really haven't, no." She sat up and wiped her cheeks with the back of her hand.

"In fact, I hoped that coming here would give me more information to help me decide."

"Well, then…" Doctor Mendez nodded. "Let's at least go over the treatment schedule."

DAN ALATORRE

CHAPTER 37

ACCORDING TO HER FLORIDA DRIVERS LICENSE, the little house at the end of the street was the current residence of Crisalyn Hartford. Sergio and Avarie approached the front door, passing a small sign near the stoop that said Gonzalez Property Management. A video doorbell stared at them from the side of the entry.

Sergio pressed the button and took a step back, holding his hands in front of himself as the electronic door chime alerted the residents to a visitor's presence.

"Remember," Avarie whispered, "she's the daughter of the chief's sister."

"Yeah…" He peered over his shoulder at the PR rep. "And she's the younger sister to Gabriella Romain, our recently-married and now-missing woman who's presumed dead. So what?"

Avarie stood up straight and adjusted the neckline of her blouse. "So, her uncle might fire both of us if we upset his niece. You might wanna keep that in mind during the interview."

As the detective opened his mouth to reply, the sound of a metal latch being unlocked came from the other side of the entry. The door opened an inch, allowing the face of a twenty-something redhead to become visible in the gap.

Her long locks were darker at the root, a deep brown, almost black.

She dyes her hair, probably with an at-home hair coloring kit. And she doesn't do it often enough to keep the color consistent throughout her head because she can't afford to.

The young woman squinted in the bright morning light, her youthful olive skin barely allowing a wrinkle as she scrunched up her face. "Can I help you?"

"Yes, ma'am. I'm Detective Sergio Martin." Sergio gave her a warm smile, the kind he put on when talking to attractive women in bars and clubs. He gestured to his associate. "And this is Avarie Fox. We're with the Tampa Police Department. We'd like to speak with Crisalyn Hartford. Is she here?"

"Crissa? Yeah…" The young woman stifled a yawn. "What's this about?"

Sergio recoiled.

This woman doesn't know that her roommate's sister is missing and could be dead?

Are they not close, or was she never told? If you're Crisalyn Hartford, why would you keep that from her?

His gaze wandered to the woman's hand. A faded dragon logo had been stamped on the back.

A nightclub stamp. Maybe she's more of an overnight guest.

"May we come in?" The detective flashed the smile again.

"Uh, sure." The woman disappeared behind the door as it swung open.

"Aliandra, no." Crisalyn Hartford walked into the tiny living room. Her mussed-up hair and smeared mascara indicated she had been asleep until a moment ago. "My mom said not to talk to the police." She turned to Sergio, scowling. "Not without a warrant."

He peered at her. Baggy pajama bottoms, bare feet, crop-top Henley t-shirt. A hand stamp similar to the other woman's.

What kind of person goes clubbing on the night they found out their sister went missing?

"Crissa," Sergio said. "We're here to help you. To help your sister, if we can. I just have a few questions. It'll only take five minutes."

"No." Crisalyn shook her head, reaching for the door. "I'm sorry, officer. My mom said we're hiring a lawyer and that I shouldn't talk to any police right now."

The door inched shut. Sergio leaned forward. "Ma'am—"

"Can I use your bathroom?" Avarie slipped in front of the detective, pressing her knees together. "It was a super long drive over here and I had a *lot* of coffee." She stretched her lips into an exaggerated grimace, raising her eyebrows as she looked at the roommate. "Please? Would you mind?"

The redhead opened the door, pointing to a short hallway. "It's right there."

"Aliandra!" Crisalyn glared at her.

"What? She needs to pee! Geez." As Avarie disappeared down the hallway, the redhead walked to the couch and plopped down. "Would you rather hose off the front stoop? Get real."

Crisalyn sighed. "Mom said not to talk to the cops."

"Then don't talk to them." The redhead turned to Sergio. "Would you like some coffee, sir? I was just about to make some."

"Aliandra!" Criaslyn's eyes widened. "Stop!"

Sergio nodded to the redhead. "A glass of water would be great, please, if it's not too much trouble. Thank you."

Exhaling sharply, Crisalyn sat down and put her hands to her head as Aliandra got up and went into the small kitchen. She picked up a coffee pot and rinsed it in the kitchen sink.

"Your friend is right." Sergio looked at Crisalyn. "You don't have to talk to me." He gestured to the loveseat. "May I?"

"Sure." Crisalyn shrugged, hanging her head. "You're already having coffee. Why not?"

"Water," Aliandra said, filling the coffee pot.

Sergio sat, leaning forward and resting his elbows on his knees. The fabric of Crisalyn's couch had almost worn through at the corners, and the home's walls were practically devoid of any homemaking decorations. The living room had no

TV, no coffee table or end tables; and the loveseat was a different color from the couch. The room was illuminated by the light from the windows and an end table lamp that sat on the floor.

These ladies don't have any money to speak of. An insurance payout might be considered a big windfall to Crisalyn.

Sergio kept his voice soft and low. Soothing. "I just have one question for you, Crisalyn." He kept his eyes on her, but held onto his question.

She raised her head slowly, her disheveled brown hair falling around her young face.

Aliandra returned with a drinking glass, filled with ice and water. "Here you are, sir."

"Ah, thank you." He beamed at the redhead. "And please, call me Sergio."

A tinge of red appeared in Aliandra's cheeks. "Okay. Sergio." She swayed back and forth. "Are you sure you wouldn't like coffee? It's vanilla French roast, and it's really good."

In the kitchen, the coffee pot gurgled.

"It does smell good." He glanced at Crisalyn. "But I don't want to overstay my welcome."

Crisalyn scowled again. "You're *not* welcome."

"Crissa! Don't be such a witch." Aliandra smiled at the detective. "How do you take it, sir?"

Sergio shrugged. "Oh, black would be just fine, Ali…"

"Aliandra." The redhead's blush deepened.

"Aliandra." He said it musically, his smile widening. "What a beautiful name. Is that Italian?

You look like your family might be of Sicilian descent."

Her jaw dropped. She sat down on the couch next to Crisalyn, leaning forward and smiling. "I am! My grandma was from Sicily. Wow, you must be psychic."

"Well, no," Sergio said. "I'm a detective."

"Oh. Yeah." Aliandra bobbed her head from side to side. "Duh."

Sergio leaned closer to her. "See, it's that wonderful olive skin and those irresistible big eyes. Total giveaway for Sicily." He took a sip of his water, intentionally keeping his gaze on Aliandra for almost too long before he spoke again. "You know, they say the beauty of the Sicilian women is so distracting to the police, it makes them completely unpredictable in interviews."

"Really!" Aliandra put her hand to her mouth, giggling. "Oh, my."

"Oh, gawd." Crisalyn raised her head.

"Or maybe the women are just unpredictable in general." Sergio chuckled. "I forget which."

The redhead laughed, bringing her knees up and falling backward into the couch cushions.

"Okay." Crisalyn sighed. "What's your question?"

Sitting back, Sergio lowered his hand and placed his water glass on the thin carpet. "I have two, actually. First…" He glanced at Aliandra. "I think the coffee's ready."

"What?" She swung her head toward the kitchen. "No, I just put it on."

Sergio winked. "I... kinda need to ask Crissa these questions in private, you know?"

"Oh. Right." Aliandra got up from the couch, nodding. "I'll, uh... I'll just be over here if you need anything." She walked to the kitchen.

Crisalyn lowered her voice, scowling at Sergio again. "Don't call me Crissa."

"Sorry." He crossed his legs. "Is that a nickname your family gave you? Did Gabriella call you that?"

Crisalyn squeezed her eyes shut and shook her head. "Just—what's your question?"

"Okay." Sighing, the detective leaned forward. "First, why would you go out dancing last night? I mean, under the circumstances?"

"That was *her* idea." Crisalyn glanced toward the kitchen. "She said I was acting all down in the dumps and I needed to get out."

"So, she doesn't know about your sister?"

Crisalyn shrugged. "Aliandra's family and my family are old friends. I used to babysit her. She kind of looks up to me. I let her move in to help with the rent, but..."

The detective nodded. "But you kept her in the dark because..."

"I just... I didn't wanna talk about it." She slouched, flipping her hands up at her sides. "Aliandra's a happy spirit. She's innocent. You can see that. It makes her a good roommate. It didn't seem right to... to spoil that."

Sergio chewed his lip, observing the young woman on the couch.

Protective instincts. Or is it an act?

"Anyway," Crisalyn looked at him. "What else?"

"Hmm?" Sergio said.

"What else? You said you had two questions."

He sat back, running his fingers over his chin stubble. "No, I think that's it."

"Really?" Crisalyn smirked, sitting up and sliding her hands down over her thighs. "You came all the way out here to ask me about going dancing? You didn't even know I went out dancing until you got here."

"That's true. But our little visit has answered my other questions." He stood up. "I'll show myself out. Thank you." He stood and waved to Aliandra in the kitchen. "And thank you, Aliandra. It was an absolute pleasure to meet you."

"Oh, you're leaving?" Aliandra stuck out her lower lip. "But... you haven't had your coffee."

"Another time, maybe." He turned to Crisalyn. "Thank you for your hospitality and for seeing me at this early hour. I really do appreciate it." Reaching into his pocket, the detective took out a business card. "If you need to contact me for any reason, just call."

She didn't look up. Sergio slipped the card under her hand.

Avarie appeared in the hallway, walking toward the little living room. "Hey, didn't we need to tell them about... that thing?"

"No." Sergio headed for the door.

Crisalyn looked up. "What thing?"

"Uh, well..." Avarie glanced at Sergio. "There was a situation we thought maybe you oughta be aware of."

"No, we don't." He waved a hand. "We don't need to bother these ladies with that stuff." He nodded to Crisalyn and then to Aliandra. "Goodbye. And again, thank you."

Avarie cocked her head. "But didn't you... In the car, you said—"

"Nope. We're good." He reached over and took the PR rep by the hand. "Let's go. Goodbye, everybody."

Avarie stepped quickly to the exit. "Bye."

"Wait." Aliandra raced to the doorway. "Can I have a card? I mean..." She clasped her hands in front of herself, swaying back and forth as her cheeks reddened again. "I might want to call you."

Sergio grinned. "You're adorable. Here's what I want you to do." He handed her a card. "I'd love it if you'd call me. Then I can introduce you to several nice young police officers who are around your age—and not old enough to be your grandfather." Chuckling, he shook his head and exited the residence. "Sicilian women. Completely unpredictable."

CHAPTER 38

"WHAT HAPPENED IN THERE?" Avarie rushed to catch up to Sergio as he made his way toward his car.

"Change of plans." He pulled out his car keys, squinting in the bright light. The heat of the day had already started, and it was only going to get worse. He glanced at his PR companion. "Thanks for the decoy, by the way. Asking to use the bathroom was smart. They'd have said no if I had done that."

"You're welcome." Avarie frowned. "But as I was standing by the toilet, stalling for what seemed like *hours*, I didn't hear you ask any of the questions we talked about. And what about the phone tapping story? Crisalyn is probably calling her mother right now."

"Yep." Sergio clicked his remote as he reached his sedan. The doors unlocked with a mechanical thump. "And we'll come walking up on good ol' Mom's place in about two minutes."

"Where she won't talk to us—having been warned by her daughter."

"Probably."

The PR rep huffed. "So—why?"

"Because..." Sergio leaned on the roof of his car, lowering his voice. "Who would go dancing in a situation like that? Could you? When your sister had just disappeared?"

Avarie held her hands out. "People grieve in different ways. Crisalyn said her friend made her go out."

"Yeah, she *said* that." He wagged the keys at her. "Doesn't make it true. But if it were you, and you just found out the police thought your sister was dead, could you go dancing that night?"

"No." Avarie pursed her lips, looking at him across the roof of the sedan. "And I'd tell my roommate about it. Women who live together for a while are gonna share stuff."

"Right." He nodded. "And these two have known each other for a long time. So again, the main reason to not cooperate with us is..."

"Ugh!" She threw her hands out at her sides. "Because Crisalyn did it. But I don't think Crisalyn killed her sister. And you don't, either. Do you?"

"Well..." The detective opened his car door. "Get in. On the way to the mother's house, propose a different theory."

"I don't have one," Avarie said. "I'm just saying—"

"No, think about it." He pointed at her with the keys again. "If you were Crisalyn, what would the circumstances have to be before you could act the way she acted just now?"

"Oh, I don't know…" Avarie exhaled slowly, looking down. "Maybe she hated her sister and was happy she's dead."

"Yeah, that would do it. But I didn't get a hate vibe back there, did you?" Sergio cocked his head, keeping his eyes on the PR rep. "Let your mind roam. What possibilities can you come up with?"

Avarie studied the ground, the hot morning breeze pushing her hair onto her cheek. As she tucked it behind her ear, a car drove by, slowing down at the corner and turning, before continuing on its way.

She raised her eyes to his. "We know the sisters had arranged to meet at the fairgrounds. And I don't think they were working against each other…"

The detective nodded, stretching his arms out over the roof of the car. "Think about the evidence we have, and then imagine what scenario would have to transpire for you to behave the way each person is acting—one at a time, not as a group—within the framework of that evidence."

"Do you know?" she asked.

He waved a hand, looking away. "Eh, I've got some pieces of ideas, but I'm pretty much still guessing, just like you. But in an investigation, I want to be open-minded and take input from every informed source. There are no wrong answers until something doesn't fit the evidence. The building blocks either line up or they don't."

Sergio pushed his car door open further and slipped behind the steering wheel, starting the engine. Musty, warm air blasted out from the A/C vents. He pressed the buttons on his armrest to crack the windows and let the built-up heat escape.

Avarie climbed into the passenger seat. When her seat belt was buckled, the detective began the short drive to Ms. Hartford's house, but drove slowly. The air from the vents grew cool with the motion of the vehicle.

"Okay, what about this?" Turning to him, the PR rep brought one leg up and tucked it under herself, leaning forward and clutching her shin with both hands. "The evidence says Teodoro was abusive to Gabriella. Crisalyn doesn't appear outwardly hostile to her sister. What if the two sisters planned to kill Teodoro because he was getting out of control? Maybe he moved from yelling to getting physical."

"It's a possibility." Sergio made a gentle turn, creeping toward the mother's house. "He was poisoned, and that's usually considered a female's method of murder."

"And Teodoro had already gone too far. Gabriella secretly recorded him threatening to kill her—and she believed him, so she took action, and arranged to poison him." Leaning against the door, Avarie pulled a strand of blonde hair from behind her ear and twisted it between her fingers. "But Teodoro's smart. He knows that if he actually does kill his wife, he'll be our main suspect—so he arranges for an associate to do the deed." She looked at Sergio. "Maybe one of those Miami thugs your dancer friend told us about. The ones that came to see

Teodoro at the club. So the wheels are in motion to have Gabriella killed, but the sisters strike first. Gabriella poisons the leftovers, and her sister's ready to help get her out of town, but the thug from Miami arrives at the fairgrounds before they can complete the escape. He manages to take Gabriella out, but this guy has no idea who Crisalyn is, or her involvement, so she gets away."

Sergio glanced at her. "Why wouldn't Crisalyn help us, then? Why lie?"

"Because she knows her sister just got murdered," Avarie said. "And… She's scared. If she talks to us, we might accidentally let something slip to the media about why she was really at the fairgrounds—which would put her sister's killer right on her tail."

Sergio glanced at her. "If Crisalyn's so scared, why did she go out dancing and having a good time?"

"Okay…" Avarie shrugged. "Then, Crisalyn *didn't* like her sister. It's the other way—a sibling rivalry gone bad. She hates Gabriella, her drug-using, semi-prostitute of a sister, who suddenly strikes it rich with a handsome guy from Miami. Crisalyn's super jealous. Her no-good sister suddenly has money, a big house on Bayshore Boulevard, and a fancy yacht at the Tampa Yacht Club, while Crisalyn is struggling to make the monthly rent payments. Then, Gabriella comes to her, and Crisalyn sees a way to help make her disappear. Next thing you know, the hated Gabriella is gone, and the sibling rivalry ends in victory for Crisalyn. She goes out and has a literal victory dance."

The detective made another turn. "That fits the evidence better, but based on that theory, both sisters are on the hook for Teodoro's murder."

"Right. Okay..." Avarie nodded, twisting the hair tighter around her fingers. "Well, they're a close family. Crisalyn tells her mom what's up. So, Ms. Clemmons-Hartford, the sister of the Chief of Police, steps in. She could have laid out a self-defense plea for Gabriella, but she knows that won't work for Crisalyn, so she gets us to focus on how bad a guy Teodoro is, and hopes we don't look any further." Avarie released the twisted strand of hair and let her hands drop to her lap. "Ms. Hartford has to protect her one remaining child from going to prison."

Nodding, Sergio pulled the car to the side of the street. "Lose one daughter, not both." He put the car in park, a block away from Ms. Hartford's house and turned off the engine, peering over his arm at Avarie. "That would explain a lot. Think that's what happened?"

Smiling, the PR rep glanced toward the house. "Why don't we ask good ol' Mom and find out?"

* * * * *

Heat seemed to radiate up from the sidewalks of the tidy little neighborhood. Sweat formed on Sergio's brow as he approached Ms. Hartford's home.

Avarie tugged at the front of her blouse, sending air through it. "Could you have parked farther away?"

"I want good ol' Mom to see us walking up," Sergio said, "so she has time to get nervous."

Avarie glanced at him. "You never explained why you didn't ask Crisalyn any meaningful questions."

"I didn't want to pollute your thinking with any of my theories. I wanted to see what you'd come up with on your own."

The PR rep scrunched her face up. "Really?"

"Sure." He smiled. "You thought up that bathroom stunt all by yourself. Who knows what other good ideas you might come up with?"

"Thanks," she said. "But since you didn't ask Crisalyn any real questions, you can't ask her mother the same questions and see if her answers are different."

Sergio stopped in front of Ms. Hartford's house, a small beige home with white trim and a freshly-cut lawn, nearly identical to her daughter's place—and every other house in the neighborhood.

The detective turned to Avarie. "If you ask three different people the same question, you look for inconsistencies. Whoever gives a different answer from the other two is probably lying. But if you say something to them that isn't true, and they know it's not true but they pretend it is anyway, then you've accomplished almost the same thing." He glanced at the house. "Ms. Hartford is about to tell us a lot by trying to not tell us anything."

Wiping his forehead, he proceeded up the concrete walk to the front entry and rang the bell.

The Tampa Police Chief's sister opened the door almost instantly, dressed in jeans and a t-shirt, shaking her head. "I'm sorry, Detective. This isn't a good time."

"I understand." Sergio nodded. "You're on your way to church—don't worry, I won't make you late. This'll only take two minutes. You'll still get your regular seat."

Ms. Hartford cocked her head. "Excuse me? Church?"

"Yeah." Sergio hooked a thumb over his shoulder. "We just came from your daughter Crissa's house. She mentioned that you're both on your way to the regular Sunday service—that you always get the same seats together, right in front of the altar." He pulled a notepad from his pocket and flipped it open. "Now, we've just received some very incriminating information about a piece of evidence, and I wanted to talk to you about it. I just need two minutes, I promise."

"Uh, well…" Ms. Hartford shifted her weight from one foot to the other, peering over Sergio's shoulder toward her daughter's house. "Yes, we're on our way to church right now, so there's no time, but…" She pursed her lips and wiped her hands across her thighs. "Okay. Two minutes."

"May we come in?" Sergio tugged at his collar. "It's a real oven out here."

Wincing, the homeowner moved back and opened the door for them.

"Thank you." He took a step inside the house, the home's air conditioning a welcome relief from the heat. As Avarie joined him, Sergio glanced around the room. A few pictures of Ms. Hartford's daughters hung on the wall—each girl's individual class picture from their senior year in high school, from the look of it—as well as a few framed family photos.

He turned to Ms. Hartford. "So, there's this one thing that's been bothering me about your daughter's case." The detective slipped his pencil from the notepad's coils. "When I was in her house—well, the house she owned with Teodoro Romain, of course—I couldn't help but notice a few things."

Gabriella's mother clutched her hands together. "What kinds of things?"

"Well, the portrait of your daughter, for one." He stepped into the living room, observing the family photos on display. "You know, that big oil painting hanging over the fireplace, with your daughter looking out over the bay. Gabriella looks beautiful in that portrait. In real life, she had a few blemishes—I mean, on her record, of course. Marijuana, soliciting… but really, other than that…"

Ms. Hartford cleared her throat. "Detective, you said you had some new information."

A picture of a gray-haired man resembling Chief Clemmons was the last framed print. It had a black ribbon over one corner, but the man was more muscular than the chief, with bigger eyes and a more rugged face. Next to it on the wall, an elderly woman stood with her hands on the shoulders of two boys—a young Chief Clemmons and his brother—and the younger version of the man in the ribbon-draped frame, apparently his father. She wore a small ruby brooch on her blouse, with a gold V in the center.

The detective stopped walking and stared at the picture.

Putting a hand to her throat, Ms. Hartford stepped up next to him. "Detective?"

"You know..." He faced her. "We located a ring that matches the brooch in this picture. It was on Gabriella's dresser, behind some picture frames. It'll go into evidence tomorrow morning when we start the investigation back up—the chief is pulling everybody off tonight, so it doesn't look like we're giving his niece special treatment, but everyone will be back tomorrow morning." He turned back to the picture. "Yeah, that beautiful ring will be tied up until the case is resolved... Then, of course, the probate courts'll hold onto it, dragging their feet for a year or so while they settle all the assets of the estate, but eventually it'll be returned to you. Close families should keep their heirlooms, you know? At least now you know where it is."

"Yes." Her voice a whisper, she massaged her throat with trembling fingers. "Uh... Thank you, Detective."

"Oh, yes, ma'am." Sergio stepped away, glancing at his notepad. "So anyway, I was wondering—I mean, what with the brief courtship of your daughter and Teodoro, getting married so quickly after they met and everything..." He turned to her, scratching the back of his head. "Well, I never asked you how the two of them met."

"I don't recall." The lady of the house stared at the wall picture, her attention slowly returning to the detective. "Gabriella just called me one day and said she'd met a man, and that they were getting married."

"Just like that?" He pretended to make a note on his pad. "And when was the last time you spoke to her?"

"That was... uh... I think she..." Ms. Hartford's voice faded, her fingers sliding along the edge of her collar, pinching at the material.

"Ma'am?"

Her head snapped upright, her eyes narrowing. "He threatened her. That's why she called me. It was the day before she disappeared." Ms. Hartford's face grew firm. "She said Teodoro had threatened to kill her. That's why she called. She said she was afraid of him."

Sergio kept his eyes on the notepad. "Did the two of you speak often? You and Gabriella?"

"Not every day, but a few times a week. But we spoke that day, because he threatened her. She was horribly afraid."

"You have a close family." He looked over at her, tapping his pencil on the pad. "I figured that. With Crissa renting a house just a few blocks away, and her roommate being the girl she used to babysit, and going to church together every Sunday... That's a close family. That's nice."

"Yes, we're a... we *were* a close family." She licked her lips and swallowed hard. "Things changed when that criminal from Miami entered my daughter's life."

Pursing his lips, Sergio nodded. He flipped the notepad closed and headed for the door. "Well, I won't take up any more of your time." He pulled a card from his pocket and held it out to her. "If you think of anything that might help us with the case, just call me."

Ms. Hartford took his card with one hand, the fingers of her other hand twisting her collar. "Detective, you said you had some incriminating information you wanted to discuss."

"Uh, well yes, I did." He shrugged, looking back at the picture of Chief Clemmons' mother. "But I don't want to keep you any longer. Thank you for seeing me so early on a Sunday morning."

"Please." She stepped toward him, placing her hand on his forearm, then backed away. "I mean, if it could help the case…"

The detective took a deep breath and let it out slowly. "It was about the ring, ma'am—the one on your daughter's hand in the portrait. But it's probably better if I don't get into all that right now. You'll be late for church."

"My daughter may have been murdered. Church can wait."

"Yeah, but…" He pulled his phone from his pocket and checked the time. "No, I can't get into it right now. I have another interview scheduled and I can't be late for it." He took a step toward the exit. "You'll have to excuse me."

Ms. Hartford followed him. "Detective…"

Sergio stopped and snapped his fingers. "Oh, I *did* forget to tell you something earlier, though. Tampa PD's Drug Crimes unit was wiretapping Teodoro's phones. As part of that, the officers also get warrants to tap the phones he contacted frequently—including yours, your daughter's, and a few others that I can't mention for obvious reasons.

Anyway, they have people listening in on all your calls, so you might want to keep that in mind while you're using your phone. That's just temporary, though. It'll be down in a few days."

"But..." She wiped her hands on her jeans again. "What—"

"Ma'am." Sergio shook his head. "I really am sorry to be short with you, but I have to go. Somebody's been lying to us, and now, after talking to you and your daughter Crissa, I know who it is."

She opened her mouth to speak, but no words came out.

Sergio let the smile fade from his face, staring at Ms. Hartford in the silence of her home.

"Again, thank you very much for your hospitality this Sunday morning," the detective said.

As Ms. Hartford stood in her foyer with her mouth hanging open, Sergio and Avarie left the house.

DAN ALATORRE

CHAPTER 39

Avarie climbed into the passenger side of Sergio's car. "Why did you ask about church? I didn't hear Crisalyn mention that."

"She didn't." The detective started the engine. "So why would the mother agree that she was going to church when she wasn't?"

"Good question." Avarie clipped her seat belt. "I don't know."

"Well, I know one thing. Ms. Hartford is lying." He gripped the wheel and pulled away from the curb. "And if she'd lie to us about something as insignificant as going to church, she's probably lying about a lot more. So is the sister. Neither of them is upset or grieving. The mom looked relatively well-rested. The only time she got the least bit worried was when I baited her by saying I had new evidence. Then, she got very anxious." He looked at Avarie.

"You know who lies about a murder? The people who did it."

Avarie sighed. "Yeah, I've heard. So now you think the mother and sister killed her? I'm not sure I can believe that. I guess I just don't want to."

"They're lying for a reason. Usually, family members are trying to help us." He plucked his phone from the cupholder in the center console, hitting the speaker button and calling Carly.

As the phone rang, Avarie glared at him. "Do you really think Gabriella's mother and sister killed her?"

The detective chewed his lip, gripping the wheel as he steered his car toward the interstate—and the temporary trailer residence of Scarlet Salazar.

In the right circumstances, anyone can kill anyone. That much, he knew. Eighteen-year-olds—nice kids, barely a year removed from playing varsity football for their high school team—could pick up a gun and shoot an enemy soldier. Petite women killed their husbands, sometimes because he was beating her up, but sometimes because she found a new guy who gave her a thrill she hadn't felt since she was a teenager—and now hubby was an irritating pain in the butt with a 401(k) and good-sized insurance policy. One old man killed his best friend during a drunken argument in a poker game; just took out a .38 and blasted him in the chest, over an eleven-dollar pot. A young, beautiful woman killed her sister to take over the family business. Psychopaths slashed the throats of joggers in the dark of night because it gave them a rush.

People killed people.

In his line of work, Sergio had seen quite a spectrum of murder.

"Do you think Gabriella's mother and sister killed her?"

He peered at Avarie. "In a word, yes."

Carly answered the phone on the fifth ring. "Hello?"

"Hey, partn... uh, hey Carly." Sergio grabbed his sunglasses from the console. "Did I wake you? Doing better with that bug thing that's got everybody sick?"

"I didn't really sleep," Carly said. "And it's not exactly early. But no, you didn't wake me. I've been up for a while. What's going on?"

"Avarie and I are on our way to re-interview Scarlet Salazar," Sergio said, "and I wanted to get your thoughts on something."

"Okay. Go."

Sergio glanced over his shoulder as he changed lanes. "What's your take on Gabriella's mother and sister? We know they're lying to us, we just don't know why."

"We don't need to know why," Carly said. "It's enough if we can show they're lying. Obstruction of justice in a murder investigation? I wouldn't want that hanging around my neck."

"Yeah, but a good lawyer could rip that to shreds." He maneuvered through traffic, watching for the off ramp. "Why would they lie? Are they in on it? Is there an insurance angle we haven't thought of?"

"What about wills?" Avarie asked. "Do the mom and sister inherit Gabriella and Teodoro's assets, like the house and nightclub?"

Carly exhaled. "Teodoro just bought those properties, and according to Max, there are big mortgages on both, so there won't be a lot of equity. But if somebody was desperate for money and had a grudge... Teodoro had drug connections, though. He might have a stash of gold bars and cash somewhere, but good luck finding it. Drug guys are bad at hiding stuff like that, but cops are even worse at finding it until..."

Sergio glanced at the phone. "Until..."

"Well," Carly said. "A lot of times, when somebody buys a drug dealer's house, any stashed money stays hidden until the new owner knocks down a wall for renovations and they find bundles of hundred-dollar bills stuffed into the hollow spots of the walls. Teodoro's house has been under construction since he moved in."

Avarie grabbed the sides of her seat. "They don't need equity in the properties! They just need to take possession and start opening up the walls." She smiled. "Time to call in a currency detection canine unit."

"For the home and the club," Carly said. "And anything else Teodoro owns."

Sergio nodded. "I'll put Mark on it. Maybe they can have it done before I finish this next interview."

"More police personnel deployed." Carly sighed. "Clemmons won't like that. He barely let me send the extra officers down to the Romain house.

And by the way, you never said why you needed them."

Sergio reached for the phone. "I'll explain later. And Clemmons will like everything just fine when we solve the case. That's all we need to do."

Carly snorted. "Oh, is that all?"

* * * * *

When they reached the decorative magic trailer in the fairgrounds parking lot, the mobile motel was quiet inside, and locked—and no one answered the door. Sergio and Avarie retreated to his car to make calls until they located Scarlet Salazar or she showed up.

After about an hour, a gray sedan pulled up to the trailer. Scarlet stepped out of the car's rear passenger door, dressed in a slinky white dress and dark sunglasses. Her phone in her hand, she sauntered up to her front door as the sedan drove away.

The magician's assistant's dress was so tight to her body, it could have been a coat of paint. The sleeves of the sheer garment were long and sleek, draping down over her wrists, with a hem line that barely covered Scarlet's petite, round butt. The right side of the dress had little cutaway holes going up from the thigh, like big links in a short chain, letting any observer know the wearer was free of any panties or bra; and the wide, plunging neckline showcased the tops of her suntanned breasts.

The finishing touch was a pair of tan suede boots that came up to Scarlet's knees, with heels as long and thin as ice picks.

The blonde magician's assistant turned and put her hands to her head, fluffing her hair as if she were a model at a fashion shoot. She strutted toward Sergio's car like a tiger stalking prey, swaying her hips and rolling her shoulders as she covered the short distance between the ostentatious trailer and his vehicle.

The detective opened his door and stepped out. "Good afternoon."

Scarlet frowned, looking up at the sky. "Is it afternoon already, sugar? The night was just getting started." She lowered her sunglasses and winked at the detective with semi-bloodshot eyes, her southern accent cutting through the hot morning air. "Are you here because you missed me?"

As Avarie exited the vehicle, Sergio leaned against the side of the car and hooked his thumbs into his belt. "Oh, I've been thinking about you all night." He nodded at Scarlet's skimpy dress. "Is it necessary to always dress so… over the top?"

"Cops wear uniforms." She shrugged, pushing her sunglasses up over her nose again. "This is mine."

Avarie slammed her car door. "Your uniform's a bit much. Or, actually, it's not much at all."

Holding her hands out at her sides, the magician's assistant smiled. "Baby doll, every time I set foot outside, I represent the act. The dazzle, the spotlights… I need to be larger than life whenever the public sees me—walking down the street or appearing on stage. Dressing flashy is part of that." She turned toward the trailer. "Now, would y'all like to come inside? It's hotter out here than it is between my thighs."

Shaking his head, Sergio fell in line behind Scarlet, and Avarie followed.

The inside of the trailer was dark, and the air was cold. The screens had been pulled down over the windows that were visible from the doorway.

The flamboyant entertainer flipped on the lights and tossed her sunglasses to the side as she strolled to the kitchen area. "Anybody want a beer? 'Cause I'm sure having one."

"Sorry," Sergio said. "It's against the rules."

Scarlet yanked open her refrigerator door, peering at Sergio over the edge. "So? You like bending the rules, don't you?"

She ran her tongue over her full, red lips.

"Not as much as you do, apparently." He sat on the sofa and took out his notepad, nodding at Avarie as he patted the cushion next to him. The PR rep sat, and Sergio returned his attention to Scarlet. "How does the Six Sisters act work?"

"Uh-uh." Wagging her finger, Scarlet cracked open a can of beer and took a long swig. She wiped her lips with the back of her hand and walked out from the kitchen. "A good magician never reveals her secrets."

"Then you can tell me," Sergio said, "because you're not a good magician."

"Ow. You're playing rough this morning." Laughing, the entertainer swung her rear end over the arm of the couch and placed her feet on the cushion next to Sergio, pointing her knees at him. Scarlet's skirt barely covered the top inch of her well-toned thighs.

The detective kept his eyes on hers. "How does it work? Not the physical stuff with the trap door, but the other part."

Scarlet cradled her beer in her hands. "How do we get audiences to believe something that's obviously not true?"

"Yes." He nodded. "That."

She leaned forward, resting her elbows on her knees, the thin material covering her breasts straining to keep them inside. "We create a plausible outcome and entice them to go with it. And we offer distractions so they aren't focused on anything other than what we want them focused on. People want to believe the fantasy. That's why they come. But…" Pinching the side of her dress, she pulled the material away from her skin and let go, allowing it to snap back into place. "The sexy assistants are part of that. Flashy costumes. Bold makeup. Bright lights and big explosions and colorful laser beams. That's how Six Sisters works, sugar. That's how all magic works."

The detective looked down at his notepad. "I watched the recordings you gave us of your show—several times, in fact. The volunteers all waved and shouted, trying to be chosen, but not Gabriella. She never even raised her hand, but you went right to her. Why?"

"She probably didn't raise her hand because she was shy." Scarlet shrugged and took another drink of beer. "But I do this every night, Detective. Gabriella looked like she'd make a good volunteer. She was young and pretty—and that's just perfect for our show. And y'all saw the crowd's reaction in the recordings. They sure seemed to like her."

"You're shy but you go onstage?" Sergio asked. "I don't buy it."

"Hey, people go against their natures all the time." The entertainer held her hands out at her sides. "The quiet librarian with the big glasses and the pinned-up hair, who takes a solo vacation to Miami Beach and ends up sleeping with half a dozen men she met at nightclubs. It happens all the time."

"In movies," Sergio said. "Not in real life."

Scarlet sighed, gazing at him. "It must be nice to have such a sheltered life. Look, this act is a loose band of wild nomads, traveling from state to state in an endless string of forgettable cities. Every night, some lonesome guy or gal comes knocking on our door after the performance ends. Honest, hard-working citizens who'd never think about straying from their quiet, boring lives until they buy a ticket and step inside the auditorium to watch the magic show. Then, something happens, and they think they wanna run away. And whenever y'all finally let us leave Tampa, it's all gonna start again."

Avarie sat upright. "Gabriella basically did an infomercial about her husband's real estate holdings. Why would she do that?"

"PR?" Scarlet held her hands up and looked around. "Advertising? Ego? How would I know?"

Avarie narrowed her eyes. "She wanted everyone to know it was Tampa socialite Gabriella Romain going on stage."

Scarlet waved a hand. "People get nervous under the bright lights, on a stage." She looked at

Sergio. "I read an interview that said your partner Carly used to freeze up whenever she had to speak in public. Maybe Little Miss Socialite Gabriella Romain lost it a little."

"Oh, she did." Avarie said. "That's right. She lost it. She lost herself. And she wanted everyone in the room to know who was about to disappear."

"Well, then it worked." Scarlet gave her a nod. "The crowd was convinced."

Folding her arms, Avarie huffed. "She didn't do it for the crowd."

The entertainer slid off the couch and sashayed her way back to the kitchen, the material of her little dress stretching across her butt. "Games. Y'all came out here to play games with me." She set her beer on the tiny counter and turned to them, her long blonde hair cascading over her shoulders. "Seems like this investigation is going about things the wrong way. If a volunteer wanted everyone to think she was dead, that was a pretty good way to go about it. You announce your name on stage, into a microphone, with cameras and a big crowd, and you make sure anybody who doesn't know your name at least ties you to the big theater renovation that's been in the news, or to the expensive house down on the bay. Now, the whole crowd knows you're rich and powerful—and ten seconds later you're missing and presumed dead." She threw her hands up. "But everybody knows it's a trick, too! What y'all gotta figure out is, if somebody *wanted* to do all that, how would they *know* to do it? Carry some blood, squirt it around, and slip out the back door?"

"Could that be done?" Sergio asked. "If I had volunteered in your show, would I be able to do that?"

"Well, sugar pie, the thing is... Every volunteer who ever did Six Sisters knows how it works. So would anybody who watches those 'magic tricks revealed' shows online. Or maybe they worked in a magic act before."

"Or..." Avarie glared at the magician's assistant. "Maybe they simply weren't selected at random."

Scarlet stared at the PR rep and slid her hand under the counter, opening a drawer and taking out a pack of cigarettes. She slipped one between her lips and lit it with a disposable lighter, then blew the smoke out toward the living room.

"I've had a long night," Scarlet said, "and I'm very tired. It's been a delightful conversation, but would y'all mind if we finished it another time?"

She turned her back to them and held the top of her left sleeve, sliding her arm out of the tight material, then switched hands and did the same for her right sleeve. Crossing her arms, she turned back around to face her guests, holding her arms over her breasts as the top of her dress dropped several inches below her belly button.

Scarlet gazed at Sergio, then Avarie, her tan skin glowing in the overhead light of the kitchen. "Unless there was something else either of you wanted."

Sergio stood up and turned away. "I already got the only thing I was interested in." Extending his hand, he helped Avarie to her feet and proceeded to the door. "You've been lying to us, lady. And the final curtain is about to come down on your stage." He opened the door and didn't look back. "Thanks, though. The act was entertaining—it's complete BS, but it's entertaining."

CHAPTER 40

Avarie sat upright and rigid in her seat, not saying a word as Sergio's car pulled away from the trailer area. She eyed him as he gripped the steering wheel, clenching his teeth as he drove to the long exit road of the fairgrounds property.

He brought the car to a halt when he reached the stop sign at the main road, and he looked both ways.

Then he pounded on the center console with his fist.

"Lies! Lies! Lies! Lies! Lies!"

Avarie exploded in laughter. "Whaaaat happened back there in that trailer!" She pushed her hair out of her eyes with both hands. "Telling Scarlet her act was complete BS? When you said that, I thought that little bimbo's eyes were gonna pop out of her head the way her fake boobs were popping out of that cheap dress. What set you off?"

"Nothing." Sergio clenched his jaw and glared out the window, his foot still on the brake. "I'm not upset."

"You sure fooled me. Miss Scarlet Hoochie Momma was doing her slutty little routine, and you were totally cold. I mean ice cold. Like, Antarctic glacier."

The detective took a long, slow breath and peered at his passenger. "Impressed?"

"It's about time, I'll say that." Avarie chuckled. "So, what gives? Why did you provoke her like that?"

Sergio relaxed his grip on the wheel and returned his gaze to the road. "I told you, I was letting her think she was playing me. Now, we've subtly managed to let all three of our key interviews know we don't believe their stories. Or, in Scarlet's case, not so subtly." He poked a finger at the air. "But if these people are talking to each other at all, they're huddling up right now, and they are scared to death. They think we're listening to their phones, and they're freaking out about what they might have said. These are smart people, so they're trying to recall any conversation, any mistake—anything that they know ties them to what happened with Gabriella—while their blood pressure goes up and up."

Nodding, he placed his hand on the dashboard. "Carly mentioned obstruction of justice earlier. In a capital crime investigation, that carries a five-year sentence per count, and they're all on the hook for at least one count."

He slapped the dashboard. "Boom! Gotcha! Every lie they told us is a separate count."

He slapped the dashboard a second time. "Boom! Gotcha again! And as soon as these phonies do an internet search, they'll find out they could be spending the rest of their lives in jail."

Raising both hands, he brought his fingers down onto the dashboard several times in quick succession, slapping out a fanfare.

He sat back, his hands dropping to his sides, and exhaled. "Thank goodness it's Sunday, so they can't call a decent attorney right away. But I'm not sure that matters, since none of them look like they could afford a decent attorney anyway."

"Man, what a ride." Avarie shook her head, smiling. "But still, the best part was seeing Scarlet being all trampy, and you not looking at her at all."

"Oh, I looked," Sergio said. "I just didn't care. Because Six Sisters is all about a bunch of horse crap distractions, and so is Scarlet Salazar."

Avarie deepened her voice, imitating Sergio as she pointed a finger at him. "You've been lying to us, lady. And the final curtain is about to come down on your stage." She threw her head back, laughing. "That was pretty sweet."

"She *is* lying." Sergio put his elbow on the door frame and rested his head on his hand. "The sister is lying, too. And the mother. They all are. Even the calendar in Gabriella's kitchen is lying."

"The calendar?" Avarie asked.

"Yeah. Remember I asked you and Max and Mark to think about things that struck you as odd? The calendar struck me that way."

"Yeah." Avarie nodded. "You said people younger than your mom don't write on paper calendars."

"There was something else." Sergio sat up. "If the cursive handwriting is Gabriella's and the other writing is Teodoro's, fine. But all her appointments were written in blue ink. Everything, for the whole month. When people write on a calendar, it's on a semi-random basis. They jot down each appointment as it happens, and they use whatever pen or pencil is handy. On the other hand, when my mom gets a new calendar each year, she sits down and writes all the family birthdays and anniversaries on it for the whole year. My aunts and uncles, my cousins, my nieces and nephews, neighborhood friends…"

Avarie nodded, her mouth hanging open. "So, it all ends up being in the same color ink, like Gabriella's and Teodoro's were. The Romains wrote all their appointments at once." She glanced at Sergio. "Why would they do that? The appointments are fake? What does that do for them?"

"Well…" He drummed his fingers on the dashboard. "It would make anyone looking at the calendar think the people living there were planning on going to meetings and doctor's appointments over the next few weeks—when they weren't."

"Maybe it's a show," Avarie said, "to throw off any hit men coming up from Miami."

"Or to throw us off." He shrugged. "And then there's that painting. Like you said, only robber barons of the gilded age had portraits made of themselves. I doubt Gabriella thought of herself that way. So Teodoro commissioned it. He put the most important thing in his life in it—her. And she put her ring in it. That same ring she left behind when she planned her escape. She took cash and a passport, but not something as small and portable as a ring that just happens to match a brooch her grandmother was wearing in a picture at her mom's house." He shook his head, voicing thoughts that seemed to wander but went nowhere. "A piece of jewelry that was important enough to put in a portrait Gabriella would have to look at every day, but it stayed behind. Why? It's important, maybe a family heirloom. Why leave it? If you're running away forever, why leave that?"

"It was upstairs." Avarie turned to him. "I spotted it when I was looking at the picture frames on Gabriella's dresser. Maybe she was in such a rush, she dropped it. I'm sure she doesn't usually keep it on the dresser behind some random picture frames."

"Maybe." He sighed, chewing his lip. "Meanwhile, everybody in this stinking case is lying. It's really pissing me off."

"I can see that." Avarie chuckled. "I'm kinda getting tangentially upset just sitting here watching you steam. But I have to admit, I don't really see how the case is any farther along than it was this morning." She glanced at Sergio, softening her voice. "Have you considered that part of your enhanced irritation might be from being tired? I know I am."

"I'm tired, all right." He scowled. "Tired of everyone's BS."

The detective's phone pinged with an incoming text. He picked it up and glanced at the screen. Two missed calls from the chief, and a message from Max.

He opened the text and read it out loud. "Max says, 'Got the currency dogs to check the Romain house and the yacht. Nothing found at either location. Took them to Teodoro's warehouse next. It's clean, too.' Well, crap." Sergio dropped his hand to his lap.

The building blocks still aren't lining up.

"Then I guess we'll go back to the original plan," he said. "It's time to call in the Marines. Or, to be more accurate, it's time to call off the reinforcements at the Romain house and clear the place out." Sitting up, the detective looked at Avarie. "Maybe I can go home and catch a few hours of sleep. What are you doing later?"

"Gee, let's see..." The PR rep raised her index finger to her lower lip, tapping it as she looked upward. "I haven't stopped working this case for almost two straight days. I should probably ask you what I'm doing."

"Oh, I'd like you to go out with me."

"Out?" She recoiled, her jaw dropping. "Like on a date?"

Sergio shrugged. "If you wanna call it that."

"Would *you* call it that?"

He cocked his head, a smile tugging at the corners of his mouth. "I want you to go out with me tonight. In fact, I think we should think about spending the night together." Sergio put on an exaggerated, thick southern accent. "It's where the action will be, sugar pie."

Avarie narrowed her eyes. "What kind of action, sugar pie?"

The smile spread across his face. Sergio took his foot off the brake and picked up his phone, driving his car out onto the main road.

DAN ALATORRE

CHAPTER 41

Carly had spent most of her day alternating between sleeping, cleaning, reading updates on the Romain case, and trying not to think about her dilemma.

None of it had been successful.

Commencing a deep clean on her sons' shower only freed up her mind to roam to places she didn't want to go. The heaviness of the situation made her want to lay down; stretching out on the couch and closing her eyes only turned into fits of tossing and turning.

If you start treatment, you could lose the baby. If you wait, you could die.

If you terminate the pregnancy, you rob Sergio of his offspring. If you tell him first, who knows where that conversation goes? He might want you to get an abortion, but do you want that?

And having the baby... what issues does that cause for your sons and Kyle?
Do you want to have a baby?
Do you really want another child?

It was more than long days of waking up in the middle of the night to change a diaper or to pat a tummy because the new baby food wasn't settling right with its tiny recipient. She had hated being pregnant. She'd thrown up almost every day when she was carrying Ethan, and twice as often when she was pregnant with Isaac.

But enough of the bad memories of queasiness-filled mornings and evenings had dissipated between the first and second pregnancies to decide to *have* a second pregnancy.

Ethan slept through the night pretty early on. Isaac, on the other hand, had turned her and Kyle into zombies, with enough middle of the night antics for three babies.

But somehow they weathered it.

And after it ended—which seemed forever while they were in the middle of it and seemed to not have happened at all once it had passed—there were the joys of motherhood. Holding that sweet, tiny infant against your skin. Watching a first step get taken. Celebrating the utterance of the first word.

Big Wheels became tricycles became two-wheelers with training wheels, and then a "big kid" bike.

A bassinette became a crib, then a small bed, then a real bed.

And a million other amazing moments, too small to take note of but so big they etch themselves into a parent's brain forever, recalled in any random instant years later for a tear-filled fond memory, would all happen over the child's life.

Or... not.

A pregnancy could get terminated, a very treatable cancer could get treated, and neither Sergio nor Kyle nor her sons would ever know the difference.

Her boys would never know there could have been a sister. Sergio would never know there could have been a daughter.

No one would know.

Carly sat on the living room couch, the sights and sounds of the neighborhood coming through the windows of her family's home. Mr. Durrows mowed his lawn. The Coniglio kid kicked a soccer ball around in their yard. Jennie Tate strolled past on the sidewalk, walking her dog Buddy.

As long as she kept all of the lies to herself, no one ever needed to know anything but the reality she told them.

Carly sighed.

But I'll know.

And what do you want, Carly?

She took a deep breath as she shifted on the couch.

I don't want to cause a bunch of problems. I don't want morning sickness, and I don't want months of sleepless nights changing diapers and doing feedings. I don't want the expense of baby clothes that only fit for two weeks and pediatrician's bills and worrying that my kid isn't learning to walk as soon as that kid did.

I don't want to worry about who I'm hurting by doing something, and who I'm hurting by not doing something.

She kneaded her fingers as Mr. Durrows' lawn mower turned a corner and went down the other side of his yard.

And I don't want to lie. That's not who I am. That's never been who I am, and that's not who I taught my children to be.

A warmth came over her, like a log tossed onto a campfire on the cold night, releasing a flock of tiny orange embers that floated upwards like fireflies.

And I want to have that little girl.

She nodded, getting up from the couch.

I do. I want the chance to make it happen.

Everything else will pass—the awkwardness of telling people, the inconveniences, the sleepless nights. If the stars have aligned to give me a second chance for something I've quietly been hoping for, I'll say yes.

Her mood brightened. The sky was bluer, the grass was greener, the air was easier to breathe.

"Oh, boy." Carly smiled, her heart pounding. "I'm really going to do this."

Nervous energy swept over her—and relief.

She jumped up, wrapping her arms around herself and smiling as wide as her cheeks allowed.

"It'll be okay. It's crazy and it's not like you—at all—and it's going to cause a lot of people a lot of waves, but it'll be okay."

Walking to the front window, she peered out on the world.

Kyle can just deal with it. Ethan and Isaac will be thrilled to learn they're going to have a baby sister. And Sergio will either be happy and be a part of a mixed family like a lot of other families, or he won't and we'll move on without him.

But he will.

Sergio loves kids and he loves families. I've seen it.

He'll come and see her and be a part of her life just like he was becoming a part of the boys' lives. And when he finds the woman he wants to settle down with, it'll be like a lot of other families—there'll be a child from before he met her. That's super common.

"Other people have made things like this work, so I'll be able to make it work." She hugged herself. "Everything's going to be just fine and—"

A jolt of pain rippled through her abdomen.

"Oh!" Gripping her right side, Carly dropped to the floor.

She curled up, pressing her cheek into the carpet. As nausea welled up inside her, Carly squeezed her eyes shut and waited for it all to subside.

A moment later, it did.

Panting, Carly got to her feet, holding her belly as she crept to her bedroom and eased herself onto the bed.

CHAPTER 42

Mark Harriman informed Sergio that the chief was on his way to the Romain house to send everyone home, and that Sergio could probably get there first if he hurried.

Sergio didn't hesitate. He drove back to Bayshore Boulevard.

Sleep could wait. It would have only been a few hours—which might have resulted in making him even sleepier, anyway—but Sergio wanted to bear the brunt of any wrath Chief Clemmons dished out, and he felt it best to let the uniformed officers witness him taking it.

He did a quick walk-through of the house, upstairs and down, before finding the chief in the garage with Harriman.

"I'll speak with you outside, Detective."

Sergio followed the chief down to his vehicle. Their conversation was professional, stern and brief.

"Stop wasting the department's money on excessive personnel, and start answering the phone when I call. Understand?"

"Yes, Chief," Sergio said.

"Send these people home." Clemmons scowled. *"From here out, you work the case with only the team I originally approved."*

"Yes, Chief."

Avarie, for her part, spoke to the press in attendance, heavily implying that the additional officers had been recalled due to budget constraints.

After the chief departed, Sergio walked to the sidewalk in front of the Romain residence and doused himself with two more bottles of water. Mark Harriman approached, carrying two canvas gear bags in one hand and a foil tray in the other, with a clipboard held in place under his arm.

"That's about it." Harriman placed the gear bags at his feet. "The last of our people will be gone in about five minutes. Then, it's just you and me." He handed Sergio the clipboard. "And a stack of catering bills. It's… almost three grand. But I managed to save a rack of ribs for you." He handed Sergio the foil tray.

"Three grand!" Sergio grabbed his chest, gasping. "Good thing Clemmons didn't see that. He'd have run me over on his way out."

"Just sign on the dotted lines," Harriman said, "so it's on your credit card and not mine."

Sergio took the clipboard and signed the papers. "Did the guys enjoy the food, at least?"

"Ribs and subs? Sure. The gang loves you."

"It's nice to be loved," the detective said, "but three grand for a few hours is more expensive than a Miami Beach hooker."

Harriman chuckled. "They were sad to leave. I am, too, but for different reasons." He lowered his voice. "I'm not questioning what you're up to. I don't understand it, but I'm not questioning it. But…"

Sergio shook his head, handing the clipboard back and patting Mark on the shoulder. "Don't worry about a thing. I told everybody the place would be swarming with cops again in the morning, that it's just a budget thing. And Avarie's telling that to the reporters."

"But it's not true." Harriman glanced toward the reporters clustered around Avarie. "There won't be an army of officers coming back here tomorrow. You'll have a skeleton crew at best."

Sergio smiled. "It'll be fine, Mark. Go on home, now, and get some sleep."

Sighing, the junior officer bent down and grabbed his gear bags. "You should follow that advice yourself. You look terrible. I hope you know what you're doing."

"You worry more than my mom." Sergio waved a hand. "I'll see you tomorrow. And don't forget, Mina's party is tomorrow evening. Bring your appetite and a nice present."

"Yeah, I'll pick up a bottle of kosher wine." Grinning, Harriman took a step towards his vehicle. "Is your mom making fried shrimp?"

"Yep." Sergio nodded. "And lechón, and her paella Valenciana, and arepas, and buñuelos…" He winced, shaking his head. "Geez, I should have had her cater this afternoon's feast. I'd have spent a lot less."

Chuckling, Harriman headed to his squad car. As he pulled away, the last remaining Tampa PD vehicles did, too.

Sergio sighed, turning to Avarie as the sun inched toward the horizon. The cluster of media personnel surrounding her wasn't as tightly packed as it had been a moment ago.

Looks like her press conference is wrapping up.

Some of the reporters left right away; a few did wrap up shots for their B-reel coverage. Kerri Milner chatted for a few minutes, then walked to her car and drove off.

A warm breeze swept over the bay and across Bayshore Boulevard, lifting Avarie's golden locks as she walked toward him.

He smiled as she neared. "You look great—unlike me. How'd you manage that?"

"Makeup," the PR rep said. "And lots of it. I think I used half a pound of concealer to hide the bags under my eyes, and a bottle of Visine for the redness. Good thing the reporters took mercy on me and didn't ask me to be in their shots for very long." She took a deep breath, looking up at the Romain house, then turned her eyes to him. "All the troops gone?"

Sergio nodded, walking down the sidewalk. "Clemmons pulled everybody, and I sent Mark Harriman home—he looked exhausted."

"The poor baby." Avarie walked with the detective. A hot breeze swept over the bay as the sun moved closer toward the horizon. "Mark probably only logged close to twenty-four straight hours. I think I'm coming up on forty-eight."

Sergio stopped at his car and turned to her. "If you're tired, there's probably some coffee up at the Romain house."

"I'm not sure I want to consume anything from Gabriella Romain's pantry right now. I'll make do with water from the caterers." She looked at Sergio's car, then at him. "Are we waiting out here?"

"Nope." He opened the passenger side door for her. "We're leaving, too."

* * * * *

Sergio drove his car down the street on the side of the Romain estate, turning right at the corner and left at the next block, stopping in front of a sign that said No Parking.

He turned to Avarie. "Where'd you park your car when you came here yesterday?"

"On the next block," she said. "They wouldn't let me park any closer."

"Okay." He nodded. "Leave it there for now. Let's get up to the house."

He turned off the engine and opened his door.

"Hey, Detective." Avarie pointed at the sign. "Doesn't that sign say no parking?"

"Yep." Sergio grinned. "Think I'll get a ticket?" He grabbed the tray of ribs that Mark had given him and exited the vehicle.

Swinging her purse over her arm, Avarie climbed out of the car. "I don't get it. What are we doing?"

"Going back to the Romain house," Sergio said.

"And why are we doing that? We just left."

He grinned in the fading light. "We did, didn't we? Come on. And we need to stay quiet until we're inside."

She followed him to the rear entrance of the estate as he lifted the crime scene tape to go onto the property. They passed the guest house and walked across the brick pavers of the pool, to the massive sliding glass doors of the main residence's rear entry.

The detective stared up at the glass panes of the doors, one hand in his pocket, the other holding the foil tray. "You know," he whispered, "I really like these doors. They're so easy to open. I wish mine opened like these."

"Yeah, you mentioned that." Avarie nodded, her voice low. "You should get a set for your mansion—when you get a mansion." The PR rep glanced over her shoulder. "Should we be here like this? It feels strange."

"We could kick back on the pool chairs. It'd be nice to sit in the A/C, though. Too bad the doors are locked." He pulled his hand from his pocket and extended his index finger, pressing it to the glass frame.

The door slid open.

"Or are they?" He glanced at Avarie, smiling. "Oops. I guess I forgot to re-lock this when I was touring the house looking for Chief Clemmons earlier. Come on."

She crept forward, looking around. "Don't these people have an alarm?"

"They have several." He strolled into the ornate living room. "None of them are hooked up right now." Walking up to the fireplace, the detective gazed at the portrait of Gabriella Romain in the dim light.

Avarie shut the door and turned to him. "Okay—what are we doing?"

"Playing out a hunch." Sergio shrugged, sliding his hand back into his pocket. "That's about all I have left, but I think it's pretty solid." He moved to the big white couch and sat down, placing the foil tray on the coffee table, alongside the stacks of hardcover books. "Come on. Have a seat over here."

"What are we, security guards now?" She shook her head, looking back outside. "If I sit down, I might fall asleep."

"Suit yourself." Lifting his arms, Sergio tucked his hands behind his head and stretched his legs out. "It shouldn't be long now, anyway." He glanced at the foil tray. "Want some ribs?"

"I want you to tell me what we're doing here."

"You know, these books—they're just for show." He leaned forward, lifting a book from the top of one of the stacks. "They're the kind that people buy but don't ever read."

"How do you know?"

"Oh, come on." He smirked, reading off a few of the titles. "The Metamorphosis by Franz Kafka? The Complete Sherlock Holmes? Hemingway's A Farewell to Arms?" Shaking his head, he looked at her. "Nobody reads Kafka after high school. Not even at gun point. Most kids don't even read this stuff *in* high school. They read the Cliffs Notes or skim a Wikipedia summary."

"Maybe Gabriella and Teodoro were trying to improve themselves through reading classical literature."

"Maybe." Sergio gently raised the book's cover. The spine crackled. He glanced at Avarie. "Or maybe not. Most books only do that the first time you open them."

He sat back again, gazing around the room.

Sighing, Avarie walked to the couch. "Just for the record, when you asked me to spend the night with you, I had something a little different in mind."

"Relax," Sergio said. "The fun stuff doesn't happen until after it's dark anyway. Have some ribs."

She lifted the corner of the foil covering the tray. "We're sure these aren't from inside the house?"

"Harriman wouldn't poison us. Well, he wouldn't poison *you*." Sergio picked up a rib and took a bite. "Okay?"

She reached into the tray. "Be careful you don't drip sauce on the couch. Neither of us makes enough to afford a cleaning bill for this place."

After a few ribs, the inside of the house was almost pitch black. The streetlights outside allowed faint illumination to get past the palm trees and high rows of hedges, filtering through the front and sides of the residence, but not the living room or kitchen.

Avarie tapped her phone, sending a white glow onto the living room ceiling.

"Whoa." He put his hand over her phone. "Don't do that."

"Why not? I was gonna show you some research I've been doing." She pushed his hand aside and tapped the screen again. "I found these videos about magicians. See, the assistants dress in crazy outfits to distract the audience, but another reason they dress alike is so that they can—"

"Not now." He grabbed the Kafka book and placed it on top of the phone, dousing the light. "I need it dark in here."

Avarie huffed. "Why?"

Glancing over his shoulder toward the courtyard and the pool, Sergio nodded at two small beams of light bouncing back and forth across the paved walkway.

"Because we're about to have visitors." He stood, looking toward the pantry in the dim light. "Would you mind waiting in the pantry?"

"As long as I don't have to eat anything in there." Avarie got up, patting the side of her purse. "I have my .45 if we need it."

Sergio nodded, following her to the pantry. "Unless I miss my guess—by a *lot*—I don't think we'll need it." He glanced toward the courtyard. The two lights came closer. "But… keep it handy just in case."

As Avarie stepped into the Romains' large pantry, the detective hunched over and tiptoed back to the couch. He lowered himself onto the overstuffed cushions in the darkness, holding his breath as he peered at the courtyard.

"I can't see much from back here," Avarie hissed. "It's too dark."

Sergio cringed.

The little beams of light stopped at the massive, glass doors. Sergio sat still and rigid, his eyes locked on the two silhouettes crouching outside the Romain residence.

The tiny beams of light went out, and the sliding glass door opened.

CHAPTER 43

"Hurry, my love." The man's voice was low and calm, but firm—and tinted with a Latino accent. It carried through the dark, quiet living room of the Romain residence.

"It's just upstairs," the woman said. "On the dresser, behind some pictures." Her words were unencumbered by any noticeable accent, to Sergio's ear.

As the two silhouettes moved across the living room, Sergio reached up and turned on the table lamp.

The house flooded with light. The intruders whipped around to face him, squinting in the brightness.

One was a dark-haired man with an athletic build and a face handsome enough to be a model. The other was a woman with long blonde hair, a slender waist, and legs that could have belonged to a gymnast.

The sudden illumination bothered Sergio's eyes, too, but he managed a smile for the blonde magician's assistant.

"I'd say it's nice to see you again, Scarlet—but I'm not sure it is." Glancing at the man, the detective nodded. "And you must be Teodoro."

The handsome stranger held his hand up, blocking the light, but saying nothing. Scarlet's mouth hung open.

She was dressed plainly this time—faded jeans, a dark blue t-shirt, simple sneakers—but her striking beauty penetrated the bland attire.

Sergio ran his hand over his beard stubble. "I've had a rough couple of days—not much to eat, and zero sleep. But I can't help but think Max was right, and that I'm looking at a couple of dead people. Because as much as I think I'm talking to Scarlet Salazar from the magic show, I'm convinced I'm really talking to Gabriella Romain."

Sighing, the blonde beauty reached up and put a hand to her hair, pulling the golden locks off and revealing the light brown mane underneath.

It was the identical color hair as the woman in the portrait behind her, and the same length, too. The same legs and curvy figure, the same shape of the face. The same nose and eyes and lips from the pictures upstairs on the dresser.

Sergio shook his head. "I can't believe I was face to face with you all this time and still didn't notice—Gabriella."

"You aren't supposed to notice." Gabriella shrugged. "That's the trick, Detective. Just like you didn't notice I was also the mousy New York accountant when you first stepped inside the trailer." She held her hands out at her sides, taking a slow step toward the staircase. "In some lines of work, skill with costumes and makeup is a necessity. Using frumpy, padded clothes to look like one way, and then changing to skin-tight, glamorous fashion to look like someone completely different."

She sighed, glancing toward the blonde wig in her hand. "A few of these—professionally made and fitted, of course, and in different colors and hair styles... some colored contact lenses... High heels versus flats..." Gabriella glanced at Sergio, her features warm and soft in the glow of the lamp, her voice like velvet. "One version gets makeup to create the illusion of full lips, and some teeth overlays, maybe some shading around the nose to make it perkier—and a flamboyant demeanor for good measure. The other version gets thin lips and a shy disposition. And, for sure, you dress one of them *very* sexy, to keep the attention away from the disguise." She chuckled. "A pushup bra and a low-cut dress for one version of yourself, and a tight-fitting sports bra and t-shirt for the other version. There are lots of ways to be lots of people." Taking another step toward the stairs, she smiled, stroking her fingers through the hair of the wig. "I like you, Detective. You're a good man. I felt bad about deceiving you, but I didn't have a choice. Don't feel bad about it. Anyone would be hard pressed to think a five-foot-eight-inch buxom blonde bombshell from the deep south of Mississippi, with blue eyes and big teeth and a sleek physique, was the same person as a shy, five-foot-four brunette, with brown eyes and small teeth, from Tampa."

"Distraction." Sergio nodded. "Just like in Six Sisters."

Gabriella's smile broadened, her voice as soft as a lullaby. "The distraction *is* the magic, Detective. I told you that."

"What about the getaway from the fairgrounds?' he asked. "Everything was hidden in the oversized bag?"

"Two bags—one inside the other. The blue and white one was left in the trash for you to find, and the other one went with me."

Sergio nodded. "And inside the bag was a squirt bottle full of blood?"

"A good magician never reveals her secrets," Gabriella said, "but it might be just that simple. They sell kits online, to draw blood at home. It starts to deteriorate after a while, though. Your coroner will find that out, if he didn't already."

"She mentioned it." The detective narrowed his eyes. "And Max will figure out that Scarlet Salazar is a fake ID, just like that other name you gave me. Katherine Tanya Jameson, was it?"

"Oh, Scarlet's real enough." Gabriella waved a hand, her eyes drifting over the walls of her home. "Katherine Jameson was an ID that I bought, but Scarlet's actually a friend from high school. She moved to Key West and created a magic show with some girls she met there. Whenever she brought the act to Tampa, I'd substitute and she'd take a vacation—this time, we just overlapped a few days. We... look a lot alike, actually."

Sergio gestured to the wig. "You mean you look a lot alike when you're both dressed as Scarlet, so you can swap yourself out for her and disappear from under the stage." He sat up, folding his hands in front of himself. "So, you went down the ladder under the cage, walked out of camera view, sprayed the blood that you'd stored up, and made a few smears on the floor. Then changed clothes and walked right out the side door."

Gabriella nodded. "To my loving husband's waiting van, and a friend of his as my driver—the same friend who made the calls from Teo's phone at the fairgrounds. And since your people didn't need two Scarlets, the real one quietly went to her trailer between interviews by the police."

"Where she left," Sergio said, "and you replaced her when I showed up." He shook his head. "It's all just Six Sisters again, over and over. I should have had the dogs come sniff the trailer." His gaze went to Teodoro. "Well, that brings me to you, Mr. Romain. You're obviously not dead, so who was the guy we took out of the dinghy?"

"A very bad man," Teodoro said. "When your DNA search comes back on the body, you'll see that. He was a Miami mobster who kills for fun. He makes his money by putting innocent women into cargo containers and sending them to places like Venezuela."

"Yeah?" Sergio cocked his head. "I thought you were that kind of guy."

"Ah, the video—the one in the café." The handsome Latin man nodded slowly. "Yes… Sometimes, in certain circles, it's good to create a little reputation for yourself. My brother's business was in trouble—which is to say, my brother was in trouble. That's the life he picked for himself—danger, drugs, excitement—and a few days ago, it cost him his life. But my side was always legitimate. Your police contacts in Miami will verify that. I've never even had a parking ticket. That video you saw was merely a bit of acting, with some friends—the one who drove the van for Gabriella at the fairgrounds, and who later moved the hit man into the dinghy so your people could find it." He put his hand to his heart. "I created nothing but honest, profitable businesses."

"From drug money."

"Perhaps," Teodoro said. "But it was laundered before it ever got to me."

"Murder is murder." Sergio shrugged. "I gotta come after you for the guy in the dinghy."

"Do you? *He* broke into my home and ate the food he found there. Nobody forced him to do it."

The detective glanced toward the living room. "It was just an accident that he ate food laced with strychnine. You intended to kill some rats, by serving them a meal on your best dinnerware."

"No, I set a trap." Teodoro stood up straight, his chin high. "But I didn't make a hit man bring a .38 with him all the way from Miami to walk into it."

Shifting on the couch, Sergio looked at the couple. "What's the end game here? Why'd you do all this?"

Gabriella walked to her new husband's side, putting her arms around him. "Teo's brother is dead. The people in the Miami crew are going to fight for the top spot now. If they think Teo's alive, they'll kill him, too—and me." She looked at the detective. "But now they don't have to. We're both already dead. It's been all over the news."

She looked down, her big eyes taking on a sadness. "In the trailer, I acted like I could see into your soul, but I just recited what I'd read about you online. But I still see the white knight—the man who does the right thing even when it's unpopular."

The wind picked up outside, rustling the long fronds of the estate's palm trees.

Gabriella raised her eyes to Sergio's. "We could just slip out the door and disappear. Five minutes. I just need to go upstairs and get something off my dresser. We'll be gone forever."

Sergio leaned his head back, peering down his nose at her. "There wouldn't be a gun upstairs somewhere, would there?"

"A ring." Gabriella clasped her hands together, turning around and looking at her portrait. "My grandmother survived the blitz in London. She made a brooch for my sister and a ring for me. V for victory—to show us that people can do anything if they set their minds to it." She looked down, massaging her fingers. "I haven't done much in my life to live up to her standards, but saving an innocent man's life might be a good start." She looked at her husband, then turned back to Sergio, her voice falling to a gentle whisper. "May I go get it, please?"

The detective reached into his pocket and took out the ruby ring, setting it on the side table. The gold V reflected the light of the lamp.

"It was all Six Sisters, wasn't it?" Sergio scowled. "Distraction. Your whole plan would have fallen apart in a few days when the DNA came back."

"A few days is all we need." Gabriella went to her husband, putting her hand on his arm. "Teo has some money stashed—clean money. We're going to disappear."

The wind from the bay picked up again, banging the distant treetops together and making the windows of the great estate moan and sigh.

The detective stared at the young couple.

A new life. A fresh start.

The story sounds true enough. All the puzzle pieces finally fit.

Gabriella took a step toward the couch, slowly and silently. Then, she took another. She gently crossed the living room, reaching her slender hand out, and picked up her ring.

Then, she turned away and crossed to the sliding glass doors.

She stopped, clutching the ring to her heart, and waited until Teodoro met her there. The handsome husband joined his beautiful wife, wrapping his arms around her.

They peered over at Sergio where he sat on the couch.

Gabriella put her hand on the large glass panel. "Thank you, Detective."

The wind from the bay pushed past the house, the trees rustled one more time. When it died down again, the young couple was gone.

Avarie stepped out of the pantry, her gun in her hand. She slipped it back into her purse and went to Sergio, extending her hand. "Come with me."

He looked into her eyes, then gazed at her outstretched arm, and placed his hand in hers.

Avarie guided him up the steps, across the Romains' bedroom, to the balcony.

She opened the door and stepped onto the tile surface, the warm wind pushing her hair back as she went to the stone railing. She slid her fingers across the cold, polished surface. "Quite a view."

"Yeah." Sergio nodded, stepping to the railing. "It's been quite a view." Turning around, he rested against the stone restraint and stretched his hands out onto the cold, hard surface, hanging his head.

I was brought in to find a missing person. She's not missing. They asked me to look into a murder. There's no murder. As far as I'm concerned, my job is done.

The job was done—with the best possible outcome.

Sergio frowned.

So why doesn't it feel like it?

Ego?

Someone got the best of you? But you still figured it out.

The DNA will check out, like he said, and everything else is peripheral. Her mother and sister were lying, to help her get away. The other stuff is insignificant.

Isn't it?

Avarie moved next to him, placing her hand on his. "If it's any consolation, I think you did the right thing. I think they're telling the truth. Don't you?"

He nodded, taking a deep breath and looking away.

It's a happy ending, it's just a messy one.
Take the win.
The building blocks lined up.

She gave his hand a squeeze. "Wanna go?"

Sergio gazed out over the dark waters of the bay. In the distance, the running lights of a large ship cut across the black horizon.

"No," he said. "Let's give them the five minutes."

CHAPTER 44

For Sergio, the night of sleep was more refreshing than a drink of cool water would be to a man who'd just walked out of the desert. It was rejuvenating. It was energizing. Restoring.

It lasted until mid-afternoon, and could have gone longer, but the neighbor's dog was apparently trying to assault a squirrel.

"Holy cow!" Mr. Givens shouted, rushing past Sergio's condo window. "No, Roscoe! Leave that squirrel alone!"

Smiling, Sergio wiped the sleep from his eyes and rolled over, checking the time on his phone.

Three-nineteen.

He took a moment to stretch, then picked the phone up and called Avarie.

"Hey," the PR rep said. "Princess Aurora has awakened—finally."

"Huh?" Sergio held the phone to his ear as he crawled across his bed. "Prince who? What time did I say we needed to head to my mom's?"

"Princess Aurora," Avarie said. "Sleeping Beauty. Her name was—forget it. Welcome back to the land of the conscious."

"Yeah, thanks." The detective swung his legs over the side of the bed and sat up, twisting his bare torso from side to side. "I think I could have slept straight through until Tuesday—and I still might."

Avarie chuckled. "You said we were going to your mom's for dinner. She doesn't eat at three in the afternoon, does she? My Great-Grandma does that. It's super annoying."

"I… uh…" The detective lowered his arms and stared at the bedroom wall. "I have completely lost track of this conversation."

"You were inquiring as to what time you should pick me up."

"Oh. Right." He nodded. "I need to shower, and we need to stop for ice."

"Will that take three hours?"

He got up, adjusting the waistline of his boxer-briefs as he staggered into the hallway. His hand went to his lower back for a thorough scratch. "It might. I'm not planning on moving very fast."

"Then… Pick me up at six? Five-thirty?"

"Six. We don't need to be the first ones there." He glanced at the shower. Immersing himself in jets of warm water was tempting, but a workout would take out the kinks in his back and actually wake him up. He pushed away from the bathroom and stepped inside his closet, rummaging around for his gear bag. "Whatever setting up they need to do for the party, it needs to happen without me this time. I'm footing the bill for the shindig, so I get a pass. And I'm too tired."

"Hmm. Maybe I should pick you up."

"No. But I think I'm gonna work out first." He opened the gym bag and checked the insides.

Clean towel, deodorant, t-shirt, shorts, socks, grip gloves...

He grabbed a pair of old running shoes and another pair of boxer briefs, adding them to the bag. "Is that okay? I'll see you at six?"

"Six it is," the PR rep said. "See you then."

"Okay. Oh, and Avarie..."

"Yes?"

Sergio pursed his lips, holding his phone close as he stood in the closet. "Thanks."

"You're welcome." She chuckled. "For what?"

"It was a long couple of days. You hung in there like a champ. I appreciate it."

"Show your appreciation by not mentioning the gigantic bags under my eyes when you see me. I'll do the same."

He nodded. "Done."

Lowering the phone, a smile crossed his face as he ended the call.

* * * * *

Mrs. Sanderson opened the door to Carly's house and strolled to the kitchen, setting two bags of groceries on the counter. "Carly, I bought that water you like." She plucked a long, thin bottle from the sagging bag and held it up, frowning. "It's got artificial sweeteners in it. Should you be having that?"

Mrs. Sanderson walked toward the bedroom. "We'll have to ask the doctor if these things are going to interfere with your cancer treatment. We don't want—"

She stopped, her mouth hanging open.

Carly lay on the floor by her bed, curled up in a ball.

Her mother raced to her side. "What happened? Can you tell me?" She pushed Carly's hair away from her face and took her hand. "Talk to me, honey. What happened?"

Carly nodded, looking at her mother through half-open eyes. "I got up to make some breakfast, and..." She winced, clutching her abdomen.

"Okay. Don't talk." Mrs. Sanderson licked her lips, looking her daughter over. "I'll... How bad is it? Do you need a doctor?"

Wincing, Carly squeezed her mother's fingers. "I think so."

"Okay." Heart racing, her mother nodded. "Okay, I'll get help. I'll call an ambulance. Stay right there, sweetie. Don't move."

Mrs. Sanderson sprinted to the kitchen and grabbed her purse, taking out her phone and calling 911.

* * * * *

Avarie opened the trunk of Sergio's car as he heaved two massive bags of ice into it.

Wiping the wetness from his hands, he glanced at her. "Mom always needs ice. It's like she thinks people enjoy drinking their beverages at room temperature or something."

"She's old school." Avarie handed the detective his car keys.

"Old school is right." Sergio chuckled. "She'll probably ask you to take a marker and write your name on whatever plastic cup you use."

"Well…" Avarie walked to the passenger door. "If she does, I'll do it."

* * * * *

They parked almost two blocks away because there were no spots closer to his mother's house.

Avarie stared out at the rows of cars lining the street. Music pumped from the direction of his mother's yard. "Wow, is this all for you?"

"It's for Mina." Sergio opened his car door and got out. "Half graduation party, half birthday party, half family reunion."

Smiling, Avarie exited the vehicle. "That's three halfs."

"Yeah." Sergio nodded, putting his key into the trunk lock to retrieve the ice. "That's why there's no parking."

His sister spotted them from the front porch when Sergio and Avarie were still half a block away.

"Sergio!" The slender brunette dashed away from a group of young ladies and sprinted down the sidewalk, throwing herself into her big brother's arms.

He dropped the ice bags and spun her around. "Congratulations and happy birthday, baby sister!" He set her down and smiled at her, looking her over. "The dress looks new. And it looks beautiful on you—as if it had a choice. Any dress would look amazing on my sister."

Mina blushed, swaying back and forth, as she batted her big brown eyes. A mob of family members came down the street, voicing their welcomes.

Sergio put his hand on Avarie's shoulder. "Mina, this is Avarie Fox. Avarie, my scientist sister Mina, the family's newest college graduate."

The ladies greeted each other.

As the trio walked toward the house, the festive music grew louder. Colorful banners hung from the porch, announcing the new graduate to the world. The front yard was filled with cousins and neighbors, tossing a football while trying not to mess up their good clothes; the back yard was brimming with uncles, debating the proper arrangement of the meat on the grill. Inside, the house was a mob of mostly female relatives and more family friends, arranging the side dishes they'd brought and fussing at their children to use paper plates for the food.

They shouted their warm salutations to Sergio as he entered, kissing and hugging him—and Avarie—as they made their way to the home's small kitchen and Sergio's mother.

Mrs. Martin was stationed at the stove, wearing a fancy dress and an ancient apron, overseeing a bubbling cast iron skillet with her wooden spoon. The aroma of fried shrimp filled the air.

"Mama!" Mina shouted. "Sergio's here."

His mother turned to him and gave her son a big smile. "Moochie!" Wooden spoon in hand, she stretched out her arms.

Avarie glanced at the detective, a wide grin on her face. "Moochie?"

"Oh, no," he said. "You are not allowed to call me that. Ever." He reached for his mother.

Mrs. Martin embraced her son in a bear hug. Reaching over her shoulder, Sergio snagged a fried shrimp from the massive pile on the platter by the stove, and popped it into his mouth.

After a kiss on each cheek, his mother released him and glanced at Avarie. "Welcome to my home. Forgive my son—he was *taught* the manners to introduce his mother to his guests, but he shames me instead and eats a shrimp first."

Smiling, Sergio put a hand to his bulging mouth. "Mom, this is Avarie."

Mrs. Martin hugged the PR rep. "You're too skinny, girl. Don't you eat?" She turned to Sergio, smacking him on the arm. "Why don't you feed this girl? She's thin as a nail."

Sergio chuckled. "Rail, mom. Thin as a *rail*."

"Either way, she's too thin." His mother waved the spoon. "Get her some shrimp, and a drink. The cups are over there."

Mrs. Martin pointed to the other side of the little kitchen. Sergio and Avarie worked their way through the mob, saying hello to his relatives along the way, until they reached a small, square table with a worn vinyl tablecloth.

A bundt cake-shaped Jello mold sat on one end of the table, filled with various chunks of fruits, and surrounded by little paper plates. On the other end of the table was a row of red Solo cups and a black felt pen.

Sergio smiled. "Told ya."

Grinning, Avarie picked up a plastic cup. "Can I just draw a picture of a blonde girl on it? It'll be the only one in the place."

* * * * *

The highlight of the evening was a big sheet cake, congratulating the graduate, and Mina announcing to everyone that she was *not* going to go to graduate school but instead had decided to accept a paid internship with a pharmaceutical research company just outside of Orlando.

Mrs. Martin was especially happy at the news, because graduate school was to take place in California, as was Mina's other internship offer.

As the sun set, and the crowd settled into dessert and conversation, the children played a game of tag across three or four back yards. One of Sergio's great aunts somehow corralled Avarie into a lengthy diatribe about politics and international relations. The PR rep looked at Sergio, mouthing the word "help," but Aunt Terri's rants were legendary. Instead, the detective decided he desperately needed a refill on his drink, and excused himself to stroll to the long dessert table, filling a Solo cup with ice along the way and pouring a can of room-temperature Coca-Cola over it.

As he sipped his drink, Mina sauntered up to him. "Are you enjoying yourself, big brother?"

"I am." Sergio inspected a piece of Aunt Maria's carrot cake. "I have to admit, I'm a little nervous, though. The charges from Party City haven't hit my credit card yet."

"They won't." Mina smiled. "I've been putting away a little bit each month from the allowance you send me." She looked out of the sea of party guests. "It paid for this whole soirée."

Sighing, Sergio put his arm around his sister. "Smart. You were always the smart one."

"That's why Mom and Dad liked me best." Mina chuckled, looking toward Avarie. "I like your friend Avarie. Is it serious?"

"I don't know." He feigned great interest in the carrot cake, then in the Tupperware dish of heavenly hash next to it. "How does someone decide something like that?"

"Well..." Mina shrugged. "Have you slept with her?"

He looked over at his sister, his eyes wide. "Hey, come on." The detective glanced over his shoulder toward his mother, then turned back to Mina, lowering his voice. "No."

"Oh, my." Mina's hands flew to her mouth. "It *is* serious."

Frowning, Sergio moved on to the sheet cake.

"I think that's great. She seems smart, and she's very pretty." Mina's smile widened as she slipped her arm around Sergio's. "You like her, I can tell. You have a good heart, big brother. Listen to it. Avarie seems like a keeper."

He looked across the crowded lawn to where the beautiful PR rep stood. She had disentangled herself from Sergio's aunt and was now conversing with his mother.

He stifled a cringe.

Oh, boy. Out of the frying pan and into the fire.

Avarie held her hands up, moving one in a circle as if she were stirring an invisible pot of soup. Mrs. Martin watched attentively, nodding. After a moment, Avarie smiled and threw her hands up into the air. Sergio's mother burst into laughter, as did the other ladies nearby. Mrs. Martin put her hand on Avarie's shoulder, wiping the corner of her eye and grinning, then gestured in the air with her other hand.

Avarie's mouth formed an O and she laughed again, the women laughing with her.

"Look at her," Sergio said. "She's getting along with everybody. A hundred strangers at your party, and she'll probably leave knowing all of them by their first names."

Mina nodded, a light chuckle escaping her lips. "How terrible. She might want to come back sometime. Then what would you do?"

Sergio turned to his little sister. "I know what you're doing."

"Do you?" She sauntered toward the sheet cake. "Are you sure? I'm the smart one, you know."

"Yes, you are," Sergio said. "You are turning out to be quite a woman. Whatever guy ends up landing you is going to be very lucky."

"Oh, I know. But I'm not doing anything, big brother." Mina smiled at him over her shoulder. "You are."

A young boy raced up to the detective, red-faced and sweaty. "Cousin Sergio, someone's here to see Ms. Fox."

"Here?" Sergio looked around. "Who even knows…"

Kerri Milner stood at the side of the house, in a dark hoodie sweatshirt. She peered at Sergio from under the hood and gave him a wave. "Hey, Detective. Avarie around?"

"Yeah," Sergio said. He gestured toward his mother. "I'll get her for you, Kerri."

"Oh, I can manage." The thin brunette walked toward the crowded lawn. "Enjoy your party."

When the reporter reached the PR rep, Kerri gestured to the side yard. The two women walked over to the space between Mrs. Martin's home and the next-door neighbor's, continuing on until they reached the front of the Martin residence, and disappeared around the corner.

* * * * *

Kerri shrugged, taking her phone from her sweatshirt pocket. "Since my chase video from the fairgrounds caused you such a problem, I thought I'd ask about this one before I aired it."

She opened a video file and pushed play.

The camera followed Avarie and Sergio as he drove around to the back of the Romain estate, until they exited the vehicle. The video footage was grainy and dark at times, but it was clear enough. The next segment showed Gabriella and Teodoro Romain as they stepped out of a van and walked onto the property.

Avarie grimaced.

"It could be a big story." The news woman shut off the video. "Or... it could not be a story at all." She looked at Avarie.

The PR rep shifted her weight from one foot to the other as she searched for the words to explain what Kerri had recorded. No doubt the young news woman understood what was on her phone; she had been following the case from the start.

That's why she was here. She understood *exactly* what was on her phone.

Avarie pursed her lips. "Kerri... that video could hurt some people if it got out."

"I guess that explains the lack of official announcement and calling for a press conference." Kerri nodded. "I figured you'd prefer it if the footage didn't run." She peered down at her phone. "And that maybe I could know the reason. But maybe not."

"A video like that..." The PR rep chewed her lip, sighing. "It could really help put you on the map, Kerri. It could. It's a solid piece of reporting. But..." She shook her head. "I can't comment officially, but let's just say, I think the victims in this case would consider it a big, life-saving favor if that footage just kinda disappeared."

Kerri pursed her lips, looking down.

"I guess I'd consider it a favor, too," Avarie said.

The reporter lifted the phone, her index finger tapping the side. The screen still displayed the frozen image of the Romain house, as the homeowners walked toward the sliding glass doors.

"I guess a story like this," Kerri said, "helps determine what kind of news organization I'm going to have. One that breaks big stories and is wildly successful, or… one that can do all that and have a conscience, too."

She brought her other hand up and tapped the screen, deleting the file.

"Oh, well." Kerri slipped her phone back into her pocket. "There's always next time. Favors are meant to be returned, right? Maybe you can buy me lunch on Thursday."

"Sure," Avarie said. "Thursday or any day."

"Thursday. One P.M." The slender young reporter turned toward the street. "At the Cuban Cigar Club. Bring Sergio."

"I'm intrigued. Do I get to know more?"

"Yeah. On Thursday." Kerri smiled, turned her back to the PR rep, and strolled away.

Sergio walked up to Avarie. "What was that all about?"

"We're having lunch, I guess." She turned to him. "The three of us. On Thursday."

"Okay." Sergio nodded. "What's the occasion?"

"I don't know." Avarie took his hand and led him back toward the party. "We'll find out on Thursday, I guess."

DAN ALATORRE

CHAPTER 45

Sergio drove his car to the end of his mother's dark street and made the turn toward home. "Did you have a good time?"

"I did." Avarie's smile was visible in the illumination of the passing streetlights. "Your family is fun." Leaning back into her seat, she closed her eyes and folded her hands across her waist. She kicked off her shoes and slid her feet up onto the dashboard. "I ate too much, though."

"That's part of the family tradition." Sergio glanced at the foil-covered paper plates on his back seat. "That, and being forced to take home more leftovers than you could eat in a week."

Piles of fried shrimp were making the journey with them, accompanied by pieces of cake and globs of Jello—two gigantic portions of each, one for him and one for Avarie.

"Yeah." She sighed and peeked at Sergio. "I don't know what I'm gonna do with all that food."

"Oh, I'll take it." He glanced at her. "I said it was more food than *you* could eat in a week, not more than I could."

Nodding, she lowered her chin and leaned her cheek against the seat.

A few minutes later, the car pulled into Sergio's parking lot. Avarie raised her head and peered over the dashboard. "We making a pit stop?"

"I'm just gonna pop the food into the fridge real quick. Then I'll run you home." He rolled into his parking spot and shut off the engine. "I don't want Aunt Lili's heavenly hash melting all over my seat."

"I hear that." Avarie unbuckled her seat belt. "Let me give you a hand."

They stacked paper plates in their arms and headed toward the elevator. At the door to his unit, Sergio performed a minor balancing act to get his key into the lock and shove the door open without dropping any of the food.

Avarie entered the home and set her plates on the kitchen counter. "Mind if I use the bathroom?"

"Help yourself. It's right down the hall." Sergio slid the leftovers onto the counter and opened the refrigerator door. The nearly-empty fridge easily accommodated the volume of paper plates.

He stood up and closed the refrigerator door, wiping his hands on a dish towel. Leaning his back against the kitchen counter, the detective peered into the living room. Avarie had set her purse on the coffee table.

As he stared at it, a calmness came over him. It was as if he had been holding his breath a little somehow, and didn't even realize it.

Avarie's purse looked natural on his table, like it belonged there.

I could get used to that.

The bathroom door shut, and she walked down the hallway toward him.

It had been a long couple of days, working the Romain case, and now it was over. But that wasn't the reason behind the good feeling.

Avarie picked up her purse. "Ready to go?"

"Uh, yeah. Absolutely." He pulled his gaze away from her and patted his pockets. "Just... gotta find my keys."

She stepped to the front door and reached a hand out, tugging his keys out of the door lock.

"Ah." Sergio nodded. "Thanks. Let's go."

"Actually..." Avarie walked toward him, twirling the keys on her finger. "I wanted to ask you something first."

She leaned forward, rising up on her tiptoes, and pressed her lips to his.

The warmth and softness of her touch sent electricity through his insides. Sergio found himself slipping his hands around Avarie's waist and pulling her close, unable to stop from pressing her body against his. His heart thumping, he moved his mouth over Avarie's, soft and slow and wet and deep, as her fingers glided up his arms and across his shoulders, coming to a rest at the back of his neck.

Avarie pulled away slowly, biting her lip as she smiled at him, her big, beautiful blue eyes shining in the light from the hallway.

"Sorry," Sergio said. "I don't think I heard your question."

"Oh. Let me ask it again."

She kissed him a second time, more passionately than the first, moaning softly. As she held him, her lips drifted over his cheek and along his neck in a line of gentle kisses, until her head rested against his chest.

Sergio exhaled, stroking her soft, golden hair. "You're a very good question asker."

A warmth filled him, like nothing he'd ever known before.

The sensation of Avarie's body against his was like sunshine. Avarie was smart and strong and funny and talented. She was beautiful and she was sexy. He laughed at her jokes without forcing it, and she got his sense of humor, too.

He'd simply been afraid. He knew that now. Afraid of Avarie, and what could happen.

And now, despite those reservations, his apprehensions were gone. Vanished, like a drop of water falling onto the sand of a beach on a hot summer day.

"Avarie..." He almost didn't want to speak, but he couldn't stop the words from coming. "I've screwed up every relationship I was ever in. I did everything backwards, jumping into bed with a woman before I even learned her last name... And the one time I didn't do that, I still managed to screw it up." He sighed, closing his eyes. "I guess I just figured, if I was ever going to meet the right person, I probably should quit doing that. I wanted to go slow because... I mean, I've known you for a while now, and I just thought... Some things are worth waiting for, you know?

"You?" She lifted her head from his chest, smiling. "That's a little arrogant, don't you think?"

"Not me." Sergio grinned. "You. You're worth waiting for."

Cocking her head, she looked at him with her big, beautiful blue eyes. "I agree. And I think you've waited long enough. We both have."

Taking him by the hand, Avarie stepped backwards, smiling as she pulled Sergio down the hallway.

"I want to warn you, though." Her voice was soft, with a playful tone. "If you aren't careful, saying stuff like that is going to make me fall very hard for you."

"Good," Sergio said. "I don't want to fall all by myself."

When the backs of Avarie's legs ran into the edge of his bed, she gave him one last tug and pulled him forward, wrapping her arms around him as they collapsed onto the mattress.

* * * * *

Carly's mother put her hands to her cheek, sighing. "I'm sorry, dear. This whole situation has me stressed." She shook her head and softened her tone, placing her hand on her daughter's hospital bed. "We've spent the day getting tests and listening to these medical professionals conjecture about what happened... it's too much."

Carly smiled from the bed. "I'm sorry it's been so hard on you."

Her mother lifted her chin. "Rather than reply to your snarkiness, I think I'll take a stroll. There's a little snack room at the end of the hall. Would you like anything?"

Carly nodded, her eyes fixed on the ceiling. "Coffee."

Mrs. Sanderson cringed. "I'm not sure coffee is a good idea under the circumstances. What about a bottle of water?"

Carly withheld the sarcastic tone that was clawing at her to get out. "Water would be great, Mom. Thank you."

"Of course." Mrs. Sanderson patted the edge of the bed. "I'd do anything for you dear."

Carly nodded.

Except get off my ass.

As her mother left the room, Carly reached for her phone.

* * * * *

Gasping, Avarie collapsed on top of Sergio, their naked bodies hot from their love making. As her forehead nestled into the pillow under his head, she kissed his ear. "Mmm. Some things really are worth waiting for." She rolled over on her side and stroked Sergio's hair. "I had fun tonight. And not just, you know… here in your bedroom."

"I know." He smiled. "I had fun, too."

Sliding naked off the mattress, she grabbed her blouse from the floor. "Sadly, I need to get going now, though."

"Huh?" Sergio sat upright, the sheets falling away from his bare torso. "What's up?" he reached across the bed and swept his hands around Avarie's firm, round butt, pulling her back down to him. "Let's have a drink, and then let's have some more fun." He kissed her thigh and began working his way across her flat abdomen.

Giggling, she let him continue for a few seconds. "Mmm." Avarie put her hand in the tangles of his hair as he nuzzled her belly button. "I wanna stay, but I have to work tomorrow." She kissed him again and rolled off the bed.

Sergio gazed at her long legs and toned thighs as she pulled on her panties. "Call the duty officer like I did and tell them that you just worked forty-eight straight hours, so you're taking some comp time. Or just call in sick."

"Can't. Contract players don't get comp time or sick days." She stepped into her jeans and did a little jump, yanking them up over her slender hips. "I have a briefing with the mayor at seven-thirty and a press conference at ten, so I need to be there." Plopping down on the corner of the bed, she jammed her feet into her shoes. "And I need to be alert to ensure the department looks good. Can't do that if I'm late and have bags under my eyes." She leaned over and gave him another kiss.

"Just sleep here, then," Sergio said. "It's a lot closer than your hotel."

Avarie's gaze wandering over the nude detective's backside. She sighed and smiled at him. "As nice as that sounds, if I stay here tonight, neither one of us will get any sleep."

Sergio grinned. "I hope not."

"Right. And I'd probably still be late for work in the morning." She stood up and swatted his naked ass. "I'll call an Uber and I'll see you tomorrow afternoon." Tucking in her shirt, she grabbed her phone and exited the bedroom, heading down the hallway. "Then, I want to pick up right where we left off."

"Hold on." Sergio jumped out of bed and glanced around for his pants. "I'll take you home."

"The app says they have a driver two minutes away." She stuck her head back into the bedroom, holding her phone up. "Go back to bed and—"

On the dresser, his phone rang with an incoming call.

Avarie shrugged. "Or answer your phone."

The nude detective walked over to her and wrapped his arms around her. "They'll call back." He lowered his face to hers and the two of them engaged in a long, slow kiss.

Avarie pulled him closer, stopping her kisses long enough to look up into his eyes. "I want this. So much." She dropped her head to his chest and kissed his warm skin. "And I hate to leave, Sirgy. But I have to."

He released her and stepped back.

Gasping, Avarie righted herself and brought her hand to her mouth, a hint of a smile tugging at her lips. "I'm sorry. You don't like that name, do you? I won't call you that."

He shook his head, his voice falling to a whisper. "I don't like it... unless you say it. Then, I like it a lot."

Avarie's porcelain cheeks turned red. "Okay. If I don't leave right now, I won't leave at all." She fanned herself. "See you tomorrow afternoon."

The beautiful PR rep sashayed down the hallway to the front door, then gave him a wink and let herself out.

Grinning, the detective walked back to the bedroom and fell sideways onto the bed. As the mattress bounced, he answered his phone and put it to his ear. "Hello?"

* * * * *

Avarie strolled along the walkway toward the elevator, trying not to smile too big and look like an idiot.

Sergio was turning out to not be at all like what she'd heard—a Valentino, a player... a love 'em and leave 'em type, who was good for a one-night stand, but not much else.

He's not like that at all. Or, he's not anymore.

She'd met his family. She'd met his last girlfriend, who may have broken his heart, but he seemed to have moved past that now.

Finally.

She opened her phone, daydreaming about their time together. The shooting range, the taco stand, the night in the hotel where he slept by the door to protect her, the cases he seemed to solve better than anyone else.

I was right about Sergio.

There could be a future with this man.

Her eyes drifted back to her phone. A follow-up email had come in from one of the many Florida police departments she'd send contract offers to. Her arrangement with Tampa PD allowed her to leave at any time to work with a city paying fifty percent more money. If Tampa did not match the offer, Avarie could move on to the better paying gig immediately—which is exactly how she had wanted it.

Until Sergio came along.

Now, she didn't know if she wanted to leave Tampa, even for a fifty percent raise.

No, I do know.

I don't want to leave.

They'd spent time together. Enough for Avarie to believe there was a good foundation to build on. And the look she saw more and more in Sergio's eyes told her that he felt the same way. He'd said as much, on the Romains' balcony yesterday and in his own kitchen tonight.

She strolled toward the elevator, smiling and imagining the possibilities as she idly scanned the email from Chief Lissette Anderson of the Daytona Beach Police Department, musing aloud to herself. "Will Chief Anderson's rejection letter start with, 'We regret to inform you,' or will it be the old 'Due to budget constraints, we are unable' crap, the same way all the other letters began?"

She read the first line as she walked.

Dear Ms. Fox,

Thank you for sending us your recent offer. The Mayor of Daytona Beach has reviewed your proposal.

Avarie's shoelace slapped against her ankle. She glanced down to see her shoe had come untied.

Squatting, she set her phone on the concrete walkway, reading on as she grabbed the loose laces.

The Daytona Beach Police Department wishes to inform you

"Roscoe! Stop!"

Mr. Givens' voice pierced the calm night air. As Avarie looked up, the big brown dog crashed into her, knocking her over as he sprinted down the walkway.

"Oh, I'm sorry about that." Mr. Givens wheezed, limping toward Avarie on his booted foot. "That dog just gets so excited." He extended his hand to Avarie.

She got up, peering down the hallway. "This is kind of a regular thing for you two, isn't it? Don't worry, I'll get him."

"Oh, miss. He's so fast."

Avarie smiled. "Haven't you been watching the internet? So am I. But watch this." She cupped her hands around her mouth and turned toward the fleeing canine. "Roscoe!"

Her shout echoed off the walls of the condo building, making Mr. Givens jump. Roscoe stopped at the end of the corridor and turned around, looking at her.

"You come here!" Avarie yelled, pointing at her feet. "Right now!"

Lowering his head, the big brown dog tucked his tail between his legs and slinked back to where Avarie stood. When he reached her, he whimpered and sat down at her feet, looking up at her.

"That's a good boy." She shifted her tone to sweet baby talk, rubbing the dog's head enthusiastically with one hand as she picked up his leash with the other. "Here you go, Mr. Givens." She handed the shocked pet owner the leather strap.

"That's amazing." Givens' mouth hung open. "He's never done that for anyone before."

Avarie put a hand on her hip, nodding. "When you've been a single woman on the dating scene for as long as I have, you learn how to deal with animals." Leaning over, she massaged Roscoe's neck with both hands. "You're just a big play baby, aren't you, Roscoe? Yes, you are." She wagged a finger at the dog, his tail thumping on the concrete. Avarie smiled. "Now, you behave and don't give Mr. Givens any more trouble."

Roscoe licked her finger and moved to his owner's side. Mr. Givens waved, heading back down the hallway. "Thank you, miss."

"You're welcome," Avarie said. "Take care of that foot."

She pressed the call button and waited for the elevator.

* * * * *

Sergio held his phone to his head, listening to his former partner.

"It's just..." Carly's words were strained. "I'm sorry to call you so late."

"No, that's okay." He sat up, pulling the bed sheets over his naked frame. He'd known Carly long enough to know when something was wrong, and the stress in her voice came right through the phone. "I wasn't sleeping. What's going on?"

"I…" She sighed into the phone. "I'm sorry I missed Mina's party. I heard you went with Avarie. I think that's great. Really."

Sergio ran his fingers over the stubble covering his jaw, letting her talk. This wasn't a drunken call to an ex; Carly was making small talk—in her own awkward way—as she built up to the real reason for the call.

He replied in the plainest tone he could muster. "Yeah, I took Avarie. It was a fun party."

"Oh… good," Carly said. "Well, I'm sure I've interrupted the second half of your date, so I'll let you go…"

"No, it's fine." His eyes searched the bedroom walls as he listened for any hint of what was actually bothering her—because something was, and it wasn't him taking Avarie to his sister's party. He kept his voice soft and low. "What's bugging you, Carly? Whatever it is, it's okay."

"Okay." She sighed, exhaling hard. "There's something I should tell you. Something I think you need to know."

He nodded, clutching the phone to his ear, but saying nothing. Carly would get to her message in her own time, in the way she needed to deliver it.

"Oh, Sergio. I'm sorry. This is harder than I thought it would be."

A knot formed in his stomach.

What could make her like this?

He pursed his lips, working hard to sound calm and reassuring. "Hey, Carly. It's me. Whatever you need to tell me, it'll be okay."

On the other end of the line, Carly sniffled.

Sergio bit his lower lip.

Something must be wrong with one of the boys. Maybe they got hurt on that cross-country hiking thing they're doing.

No. She wouldn't call me for that. Kyle's with their sons.

It can't be work. She just got a promotion. Unless she's firing me. But she wouldn't do that right after I just finished a big case for the chief.

So what is it?

A metallic tone came over the line, followed by a woman's faint and fuzzy voice. "Doctor Venarro to room three-thirty. Code blue."

Sergio flinched.

She's in a hospital.

His breath caught in his throat.

* * * * *

Avarie climbed into the back seat of the Uber, verifying her destination with the driver. As the car pulled away, she reached into her back pocket for her phone.

Might as well finish reading my newest rejection letter, courtesy of Chief Anderson in Daytona Beach.

Her phone wasn't in her pocket. She pressed her hand against the other side of her jeans. Nothing. And nothing in her front pockets.

A quick glance through her purse showed the phone wasn't there, either.

"Uh, wait a minute, please. Hold on." She glanced at the Uber driver. "I'm so sorry. I must have dropped my phone when I was getting in your car. Give me a sec."

As the vehicle stopped, Avarie opened the door and peered back at the sidewalk. No phone was visible.

Wait.

Roscoe.

She winced.

I set my phone down right before that big crazy dog plowed into me. My phone's upstairs, on the landing.

* * * * *

Sergio held his breath, keeping the phone tight to his ear.

Stay calm. Carly's already stressed out. It's probably another health scare with her mother.

"Hey, uh... Carly, where are you?" He tried his best to sound casual. "Do you want me to come there?"

Carly exhaled sharply into the phone. "I'm... at Tampa General." Her voice broke as the words came out. "I might not be doing too hot."

Sergio slumped back in his bed, sagging against the headboard.

She wouldn't call if it wasn't something serious.

Your friend Carly needs a hand to hold, and her husband and children are a thousand miles away.

"I'm on my way." He rushed to the dresser, throwing open a drawer and yanking out a pair of pants.

"Sergio, you... you don't have to do that. And what will your date think?"

"Hey, you're my friend. Nobody should be alone in a hospital. I'm coming, Carly. I'll be there in fifteen minutes."

* * * * *

The elevator doors opened and Avarie stepped onto the landing. She rounded the corner as she headed toward Sergio's unit, scanning the concrete. About twenty feet from his doorway, her smart phone glimmered in the illumination of the building's wall lights.

Right where I left it. Thanks, Roscoe.

As Avarie bent down to grab the device, Sergio's door flew open.

He rushed out, his phone to his ear, and raced toward the staircase at the other end of the hallway. "No, don't worry about Avarie. She just left, Carly. She won't even know."

Avarie stood up, the condo door easing shut as Sergio sped to the corner and disappeared down the steps.

"I'll be with you in fifteen minutes, Carly. I'm coming right now."

Avarie stood there, a knot gripping her insides, unable to utter a word.

He's going to Carly now?

We just made love, and he's already running off to... to see her?

She stared down at the parking lot as a vehicle started. A moment later, Sergio's car sped off the property.

A deep ache permeating the PR rep's insides, like a cold, hard, hollow balloon.

He isn't over her.

His reputation with women was accurate after all.

A lump formed in her throat. Swallowing hard, she turned away from the railing.

I thought we were really vibing. How could I be so wrong?

Her phone buzzed in her hand. Avarie lifted it and tapped the screen. A notification from the Uber driver appeared, asking if everything was alright.

Shoulders slouching, she went back to the elevator and down to the waiting Uber, climbing in and riding all the way to her hotel in silence.

* * * * *

Mrs. Sanderson stirred her coffee as she re-entered Carly's hospital room, a bottle of water under her arm. Wincing, Carly slid her phone onto the little table by her bed.

Her mother gasped. "What did you just do?"

"He deserves to know," Carly said. "It's his child."

Mrs. Sanderson raced to the side of the bed. "It's *your* child. You would ruin your family over this? You have a husband and children. What are they going to think?"

"They're going to think their father walked away from their mother, and that she—" Carly winced again and clutched her abdomen.

Mrs. Sanderson leaned forward. "What did you say to Sergio?"

"Nothing." Carly gasped. "I said I was in the hospital, that's all. It didn't seem right to say anything more. That's... not the kind of news you give someone over the phone."

Sighing, Mrs. Sanderson patted the bedrail. "I can't stand to see you hurting like this. Let me get someone." She turned to the door and flagged down a passing attendant. "Excuse me. My daughter's in pain. Can you give her something?"

The nurse practitioner appeared over the attendant's shoulder. "We can only administer Tylenol until she's seen by Doctor Mendez."

"No," Carly said. "Tylenol puts me right to sleep. I need to be awake when Sergio gets here."

Mrs. Sanderson whipped around to her daughter. "He's coming here?"

"I need to talk to him and—" Wincing again, Carly clutching her abdomen. "Oh, good grief, am I giving birth already?"

Mrs. Sanderson turned and nodded to the nurse. "Get the Tylenol."

* * * * *

Sergio raced down the corridor of Tampa General Hospital's third floor, glancing at the room numbers as he passed. Ahead, he spotted Carly's mother standing outside an open doorway, speaking to a nurse.

Her eyes locked on his. Mrs. Sanderson stepped away from the nurse and put her hand up, shaking her head as she walked toward him. "Slow down. Carly's asleep."

"She called me." Sergio tried to peer into Carly's room. "She said she needed to talk to me."

"I'm sorry about that. I tried to talk her out of calling you, but she was being unreasonable. My daughter is in a lot of pain, Detective." Mrs. Sanderson lowered her voice. "Frankly, she's having some... female problems. It's a very personal situation, you understand."

Sergio scrunched his face up. "Female problems landed her in the hospital?"

He looked into the room. Carly was asleep on the hospital bed, the monitors beeping and humming calmly.

"Well, she was scared." Mrs. Sanderson shrugged. "And rightly so. After all, her husband isn't here. So, Carly reached out to her best friend—you, Sergio." She sighed, putting her hand on his arm. "A hysterectomy is a—"

Sergio recoiled. "Hysterectomy? Oh, wow..."

"Me and my big mouth." Mrs. Sanderson looked away.

Swallowing hard, Sergio shifted his weight from one foot to the other. "Ma'am, I... I'm sorry. I had no idea."

"Well, why would you, dear?" She patted his arm. "Sergio, women of a certain age—" She glanced over her shoulder, to where Carly lay asleep in the bed. "Let's step over here." Wrapping her arm around his, she led him away. "Sometimes women of a certain age can have problems—female problems—and... the doctors recommend surgery. And it's a big deal. It can be very scary. Now, Carly is a little young for a hysterectomy, but it's not unheard of for a woman in her late thirties. And of course, she was scared because she couldn't get in touch with me when they told her they'd like to admit her to the hospital, so she reached out to you. But I'm here now."

They stopped halfway down the hall. "Give her a day or two to recover." Mrs. Sanderson patted his arm again. "She'll call you when she's feeling better. This… really isn't something you need to be involved in. It's really a family matter. You understand."

"Yeah, I guess." He slipped his hands into his pockets, gazing at her doorway. "She sure sounded stressed on the phone, though…"

"Well, of course," Mrs. Sanderson said. "It's those pain medications. She's not thinking clearly. I'm surprised she asked you to come all the way down here. This is a very private situation."

"Well, actually…" Wincing, Sergio rocked his head back and forth. "She didn't ask me to come. I kinda volunteered."

"I see." Mrs. Sanderson nodded. "Well, as I said, this is really a very personal female matter. Let her call you in a few days. After she's recovered and had a chance to go over everything with her husband."

Pursing his lips, the detective turned away and walked to the elevators to leave.

* * * * *

In the Tampa General Hospital parking lot, Sergio got into his car.

Man, that's some rough news for Carly. I hope this turns out okay.

I'm sure it will, though. Mom went through this.

He drove his car out of the lot.

Her mother says Carly will need some time and space, so give her that, and be ready to roll with the punches. In a week or two she'll be back to her old self again.

At least she's got her mother with her, to help.

As he reached the main road, his anxiety calmed and his thoughts settled. He needed to consider what he'd tell the chief about Gabriella. Not what to say, exactly, but how to say it.

Bottom line, sir, your niece kinda ran away to join the circus—one of her own choosing. She's a legal adult, and if she doesn't want to tell people what she's up to, she doesn't have to. Not even her uncle, the Chief of Police.

He shook his head.

Nope, that won't do it.

Good thing I know a PR expert. Avarie can help me figure out a way to deliver the news and still keep my job.

A smile stretched across his face, and he reached for his phone, to call her. Not to discuss work, or a statement to the chief. All that could wait. He just wanted to talk to Avarie.

And say what? Thanks for a great evening?

It didn't matter what they spoke about. He wanted to call her. Thinking about Avarie made him suddenly feel warm and happy inside.

He tapped his phone in the cupholder and checked the time.

It's not super late.

But she said she needs her sleep. Just call her tomorrow.

He drove in silent bliss, recalling how Avarie hit it off with his mother at Mina's party—and with everyone else in attendance, for that matter. She did well with key elements of the Romain case, and the cases they'd worked before that.

Chief Clemmons said she'd make a good cop. So did Sergeant Schmertz. Maybe she reinstates in Orlando and transfers here after a few months...

It was a possibility. They'd discussed it, and Avarie seemed open to the idea. Even enthusiastic at times.

Sergio's smile widened.

You're lucky to have that woman in your life. Like Mina said, she's a keeper.

He switched on his radio and turned the music up loud, tapping the steering wheel to the beat as he drove home, a warmth filling his insides like he'd swallowed the sun.

I can't wait to see Avarie tomorrow.

* * * * *

Avarie sat on the edge of the chair in her hotel, her elbows on her knees, staring at the wall. Her heart ached so much, it no longer seemed possible to take a regular breath.

Sighing, she slumped back into the chair and covered her face with her hands.

Sergio couldn't wait to leave me to be with Carly. All she had to do was call, and he ran to her side. He couldn't get there fast enough.

I'm so stupid. How did I not see this? Why did I let myself be so blind?

She swallowed hard, holding back the desire to collapse into Jello.

He never got over Carly, and he never will.

He used you, just like everyone said he would. He doesn't care. It was all an act.

So stupid. You thought you knew him. You thought he'd changed.
You thought you changed him.
So, so, so stupid.

She sagged lower in the chair, holding her phone, wanting to call him—and afraid of what he might say if she did.

Just admit it. He still loves her, Avarie. He's still in love with Carly, like everyone said.

Her phone screen lit up with a reminder notification. "Uber wants to know how your trip was. Rate your driver now."

Blinking hard, she tapped the screen to clear the notification away. As she did, the email from Chief Anderson of Daytona Beach reappeared.

Sorry for the delays in confirming your bid to work with our department. The mayor has approved your contract, and we would like you to start as soon as possible—the sooner, the better.

Regards,
Chief Lissette Anderson,
Daytona Beach Police Department

Avarie's hand fell to her side.

She thought about Sergio's car, racing away to take him to Carly.

The lump in her throat grew larger.

"Don't worry about Avarie," Sergio had said. *"She just left. I'll be with you in fifteen minutes, Carly. I'm coming right now."*

Avarie groaned.

"Don't worry about Avarie."

The ache in her heart swelled, forcing out everything else.

Her shoulders slouching, Avarie lifted her phone again and looked at the message from the Daytona Beach Police Department. She sighed, the screen blurring as she typed out her reply.

That is great news, Chief Anderson. I will be there tomorrow to start work.

She sent the message and placed the phone on the dresser, walked to the closet and took out her suitcase, and silently began to pack all her belongings.

THE END

Carly and Sergio will return in
DOUBLE BLIND BOOK 7

SEVENTH AVENUE

Go to www.DanAlatorre.com and join my readers Club to learn more about when Seventh Avenue will be released.

Three new college graduates are abducted during a murderous shooting in Tampa's popular drag show theater, the Cuban Cigar Club. One of the female hostages happens to be Mina Martin, the younger sister of Tampa Detective Sergio Martin.

Was the nightclub attack a random act of unspeakable violence, a targeted hate crime against the club's patrons, or a move by a drug lord to take over a lucrative market?

Sergeant Carly Sanderson will have to work with her ex-lover's new girlfriend to keep Sergio from seeking revenge, while still working to rescue Mina from the murderous hands of her abductors.

But as Carly gets more and more involved in the suspicious case, the evidence indicates that Sergio's sister was not taken by accident.

**Find out when and where you can enjoy this new book by joining my Readers Club at www.DanAlatorrer.com
as well as getting the inside scoop on other stuff before anyone else.**

And if you liked Six Sisters, please pop over to Amazon and Goodreads to say so.
Just a few words from you helps other readers find a new book they'll love.

A NOTE FROM THE AUTHOR

Dear Reader,

Thanks for reading *Six Sisters*. This book really took some interesting turns, didn't it? Especially at the end! So many readers refer to the Double Blind series as "Carly and Sergio books" – as in, "When is the next Carly and Sergio book coming out?" or "I can't wait for the next Carly and Sergio book!" I agree! I love these characters, and we'll get to know them even better in the next book, trust me. Right now, it's hard for me to imagine Carly and Sergio *not* being Carly and Sergio anymore, but who knows? I mean, never say never, right?

Even though by some standards I write pretty fast, Six Sisters took a little bit longer to write than most of my other books, because I really was *not* liking dealing with Carly and Sergio not being together. They're a great team and I hate to think about them not being a team anymore. Well, don't worry. The questions you have will be answered very, very soon. It's my opinion that Sergio might actually still have a thing for Carly, even if he won't admit it; and I tend to think Carly also has a lingering interest in him, too, no matter how much she denies it. But the only way to find out is to read the next book in this series!

I love the conversations these characters have. The "banter" is one of the things I look forward to the most when I write the Double Blind series. It's just fun for me. And as much as I care about these characters, it's my job to put them into difficult situations and then see how they'll get out of it again, so you have a fun story to enjoy.

Readers always ask what's next? What's gonna happen with Avarie, or Big Brass? And is Sergeant Schmertz ever going to be dealt with? (Remember what happened to Lieutenant Davis!)

Well, YOU are the reason that I will explore the future of these characters! So, tell me what you liked, what you loved, what you hated... I'd love to hear from you. You can write me at www.DanAlatorre.com using the "Contact Me" button and visit me on the web. I LOVE reading your emails. Honest.

Finally, I need a favor. If you'd be so kind, I'd love a review of *Six Sisters*. Love it or hate it, I'd really enjoy your feedback. Your honest review will help readers who like what you like to find my stories, and help those with other tastes to not pick up a book they won't enjoy.

Go to my author page on Amazon, too. You can find all of my books there.

Thanks a bunch for reading *Six Sisters* and spending time with me. It's an honor to know you enjoy my stories.

In gratitude,
Dan Alatorre

ABOUT THE AUTHOR

Dan Alatorre has published more than 50 titles in over a dozen languages. His unique page turners will make you scream, chuckle or shed tears—sometimes on the same page. His novels always contain unexpected twists and turns, and his amazing characters will stay with you forever.

Readers agree, making his thrillers #1 on bestseller lists across the globe.

You'll find heart stopping chills in the medical thriller series The Gamma Sequence, intense crime drama in the thriller series Double Blind, action-adventure in the sci-fi mystery The Navigators, a gripping roller coaster ride in the paranormal mystery A Place Of Shadows, an atypical comedy-romance story in the hilarious and very sexy The Italian Assistant, spine-tingling chills in the short story horror anthology series Dark Passages, and much more.

Prior to becoming a bestselling author, Dan achieved President's Circle with two different Fortune 500 companies. He resides in the Tampa, Florida, area with his wife and daughter.

To join his Readers Club and learn about new books and special offers before the general public, go to DanAlatorre.com and click the link!

DAN ALATORRE

OTHER BOOKS BY DAN ALATORRE

NOVELS

Double Blind Murder Mystery Series
Double Blind, *a murder mystery*
Primary Target, *Double Blind book 2*
Third Degree, *Double Blind book 3*
Fourth Estate, *Double Blind book 4*
Five Sparrows, *Double Blind book 5*
Six Sisters, *Double Blind book 6*

Jett Thacker Mysteries
Tiffany Lynn Is Missing, *a psychological thriller*
Killer In The Dark, *Jett Thacker book 2*

The Gamma Sequence Medical Thriller Series
The Gamma Sequence, *a medical thriller*
Rogue Elements, *The Gamma Sequence, book 2*
Terminal Sequence, *The Gamma Sequence, book 3*
The Keepers, *The Gamma Sequence, book 4*
Dark Hour, *The Gamma Sequence, book 5*

OTHER THRILLER NOVELS
A Place Of Shadows, *a paranormal mystery*
The Navigators, *a time travel thriller*

OTHER BOOKS
The Water Castle, *a fantasy romance novel*
The Italian Assistant, *a very funny, very sexy romance novel*

Dan Alatorre Short Story Horror Anthologies
Dark Passages
Dark Voodoo
Dark Intent
Dark Thoughts

DAN ALATORRE

Short Story Horror Anthologies With Other Authors
The Box Under The Bed
Dark Visions
Nightmareland
Spellbound
Wings and Fire
Shadowland

Family Humor
Savvy Stories
The Terrible Twos
The Long Cutie
The Short Years
There's No Such Thing As A Quick Trip To Buy-Mart
Night of the Colonoscopy
Santa Maybe
A Day for Hope

Illustrated Children's Books
Laguna the Lonely Mermaid
The Adventures of Pinchy Crab
The Princess and the Dolphin
Stinky Toe!

Children's Early Reader Books
The Zombunny
Zombunny 2: Night of the Scary Creatures
Zombunny 3: Quest for Battle Space

Writing Instruction
A if for Action
B is for Backstory
C is for Character
D is for Dialogue
E is for Emotion
F is for Fast Pace

SIX SISTERS

SIX SISTERS